Lojze Kovačič

NEWCOMERS

BOOK ONE

Translated from the Slovenian by Michael Biggins

archipelago books

Copyright © Slovenska matica, 1984,
published in arrangement with Michael Gaeb Literary Agency

English language translation © Michael Biggins, 2016

First Archipelago Books Edition, 2016

All rights reserved. No part of this book may be reproduced
or transmitted in any form without the prior written
permission of the publisher.

First published as *Prišleki I* by Slovenska matica in 1984.

Archipelago Books
232 3rd Street #A111, Brooklyn, NY 11215
www.archipelagobooks.org

LIBRARY OF CONGRESS CATALOGING-IN-PUBLICATION DATA
Kovačič, Lojze.
[Prišleki. English]
Newcomers / Lojze Kovačič ;
translated from the Slovene by Michael Biggins.
pages cm
ISBN 978-0-914671-33-6 (paperback)
I. Biggins, Michael, translator. II. Title.
PG1919.21.O87P7513 2016
891.8'435—dc23
2015031469

The publication of *Newcomers: Book One* was made possible
with support from Lannan Foundation,
the National Endowment for the Arts,
the New York State Council on the Arts, a state agency,
and the New York City Department of Cultural Affairs.

PRINTED IN THE UNITED STATES OF AMERICA

AND HE CONTINUED talking about himself without noticing that this couldn't interest the others as much as it did him.

Leo Tolstoy, *The Cossacks*

SINCE THIS ISN'T A NOVEL, there isn't a thing I can change about my hero.

From the epilogue to *Book Three*

A CERTAIN INDEPENDENCE exists by the grace of God. In each individual person. Every single one. Everyone carries his own head on his shoulders.

Alfred Döblin, *A Trip to Poland*

INTERESTING IS AN IMPORTANT WORD. Interesting doesn't lead into that opaque, torturous "depth" that we know so well, and it doesn't immediately lead to Goethe's realm of the "mothers," that popular German destination – interesting is by no means identical with entertaining. Translate it literally: inter - esse: amid being, which is to say amid its darkness and its glimmer. – "The Olympus of Seeming." Nietzsche.

Gottfried Benn, *A Double Life*

NEWCOMERS

That's how we left Basel. The Gerbergässli ... rue Helder ... Steinenvorstadt ... Nadelberg ... rue de Bourg. A lot of people came to our building, mostly police. Some wearing uniforms, others in plain clothes. Among the latter were some who looked like businessmen from the city center, while the wide-brimmed black satin hats on some of the others made them look like dancers from the variété. Two in uniform accompanied us with our most essential luggage across the Luisenplatz to the train station as people stopped and stared. We crossed a footbridge over a tributary where scarcely two hours before I had been playing with the yellow riverbed gravel at the foot of an artificial cliff. So we were going after all ... So long, Basel!

We were underway by one in the afternoon ... I walked in and out of the compartment ... the windows on both sides of the train car offered interesting views of the buildings and people ... In the corridor I had a whole window to myself. Every now and then mother would call out to me not to lean on it so much or I'd get filthy, and to come back and join Vati and her in the compartment where they were sitting with Gisela ... I ignored her, I felt ashamed to sit next to her ... I pressed my ear up against the pane to drown out her voice. This was my first proper train trip ... All I could remember of my first actual trip, when I was five years old and went with Vati to a sanatorium in Urach and back home to Basel, were the blue upholstered benches in the Pullman car ... Now I could see what Basel was like when it got dizzy. At first like a fat, gray-green snake flying backwards, half on the ground, half in the sky ... into a sort of huge sucking tube in the distance behind us ... a proper dismemberment, a torrent, a hurricane. Then I saw a glass ball slowly swimming across the sky. I couldn't tell whether it was the cupola of the exhibit hall at the fairgrounds or the main railway station. Buildings wriggled by under the train ... I recognized some of them, but only from the street side. What was disappearing behind us was more interesting than what was coming toward us from up ahead. So I turned my head back ... The red, star-shaped roof of the St. Alban's gate that I'd run through at least a thousand times leapt into view ... Adieu, adieu ... then a long street appeared, perhaps the rue de la Couronne ... with buildings washed yellow from exhaust or sulphur ... A chain-link fence started to reach higher and higher up the window until it took over the whole field of vision, with numerous red tennis courts behind it. Vati and I had come here once on a long walk and watched from the shade as two couples played ... The pictures in the window changed quickly, as though I had rapidly multiplying eyes. The tops of chestnut trees swarmed into view, and before I got a good look at the expanse of black, grassless earth full of bicycles and benches where they stood, I heard shouts and squeals and splashing water as the train went straight up over the white wall of the Eglisee. It was full of swimmers in bathing caps with inflatable balls in the water, and swimmers on the steps, on the wall ... I didn't see the big white ball with handles in the pool. I used it to learn how to kick in the water when Margrit and I came here ... I noticed it by the wall, in the grass, where a bunch of hands were reaching for it ... The white, square tower with its clock and pennants on halyards appeared ... but the roof of the Eglisee had already evaded the train car in a wide arc, and all I could see at this point were some legs on the roof and a man's feet ... Then trees concealed the frolicking little hollow with their crowns.

It's hot out there, I thought smugly, but in here there's a breeze. All up and down the shady corridor the drapes kept battering against the windows and doors ... God had chosen a totally ordinary, totally stupid day like this to send me on this train trip ... far, far away to a country where Vati had lived as a child and then later as a slightly older boy. Up ahead, beyond the buildings and trees that were flying back into Basel like drizzle ... on the far side of the clouds and the arrogant mountain that kept retreating ahead of us, no matter how much the train tried to reach it ... on the far side of some mountain slope I was going to encounter all kinds of things that were appropriate for my age ... whether those were toys or buildings, animals or people, cars or airplanes. At night nothing like it would ever have occurred to me ... and I had never even dreamed about Vati's country, let alone imagined anything like it during the day ...

After Vati's and mother's compartment, right next to the bellows-like connector, there was also a WC. It was so tiny and silly, like part of a gnome's house. The toilet bowl shook and creaked crankily as I peed, as though it didn't like being a toilet and would rather have been a milk jug, a chair, or at least a vase ... The other door leading to the back of the train opened and people came out of it into the corridor ... Through the narrow door I could see the other cars swaying like drunken houses ... The people were carrying waxed yellow or round, red, lacquered suitcases that were too big and too heavy, they were as excited as I was, and happy ... Their clothes exuded a smell that I inhaled with that of their skin and their hair. What a lucky coincidence that I was traveling with such childlike people, such scampish jokers ... A splendiferous gentleman closed the car door behind him and put his bag in the compartment where Vati and mother were sitting. He stood by my window. He smelled of all different colognes, different down below than up above. He was wearing white trousers, a serious, striped jacket and a stiff red necktie. His eyebrows and mustache were equally thick and black, and could have been switched out with each other and replaced at random. He looked like a millionaire or a gangster from America ... there was something of a boxer about him, or a trained horse, or even a camouflaged tank. Around his wrist, which he held next to the ashtray, was a watch that I'd seen in store windows: it had a green frigate riding atop its second hand. He smiled at me, which made me feel awkward, and I didn't know where to look ... and so he smiled again, revealing such brilliantly white, perfect little tiles between his red lips and black mustache that I couldn't believe a person could have teeth like that ... I lost so much time with smiles and furtive glances that in the meantime a completely different picture came through the window ... We were riding through a pale blue sky with the sun up above in one corner of the window, like an unleashed crown. Dark red brick bell towers, one bigger than the next, appeared and rotated with pairs of saints, the peaks of their roofs articulated with spikes and balls and a different cross on top of each tower. The biggest one of them was probably the Münster with its fountain down below that I liked wading through up to my knees. Now we're going, now we're going, I sang into my lips... Suddenly there was a huge rumble and through the window steel girders flickered past this way and that, and below them the Rhine appeared with black bands of waves... On it were long, flat barges with closed hatches that carried coal and charcoal for irons... Above the Rhine stood a white building marked NEPTUN right on the water amid train tracks and coal cars, and through the window of the compartment I could also see the Mittlere Brücke with people and struts. The racket was so loud that I could have screamed and kicked doors and nobody would have scolded me for it... I touched the door and, as in some noisy dream, I wanted to say something special, but all I could say was "Wie schnell wir fahren,"* and then I shut up, disappointed... I started to hum Vati's song, "Ljuba Kovačeva, two beers, we've got no cash..." of which all I understood was the surname, which sounded like ours. The infernal clamor died away and was replaced by a soundless silence, as though the train had become a balloon, a zeppelin, a glider slicing through the air with a whoosh as though it were silk... then came small, withered bushes and smaller houses... Basel was strangely disappearing through the windows... a building from the city had just been here, and now instead of it there was already a big hill.

*We're going so fast.

This was a speed I could appreciate ... I could feel a jaunty tick-tock at the back of my head ... I was traveling, traveling through an endless expanse to a country that had lots of horses waiting in stables, and I would unhitch one of them and ride him down to the river so he could drink water ... and there would be red boats, so I could row from one riverbank to the other. On the rooftops there would be biplanes ready to take off, and I would fly around in them ... over the rooftops and the water ... and when they called me to dinner, I would land on the roof and climb down the chimney on a ladder back into the house. I pictured the short, stodgy airplanes that they used for acrobatics at the amusement park, with an open cabin for the pilot ... one of them, a red one, would have my name stenciled on it ... and I would fly all around in it, over the ponds and white gravel paths of the parks ... If I stood by the window, the train went forward faster than if I left it alone ... Outside all that was left was greenery, and only here and there some tree would try to finagle its way into the corridor, but of course it couldn't. My legs became wooden from all the standing, and my eyes ... and when the sun started to go down ... a huge red tunic ... I went back into the compartment.

Vati was sitting by the window, with nothing to do of course, so he either looked out or dozed. Mother was still completely beside herself ... red in the face and neck, she kept fidgeting ... but thank God she was no longer complaining or whining. Our luggage, which had formerly been kept in the attic, was stowed on shelves up above:

there were several brown and gray canvas bags with rusted corner pieces, a round carrying case made of shiny black leather, two cardboard suitcases and one made out of wicker. Gisela was sleeping with her head on a small comforter and her overcoat for a blanket. Mother offered me a slice of home-baked apricot bread on a napkin ... I didn't feel like it, I was more thirsty. "Iß, sonst wird's dir schlecht."*
I ate one, two, three slices and then stretched out on the seat next to Vati. I didn't want to rest my head on his knees, because I knew how he stank of fur down there, but also how uncomfortable my head would be. The gentleman from the corridor with the frigate on his watch sat and talked with both of them for a while. Was he Italian or French?

"Nach dreißig Jahren Leben in der Schweiz haben sie uns hinausgeworfen,"** Vati blurted out ... and what other voice came next, but mother's ... here came the tears down her nose, and again I felt ashamed for her. Oh, I knew all of her reproaches by heart, even if I didn't understand all of them ... Vati turned attentively toward the dandified man.

"Das macht der Krieg,"*** the visitor answered thoughtfully. "Wenn es nicht die Gefahr von Krieg gäbe, wäre die Auslassung aus der Schweiz niemals passiert."****

---

*Eat, or else you'll get sick.
**After thirty years living in Switzerland they've thrown us out.
***It's the war.
****If it weren't for the threat of war, you would never have been expelled from Switzerland.

"Ach, wenn wir doch damals, in den zwanziger Jahren die schweizerische Staatsbürgerschaft angenommen hätten. Aber mein Mann wollte seine Länder zurück ... Bis wohin fahren Sie mit uns?"*

"Bis zu der Grenze,"** the gentleman said. He was the one who had locked the compartment door and had a key to the whole train car in his pocket.

They woke me up in the night with the electric light bathing the compartment in yellow. "Schnell, schnell, wach auf," Vati said as I sank back into a pleated sort of sleep. He took hold of me and set me on my feet. I raised my arms over my head and fell to the floor. Gisela was already wrapped in a blanket and sleeping on mother's shoulder. The gentleman was standing outside the train car. They hurriedly dressed me in my sailor's coat with the anchor. Outside nothing was visible through the watery darkness except for some lights. I jumped from the high door out into the drizzly rain. We ran from the train that had brought us across tracks and ties that looked like ladders scattered over the gravel ballast. Mother ran with Gisela across a track toward a long, dimly lit roof. Vati was hurrying with me, pressing one of my hands to the handles of two suitcases he was carrying, because in the other he was carrying two more, while I had the round one in my other hand. Mother was shouting back at us, worried crazy as usual ... In the light of the locomotive the rain turned into Christmas tree tinsel. The roof turned out to be a station with posters and numbers, but no people.

*If only we'd taken Swiss citizenship back then, in the twenties. But my husband wanted to get his land back ... How far are you traveling with us?
**To the border.

Mother sat on a black iron bench holding Gisela in her arms, who was awake now and had the eyes of an ermine... Vati, accompanied by a gentleman disappeared into some black hole, because he had to take care of something with our green travel booklets. I was freezing. It was strange, that same day I'd been knocking around Basel. When I got to Barfüßerplatz across from Gerbergässli, Gritli had called to me from the other side. At first I thought she was trying to trick me, as she had often done to get me to go home. But this time she was shouting in such an urgent voice and with such an earnest face, even after a streetcar came between us, that I finally ran across the street on my own... She didn't slap me, she didn't touch me at all. Outside our building there was a policeman in a short cape. On the other side of the door there was chaos and running around, and suitcases were lined up one after the other on the steps, as though they'd walked out of the room on their own... "Schnell, schnell," mother shouted from upstairs. "Wasche dich, wir fahren nach Jugoslawien."* ... Had I heard right? Was that even possible?... They literally ripped the clothes off of me, causing the buttons to fly, tossed me into the bathtub, soaped me up and scrubbed me so hard I had scratches, dried me with a towel, and dressed me in white... in a shirt with buttons that I tucked into my shorts. All the rooms – the workshop, the showroom, the salesroom – were full of strange gentlemen, plainclothes policemen, some of whom looked like businessmen and others like dancers, walking back and forth holding papers, writing things down, counting on

*Hurry, hurry! Get washed, we're going to Yugoslavia.

their fingers and pushing us the whole time, "Schnell! Schnell!" We walked to the train station with our luggage, accompanied by two uniformed policemen and two in plain clothes. It was so hot that we all had dark spots on our clothes from sweating ... At the station a nurse with a red cross on her cap met us. She wanted to take Gisela and me to the dispensary for coffee with milk, because we hadn't had lunch. "Nein, das erlaube ich nicht,"* said mother. Lots of people crowded around ... Mother held me by the hand and refused to let me go ... but the nurse pleaded with her and gently took hold of me by the shoulder. Finally, with Gisela in her arms, mother went with me into a sooty office where the huge black plate of a locomotive loomed right outside the window. The nurse pushed a cup of gray-white coffee across the table ... Mother picked it up with her left hand and tried it. "Ein schlechter, lauer Kaffee,"** she said. The nurse gave me a friendly nod. I knew that when adults were this nice it wasn't right for children to turn down whatever they offered or else they could suddenly get angry. There was a gray membrane floating on top of the coffee. I took a swallow and a revolting, cold slime slid down my throat ... I couldn't get it down or out ... I spat it back out into the coffee. I set the cup down and climbed out of the chair, regretting that I couldn't oblige myself for the sake of the nurse. Vati arrived with the papers and black booklets that had little windows in them for our names. Finally we boarded the train, where I spent the whole time standing

*No, I won't permit it.
**Bad, tepid coffee.

by a window. Mother of course was crying and complaining, which made me draw in my head and wish I could hide. The policemen and two gentlemen showed us the compartment we would be traveling in. They stood at the doors at both ends of the car, and there was a policeman in the corridor too ... until the conductor came and locked the compartment. The train stood fairly far out from the main building and it wasn't until it began to move that Clairi and Gritli appeared on the platform, both of them dressed like mother in white dresses and broad white hats. "Warum fahren sie nicht mit uns?"* I asked mother. "Clairi kommt später, das Gritli bleibt und wird alles machen bei den Behörden, daß wir zurückkommen."** So we can come back? No, I don't think so ... Mother wept and kept casting looks at father as though he were some sort of lizard or crocodile. My sisters waved to us from next to a pillar. Clairi, Gisela's mother, I liked better because she was always sad, but I looked at Margrit, who was mean, because she had begun to interest me more and more ... As I was standing next to a pillar now, everything that had happened seemed as colorful and abrupt as in some comic strip ... Despite the scrubbing, my fingernails were still black from the dirt and sand I'd been playing in by the water under the cliff ... Vati came running alone out of the black hole and shouted, "Da ist der richtige Zug!"*** as he pointed toward the headlights of a locomotive that was puffing in the rain, "woo-woo-woo" ...

*Why aren't they traveling with us?
**Clairi will come later, but Gritli is staying and will do everything she can with the authorities so we can come back.
***That's the right train!

The car we got into was empty, cold, and poorly lit. There were no compartments so we could be together as at home, just benches on either side beneath baggage racks that looked like bird feeders... and it smelled vaguely of the toilet. It resembled an empty, unheated room. Little white porcelain markers were attached to the windows and doors. The black, arched letters on them resembled drawings of hummingbirds, frogs, and crabs. Except for the vowels, I couldn't make out a single letter or a complete word in a language I knew. Mother tried to read them – father, too – but with no success. I went to the far end of the car, which was in semi-darkness, so I could take its full measure from door to door, but mother, who had been soaked through by the rain, shouted at me so loudly to come back immediately that I hurried to take my seat next to Vati, because if she shouted again something in the car was bound to explode. Outside the windows there was nothing but blackest rain... Without any ado, blowing of whistles or shouting of railway men, and without my noticing it, the train had begun to move... Through the rain and the dark, its black windowpanes covered with millions of raindrops... It pushed into the tracks with its wheels, as though it were kneeling, then its shock absorbers collided with something, and then it was pushing into the tracks again... The car leaned out to one side and repeated this motion several times and each time it did, I didn't know if I could move up or down its steep incline without the car breaking in half or my weight causing an accident... A narrow caged door kept opening and closing by itself... nothing was visible through it, except for darkness and some toilet paper on the floor, crumpled and filthy, a whole roll of it, a regular paper garland, like in the boys' bathroom at school. The floor didn't have rows of tiny gutters like the car on the train from Basel, it consisted of ordinary wooden floorboards. This fact bothered me, as though they'd removed something essential for the operation of the train... In the windows I could see dim reflections of the benches, the poles and the shapeless white mass of my own figure... I went straight toward myself and pressed my face to the window... to see what I was like since I'd been traveling... I couldn't see, but I could sense that it was still pretty much me... though blurred, so that I could have taken the image for some counterfeit or substitute for myself... For a tenth of a second I felt uncertain and would have liked to send my ghost to check where I was... inside the train or stuck somewhere out there, flitting through an unknown land... I turned away perplexed, because I couldn't make out if something had happened to me or if I really was someone else... Did this strange train car have any connection at all with the locomotive, the tracks, the railway, the ventilators on the roof... I knew trains well, every Christmas I got a new one, which I would immediately disassemble down to its motor... It was moving, all right... lost in the darkness, but neither over the earth nor through the sky... so where, then?... it had to be racing toward the place where there were lots of animals in the barns... horses, cows, colts, calves... red boats and little biplanes for doing aerial stunts... I looked at my legs jutting out of my shorts. Sometimes I was amazed I was still so little and hadn't grown up yet... and sometimes I got angry that parts of me were growing so fast and gawkily, and that I wasn't a child anymore... Fortunately my family was sitting at the other end of the car ... mother in her white hat, which she'd put on over a kerchief, Gisela covered with her little overcoat, Vati with his long graying hair and dandruff on the collar of his blue suit ... they were sitting there as if in one of our rooms at home ... and for an instant I sensed that this image would stay with me forever ... It occurred to me to go check the time on Vati's watch. It was ten. We had left Basel at one. "Wie komisch das ist ... vor neun Stunden waren wir noch in Basel,"* I said. Father's lips stretched out in a smile. Mother was turned away, scratching a corner of her mouth with her index finger. Oh, these two were never going to get along if they couldn't come together on such a nice trip ... I had never seen Vati at rest before ... in a train, outdoors, on a streetcar ... except for once in the sanatorium when he took me there and then came back and fetched me, in the zoo, and on rue de la Couronne ... He sat holding his hands between his knees because it was cold, his eyes blinking behind his glasses. Then he got up and went to the bench behind me. He took off his shoes, wiped his feet with the newspaper and then stretched his legs out on the bench. "Dort ist es schmutzig,"** mother said. Vati lay his head on the arm rest. He had made a pillow for himself out of the *Basler Nachrichten*, put his glasses into their case and covered himself with his coat, so that he now vanished. Nobody was inclined to say anything unusual or amusing. I climbed up on my knees and stretched out on the bench the length of the backrest, on the other side of which he

*How funny, nine hours ago we were still in Basel.
**It's dirty over there.

lay. Mother covered me with a coat and tucked a scarf under my head. I could just feel the warmth of my body or of the coat where it covered my face without warming the cold air above me. Although the whole car was ours, with only our luggage on the racks up above, the train chugging and racing, I was spellbound by the blue, dreamlike lights above me ... and wished I could be, if only for the short time it took me to fall asleep, back in my bed in Basel, under that fluffy comforter of mine ... Mother was dozing in the corner with a scarf on her head and her hat pushed down over her eyes, and Gisela lay in the hollow of her lap, while Vati had begun snoring, invisible on the other side of the bench.

WHEN I OPENED MY EYES, all three of them – Vati, Gisela and mother – were sitting across from me. Judging from the thick tobacco smoke that filled my head and my lungs, I could tell that something must have happened in the meantime, and I could hear various languages and murmuring voices intermingling around my head. The train car was full. Thick with people ... but I had to shake off the sleep and the smoke in order to see them. "Sind wir schon über die Grenze?"* I asked randomly, because I didn't know ... "Ja, jetzt sind wir schon in Jugoslawien,"** Vati said, smiling. I was crestfallen. There had been no flash, no thunder when the locomotive penetrated the

*Have we already crossed the border?
**Yes, we're in Yugoslavia now.

border, there was no sign that anything had been split or changed outside ... all around in the blue darkness there was a huge number of people just sitting ... I pressed my eyes shut to see if somewhere in the darkness of my body, my chest, my head, I could find a bright line of lightning, some afterglow of the border, an echo of thunder ... Because although I'd been sleeping, my body must have perceived the transition from darkness to light ... and in my darkness there must be some trace at least, some dim glow, some smoldering bulb ... There was nothing ... it was mute, black, weightless, thick. I was just terribly sleepy. People were sitting in the shadows ... on all the benches, dressed almost for autumn, although it was June. They had scarves and hats on their heads ... Their heads, their heads. What were they like? Blurry. They were holding baskets, bags woven from straw, brightly colored, a man in a black suit and white shirt sitting on the bench across the aisle from me had the ugly remains of an old backpack slung over his shoulder. On the luggage racks there were baskets covered with napkins like pillows. I wanted to inspect them from head to toe, but that wasn't possible on account of the weak, dim light ... Who were they? They were sitting, from right next to me all the way to the door at the far end ... there wasn't even the tiniest free space remaining in the whole train car ... They just went on forever at the back, as if in the rain. But some of them were seated facing toward our bench and seemed to be alert. What were they like? They had darkish, old faces, like leather soccer balls ... and big, black cavities of various depths where their eyes were. I couldn't make out their speech. They stared at mother, who in contrast was as white as snow, and at Gisela, even at me, and especially Vati ... But he was one of them and could have blended in ... They stared at us, languidly, from head to toe, causing me to feel a flush of warmth that cooled as soon as it reached my face. Vati turned to a man who was dressed in an ordinary jacket, although on his head he was wearing a uniform cap with a cockade. He said something, his mouth moving so slowly that his jaw muscles tightened, turning his face into a mask ... he said something in a strange, soft language, as though he had some new, unusual mashed food in his mouth. They looked him in the face, in the eyeglasses, the mouth, his hair ... "Was hast du gesagt?"* mother said. Our language was sharper and firm, but understandable. Now everyone turned to look at mother, even the ones sitting in the back ... Still holding his hands between his knees from the cold, father turned toward where the other man was sitting ... and again he said something in that extraordinarily pliable language in which I could barely make out even the more distinct consonants. The man in the cap didn't answer, even though he was the one facing him. Instead, the voice of someone in the packed car who was sitting in shadow by the window across from us answered. I couldn't distinguish him from the other dark-clad figures around him ... He answered quickly, as though issuing some call, but again in the same strangely drawling language where I couldn't distinguish friendliness from hostility, nor could I detect any melody, if it had one. The same man, now with his head stretched out, continued to speak, while the others kept stealing glances at Vati

*What did you say?

from over the backrests. The man with the backpack said something like thunder. Using a black, bushy umbrella that had a knotty handle resembling a roasted lizard on it, he drew something on the floor with its tip. Vati pointed at the drawing, invisible on the dark floor, which was now caked in mud and covered with sand that had been tracked in... and bent over the floor, he said something in their language that sounded very childish. Suddenly everyone started talking at once, a veritable barrage of yarn and wool... and somebody got up from the seat by the window behind me, revealing the unbuttoned panels of their vests and white expanses of the shirts underneath... "Worüber sprecht ihr?"* mother asked, and all eyes fastened on her, including mine. "Wo wir billing essen und schlafen können,"** Vati answered from the door of the car, where he now stood, looking rumpled and very pale.

Maybe these ones crammed into the train car weren't yet the real ones. The real ones lived in houses, had stores and horses and all kinds of machines.

W<small>HEN WE GOT OFF THE TRAIN</small> they didn't even give me enough time to look up at the sky and catch my breath... There was a gray, illuminated, covered passageway on the platform with a few people... and beyond it was pitch darkness all the way to the sky. The air was

---

*What are you talking about?
**Where we can eat and sleep cheaply.

warm, dry and a bit oily, with a fine mist slowly drizzling ... We set our luggage down on the stone floor of the illuminated passageway ... It was quiet, extremely quiet. The passageway didn't have any interesting posters or different-colored light bulbs, just iron pillars curved at the bottom and top ... Some people were standing around at the far end or were walking back and forth ... many of them in black trousers and white shirts, with hats on their heads ... Nobody spoke ... laughed ... or waved ... There were a few dark-skinned women with scarves on their heads and men's shoes on their feet ... just one woman, running across the tracks in the distance, was dressed in cheery, colorful clothes like the women in Basel ... but she vanished among the trains ... The people were milling around as if waiting, looking around, especially at us, although they moved as though they were slightly crippled ... They had umbrellas as big as the one on the train ... I couldn't believe that we had arrived here so quickly and that I was still awake in the middle of the night ... maybe because we were so tired and sleepy, someone had tricked us and we'd been directed to the wrong place ... and now we were who knows where ... It was a shame I couldn't see the sky and a shame it wasn't daytime so I could find out whether all of this was just some prank ... Vati was in a conversation with some short, stocky, swarthy man. He was speaking to him in his language that felt as soft as pastry ... was he asking him something? This man, too, instead of listening to Vati, looked him square in the face, and then answered him the same way ... straight in the eyes, the mouth, the nose ... in a voice that resounded way up toward the ceiling. Was he a woman, perhaps?

There were so many people in shirtsleeves jostling in the enormous, poorly lit waiting room with ticket windows and bars over them!... And such a big clock hanging way up on the wall, as white as a moon that had escaped indoors ... but it was still outlined with those big, disgusting numbers from the first grade arithmetic workbook ...

Outside there was a street with trees that ran parallel to the train tracks, but everything else lay in darkness. It was monotonous and dreary, like some side street.

"Kommt, ich werde euch etwas zeigen,"* said Vati. "Laß die Kinder in Ruhe, wir gehen schlafen."** ... Vati took me assiduously by the arm in a way he'd never done before, and we proceeded to walk the length of the gray station building. From around a dark building on the other side of the street it got lighter and lighter. "Schau nur!"*** he said. All at once, in the middle of the black sky, there appeared a dazzling glass castle. So that was it!...

"Ein Schloß aus Glas,"**** I said. So this really was it now. The light permeated my skin, coat and hair, touching me like a ghost. I had no sense that any of my family were anywhere nearby.

"Wie schön,"***** mother said behind me, holding Gisela, now

*Come and I'll show you something.
**Let the children be, it's time for bed.
***Take a look.
****A castle made out of glass.
*****How beautiful.

· 26

awake in her arms. There, you see, now even she admitted that something was beautiful. The light made us as visible as though it were day, it saturated the sidewalk and transfixed us like the sight of a Christmas tree ... The glass castle had a tower and a long main building. No windows were visible. It hung in a cloud ... did it float like the moon? What kept it up there? Was there just air between it and the city? I didn't want to risk asking questions, or they might drag me away. Even my buttons, the anchor, my whole blue navy coat from Basel was saturated with this topaz-yellow light, as though it were changing. The street that we saw the glass palace through seemed wrapped in a flannel darkness, between its tall buildings there were lamps that shone in a line going all the way down ... It was impossible to do anything but just stand and stare.

We had to go back to our stack of suitcases and take them across the road and some streetcar tracks. The front door of a tall, dark building was open and lit in the very middle of the night. A gentleman wearing a striped waistcoat was standing behind a desk, with numerous keys hanging on the wall behind him. Vati spoke to him and the gentleman spoke back to Vati in that language that even here, in this building, among chairs and tables, refused to stop being dreamlike ... We got a key with a big wooden pear attached to it. Some other man helped us carry our suitcases as we went up the red carpet covering the stairs. We went all the way to the top, bumping into some wood-paneled walls on the landings, and then turned left where there were even more stairs that appeared to have no end. In the corner of some hallway next to a small table a door opened. It was a room, not very deep, with white covered beds and a divan ... a mirror and a cute washbasin. The white castle shone through the window. I wanted to sleep on the divan next to the window. They grudgingly moved it for me. Vati and mother lay down on the double bed with Gisela between them. When they put out the light, the castle shone gently into the room at the same height as my pillow. I crouched there looking at it and at mother, who saw my head against the pane, and quietly tried to persuade me to lie down ...

In the morning ... the pillow under my head smelled funny ... and I jumped when I suddenly woke up ... Out the window, in the place where the white castle had shone the night before ... there was an old building resembling an ugly, brown ruin with a square, crumbling tower and holes in a sort of stone crown jabbing into the cloud cover above it. I couldn't believe my eyes ... But maybe, I quickly recovered, the glass castle is invisible in the daytime, because it's transparent ... The brownish-gray jagged wall with its square tower stood atop a forested hill ... above the reddish cupola of a church and the tin roof of the hotel courtyard that had been soaked black in a downpour ... It refused to be erased so that I could see the glass walls of the resplendent castle from the previous night ... Or maybe the earth moves so fast that the glass palace is already appearing to people on the other side of the world.

I called out to Vati when his eyebrows began to move. I told him that the castle was no longer made out of glass, that it had turned to stone. He jumped out of bed in his long linen skivvies and nightshirt and leaned over my shoulder at the window. I was expecting something to happen when his eyes made contact with the demolished castle... but it stayed the same. "Weisch, es its abends nur beleuchtet,"* he said.

I didn't feel like reminding him that yesterday when I'd said the castle was made out of glass, he hadn't corrected me.

"So hast du dir das nur vorgestellt."**

"Es war aus Glas."***

Then mother spoke up. "Shhh! Bleibt still, daß die Gisela nicht erwacht."**** I told her what had happened. "Schon gut, das war nur die elektrische Beleuchtung."*****

Vati hopped back into bed, because his feet were cold... but really so he could sleep some more!... How was this possible? They'd fooled me again, if not lied outright. There was nothing outside, and here in this room with them everything was the way it had always been, broken and rancid for the millionth time. I flung myself back down and closed my eyes. I could hear father as he shaved. He was standing at the sink in front of the mirror, tugging – tsht, tsht – the razor across his face. Admittedly, this was the first time I'd ever seen him shave, but the brownish gray castle with the strange tower stayed the same.

We had breakfast in a nice dining room downstairs. I had to stay with mother and Gisela while father went into town to take care of some business. I took up my position by the window. Maybe the reason

---

*You realize it's because they light it at night.
**You just imagined that.
***It was made out of glass.
****Be quiet, or you'll wake Gisela up.
*****It's all right, that was just the electrical lighting.

it was made out of old stone was because there were noblemen, old knights with their squires, horses – and maybe even a White or Black Prince living there. And maybe it was even better that way, because if it had been made out of glass, then only princesses could have lived in it.

VATI CAME BACK and mother went with him back into town to see the authorities. I had to stay alone with Gisela and look after her. She wanted to play on the divan by the window and on the carpet. I set her back on mother's bed and told her she had to be quiet ... I ran out into the hallway and looked out through a window. What a vivid picture presented itself to me! The gray train station, a locomotive with cars, trees, two or three streetcars and just a few people ... but it was all so bright, warm, slightly sticky and as colorful as Africa! Most interesting of all was a man in a round red cap with a black pompon standing right down below at the corner of the tall hotel. He had a box strapped onto him which jutted out at his belly, with all different kinds of things in it – combs, little wooden boxes, harmonicas, pinwheels ... He stood next to a door where people – some of them ordinary, others darker-skinned and unshaven – were constantly going in and coming out. Hm, what was he up to? ... My eyes went from him across the long, sunlit street to the row of skinny trees that I had noticed the night before. The tramcar was green, not red or white like they were at home ... I swear it rang exactly the way they did in Basel ... and it was passing along the row of trees ... when the bow collector and roof of another tram pulling a second car behind it came from the other direction. They weren't very crowded ... but outside the train station and on the street there weren't many people either ... Near a fence where some red train cars stood some of them were walking slowly but with a comical persistence like pairs of black scissors ... until they came close enough for me to see them ... now they were no longer mysterious in their movement, but since I could understand nothing of their language, they were mute, as if wrapped in invisible cotton. A locomotive on the far side of the fence was puffing smoke. Three grown-up boys crossed the street barefoot. But of all the people, the most interesting was the fat man with the red cap and box of goods who was still standing at ease by the door, motionless ... Gisela started to cry and I had to go back to the room to quiet her down, then back out into the hallway. Once I was back, the man in the cap down below was gone and I couldn't find him anywhere on the street or in the vicinity of the station ... a locomotive with a trumpet-shaped smokestack began puffing on the far side of a building and then pulled up to the fence, "Tshhhh, tshhhh" ...

Vati and mother still weren't home. The minutes stretched into hours. I sat Gisela down on the first bed and propped her up with all available pillows so she could sit upright. Since she wouldn't calm down, I told her everything Vati had told me about the horses, airplanes, boats and all the other things we were going to see at uncle's house, where we were going to live. Gisela grinned and, using her mouth and eyes, imitated all my expressions. I improvised a comedy about animals for her, with the two of us first riding horses – that part wasn't hard, since I'd had a hobby horse at home – and we would ride them like cowboys like this, hanging out of our saddles off to the side, and when we galloped into a meadow, we would hitch them up to a tree and climb into a little red airplane that we'd fly off into the sky... and I ran around the room, over the beds and divan with my arms stretched out... and then we'll land... and I stretched out on the carpet... All around at our feet there will be nothing but little chickens going cheep-cheep, and puppies will come racing in wearing sailor's caps, and cows moo-moo, and then a horse with two colts. We'll step into a boat and row to the other shore. That's where there's a forest. Rabbits standing in front of a bush will wiggle their ears at us and hold out their paws all covered in paint, because they've been coloring Easter eggs, and they'll say, "Salut! Guten Tag, Gisela! Guten Tag!"* I became a rabbit and held my paw out for Gisela and shook her little hand with the tiny vein in it, and Gisela said hello back, embarrassed, "Guten Tag, Häsli, was macht's?"** "Ich laufe im Walde und warte auf Gisela,"*** the rabbit said... Gisela blushed and said hesitantly, "Weisch, das Boot isch zu langsam gfarre..."**** "Er isch halt a Remorker. Gehen wir in den Wald. Der Wald ist schwarz."***** ... "Wart', dort isch a Heks," she said. "Die will uns fressen!"****** "Wir

*Greetings! Hello, Gisela! Hello!
**Hello, little rabbit, what's up?
***I'm running through the woods and waiting for Gisela.
****You know, the boat went too slow.
*****It's just a tug, anyway. Let's go into the forest. The forest is black.
******Wait, there's a witch. She's going to eat us!

schmeissen sie ins Feuer."* I grabbed the down comforter, beat it up, pushed it off the bed with some mighty shoves, fell onto it, stomped on it and then kicked it under the bed ... As we were playing we suddenly heard a knock ... We didn't breathe another word. We looked at the door. Again there was a knock and we didn't move, we just waited to see what was going to happen to the room. We didn't dare open the door. Gisela rolled toward me.

The door moved away from the wall ... In the doorway stood a tall gentleman dressed in black who resembled the men in the dining room ... and he wasn't too old, so he was safe. He looked all around the room. Then he said something to the room or himself in his foreign, monotonous language (he was probably sick, too, and this had dried out his throat). Neither the melody nor the pauses between sentences helped me understand what he was saying, though I wanted to understand more than anything. He had a bony face, resembling a skull, but without the smile ... and such a narrow forehead that he must have cracked it whenever he tried to think. He pointed around with his hand. "Allein? Mama? Papa?"** he asked, his face rearranging itself. I pointed to the open door. "Zimmer aufräumen, Betten machen. Leute schlafen."*** ... So what was this now? Something white appeared behind him. The door opened and a woman dressed in

*We'll throw her in the fire.
**Alone? Mother? Father?
***We clean room, make beds. People sleep.

white, with a white cap and a red face, the same height as me and carrying a whole armful of sheets, entered the room. Never before had something that I wished for appeared … it was always some other, surprising thing that came … The woman set the sheets down. As if he'd been wound up, the man pointed to Gisela, "Aufstehen, kleines Mädchen."* The woman, who was quite wide, pulled the pillows off one of the beds. The gentleman picked Gisela up and set her down on the divan. As long as he was standing there, I didn't move, but when he took a step aside, I joined Gisela. The woman made the bed and when she went up to the wall, she was etched in the air like a pillow moving all by itself … she picked up the down comforter and said something quick, round, and almost jovial. The gentleman leaned his hard forehead down toward me and pointed to the comforter that the midget was taking over to the window. "Kak dein Mädchen,"** he said and wagged his skinny finger at me, which must have grown at the same rate as his forehead. I felt the pressure of tears welling up and I tensed my forearm to be ready to push him away … The white woman, whom I also found it hard to look at because she had such a squat, red face and round, little eyes with too much make-up – probably a washerwoman or a baker – also threatened us with her fingers, which were like little red sausages. So, here we'd done something wrong right off the bat … oh, this was not good. I turned toward the window. Gisela was sitting on my pillow, swiveling her head back and

*Up, little girl.
**Your girl poop.

forth. Just as long as she didn't start crying. But it must not be that bad if they weren't taking us with them. The man stood at the door, looking at us. How did he look? He had drawn his lips in, an indication of scorn or something like it. I turned my back to him once more. Just as long as Vati and mother came in the door in time to keep them from sending us back to the train. The cook was changing the bed, taking the sheets that had been on it, perfectly smooth and unruffled, and throwing them on the floor ... The man kept standing there, while I looked out the window at the castle, which still interested me. Its tower was stuck right onto the buildings, onto the flat and pitched roofs ... of the city ... The door was still open when some sheets went billowing up toward the ceiling with a snap. As the man finally began to step backwards out of the room, a new person moved in from behind him, a thin woman in a black dress and white collar, who came into the room and went past the bed. As she went from the door to the bed they said something to her that sent sparks flying, like a power line. I watched the black-clad woman as she moved past the divan. She had dry, colorless eyes. She was so big and powerful that Gisela and I suddenly became tiny and flat. With her strong back to us, she went to the wall and stopped next to our suitcases, one of which was open. I became afraid that she was about to make a decision to send us both back to the train. She hurried back to the door and I kept watching her. Then the washerwoman approached the divan and with a big smile on her face bent down toward us. "Hitler, huh?" she said. I had no idea what she wanted. I knew the name. I had seen pictures of Hitler and a zeppelin with a swastika on its tail that had flown over the

Barfüsserplatz. My friend from across the street, Friederli, and his sister and I had shouted and shaken our fists at it. At one point the zeppelin stopped right over the square and we ran away terrified, because we thought it was going to drop a rope ladder for the whiskered Führer to climb down. I nodded and she threatened me with her index finger and gave such a big laugh that I could see her teeth and tongue … she was probably happy. "Aufstehen!" I got right up, then she said, "Kleine," and pointed to Gisela and me. I couldn't understand what she wanted. She put her arms around Gisela and lifted her up as Gisela beamed happily. She set her back down and pointed to me. I didn't know what she wanted. She lifted my arms up and put them around Gisela. "Up-sy," she said, lifting Gisela and putting her in my arms. She pulled the sheets off the divan, threw them on the floor, and then gestured for us to sit down. Then she bundled the sheets, went out, and came back in without them. Again she motioned for me to pick Gisela up, then she stepped backwards to the door, curling her fingers toward herself to get me to follow her. Out in the hallway she kept on like this, motioning to me. I came to a stop holding Gisela, who was heavy, and couldn't move any farther. The washerwoman stopped next to a small table and pointed to a little chair. I didn't move, but she kept nodding and pointing … and at that moment the black-clad woman marched past and waved a hand for me to go with her. I didn't want to follow these women. I stopped several times, and each time the thin woman said something out loud. Finally I reached the chair and she indicated for me to set Gisela down. When I did that, they both called me back into the room, each of them, the white and the black one, each curling a finger to get me to follow them. What do you want? I was reluctant to go with them, because I was afraid something could happen to Gisela and that they might do something to me, too. My face was buzzing with fear. Back in the room they pointed to the open suitcase and to mother's nightgown, which was draped over the back of a chair. The washerwoman lifted the nightgown, spread it out and gave it back to me folded, and motioned for me to put it in the suitcase. When I had put it there, the washerwoman lifted the things and then looked. I was supposed to close the suitcase, but because it was full, I had to sit on top of it to get it to close. The black and white women carried the other suitcases away, while I carried mother's, and we put them next to the table and chair in the hallway. Then they carried the bundles of sheets downstairs amid much talking and laughter, which echoed up the staircase so distinctly I was amazed. I put Gisela on my lap, still not understanding what had happened.

The voices had almost dwindled away in the kitchen at the foot of the staircase, when some other, agitated voices mixed in with them, becoming progressively louder and angrier... Had something happened to mother, too? She appeared at the top of the steps in her white coat, gloves and hat, with only her face red. The washerwoman with the sheets, the black-clad woman, the tall gentleman and Vati all followed behind her, but stopped at the top of the steps and watched her. "Was habt ihr mit den Kindern angestellt? In den Gang gefeuert

mit allen Koffern? Das ist eine pure Tollheit und Unverschämtheit,"*
she shouted, pointing to us and waving her other hand at them... So
were Gisela and I going to have to move from this place in the hallway
now, too? Once mother calmed down and approached us she wasn't
just red, she was drenched in tears. The white and black women smiled
contentedly. "Sag doch was!"** she said to father. Taking his usual short,
refined steps, Vati approached the gentleman, and the tall gentleman
approached him. Vati said something in his language which was like
the semi-audible sounds a person might make while eating and drinking. Both women approached and listened, practically cheek to cheek,
when the black-clad gentleman spoke. The hallway became almost
drafty with tension... and I could hardly wait for us to get out of there.
Vati went over to mother, who kept taking her coat off and putting it
back on, and he explained something to her, making small gestures
with his hands. "Und wenn! Und wenn es auch zwölfe ist, noch kein
Mensch hat das Zimmer gemietet,"*** she exclaimed. The white and
black women stood there looking, while the gentleman with the bony
face and narrow forehead had already left. At last we went down the
stairs, too, with the suitcases and Gisela, who walked by herself with
her feet turned out like a clown's. We left the suitcases behind the
desk with the keys and in exchange got a tin disk with a number.

*What have you done with the children? Kicked them out into the hallway with all of
the suitcases? This is downright crazy and an outrage.
**Say something!
***So what? So what if it's already twelve, nobody else has asked for the room.

It was warm outside when we finally went out the door, there were people everywhere, and it was noisy. Horses, trams, bicyclists, the palms outside the front door, the lace curtains over the windows, people with backpacks, women carrying wide baskets on their heads, two boys my age walking past the display windows shirtless and barefoot, which surprised me. Gisela walked on her own, dressed in her little coat and with her cube-shaped hat pushed back off her head and dangling from her shoulders. Vati walked ahead of us, blazing a trail and showing the way. Slowly we reached the corner of the big hotel and turned into the street of tall buildings with wide ledges at the windows – this was the street down which we'd seen the glass castle the night before. Despite all the noise it was muffled, tepid and thick like a warm compress over our ears. The street was full of people whom I would see just that instant, of course, and then never again, because they would disperse all over the world. A big gray building with a fence right in front of its facade resembled a building in Basel... Much farther down the street there was a brownish building with statues on top. That one was truly impressive. It was just a shame the statues didn't include any children or flags... The sidewalk was wide. Alongside it there were thin, yellowish brown carts on two tall wheels. Big white bundles of sheets lay on them... maybe the very same ones from the hotel... and milk canisters with handles. At the end of the street part of the green hill was visible and the brown end of the castle. I ran to join father. "Vati, werden wir auf das Schloß gehen?"* "Ja, nach

---

*Father, are we going to go see the castle?

dem Mittagessen."* "Es wird keine Zeit mehr übrig bleiben,"** said mother, who joined us with Gisela sitting on her shoulders. "Wir müssen mit dem ersten Zug fahren."*** I made a bad face. Then, walking in the broad shade on the right side of the street, we came to the display window of a butcher's shop where something tiny was moving. Behind the big cuts of meat and loaves of cheese garnished with parsley, there was a procession of tiny, white, spotted cows that kept disappearing into a little white house, out of which on the other side came stubby, fat, bean-colored sausages, which then turned a corner behind some cheese and bacon before disappearing from view. This was like that goose at the Macreus shop at home, that lifted its wings in the display case full of white down, and then each time it flapped, more feathers came fluttering down from the ceiling like snow. But this display was more interesting. I exchanged glances with Gisela, who also wanted to look. She was craning her neck over mother's shoulder and pushing the brim of her hat down, so that mother finally had to stand still and turn her back slightly toward the display window. The little cows kept trundling down their semi-circular path toward the little white house, coming out of it as stubby, fat sausages. Mother took just one look at the cattle being converted into ground meat, and then was ready to move on. "Nein, nein, ich schaue noch."**** But mother went on to the corner as fast as Gisela would allow, even

*Yes, after lunch.
**There won't be any time left.
***We have to catch the first train.
****No, no, I'm still looking.

though she was pounding her little fists on her shoulder. I stayed standing in front of the display window. The little cows, all identical, with bells on their collars, all came at the same speed, disappearing through the little open door one after the other. They called me to come. Gisela, who still wanted to look, was pounding on mother's back. I dawdled so I could figure out where exactly the little cows were coming from, but I couldn't make anything out. All I could see were their horned heads appearing from under a mountain of cheese, more or less out of nowhere, and advancing like a column of soldiers before going under some ham into the little white house. It was the same deal with the browned sausages. They vanished toward the back into an abyss much like the one the little white cows with their tiny black hooves emerged from. It was impossible to discover or figure out how the processing took place, much less any trick behind it. Vati came back to get me, he looked at the transformation, then he took me by the arm and dragged me away from the display pane. Mother was waiting at the corner. Oh, how pleasant it was to walk on the asphalt that was soft as dough in that warm city. At home on the Luisenplatz or in the rue de la Couronne it was always as hard as rock. "Folge ein wenig. Wir müssen eine Menge Sachen erledigen,"* mother said. As we crossed the street, people looked at her and at Gisela, but also at Vati and me, as if through wooden masks. Big copper disks had been embedded in the roadway for the pedestrian crossing and both rows of shiny buttons reminded me of Basel. There, at the intersection of rue Helder and the Bahnhofstraße there were disks just like these,

*Keep up with us, will you? We have a lot of things to take care of.

and it startled me a bit to find them here, too, so far away from home by train, and at the same time I was happy, because I knew what they were for. Now I already had two things that were like home. On the other side of the street we walked past a tall building into a rather dirty little side street. It had display windows with black ledges and black doors, like coffin lids, and in front of them there were crates with bones and ashes, but there was a gold barber's plate, which I also recognized, jutting out from the wall. Eventually we made our way to a short, one-story wooden building, painted violet blue, with small windows and tiny little shutters and with a dark blue printed sign hanging from it with white letters spelling F O T O ... Aha, this I could understand! On account of the short buildings all around in this neighborhood the sky had become even more bottomless, almost threatening, hot and glowing from the blurred sharpness of the fog-shrouded sun, and this made the building seem even older and darker from close up. The pictures in the display windows showed men with oatmeal-colored skin and fair-skinned women, girls with wreaths on their heads, soldiers wearing stiff, coarse uniforms and monstrously huge caps like kettles, with long, thin, curved sabers hanging next to the seams of their trousers ... the hand guards on the sabers were almost hidden under tassels, pompons and ribbons ... The better, more elegant, best-groomed ones had wide, gleaming tablets on their shoulders, high-peaked caps with big coats of arms that featured a half moon with stars, stripes on their trousers and boots. They sat with their sabers between their legs or next to them. They looked a little wild, and that was fine, but also a bit odd and bereft, as though they were slightly deranged. In one picture I discovered something I could relate to: a boy in a sailor's shirt and cap sitting on a wicker chair like one we had at home ... Heaps of sand and masonry stones lay in the street. Mother flushed red with anger and shame when she had to step up by crossing a board. Dark-skinned men stood in the ditches, working with picks and shovels, but without jackhammers or other equipment. They were naked down to the waist and watched as she walked over the plank. They had dark eyes, hooked noses, regular features like in the movies, prominent jaws and heads that came to a point at the crown. With their white caps and kerchiefs on their heads they looked like regular heathens or pirates. The faces lined up in the ditch, one after the other, all looking at us. They were smiling. I had never before seen such beautiful, white, powerful fangs, as though they had nothing but cream in their mouths. When we got to the end of the ditch, mother set Gisela down and began to whine. "Das ist das Gasthaus,"* Vati said, pointing down a narrow street that was literally baking in the sun. As we crossed the narrow street, my sandals sank up to the ankles in thick, hot dust mixed with bits of stone. An old lamp hung over the entrance to a modest building. On the wall next to it there was a painting of a white-haired gentleman in a dazzling, embroidered, gold-braided jacket. In his right hand he was raising a glass and looking through it. "Ist dieser Anzug aus Gold?"** I asked Vati ... "Ja, es scheint so,"*** he answered.

*That's the boarding house.
**Is that suit made of gold?
***It appears to be.

We finally arrived in uncle's town in the middle of the night. The station was an ordinary peasant house. Uncle wasn't waiting for us, even though we'd sent him a telegram. There was a dark forest right in front of us and not a single streetlamp on the road. Neither on the left, in a depression that had standing water in it ... a regular lake that was impossible to cross ... nor on the right, where the road climbed a sort of hill, beyond which it was pitch dark ... We set our suitcases down on top of some logs and a coal monger's bags in a shack next to the tracks ... We took with us only the bag in which our nightshirts were packed. Since we'd been spattered with wet coal dust, we wiped ourselves off with bits of cardboard that were lying around. We stayed standing outside the closed little station to give father time to figure out which way we should go. Mother was on pins and needles. But here, in the place where he grew up, she could at least trust him a little ... Yes, he suddenly recalled some shortcut, a path that he often used as a child to go to school and also to come home, when he'd return to the village. The path was up there somewhere, way at the top of a hill, and then led back down to the water ...

We headed uphill. To one side there was a long wall that rose up with the road from the train tracks and some monstrously mighty body of water that roared down below ... I felt the wall with my hand. It was made out of coarsely hewn stone and was full of gaps and bits of flint. A regular rampart! But I was more interested in the body of water that was splashing around down there ... It hung in the air with the rain, like an ocean that was cooling my head from afar and giving me shivers ... Vati walked so far ahead of us that he vanished from sight.

We caught up with him again at the top. He was standing next to some black bushes in front of a wall. "Da hinunter müssen wir gehen, glaube ich,"* he said with a note of guilt in his voice. "Einen anderen Weg kenne ich nicht."** He pushed some dripping branches aside. Between the leaves and the wall appeared a gap leading into a veritable abyss. "Was?" exclaimed mother, who wouldn't have been visible at all if she hadn't been dressed in white ... But there was no other way out. Vati headed down the steep slope first, with a suitcase and a lit sulphur match, then, like it or not, mother followed holding Gisela, who fortunately wasn't crying, because she wasn't a whiny child by nature ... with me, carrying mother's bag, coming last. The leafy branches all around rustled and snapped, surprised to find us hugging the ground with them ... I had never before penetrated such a jungle. I couldn't even see my hand in front of me. For an instant in the faint glow of a match I noticed some rods within a circle of blistered trees ... no, a bunch of snakes standing upright! ... and on the moleskin spread out all around them were sea shells, smashed snails and soft, white, broad-capped mushrooms, toadstools – the poisonous ones from the Schwarzwald ... I began to feel afraid, especially at my back. But here I was in Vati's country, after all! ... I seized onto every solid thing that came into my fingers ... there were so many leaves, like a dark, thick, slippery carpet, that they stood upright like weasels, scratched my hands and caused me to keep sliding forward. My God, what if I do

*We have to go down this side, I think.
**I don't know any other way.

a somersault and crack my head open on the fork of some bush! I was staring so intently into the dark that my eyes started to hurt. But each time I went flying again ... into some forked branch, hanging vine or tree trunk ... or were they all so happy to see me that they kept clumsily bumping into me? ... I tried to walk crouching down to trick anything that might have been lurking in the dark brush ... I expected Vati any instant to run into some monster, beast or robber that would proceed either to eat or to strangle him, so I got ready to beat a quick retreat back uphill or die here on the spot. And why shouldn't I die? Alive or dead, I was in some sort of paradise here ... I never imagined that a tunnel like this would await me in Vati's country ... full of branches, endless, dark and with no way out. Here and there to the left or right I smelled something that was ready to leap to my rescue ... It was the stench of rotting trees and human excrement ... but there was no way I was going to be able to get off the smooth shoulders of this slippery earthworm that I was sliding down. Various things that I had just barely avoided or at least forced into submission resumed their former shape behind me and turned wild again. No, there were no insidious ravines like this even in the hills around Urach. If I could only slide downhill using my rear as a sled, it would have been safer and so much more fun ...

Suddenly the path became lighter and I heard a hollow, insistent sound. Mother was already standing ... I stepped onto level, slushy ground ... the humid air was just as heavy from the rain as the ground was wet with it ... I saw Vati, transformed into a shadow against the bright ground ... So this was probably the meadow with molehills, and next to it some other flat space was splashing, spraying and pounding ... Water! I stumbled over to the suitcase, then to Vati, who was standing far away. His suit reeked and hung from him like a tent. Out of the dark he said to me in his usual voice, "Das ist der grosse Fluß."* The river! The same one he had told me about? I ran over to see it ... Right next to some trees and bushes turned upside down on their heads an enormous, wide body of water was gushing ... leaping and racing past like the back of some gigantic lizard ... a dance floor wildly spinning all the way to its middle, where a black shadow fell out of the sky over the unseen far bank ... But here it was spraying the trees and bushes with its foam, gurgling in the grass around my shoes, as though it were washing the trees ... In life you only rarely see anything as awful and glorious as this. My eyes practically fell out of their sockets trying to see more. So for once Vati hadn't pulled the wool over my eyes.

There was a little path wending its way under the trees by the water ... and father was first to set out on it ... It was slushier, as though it had been sprinkled with pebbles ... It led toward some black shadows that loomed tall and round against a brighter sky ... Like thrones, fortress walls, and big theater balconies ... Or maybe also like a jungle or an upland plateau ... A real exotic landscape! There was a winter chill but also such a cheerful sound wafting to us from the water, that I could have had ice cream just as though it were summer ... On the far side there was emptiness – a big, strange,

---

*That's the big river.

soft meadow that suddenly rose up in the vicinity of some shrub-like shadows ... not too far off, since otherwise our voices wouldn't have echoed as they did. It was clipped off even by a white line at the top, and above that there was a sort of mountain that ate the white line. In a way it resembled a machine I had seen before. Only its dimensions weren't such that people were like dwarves alongside it. I ran to catch up with Vati. His soaked suit and shoes made slapping sounds as he walked. He turned his head back, "Das ist die Eisenbahn mit dem Tunnel."* How could I be so stupid! Of course, this was a hillside with railroad tracks and a tunnel that went through the hill. Like the picture on the cover of the box for my train set in Basel. I was only now seeing it in its proper dimensions and from close up for the first time. This ... not some dumpy train station with schedules and wooden waiting rooms, was the proper domicile for a locomotive that roamed the whole world ...

W**HEN WE GOT TO A TREE**, we were in the deepest shadow. The path had suddenly narrowed and the water was gurgling very close by, as if somebody was brushing his teeth on the far side of the shrubs ... Vati sparked a match from his little pack. In front of us was a huge cliff face, wide and black, looming progressively farther out over us the higher it reached up into the trees ... With its belly it shoved the path out closer to the water, and us, too ... Vati pressed close to

---

*That's the railroad and one of its tunnels.

the rock face, he hugged it, and with the hand that he used to carry the suitcase, he lit a match ... the tiny, useless flame of an innocent match from Basel illuminated his mud-encrusted face and the black cliff that was thrusting its chest out, but most of all a multitude of various kinds of leaves that came fluttering down like a waterfall ... Suddenly Vati was gone from the cliff... "Wo bist du?"* mother called out tearfully. He had vanished. "Vati!" I shouted. All we could hear was the crackle of branches and kerplunk ... father was drowning amidst bushes and toads!... "Mama, Vati kommt um!"** I hollered ... Suddenly another little flame appeared ... We saw Vati's face above us, pale and with muddy streams of sweat running from the lenses of his eyeglasses on down ... he was standing over a part of the path that had been washed out. He was carrying something... "Steine!"*** he announced. He tossed them down onto the path beneath him, on the place where it went underwater ... white, gray, round, square. Any second he was going to slip and fall ... "Hast du dich verirrt?"**** mother asked. "Nein, nein," he answered through clenched teeth. "Hier geht der richtige Weg ins Dorf."***** He climbed down, stepped on the stones and reached out his hand. "Gib mir die kleine Zwetschge."****** I thought ... all right, now Gisela was going to make

*Where are you?
**Mother, father is dying!
***Stones!
****Have you gotten us lost?
*****No, no! This is the right path to the village.
******Give me the little tadpole.

a ruckus, because she didn't like Vati, who was always arguing with Clairi over her... But Gisela had character! She leaned forward and let him pick her up. For the first time ever father was carrying Gisela in his arms! Just imagine! He climbed up onto the far side of the path, which was veinous with roots, and set her down on the suitcase... Now it was mother's turn. She was soaked through with sweat. She clung onto the rock face while it shook down a rain of leaves, as though they were being dumped out of a cloud... I shoved off after her, stepping over Vati's stones, which were jutting out of the water. The path reached up to my chin, so they took hold of me and pulled me up and there I was, next to a tree that was half-entwined in clematis. Here the path was firmer, there were pines growing on both sides, and my stockings felt like bags full of mud... Nothing had been like I'd imagined it, but this dangerous path, that fearsome cliff, these raging waters... oh, this had been fun!

Now there were big, fat stones underfoot. The tree growth was below us and the river had split in two like a peaceful lake, but a little farther on still more jagged rock faces loomed... "Jetzt kommen wir in den Steinbruch,"* Vati said. "Was?"** Why on earth did mother have to shout back a question each time? I walked right behind her coat and Gisela, whose head hung over her shoulder, would tug at my hair... The path emerging from under mother's feet refused to end. Suddenly it inclined downward, with rock faces rising on both sides.

*Now we're entering the quarry.
**What?

They resembled high cliffs and the ground underneath them reflected gray triangles ... Vati suddenly came to a stop. "Vorsichtig und ganz still - da ist das Zigeunerlager,"* he whispered. We huddled closely together, seizing onto each other's clothes and buttons, and Gisela kept hold of my hair ... We stood there, each of us looking in a different direction, in case someone was about to attack us ... Behind us was the stone chute, and up ahead of us the chute descended even farther into a chasm between cliffs ... It was the quietest quiet. After a while we moved forward and down ... the path leveled off and merged with rocks all around ... Gray outlines stood pitched in all the shadowy corners – these were supposedly tents made of canvas. Inside them lurked Gypsies who weren't as noble as Indians ... I heard a high-pitched, giggling voice ... "Pferde," Vati explained. Indeed, I saw some shaggy shadows or other, the outline of a head ... horses ... and wheels, so those were their wagons. If they were going to attack us now, we were lost! My buttocks tightened and my heart held still. It became a tiny, hard nut. I knew that it could burst any second ... The path unspooled along the bottom of the ravine ... we lifted our legs at the knees, practically up to our chins ... I couldn't make out anything as we passed the tents ... but I did pick up some revolting smell. "Verbranntes Schmalz," mother whispered ... Thank God, it was burnt tallow, at least something kitchen-related ... But despite our precautions while walking, the stones underfoot began to crunch. This was a bad part of the trail. We were in a ravine that wasn't just dangerous

---

*Careful, be very quiet now. That's the Gypsy encampment.

at the bottom, but also up at the top. The path suddenly softened and rose ... Vati began to ascend toward the sky ... and I pressed my head toward mother's back in order to leave all this nonsense behind me as soon as possible ... until finally the vagabond path leveled out.

Now it became easier to walk. There were no trees. Down below it was high water. It seemed as though we were walking on air ... Still, the path had its own devilish ideas. From some rise it descended again ... and when we finally reached the bottom where it became dark and forbidding, its dark soul snarled at us again. It leveled out and opened up and showed us a bland stretch leading up to ... the end. There it confronted us with a small iron footbridge, beneath which the high water foamed and surged ... An undeniably wild stream that a bit farther on emptied into a river. How to get over it? ... We had to take care not to slip off the narrow iron walkway that kept getting sprayed from below ... Vati went first and set down the suitcase ... Then a second time, with Gisela. She didn't cry out, so he wouldn't lose his balance. Then he struck another match. Mother glided across like a ghost and kneeled down on the far side. As soon as I started out on the bridge, the froth from the stream engulfed my feet ... and the bridge shook at all of its gaps, so that I would have preferred to slip off it into the depths than go on.... In any case, on the far side the meadow was even slushier and in places completely flooded, and the molehills jutted up out of the lakes like little fortresses made of sand ... The river rushed off toward a bend, probably like someplace in South America, and there wasn't a single tree or bush beside it. I was able to walk alongside ... Big, wide and taut as a road, it was possible to see across it to the other side, where there was a thick, dark forest ... of pines and firs. Mother called out ... "Ich habe den Schuh verloren!" She had lost a shoe ... it was white. We had to go back over the squishy meadow all the way to the decisive stream. Planks ... some sort of worm-eaten wooden troughs lay all around, half-filled with water. I inspected them and turned one of them over: don't tell me these were once boats, bits of smashed river-going vessels? Excited as I was to discover it, the mud made exalted squishing sounds beneath my feet. Vati searched the waterfront and mother with him ... Who was it they'd searched an entire country for to find the right foot to fit in a shoe? ... I found it! It was lying heel up in a puddle, so it wasn't obvious ... I brought it to Cinderella. She shook the sand out of it and put it on right away ... The meadow rose like a potica ... At the end of it we came to a nice, dry sandy path that split in two: one path rose toward something white ... probably some house or other ... and the other, darker path went alongside a sort of forest of straw-like spears. "Das ist Kukurus,"* Vati said. He didn't know which path we should take. He lit a match. When it ignited, a cross with Jesus on an old lath appeared under a round tin roof. I noticed the drops of blood on his face under the crown of thorns and a bunch of flowers tucked in between the nails through his feet. So alone in the night, in a cold foreign land ... Of course he wasn't afraid, because he was the

---

*That's corn.

Son of God and he had his Father in Heaven to protect him ... It was really good that we had him for company now. "Ein Kruzifiks!" said mother ... Vati shone a match on the first and second paths. "Ich gehe dorthin zu diesem Haus fragen,"* he said. And indeed up he went to the white house, even though it could have been a trap. And indeed he knocked on the door ... I heard knock! knock! on wood ... and I even heard some human speech. I will never be so brave as to go wake a stranger in the middle of the night to ask a question ... He came trudging back down in his squishing clothes and shoes ... "Da hinauf müssen wir gehen,"** he said, pointing toward a deep, dark path through the cornstalks ... Mother began whining again. "Ich werde die Schuhe ausziehen."*** The mud on the path was black and greasy, a regular coal cream. I took my shoes off too and made contact with the cold mud through my stockings. At intervals Vati would light a match ... but the mud got deeper the farther we went, as though it were continually being kneaded and then left to rise ... I couldn't go any farther in it ... Vati began walking more closely alongside the corn, mother as well, so I tried walking on the grassy border to one side ... I tripped and went flying and got covered in mud. So I tried going farther in among the corn ... tall, knuckly reeds with dangling leaves, reminiscent of branched candelabras ... Their fuzzy tails waved at the top, while something like hard bananas wrapped in straw husks jabbed at my face. It rustled and fluttered. I couldn't see three feet

*I'm going up to that house to ask.
**We have to go up there.
***I'll take my shoes off.

ahead of me for all the fragile spears jutting up. I kept running into them ... they smelled raw ... this was a regular Africa, a savannah overgrown with reeds ... The earth was muddy here too, but at least had some sand ... I held on tight to mother's bag and sandals, but each time the leaves, the hard bananas with their threadlike mustaches slapped at my face ... I ought to have a machete, like Ali in Timbuktu. It went slowly. Here and there some shoots, sharp tiny stumps, started to stab my feet in the sandy earth. I set the sandals down and stepped into them. Amid all the corn and constant rustling I could neither see nor hear anything. Suddenly I sensed I was alone. Then there was a mighty cracking sound through the stalks and an instant later I noticed something white and black like a mole hill ... a monster went storming off right in front of me, it took off like a blacksmith's hammer hurled up into the sky. I screamed for all I was worth and raced out of there ... Mother and Vati were standing on a rise, they shone in the dark, and she was shouting desperately, "Bubi! Bubi!" ... "Da bin ich!"*

Now BOTH OF THEM were walking comfortably alongside each other down a broad path, which I had all to myself. For the first time everything around us got quiet. Went mute. The trees, the river, the shrubs. Finally they got to see something that had left them dumbstruck. Oh, it wasn't easy to surprise them! ... Down below the gray water lay still. On the far side was the railway line ... which led off into

*Here I am!

the darkness... into the excitement of the wilderness... Now the path dissolved into a plain that was thickly strewn with big, white stones... Skulls with toothless jaws, egg-shaped balls with their ends gently set one on another... all crunched underfoot. Brrrr, brrrr, they tumbled aside... Were these ruins or a riverbed? It led uphill... toward railroad tracks alongside a forest, where a striped boom barrier jutted up in the air. A crossing! And almost directly across from it a fence... a long, skinny tree trunk that lay atop two meter-high forks stuck in the ground. And next to it Christ on the cross, with ordinary rosaries left in various glasses and cups. God was everywhere in the world, and without exception he ruled here too. Perhaps this country was even a little more pious than others, because they had Jesus outdoors, at night, in the open air... I could barely see anything due to sleepiness, but I knew that from the very first day here I was going to have to be much better behaved than I had ever been up till now... Vati lit a match. Beyond the fence there was a meadow... so big that wherever you looked, green showed through the shadows. "So, jetzt sind wir angekommen,"* he said. He lifted the trunk off its forks as coolly as though it were the lattice gate on a cowboy ranch...

We proceeded along some other fence toward a house that shone white in the high grass to the left. This whole meadow that stretched off toward a fog-shrouded forest, as huge as an airport... was this uncle's? The house had to be white or at least yellow to show in the dark like that, and its windows were edged in black and had wide

---

*We're there.

ledges ... The roof came down to the level of our heads as we walked past, and from the sound of it the river was close by ... Vati went all around the house and came right back ... "Keiner hört etwas."* ... The house was asleep. Or else there wasn't a living soul in it. A whole bucket of water came pouring down off a tree behind us when father broke off one of its branches ... Did he have a right to do that? He tapped on the nearest windowpane with his stick. A face appeared in the darkness, then a light ... an actual flame in a kind of bottle. The face said something from behind the windowpane ... it was a long, white face with a mustache ... Uncle Karel! He opened the window, which was as small as the window on the door of a WC ... and he stuck his head out. "Das its der Onkel."** I was suddenly petrified with respect. Vati said something to him in his foreign language ... while I looked at uncle, at his white, sleepy face, his long, handsome head sticking out into the darkness, his dark, close-cropped hair, and the nose that shone above his mustache. But especially his eyes, which were as big and black as buttons. "Wir müssen um das Haus."*** Vati proceeded as though he were a little drunk, and walked at a slant ... The house stood on a slope. When we reached it, it was even farther down. We had to go in single file, because the hill was so steep. The water sounded closer and closer ... It washed up into the bushes, not too far down from the house ... I went past a small window with adhesive tape still stuck to it in the shape of an X at the level of my

---

*Nobody can hear anything.
**This is your uncle.
***We have to go around to the other side.

head. It was open and the smell of fresh mortar and sand wafted from inside ... At the corner stood a strange device that was two meters tall. With a big log aimed at the sky on two stakes set far apart ... and it creaked and groaned. Maybe it was some kind of machine that had no real function, maybe it was just for show ... Then there was a black heap that stank nastily and two barrels that gave off the smell of carrots or vinegar ... and now at our feet we no longer had water and mud, but cement ... When the door opened, the light illuminated a gray vaulted ceiling. Uncle was holding it open ... he was wearing a hat, an undershirt and skivvies ... we went in ... to the warm, sleeping darkness of the house, as though we were walking into sleep ... The stone entryway was black ... and warmth drifted out of some deep hole in the wall, where red coals were glowing ... My whiskered uncle opened another black door ... it had a big iron box on the door for a lock, like the ones that can be seen on castle doors. This door opened into a wide, warm room with a low ceiling ... There were two narrow beds in it, both made high with comforters and pillows ... someone was lying in one of them and next to the door there was a big stone chest with a bench around it ... "Jetzt sind wir endlich zuhause,"* said Vati. He said something to uncle and pointed to mother, who laughed and offered her hand ... to Gisela ... and to me. I studied him when he lifted the light to his eyes. He had a genuinely handsome, pale, slightly triangular face. Emphatic black eyebrows and mustache and big eyes like two buttons. Only his bare feet sticking out of his long

*At last, we're home.

underwear were strangely shapeless, as though he constantly lived in water. Otherwise he was as handsome as a film star ... Only one thing was strange: such a handsome man, yet so badly dressed and living in such an impoverished shack. I would never have been able to compare him to Vati. Vati was made out of silk ... fragile, small, with a goatee, wearing his broad-rimmed hat, narrow trousers, with a thin cigarette in a holder. His hair always shone blue and gray. I would never have guessed that he and Karel were brothers ... "Die Tante Mizi, meine Schwester. Sie ist krank."* ... On the other bed by a window in the corner an old woman with a scarf on her head lay in her clothes ... When I got close so she could look at me, too, I saw she had eruptions all over her face that were wet and as red as smeared makeup. She reached a hand out from under the quilt ... Good God, it was like some inflated bird claw, its upper side covered with little sores. Vati bent down toward her, said something cheerful and laughed ... She opened her mouth and I saw a few teeth, stumps and bits of gray metal ... she answered in a creaky voice ... She studied mother's face carefully, very seriously ... Oh, I knew instantly what she was thinking, because she took a big swallow. She looked at me and smiled, she had very bright, sharp eyes despite all the scabs and oozing eruptions ... which covered her forehead, too, like boils ... I had to look away. Mother sat on the bench by the chest, barefoot, holding her hand over Gisela's eyes. She wouldn't let her go near our aunt. I sat next to her, something stung like the devil on my back, and I stopped

*Aunt Mitzi, my sister. She's sick.

coughing ... "Ziehen wir uns aus,"* mother said. Vati and our dark-haired uncle sat in the middle of that strange ... room, one of them on a chair, the other on a footstool. Father's speech was cheerful but timid, refined and curious, while uncle spoke loudly, as though he were talking to someone in front of the house ... that was the spirit! I took off my stockings ... they came off my feet like a hippopotamus hide, and the sandals were just muddy lumps ... What hadn't they seen that night! ... Mother was dressing Gisela in her nightshirt straight out of the open suitcase ... a bit irritated, as though she were back home in Basel. Uncle sat with the knees of his long legs pulled up under his chin, and he looked at her and said something through his mustache. Vati looked over at her. "Heute Nacht schläfst du, Lisbeth, mit der Zwetschge in diesem Bett. Du kannst das nasse Zeug über den Ofen hängen."** Father pointed past me, to where there were some rods that had rags hanging from them. "Frag den Karl ..."*** mother said, but Vati headed her off in embarrassment, "Er wartete beim Zug um sieben, aber das Telegramm hat er später nicht bekommen wegen des schlechten Wetters. Es hat gehagelt und die Felder und viele Obstbäume sind kaputt."**** I looked at uncle. There was something about him that suggested he was laughing internally. Perhaps the strange

*Let's get undressed.
**Tonight, Lisbeth, you'll sleep with the tadpole in this bed. You can hang the wet clothes over the oven.
***Ask Karl .. ...
****He waited for the train at seven, but he didn't get the telegram later on account of the bad weather. It hailed and the fields and many of the fruit trees are ruined.

light was at fault for that, or his mustache, or the late hour ... Vati's sister chimed in here without lifting her swaddled head from the pillow ... I didn't care to look at her a second time, because I knew that from now on I was going to have to love and respect her. "Karel wird auf dem Heuboden schlafen, ich und Bubi auf dem Ofen. Nur für heute Nacht ..."* Mother ... who had always been fearful of touching ... spread some towels over the bed that was Karel's and that she was supposed to sleep in with Gisela. Our aunt looked at her, her cheek resting on her pillow ... "Daß ihr nicht hinunterfällt,"** mother said. "Nein, nein," Vati brushed her comment aside. Uncle lifted me ... upsy! ... onto the stove. What hands he had! Like whips! A bag lay on the stove whose contents crinkled ... straw or onion skins? "Das ist Kukuruz,"*** Vati reassured me. "In allen Betten sind Kukuruzblätter."**** I tried to catch a glimpse of uncle's face, to see if it had that smile or if it was just a shadow ... He left the room for another lamp and a blanket. The rags that hung from the rods over my head were yellow and spotted and didn't come close to smelling of Persil. Only now, from atop this odd stove, did I get a really good look at the room. Black straw-like stalks jutted out of cracks in the white plaster. Beneath a cross in the corner above our aunt's bed, two dark painted pictures stood on a small shelf alongside a tiny flame in a red glass ... they were the woman and man from church who pointed at their bare

---

*Karel will sleep in the hayloft, and Bubi and I will sleep over the stove. Just for tonight.
**Make sure you don't fall off of there.
***That's corn.
****All the beds are stuffed with corn husks.

chests with red, bleeding hearts that emitted flames and rays of light, but also had swords and a crown of thorns planted on them. That was probably Jesus and his mother, Mary... Aunt's eyes were closed. She was either sleeping or she was bored. Mother and Gisela lay hugging each other. Uncle Karel arrived with a thin, hole-ridden blanket. He stood in the doorway with a second, dust-covered lamp in hand. When he spoke with Vati, who was holding that first lamp, the clean one, I noticed under the mustache on his pale yellow face that grin like a taut string... I could see the very same grin in his eyes, which were even more pronounced... No, this wasn't a smile... this was scorn. This made me sad. Vati blew out the light. He lay down beside me. The space over the stove was hard and very hot. All I could see of the desolate room were two gray windows and the red light beneath the pictures. Aunt Mica was snoring. "Bubi! Vati!" mother quietly called out. "Ja! Ja!" the two of us answered. She always worried until everyone was home and under the covers... After that there was only the sound of the corn husks crinkling in their bed. It was great to go to sleep in this African hut, even if much of what came before sleeping had resembled dreams. But there was tomorrow...

WHEN I WOKE UP and looked out from under the rags, mother and Gisela were still asleep. Even our old aunt was still lying with her scarf over her face and her cane by the bed. Vati was gone from where I was. The stove had gone cold. The sun was shining outside both little windows... more brilliantly, clearly and powerfully than

I'd ever before seen it shine anywhere in the world, that could only happen somewhere near Africa ... but outside the third window there stretched a long, wet, almost black shadow. I could see trees, vividly green grass, blossoms ... tiny ones, big ones, of all different glorious colors. The two pictures over the little cross, of Jesus and Mary pointing to their dripping hearts, still hung there, too, but they were darker than last night, even though the red light was still burning ... Wow, at last I was here!... I was just a little chilly and there was something that smelled sour and wilted. Maybe our aunt. Gisela woke up and mother started shifting around on her corn husks. Then auntie stirred and climbed out of her narrow bed ... she slept in a long blue habit, similar to what nuns wear, only it was covered with crosses. She wasn't big when she got up. Only her nose jutted far out in front of her. Her feet had been bundled up in many layers of yellow rags. The kind that were hanging from the rods over the stove ... She looked up in my direction and mother signaled to me emphatically with her eyebrows. I climbed down onto the bench, bowed and said, "Guten Morgen, Tante." She giggled out loud and the gray eyes in her red, pustular face shone radiantly, in a way that only crazy or very intelligent eyes can shine ... Gisela and mother got up. "Wo ist der Vati?"* I asked her. "Er ist mit dem Onkel zum Bahnhof wegen der Koffer gegangen ... Ach, wir müssen zum Wasser und auch unser Zeug waschen,"** she complained.... I jumped down ... onto

---

*Where's father?
**He went to the train station with your uncle to get the suitcases. Ah, we have to go down to the water and wash our things.

the wide floorboards ... and over to the window ... Beneath it there was nothing but flowers. And such flowers! Lilac, red, orange, black with yellow stripes, tiny satiny flowers ... and big ones full of little stars. Aunt was standing in the open doorway with a paring knife in her hand and her face shone in the sun like the shard of a red platter ... Then we heard noise approaching the front of the house ... Uncle Karel entered the room dressed in black trousers, a green jacket and wearing a hat. Instead of a lantern he was carrying a nice, fat whip over his shoulder. Now, in the daylight, his face was even whiter and his mustache and hair were jet black ... His forehead shone like wax. He came up to me and tapped on the windowpane with his whip and said in his youthful voice, "Window!" Maybe he meant the flowers, aunt, the sun, or that I should should go out and wash up. Using his whip, which had little multi-colored braids at its tip, he etched out the whole pane. "Was das?"* he asked. "Oh! ... Scheibe, Fenster, fenêtre ..."** I answered. "Window!" he said. I looked at him intently. Maybe around his mouth or his eyes or someplace else on his face he had a dot ... a wrinkle ... features ... something that crept out of his mustache, his eyebrows, his nostrils observing someone and something about me, on my forehead, my cheek or even inside my head. "W-i-n-d-o-w!" he repeated distinctly. I repeated artlessly, hopelessly into the empty room, as though in some school where I knew absolutely nothing, "Vindoh!" ... Uncle laughed his head off. I wanted out of

*What that?
**Oh! Pane, window, fenêtre.

there as soon as possible. But he stopped me. He got down on his knees and used the whip to pull something like slippers out from under the bench ... in fact they were clogs that had been made out of worn-out shoes with no upper parts. "For you," he said ... So these were for me, I understood. My sandals really were just heaps of caked mud ...

What was just on the other side of the door wasn't an entryway, but a kitchen where our suitcases were standing ... Inside the black hole where last night coals had been glowing they baked bread. This ingenious device was an invention worthy of Indians ... Inside that wide, dark tunnel they heated the house, baked bread, fried things, cooked them in pots, Vati explained to mother. The hole in the wall got wider the farther in it went and on the other side it expanded into a stove as big as a monument that simultaneously kept the room warm, served as a sleeping space and even a drying area ... "Wenn wir uns so einen Ofen und Herd in Basel leisten könnten, hätten wir viel Geld gespart."* That was true. But when I looked inside at its walls shimmering with heat and saw a heap of glimmering embers, I remembered the witch from the gingerbread house and I pulled my head out of there right away ... From out of one corner Aunt Mica took one of several long poles that had a wide wooden ring on the end. Onto it she slapped a whole mountain of dough no smaller than an infant ... She showed us how she put the paddle into the oven

---

*If we could have afforded a stove and hearth like this in Basel, we would have saved a lot of money.

and then yanked it back out from under the loaf of dough ... I soon looked away ...

There was also a black table and a heavy bench in the kitchen, and a cupboard with a bin for flour, and black pots of lard. And it had two doors. One that we had come in through the night before, and the other where there were steps, uneven logs, outside which we'd stood when father tapped on the pane with his branch. There were nettles growing up out of those steps, a whole grove of them with pretty, milk-colored blossoms. Which meant that nobody used that door ... I hurried over to look at it, I was excited that green things grew right into the house, just like in some exotic hut ...

Then Uncle Karel opened the door across from the room with the stove. It was a whole place of its own, new, shiny, just whitewashed and big ... Some spattered wallboards lay on the floor, along with buckets, a shovel, some sand ... "Da werden wir wohnen,"* I told mother. "Gehört das Zimmer uns?"** I asked, full of hope and doubt. "Ja, Vati hat etwas Geld geschickt aus der Schweiz, daß es der Onkel gebaut hat..."*** So it was ours! I ran inside. A small screened window seemed somehow familiar to me. Yes, I had walked past it last night! Proudly I closed the door, which also seemed almost new ... Uncle Karel pointed to some stairs that led up to the ceiling. He pushed open a hatch at the top ... Here in the attic there was a veritable jumble of things – half storage, half butcher shop. Sausages, salamis, and

*That's where we'll live.
**Does that room belong to us?
***Yes, daddy sent some money from Switzerland so that your uncle could build it.

reddish brown shanks – hams – hung on lines from the rafters … "a veal shank," said Vati. A whole calf's leg complete with hoof and whiskers dangled in front of my face, as though from a gallows … On the floor there were pumpkins, some sort of troughs, a wooden wheel on a rope … Oh, if only I could have understood the language in which Karel was explaining things to Vati. When we went outside, the surroundings were completely different from the way they'd been the previous night … A river, dark green, extended across to a dark forest that grew a few meters from the shore on the far side … It was incredible how disciplined the trees were about stopping just shy of the water! That gave me something to think about … And the grass underfoot that was bright green and still full of dewdrops.

The unusual piece of equipment outside the house consisted of a block on two legs, a beam, a spindle with a wiry rope and a bucket with a dish-like little roof over it. It was Karel's invention! He showed it to us first thing: he turned a crank, like on automobiles … and the bucket took off down a wire and splashed into the water, which was a milky green from all the branches of bushes it had torn off in the storm … then he turned the crank in reverse, producing squeaks that reached to the far shore and up to high heavens … returning the bucket, now full of water which uncle used for the livestock, and setting it back on the shelf under its little roof. The only thing missing was for it to salute you! This was a real revolution! … But in addition to this apparatus there was also a well in front of the house with water you could drink. When we bent over it, our heads met against the backdrop of the sunny sky on its round watery bottom as if on a golden platter ... So many different things in such a small space! The casks and kettles standing on stones were pots that they cooked carrots and turnips in, then used blocks mounted on sticks to mix and strain them for the pigs ... Between this house and the neighboring house, which was much uglier, there was a handsome rooster, a glorious bird, standing atop a black heap of leaves and animal manure. His hens, as they pierced the surroundings with their eyes, pecked their way over to Gisela and me, showing no fear of us ... Then followed their chicks, little balls of yellow fluff that kept tumbling over the leaves. We reached our fingers out toward them, but uncle and aunt said something to each other and turned away, as though we'd done something bad ...

The house next to the heap was long, grayish brown and made out of stone and wood. It was covered with black straw like the one we had slept in, except it was already old and full of white and green moss. In one part of it, which was dark with a muddy window, there was a barn for the livestock ... Big, warm, handsome gray cows, rectangular and almost white ... In the pen next to them pigs jostled each other ... this was the first time I'd seen these fattest, dirtiest and most gluttonous of all animals in the world ... whose name got thrown at the most terrible people ... Horribly fat, pink under their whiskers, they shoved their snouts in their neighbors' rear ends and their rear ends at their neighbors' heads, their ears big as omelets ... I saw two or three little piglets, the poor things ... so young and already pigs ... One of them ... a big hog with its nostrils inflamed like a baby's bottom, suddenly snapped at my hand, which I was holding over the fence. Uncle laughed at this ... To the right of the entrance there was something resembling a bed, full of leaves and rags. "Da schläft der Hirt vom Onkel Karel,"* Vati said. Mother looked horrified ... finally she was getting to see a farm for the first time, too ... Up next was a narrow passageway with an old cupboard. That's where the hens slept, and up at the top in the hay is where they laid their eggs ... Right next to that was some sort of room with heaps of grain on the floor and a bunch of long sticks, each one tied with a cord to the others. Uncle showed us how it worked: he started swinging one of them, and with the others, which began to spin on the cord over his head, he thrashed at the floor ... He motioned to me to try it, but I couldn't make it work ... A free-hanging stick slapped at my face like a billy club ... In the middle there was also some equipment that resembled Vati's square sewing machine for working with fur. Uncle got it going with his leg and cut off a sheaf of straw ... bzzz! bzzz! Quickly I hid behind the grown-ups so he wouldn't call on me again to try it.

Outside there was some kind of door lying on the ground with sharp nails turned upward ... A fakir's bed? ... And a longish, bent wooden thing with handles and a sharp, wide blade, a real guillotine ... Hanging from pegs were round gray sticks with curved Turkish sabers ... Karel showed us: whoosh! whoosh! ... he used them to cut the grass, which went falling in rows. Up above there was an opening

---

*This is where Uncle Karel's shepherd sleeps.

with no door over it ... which you reached on a ladder ... I wasn't careful enough, because uncle grabbed me, put me on the ladder and shoved me up. The rungs sagged like rubber ... some dry grass was poking out of the hole way up above just under the ladder ... Uncle held onto me tight and kept pushing me higher ... but the upper end of the ladder moved and I was going to fall any second and take it with me as I splashed into the water ... Everything started to spin underneath me ... the heads, uncle, the river, the building. "Nein! Nein!" mother shouted ... When I was back down on the ground, uncle laughed so hard he stomped all over the grass in his shoes ... and the glistening grass was far more attractive than him ... Under the ladder there was a sort of hollow made of compacted red dirt. You got to it by going down a slope ... it contained firewood, axes, bags full of things, fastened, all stacked neatly up to the ceiling.

At the end of the building the meadow began to drop off ... toward the big body of water. There were smooth, wide stones on its bank. Karel said something. "Da waschen die Weiber die Wäsche," Vati translated. Fantastic! "Was?" mother gasped ... But where were the boats and horses? ... The water was gray, green, black ... full of eddying waves and ripples that sank in the middle of the river or expanded in rings. On the other side was the forest, a proper black forest of slender black pines, standing there like hundreds of bell towers ... Not until we headed back did we see how extensive the meadow was ... it was at least three hundred meters from here to the railroad tracks. There were a lot of spheres hanging in the dense crowns of the trees there. Green, red, and yellow. Small, egg-sized, blue. Apples and plums!

I barely recognized them from the ground ... until then I had only seen them in crates and at fruit vendors' stands ... "Habe ich es recht verstanden ... ich soll am Fluß die Wäsche waschen?" mother asked in shock. Uncle said something to Vati. Vati answered him. Karel laughed. But when he saw mother's face, her incensed, gaping mouth, the laugh turned into a guffaw ...

I ran off as fast as my legs would carry me. I stopped in front of the house. I had no idea where I wanted to go. But then I remembered what I had intended to do earlier: go look at the room we had slept in from the outside, through the window ... Now it was all by itself. I saw its white walls, both narrow beds, the high stove in the corner, the glass globe of the lantern (now out), both pictures with the bleeding heart over our aunt's bed, the flickering light in the red glass, the cross with Jesus ... Some straw poking down past the wooden gutter scratched at my neck.

Then we washed our shoes in water and set them out in the sun to dry. Nervously, as always, mother sewed a button onto the shirt I was wearing tucked into my pants, the button I had lost the night before ... Then suddenly from very close by we heard the whistle of a locomotive and tshhh! tshhh! tshhh!... I ran around to the other side ... It was a train just then approaching the crossing with the crucifix near uncle's fence ... A steam engine with two cars attached ... Like a ghost appearing in the wilderness. For the first time ever I saw the engineer, a swarthy man, from close up. He was leaning out his open window, wiping his hands with a red rag. Then the people in the cars appeared. Wearing scarves and simple hats, they were standing and looking out of square windows that looked like they'd been sawed out of the sides of the ordinary cars. It didn't seem like a real train to me, more like a procession of horse-drawn carts. At any rate, it made a proper "toot-toot!" The locomotive was genuine enough, with an enormous cow-catcher up front. Its movement past uncle's huge meadow was neither fast nor slow. As though it were out for a walk ... At the end of the train I could see the gray wall of its last car disappearing into the black pine forest. And then the smoke bending up out of the woods. A train right out my front door and every day, at that!

We ate out of one big dish next to the stove in the kitchen – some thickened milk that had small, sour dumplings floating in it. Each of us had his own wooden spoon ... Vati, uncle, me, aunt ... only mother and Gisela shared a spoon ... Auntie giggled to herself with all the red craters on her face as she carried the sour milk up to her mouth. When old women laugh that wholeheartedly, it means they're not quite right in the head ... And if they have so many pustules, they're probably suffering from some awful disease ... plague, leprosy – which isn't contagious ... I ate across from her and was careful not to spoon anything out from the middle ... But my stomach revolted when I put the first little dumpling with milk in my mouth. It tasted terrible ... like nothing at all. After breakfast Karel took me by the shoulder and led me outdoors ... He went to get the gray spotted cow in the barn. "Du bist jetzt der Hirte," Vati said. "Nur an diesen kleinen Baum dort darf die Kuh nich heran."* I picked up one of the sticks that were lying around. The cow came out of the barn ... It had nice, taut brown spots, as though it were dressed in a map. A chain hanging down from its collar dragged along the ground. It headed straight for the tiny tree that was tied with straw to a stake. I had lifted up my thin stick when it turned its head toward me ... as big as a gas lantern. It looked at me with its eyes ... which were at least five times as wide as human eyes. The first time it saw me, and I it, it was barely a hand's breadth away. Its horns were marbled, flinty, and slightly curved ... It curled its lips, which had thick, white spittle, milk, dangling down ... It exposed its yellow teeth set in their pale gums. I fell flat on my face in the grass. Fearlessly uncle picked up the chain that lay next to its hooves and tried to put one end in my hand. I was unresponsive. But he picked up my hand, set the hot ring in it, wrapped the chain around my wrist and pointed ahead ... to a patch of dry grass in the sun. I was now holding her head at the end of this heavy restraint. But thanks to a chin that resembled Claire's, she struck me as goodnatured and entirely trustworthy. I ought to have pulled her along behind me, but I didn't dare. Uncle Karel stepped in and pulled the chain tight from the middle. The cow strained away and Karel let go of the chain ... For a while the huge, earnest animal walked obediently behind me of her own free will. Maybe she sensed that I was alone and would care for her ... But that's not very likely ... Suddenly she was nudging my

---

*You're the cowherd now. Just make sure the cow doesn't go near that little tree over there.

back with her bazooka round of a muzzle ... And she was mooing strangely, plaintively, angrily, as she kept advancing on me. Hurriedly I unwrapped the chain from around my wrist ... and jumped aside.

When I turned around I saw two boys under the tree outside the house. Lithe and swarthy. They were wearing snow-white shirts and shorts that reached down to their knees. Barefoot. Slightly shy. "Das sind die Söhne vom Onkel Joseph oben vom Dorf,"* Vati said. Cousins, Ivan and Ciril. "Das ist Bubi." They looked at me. They had brown eyes and dark mouths, as though they'd been eating cherries. They were at least two grades ahead of me. Should I shake their hands? That probably wasn't done here. All three of us were at a loss ... They studied me from head to toe. That was uncomfortable, because both of them were handsome. Then Karel called them and they ran off.

Gisela and I went out under a tree in front of their garden. Using the sticks that lay scattered in the grass in huge numbers – you could hardly pick up one of them without three or four others sliding off – I created the outline of a ring. Gisela was going to be the black man Joe Louis and I was going to be the German, Max Schmeling. The grass was appropriately low. Both of us assumed our boxing positions. "Box match, Joe Louis: Max Schmeling!" I announced. "Bong!" I struck the gong ... It was wonderful to be fighting outside, in the open air, in the grass. In Basel we could injure ourselves if we went flying to the ground ... but here it was a pleasure to fall into the soft grass. In my excitement I actually punched Gisela and hurt her, causing her to cry.

*These are the sons of your Uncle Joseph who live up in the village.

She gave it back to me in the eyes, so that I couldn't see. Uncle Karel stood watching, once again doubled over with hilarious laughter ... but strangely, his eyes weren't laughing at all. No, this was not a good sign ... Mother came out, dressed, Vati too. "Jetzt gehen wir hinauf zum Onkel Joseph. Sie warten schon auf uns,"* he said. Ciril and Ivan, my cousins, also came galloping out from behind the house. Each of them was wearing a new green hat.

We hit the trail as we had the night before ... going past a white house with a brand new red roof. The same flowers that grew in the meadows were in various big pots and glasses at the foot of the cross. Except they had faded. It was strange that they picked flowers that grew in such numbers at Jesus's feet anyway ... And even stranger that they let them fade when they could have put fresh ones in the glasses each day ... At the railroad crossing I paused in the middle of the tracks: on one side they led from where we had just come from, and on the other side they curved along the high gravel trackbed and headed into the black forest ... After the crossing the path rose ... with houses built along the slope. Simple, unadorned, white ... A little black house made of straw stood slightly set back from the path. "Da lebt eine alte Närrin, wie der Karel erzählt," I heard Vati say. "Ihr ganzer Kram liegt vor dem Haus."** ... It consisted of a box and a colorful heap of rags, with not even a chair ... Ciril and Ivan were

---

*We're going up to visit your Uncle Joseph now. They're already expecting us.
**That's where an old crazy woman lives, according to Karel. That's all of her stuff in front of the house.

walking on either side of me. I wanted to be polite ... but it's hard to connect with boys your same age when you can't talk or play some game ... I pointed at the forest that the train had passed through ... at the iron weathercock on a roof ... and at a neat wooden garden hut in the distance. Both of them nodded, adjusted their hats over their black hair, bent down because I was shorter, laughed ... In their hip pockets they had something interesting ... a fat rubber band, a kind of sling, like David's, on a sturdy cleft stick. They picked up a stone, pulled back the rubber band and ... ping! it went flying straight into a snipe that had been perched on the mossy roof of the crazy woman's house ... As handsome as they were, and as honest and decent as they may have been, they knew all the tricks ... What would it be like? Would we really become friends? ... Along both sides of the path lay carpets of furrowed black earth. We walked past several wooden structures that had carts and ladders standing beside them. On the road there were a number of men, peasants like Uncle Karel, only shaggier, with pitchforks and shovels in hand, but friendly, I thought. Also old women in dense layered dresses and scarves, like our aunt, but minus the bundled-up feet and the pustules ... Untroubled faces, dark furrows. Some brown stinking rivulet, liquid manure, trickled right down the path ... and huge heaps of black, stinking leaves stood in front of each house. A white hen was waddling along the top of a fence above a pool of filthy urine. Yellow chicks like the ones we'd get for Easter, but alive, were chirping. No one paid any attention to them except Gisela and me, but mother called us back so we wouldn't fall into any manure. Now we could see that garden cottage from a bit closer up and next to it a house with big windows. That was probably where city people had to live.

This latter turned out to be Uncle Jožef's house. On one side it was as tall as a castle ... and that's where an enormous dung heap stood and where you entered the house by stone steps to the right or left. On the other side the house was like any other little house with small doors and windows, just like Karel's. It had a wide entryway with a stove and a fat pillar in the middle. This was the house Vati was born in. A lot of people had gathered in the main room. I felt bashful and didn't know how I was supposed to behave. There were several holy paintings on the wall, just like at Karel's house. Jesus, Mary, Joseph and lots of other saints with little lambs. A little white porcelain Mary wearing a blue shawl hung by the door. Instead of legs she had a little dish with water, which sent a sudden jolt through my hips ... Paper flowers and green branches had been tucked in around the cross. There were photographs hanging on the wall between the two small windows. "Deine beiden Onkel, die in Amerika leben,"* said Vati. These were two portly gentlemen, wearing floral silk vests and with watches on chains, who were standing on a shaggy rug. Next to them in a round frame were Vati's father and mother. If I look at them long enough, I thought, I'll learn something. I always did that with pictures. "Meine

---

*Your two uncles who live in America.

Mutter, als sie starb,"* Vati pointed to another one. In this last, long picture my grandmother was lying dead in her coffin, beneath a lace veil and covered from her feet up to her folded hands with icons of saints ... Jesus, Mary and one other, a monk in a brown habit who was holding the baby Jesus in his arms.

"Bubi! Bubi!" they called me to the table. I was flushed red with embarrassment. Uncle Jožef sat at the center of the table. He was thin, with white hair and a mustache. The eyes under his splotchy forehead were harshly blue and when he smiled, it wasn't exactly innocent mirth that showed in them. He was wearing a hat. When he got up, he turned out to be small and his long gray trousers were short enough even for me to wear. His wife was gray and tiny, with a mouth as wide as the slot on a piggy bank. I also had three female cousins at the table. The oldest was big, powerful Minka who had studied to become a postal employee ... pretty, dark-haired Stanka who had blue eyes and dazzling teeth and was so attractive she seemed almost magnetic ... and the last was little Anica, who was perhaps a year younger than me ... long-legged and skinny-armed, wearing a dirty red skirt ... as barefoot as a chicken and completely unkempt.

Anica, Ciril, and Ivan took me through a tall door to some steps leading out of the house. They were grinning like crazy ... with their eyes, their skin, their hair. We came out onto a stony slope leading downward with a tall, narrow barn made of stone. Inside it were three glorious horses. A gray, that was slightly dappled and two bays with

*My mother when she died.

extremely high-set tails and such shaggy legs that they looked like they were wearing muffs ... So these were the horses I was going to ride. Just get me saddles, stirrups, and tournament dress for over their bellies. And some plumes for their heads. Armor. All set to ride over the drawbridge into the castle ... You hurl a gigantic spear ... all the way to the altar in the castle's chapel, where your enemy kneels, the black prince, begging for his life ... Then the battle is won and bells announce my victory in war ... In a wooden barn next to it there were a lot more chickens than there were at Karel's ... its floor practically billowed from the abundance of feathers ... Then there were some big pigs in a wide pen ... and some little wooden slat coops where some white geese and those funny coral-colored ducks lived. Who would have thought! Just past the dung heap the meadow began, hanging gently like a sheet over a hollow that stretched from the house down to the road at the foot of a hill. And here at the edge of the meadow was a little building made out of nothing but timbers and full of rummage. My cousins and Anica just opened its door ... and pointed, without saying anything, and if they had, I wouldn't have understood them anyway ... All I had to do was look at their eyes and their laughter. There was a tiny round hut way up at the top of a long pole, with cooing sounds coming out of it. Pigeons. Domestic ones ... white, fat, and handsome ... handsomer than in Basel along the Rhine, or in front of the city hall ... Covered with dots, they came out of their opening, flew down onto the roof of the little building and then back home ... So these cousins and uncles of mine must be good people, I concluded. There was a wooden building in the middle of the meadow.

"Hay barn," they said. Up above it was full of dried grass, while down below there were carts with sides made of slats, lined up one after the other. And a real coach, the kind that princesses ride in, that was yellowish brown, with lanterns on each side. My cousins showed me how to climb up the struts. Anica climbed like a squirrel ... and when she was standing on the strut above me, I noticed she didn't have underpants on ... That excited me and I thought I was dreaming. The barn was on the lower side of the house. In addition to cows, black and brown smoky grays, there was also a bull and a calf. Then they were called back to the house ... all three of them had to run somewhere carrying baskets that were as big as cradles ...

Once left on my own, I headed farther down the path that we had used to come up into the village ... There were no houses anymore on this stretch, just high bushes growing on both sides, making the path quiet and dark. The deep shadow made it feel like evening. Suddenly I thought I had found the place where Vati, as he had told me once long ago, had stopped to rest when he was little. It was Easter and he was delivering a potica to the priest. He pulled the napkin aside and discovered that the potica he was carrying as a gift was full of raisins. Far more than the ones that mother baked at home for them. This made him angry, because he didn't like the priests. He picked out all of the raisins he could find and ate them, and so the potica he delivered to church was more or less gutted ... I could practically see in the dust where he had set the basket down and sat to rest a while, because he wasn't one of the hardiest boys in the family. That was right here where the path made a broad arc behind a big, bushy shrub, leaving this side of the shrub quiet and hidden behind lots of big branches, so that truly no one would bother him. But he would have had to be quick if he didn't want the path to take him around the corner with it and turn him into a stone or a bush ... They started to call my name, "Bubi! Bubi!" I had to hurry back if I didn't want to give my future hiding place away.

The table in the main room had a white tablecloth on it and practically everyone was standing or sitting around it. There was some bright red drink in unusual bottles and in the middle of the table there was a stack of neatly arranged yellow slices of some baked goods. I was as hungry as a dog. When we sat down, I took one of them. It was slightly moist, hard, compact and coarse, and when I bit off some of it, a salty, hard, watery, empty taste filled my mouth. I spat it out. All of them stared at me. Even mother. "Ich meinte, es wäre ein Biskvit,"* I said. Vati translated. All of them laughed amicably. It was made from corn. Then they poured me some yellow drink that was sour and bitter. I couldn't force it down. I took Gisela and went out with her to show her what our cousins had shown me ... and maybe also the path I'd just discovered.

But barely were we at the fence when they called me again, "Bubi! Bubi!" ... Everyone was standing outdoors on the high side of the house, on the hillside of round stones except for the horse stable ... Our cousins, Anica too, came galloping back with baskets filled with turnips and carrots. "Der Stritz will, daß du mit Ivan and Ciril zum

---

*I thought it was a sponge cake.

Fluß reitest,"* Vati said ... Mother, who still appeared to be satisfied with the food and drink, waved her hands, "Nein, nein!" Gisela drew me away when the door opened and she saw the forest of high rear ends in front of her. Everyone all around laughed. I was willing, but seized with fear ... Ivan and Ciril boosted me up onto a tall chest ... next to their wiriness and agility I was a regular fatso and cry-baby ... Then one of them jumped and held onto the horse by the head. The animal was standing before me ... tall and powerful, with a bushy blond mane and its brown coat mottled all over. A living, breathing animal, not some papier-mâché horsey on a merry-go-round. How had I missed my chance to get Gisela and myself to that nook by the path where we could have hidden? ... Ivan was pushing my feet up on his shoulders. My rectum stretched painfully when I threw one leg over the horse's back. It was as though I'd mounted a drum. I thought I was going to be torn apart, drawn and quartered ... The horse whinnied and tossed back the bright, stifling yarn of its mane. They pushed it backwards out of its stall, where there wasn't enough room for it to turn around. I lowered my head, but the door still struck me hard enough from behind that I saw stars. Now I hurt at two ends ... "Hinunter! Geben Sie ihn hinunter!"** mother shrieked. Nobody paid her any attention. I would have preferred to jump down, but its hoofs would have trampled me ... When the plump, shaggy horse began ambling down the escarpment, everyone looked up. Anica, Stanka,

---

*Your uncle wants you to ride down to the river with Ivan and Ciril.
**Down! Get him down from there!

uncle, Minka looking as though it was funny, Gisela tense, mother all red, Vati casting worried looks in every direction ... They finally managed to push the horse onto the path leading uphill. Ciril and Ivan were on the other two, the gray and the other bay ... both of them having mounted to my left. The animal was calm, even though its brown, bristling coat seemed to undulate ... I held onto it by its mane, but there was also its bridle ... Left-left, right-right ... Both of my cousins were laughing ... I had never been so high up, let alone on something so alive, with its own head and heart ... its own will! Actually I enjoyed the fact that everything was happening so fast. Barely would one thing reach its mid-point before the next thing would clip onto it and get underway ... And on and on like that ... This was a life packed with excitement and adventure! ... There was so much I was going to experience here! Row through, ride through! Now this was freedom! ... What did the world look like from horseback? ... The thatched straw roofs grazed past my feet like carpets and the windows were hidden beneath them like eyes ... The path wasn't a path at all, it was a mixture of sand, puddles and stones. Nobody was going to scold me if I set the world even more on its head. Made castles or holes, rearranged this whole part as I saw fit ... Or cleaned it up, because it was full of cow pies and horse droppings and dung heaps and rivulets that trickled down the paths. Everything was exposed, vast, free, everything was allowed ... the world was a big toilet under the open sky ... A branch of some hanging tree slid over my face, with nothing but tiny little leaves. Right, a willow. I had to half-close my eyes and squint. See this, just like the Indians did. I could feel the horse's belly under my rear end, its guts and the movements of their muscles under my calves. This short-haired brown hide was alive for a change, hot and damp, not dead like the hides of Vati's wild animals ... The horse's ears, pointed and foxlike ... flicked near my eyes ... This was a parade! Only now did I see the grassy slopes alongside the path as hills, and a bush as a single flower tossed into a canopy of starlike blossoms ... As we went Ciril and Ivan introduced me to a bunch of boys, peasants and women ... Their voices sounded like trumpets. I would blush when they pointed to me, because I was sitting so high and clumsily ... One of the peasants said something and Ivan, or Ciril, who was older, answered, provoking so much laughter I thought they would burst! ... I didn't understand a word. They spoke quickly, abruptly, as if in shouts. Which words? They laughed wholeheartedly and I laughed with them ... One, a boy in a hat and holding a hoe, who stood next to the house of that crazy woman, asked something slowly. I tried to look into his eyes under the head covering ... He wasn't satisfied with my cousin's response. He said something else ... something not very friendly, I thought ... and at this the two cousins burst out in laughter. Did they mean me ... were they trying to hang something ugly on me? The boys in Basel – Italian, French, German ... all boys in the world ... including these here ... were alike ... But when we reached the edge of the forest my cousins turned around on their horses and brandished their bridles at the one by the path. Maybe some old feud they had with him? ... By the woods we trotted over the railroad tracks. Here, on the other side, next to Karel's fence with Christ on the cross, was that white, cool house with the new red roof.

On its ground floor terrace, in a corner of its snow-white walls, for no particular reason, stood a tall, beautiful, fire-red vase with a single glorious flower in it. As though it had been placed out for public view in some display window in a city. I could have been both at the same time – the empty space and the big vase – if I could have seen myself from the outside... A young woman dressed in blue had appeared... incredibly beautiful! Like in a fairy tale! Such curls! That smiling face! Her shoulders, her movements, her apron, all of her!... She waved to Ciril and Ivan... and both of them, flushed red with embarrassment and pride, could barely bring themselves to wave back. Her eyes slid over me, too, and in terror I fixed mine on the horse's mane... Now the horses were walking over that clinking flat surface of stones, of big, flinty eggs, that we had negotiated the night before. But the horses shoved their hooves and horseshoes into the little rocks as though they were nothing, as though they were gliding through the grass and causing sparks... At a bend there were trees whose crowns bent down over us... dark green leaves with swarms of big flies... I shook them off and the horse jumped a little. From now on I'll have to quietly put up with everything!... Beyond the tree crowns there was a wooden and masonry house... On its terrace were several people looking at me, one of them dressed in city clothes... Thank God some trees rose up again and the stones became damp... And in this context I saw the river. It ate into the bank in a semi-circle, shallow and calm, not wild like during the night... When the horse waded into it up to his belly, the river noisily foamed all around him, so that it felt like looking out from a ship's prow... and when he lowered his head, I almost slid down the back of his neck ... I didn't dare get my sandals and stockings wet, but I did, immediately. This was so dangerous – sitting on an animal in the middle of a raging river! In no time other kids had gathered around the inlet and horses ... A little girl crouching down with her skirt billowing like a balloon, grinning up at me with a scab on her lips like a dozen frogs ... a little imp with his head bandaged ... and two or three others who had appeared like Liliputians out of the brush, flung themselves into the water and began splashing each other, squealing, striking its surface with sticks and walking on all fours as though they were swimming ... Ciril tossed his shirt and trousers onto his horse's back. Wearing only his undershorts, in a glorious leap off the horse he dove into the middle of the river ...

LANGUAGE, one that you don't understand, can be pleasant now and then ... It's like a kind of fog in your head ... It's nice, there's truly nothing better ... It's wonderful when words haven't yet separated from dreams ... But not always ... I could examine everything as though I was in a theater ... Before a storm the sky would get dark. The rain splashed as though a whole sea hung in the air ... The Krka flowed like a roadway from hell ... the water rose to the machine with the bucket ... a whole wagon, a haystack, half a hayrack, a small forest ... once even an ox gasping for air and lowing ... floated past quickly and slammed into the banks of the river ... You lost your voice from the wetness, your sight from the gloom, your soul from the lightning ... And then silence again. The great kingdom of fog! ... It was as though everything was under a spell ... a different world ... You couldn't see two paces ahead of you in Karel's meadow ... The house hung in a cloud, the fog tamely expanding into the entryway, slowly pressing into the dark kitchen, into our yellow room, between Gisela and mother, who was refitting dresses for Minka, Mica, Stanka ... between the cows and the pigs in the barn ... Mooing and cooing and crowing filled the space ... Especially sounds from the river below ... It seemed as if the water reached to our window ... We could hear it on the other side of the house, where just a plum and an apple tree stood ... The steam engine's whistle expanded in serpentines through its foggy soot to the sky ... A land of ghosts. You had to go back into the house right away. So you wouldn't topple into the Krka down by the bucket ... But on peaceful days red clouds floated back up above the horizon over the water and the fields became blue ... A whole parade of people ... women, men, children ... each with a hoe in hand, wearing hats, scarves, and colorful woolen caps, like the ones babies wear, would be digging out in the fields ... tossing the useless potatoes onto the gravel ... calling out to each other across the fields. A ladder wagon came racing along and stopped, causing its horses to rear up on their hind legs ... With that guillotine of his on a tall handle, the plough, Karel pushed through the meadow ... Everything that had been down below got turned up ... The meadow exposed its whole lower layer to the world, to the sun and the air, so that the huge green space by the train tracks looked something like an African's gigantic shining face. No one had ever seen anything like it. Ever. It was a miracle, a sin, something like the Indian wars, the first casualties ... with not a sidewalk, a bit of asphalt, a roadway to be seen ... you kneaded the cool, pleasantly damp, greasy lumps barefoot, till at the end of a row, next to the ploughshares and the basket-like carts, you were spattered with dirt on your chest, back and face ... like the Sioux in their warpaint ... Then all the way back, and then once more all over again to repeat the pleasure of having your legs sink into the dirt up to your knees ... Mother in her white dress smiled at me from the far end of the field and Vati, as always, rested his hands on his back and was nervously blinking behind his glasses ...

During the first week we went down into town. To the authorities to take care of some paperwork. Both uncles wearing black suits and hats. In tall black shoes that laced up high. With no stockings. They wrapped rags around their feet. "Leggings," Aunt Mica said. I couldn't repeat it ... I went with one of the uncles and Vati went with the other. Karel entertained Ciril and Ivan with much laughter ... they were very similar. All three of them had black, fringe-like hair and brown eyes, but only Karel had sideburns. Each of them had a big mouth. And the same way of shoving his hat back on his head. "Go join them!" Karel said and I ran over to Uncle Jožef, who was talking to Vati and laughing with Anka, his youngest ... I ought to have been staying at Karel's side, not running to Jožef. They were revealing their teeth and gums ... this was whole-hearted laughter ... which I could understand even in a foreign language ... The houses reached down toward the water, like animals going to drink ... Along the way there was a smithy, with the smith outside just then, nailing shoes onto a black horse. "Unser weiter Verwandter,"* said Vati ... For a while we watched the black horse – lithe, glistening, a regular racer with his head tied to a timber – put up with all the hammering on his hooves ... The nails that broke got pulled out with pliars. Uncle and Vati had a short chat with the smith. He didn't look strong enough to me for that kind of work. I couldn't understand anyone. Maybe the bellows, the fire under the hood. But when the smith's assistant began to strike the white-hot shoe with his hammer, even that *clinkity-clink-clink* sounded like a word from their language ... Other than that, my ears just hurt from the noise, but still ... Even Liska was mooing like the braune and schwarzbunte Kühe** on the slopes around Urach ... But this "moo" coming from her funnel-like muzzle was not the same "moo." Maybe Liska wasn't even a proper cow ... She went walking straight into the house, announcing herself in the kitchen. As fat as poor Mrs. Dopf from the flower shop next door on Gerbergässli in Basel, she stood between the table and the hearth in the fringe-like coat and horns of an outwardly clumsy cow. I felt sorry for her ... Now I could take her by the horns fearlessly and lead her out. I could stick my hand in her mouth and let her lick it ... There were no "Tannenbäume" in this forest. These pines grew tall and resinous, with sharp needles and lots of gaps ... they were some completely different species of tree ... A completely new one! Exotic! Straight out of my imagination, although I could touch them ... a species thoroughly mixed up by the chaos that

---

*A distant relative of ours.
**Brown and black variegated cows.

language causes. I had to give it a new name ... who knows, maybe half in my language, half in theirs ... derived from the impression the pine made on me ... "mast tree," "umbrella tree," "monk tree" ... Even the spoon I ate with wasn't a proper utensil ... but some object of driftwood and steel that would jab at the corners of my mouth as though it didn't know what it had been made for ... It would try to pry my jaws open ... pulverize my teeth, smash my tongue. And the skinny, white and brown cat that introduced itself one morning with its magical mewing in the gutter ... And then the Krka! It was a dangerous thing that flowed with its crocodilian surface as though it were flowing past us straight out of hell. It wasn't the Rhine, which was wide and had ships sailing on it ... it was meant only for drowned people, cattle, house roofs, forests and hay-wagons ... It could be quiet, gurgle, swell, subside, be peaceful, ugly or beautiful, but always as though under its mists it wore some sort of mask. I wouldn't have been afraid to wade into it ... I tried from the laundry stones, since the inlet where livestock were watered wasn't really the Krka. But Vati grabbed me under the arm. And yet I wouldn't have dared ... because it was and it wasn't real water. Were my eyes deceiving me or something? ... One morning by the pear tree outside my window I saw Ciril and Ivan, who as usual had come to get me to go with them to water the animals. They stood facing each other ... each holding a sharpened stick pointed at the other, trying to gouge him in the eyes. "Sie werden sich die Augen ausstechen!"* I shouted and ran to get

*They're going to poke each other's eyes out!

mother. Mother shouted and ran to get Vati. Then Vati to get Karel. Karel waved dismissively and turned away. For him that was a game. "Sie spielen nur. Du hast das nicht richtig verstanden,"* Vati said. I had misunderstood? I shouted, "Ich habe es gesehen! Ich habe es verstanden!"** I knew I had seen it as it was there to be seen. Then again I wasn't completely convinced ... Karel went to talk to my cousins. They were offended and sulked angrily after that. Had I seen right or falsely accused them?

We reached the little railroad station where we had arrived several weeks before. There were train cars standing there. Big, red ones. Tenders, as they were called. But for me they were circus paintings on a big canvas, cars made of red chewing gum ... When we went down into town, the buildings scattered around amid the stones of the paved town square, which was full of sewage puddles, horse droppings, cow pies, hay-carts and pigpens, were just country buildings. Not city buildings at all, these were tiny and quiet and you could practically see through them. The town hall was a building with a tower, but it was lifeless, without any guard houses or police cars in front. The little shops here had dirty windows, half-blind rummage stores. I was no longer interested in produce stores as I'd been in Basel ... with whole mountains of oranges and valleys of spinach on little bleachers ... but the bakery, instead, with its sesame and poppy buns and loaves of white bread. The barbershop with its white-clad barbers, wigs and

---

*They're just playing. You misunderstood.
**I saw it! I understood!

bottles in the display window full of scents and ointments, none of which had any trace of earthy dirtiness, mud or the unpleasantness of nature ... The pharmacy with its medicines in jars and gold bust of the first doctor in ancient Greece ... The general store. Its display window had bottles and glasses full of unwrapped candies and a stack of small, faded chocolate bars in dismal, monochromatic wrappers. That was the clearest possible proof that everything had really changed ... that it was all just a pale reflection ...

I was learning the language. My cousins Ciril and Ivan, and occasionally Stanka, too, taught me the song "Little Sunshine on Little Mountains" ... They pointed to the soft blue peak that rose up over the black forest on the far side of the Krka. Those were the "bountains." Atop them lived a shepherd who got married to a skinny girl, who was all bones when she hugged him, a fat girl, who melted on him, and a very short girl, who got lost in his bed. All of them resembled various peasant women, young or old, whom you could see walking around the village. But most of all they resembled the crazy woman from the cabin, who was all of these things at once ... she had a big rear end, skinny legs and she was short ... The worst thing was when Vati went looking for work in town and he wasn't at home. When I went out and said, "gut mornink! gott villink! gut day!" my cousins would laugh. This wasn't a pleasant laughter, I noticed that right away ... It shook them so hard that they practically bounced up to the roof. "Zerspringt nur, kleine Mistviehe,"* I thought to myself. They ran into the house

---

*Go ahead and blow up, ya bloody animals.

to get reinforcements for their laughter ... Aunt Mica or Karel. If one of them so much as touches me, I'll lose it ... Two weeks, three weeks, five weeks went by ... I wasn't going to let them trick me, no way! I wasn't yet capable of having a conversation ... All I had to do was remember Ivan and Ciril's sharpened sticks ... the endless arguments between mother and Vati, every possible gossip and threat ... all the mischief they could inflict on you with a word ... and it passed. I was fully prepared. They weren't going to get me to walk into their trap ... I had a unique opportunity to keep quiet ... to hide in a way. They thought I was sulking. Let them think that! In fact, I was unable to speak ... Karel dug a big, deep pit near the cross to hide food. I helped him send foodstuffs down on a pulley. A barrel of cabbage. A crate of apples. A case of meat. A box of flour. A tin of lard. He laid straw and boards over all of it. "Krieg! Krieg!"* he repeated, "There's going to be a war!" he said, encouraging me. "Zers koink to pea a vor!" I repeated. I turned around in the pit to face Ciril and made a sign on my forehead that meant "he's nuts" ... I ran off as fast as I could. But that afternoon I was already tending Liska at the far end of the pasture. I could see mother and uncle in the doorway of Karel's short house – her wearing white, him in black. It would have been impossible to imagine two more remote opposites. I knew they were never going to be able to understand each other ... From morning to night mother would only lament. And she would cry, which made me feel sorry for her. "Ich fühle mich so wie in einem Kerker"** she kept repeating. On Sunday

*War! War!
**I feel like I'm in a dungeon

we rode in Jožef's black and yellow carriage with the lanterns to Prečna for mass. When I got up I had to get a good wash using the bucket next to the well ... Only Vati didn't go with us, because he didn't believe in God. And Aunt Mica on account of her legs. Each of us was supposed to pray an extra Our Father for her. The carriage was full of my female cousins decked out in their Sunday best. Bright-colored dresses, loose blouses, pink satin. I was allowed to sit on the driver's box next to Jožef. He was nicer than Karel, probably because we didn't live at his place. Once long ago Vati had sent some money for the church bell in Prečna. I was proud as it rang now and echoed through the hills, fields and forest ... Its white walls rose high up over the people, and the church had just two ordinary windows without colored figures ... The peasants sat dressed in black, baggy suits, the very best of their wardrobes ... their heads and faces poking up out of them like dirt, and their lips were chapped. God wasn't a silver-haired St. Nicholas ... He sat on a cloud with a triangle behind his head and a geometrical nose ... On Sundays Stanka was prettier than usual ... Children had to stand at the rear ... My lips practically touched the bronzed back of her neck as she sat in the pew ... The temptation was great ... Her hands as she prayed were beautiful, exquisitely bronzed ... they had the same maturity as her face. Like something out of a fairy tale. The charm that passed over her face as she pronounced the words of the prayers, the way her nose twitched and her lips moved ... It was pure witchcraft. It flooded me. I heard angels singing. Her slightest smile sent out waves ... a pure magical force. I didn't dare look at her anymore ... And her hair, as the candles got lit. Black, violet blue!

Damn! She was becoming a water sprite! Right here, for all to see. I looked around, but no one had noticed... But I also knew she could be mean... like Gritli... From that time we were mowing on the slopes above Kandija, when we played tag and she hit me with a bridle supposedly just in fun, but in fact swung it as hard as she could... Up above, on a kind of stove in the middle of the chuch, stood the priest, dressed in white... whenever the organ came in, the women would start singing like waves of thin voices. Banners hung from shiny metal poles... with saints, temples, St. John the Baptist with his shepherd's staff on them. This was a different kind of God from the one I was used to. A peasant! A mower! A sower and driver!...

At that time Vati went to look for work in the biggest town, Ljubljana, where we had first arrived... Whenever he was away, we were alone. And that wasn't good... Uncle Karel gave mother one less tablespoon of lard. She had to ask him specially for flour and potatoes. He forbade her to sew for my cousins: none of those girls was going to wear her city rags. "Niks schneiderei! Arbeiten!"* he said. She had to chop up a whole mountain of carrots and turnips. I stood at the block and used a mallet – a block on a stick – to mix, crush, and strain the feed for the young piglets. Clunk! Clunk! Aunt Mica came out. "Barrel!" she said. "Carrots!... Pigs!" Her red pustular face bunched up into cute wrinkles. Encouragingly. And if only she had been God knows how much nicer!... "You pig! Your mother pig!..." I understood. And I almost slipped, but I managed to get a grip on myself.

*No seamstress! Work!

I just had to remember everything ... recognize the words, that was the key, and pick your own fights ... I opened my mouth ... wide, I looked like something was about to come out ... But nothing came ...

W<small>E HARVESTED GRAIN</small> on Jože's field and bound it in sheaves ... Vati worked in town at a branch of the Elite company ... He sewed sleeves into ready-to-wear jackets ... He would leave for work in the pre-dawn darkness and come home in the late-evening gloom ... In exchange for flour and lard mother sewed a nicer dress for my cousin Minka, who was supposed to have gotten a job at the post office ... She was a stout woman. Her round face radiated good will. She reminded me of Claire. She walked back and forth in the kitchen in her rustling bright silken dress and tight blouse with billowy pink satin sleeves ... Aunt Mica, who was mixing dough for bread, turned around from the hearth. She said something with an ominous look on her face. "Was sagt denn diese Schlitzäugige wieder?"* mother asked. I looked at my aunt. Her eyes weren't slanted, they were as bright as pebbles. "Etwas über die Messe ... daß sie mit diesem Kleid nicht zur Kirche gehen kann ..."** I answered.

A yellow dust rose up over Jože's field that pricked at your skin and burned your eyes ... An ox tied to a stake walked in circles over the grain, so that its hooves would thresh the grain out of the husks.

*What is old slant eyes saying again?
**Something about mass, that she can't go to church wearing this dress.

A regular merry-go-round. The post he was hitched to would creak. He walked in a circle for kilometers on end. That's how bread was made. No other way. It was obvious the ox would succumb, so they switched him out with a horse and then the horse with the ox again. On the floor of the storehouse next to the cow barn they also threshed grain ... I helped. By swinging the stick that had another stick fastened to it, over my head, and striking it ... I got quite good at it, although the little kids from the neighborhood would come watch me ... All little clowns, each and every one wearing too short a shirt and grinning like toads ... one hand with the thumb in their mouth, the other on their pee-pee ... Lunch was brought out from the house and set up in the shade ... A big piece of dark bread and a dish of buttermilk ... I ate so greedily I almost broke the spoon ... "This climate makes the boy hungry as a wolf," mother said. Anica and I went into the little white log building that they had shown me the first time. It was the coolest place to be. There were two benches in it and a heavy whetstone ... Anica looked me straight in the eyes. She pulled her skirt up to her chin and showed me her strange, smooth pee-pee with its pink little slit down the middle. My hair stood on end. She nodded her head toward my blue shorts, as though to say I should, too ... I unfastened the buttons and showed her my fuse, about the size of a little finger. Now I could see her clearly and with completely different eyes. And she could see me. We weren't the same anymore. She had brown eyes like Stanka. And if I looked closely, the same mouth and nose with wide nostrils. She just needed to get her hair combed. Have I got a wife now or something, it suddenly occurred to me. I'll be able to stroke her in all the most forbidden places. And she can stroke me. They called her … She ran out, but as though she were dancing. If she hadn't run, I would have fled … As a joke I tugged at her black ponytail … Outside it was very different: the dovecote, the dung heap down the hill, the ox plodding over scattered straw in a circle … I now had a friend among them, and that was more than a good thing. Maybe I would even get to talk to her … Upstairs in the house Uncle Jožef had a hayloft. That was where Ciril, Ivan, Anica and I, and sometimes Stanka would sleep. We were all dirty and sticky, our feet completely black … Anica lay next to me under a blanket. The edge of her skirt hid one of her knees from me. I wanted to squeeze it, mightily, like a wrestler. But she was a lot stronger than I was.... We had to get up early. Anica woke me up with a shaft of straw. She said something to me slowly. She was missing two front teeth. She pronounced everything word for word, so that I would repeat it … I couldn't stand that … It made me bristle when anyone tried to talk to me. Enough! I knew where that was leading … I showed her that I was hungry. I wanted to lift her skirt to see her strange pee-pee again. But I didn't want to repeat everything. We ate in the kitchen, which looked out over the dung heap. Cold corn mush from the night before, with bitter hot black coffee poured over it. Then to work … The grain was waiting for us … and then the upland meadow.

Karel forbade us to draw any water out of the well for cooking, which is why I had to go down to a spring near the timber and masonry house of a woodsman. Then I had to help Karel throw all the old litter out of the barn and carry it in baskets down to the dung heap. Then use an old bucket on a stick to scoop up the urine and pour it into an old barrel. Then carry the barrel to the back wall of the hen house, where others like it already stood in a row. Clean out the manger, then spread out new litter for the animals. Feed them ... Those poor cows that Aunt Mica milked needed a lot of attention ... The dappled, the gray, the white, all of them were prettier than Mica. How could they bear to have her crusty forehead pressing against their lovely bellies? And have her fingers tug at their udders? How could they obey her squeaky voice, endure her interminable giggling? ... They crowded together and looked at me askance from under their heavy eyelids, their yellow eyes ... When storms raged and there was lightning over the barn, when the weather overturned carts, upended baskets and carried whole bushels of meadow down to the water ... it was best to stay here with them. They weren't afraid of anything. They just rustled the hay as they chewed or rested with their eyes closed. What God was doing out there ... with those clouds in the sky, the apple trees, the carts, was just business as usual for them. They weren't available for it. They didn't recognize it.

One afternoon when I came back from raking at Uncle Jožef's, Karel was waiting for me on the path. Angry. "Du niks arbeiten da,"* he said. He put a hoe in my hand and pointed back where the potato field was ... Was he saying I hadn't done anything around the house? ... Mother had spent all morning digging up potatoes. Due to her fat goiter and I don't know how many varicose veins she couldn't do

---

*You not any work there!

any more ... So she had left her sickle and muddy shoes outside the house and staggered off to lie down. Even Gisela had helped aunt in the morning to pick through the beans in the kitchen, even though mother didn't like to see them together ... I struck once, twice at a furrow. But the sun was too strong and my bones hurt so much from bending over in the high meadow ... Let him think whatever he wants! No, I'm not going to dig anymore! ... Angrily I flung the hoe back toward the train tracks and headed for the house ... Karel, who had just been unhitching Liska from a pear tree, shouted, "Zurieck!"* and bounded after me. I took off at a sprint and he started running and because he happened to have the chain in his hand, he hurled it at me from a distance so that it wrapped around my back and chest ... I thought I was going to puke my lungs and heart out ... I fell down flat on the cement by the well ... Suddenly mother was outside, yelling "Mörder!" She literally carried me several yards past Mica, who had come out to look, and into the house ... In our room she got me out of my trousers. Across my chest there were stinging red marks that were visibly swelling from the chain links, as though they had bitten me. The worst thing was that my back hurt and I had to lie on my stomach. I couldn't get any air ... I hadn't done any less work than Ciril or Ivan ... I just didn't know how to work with as much ease, momentum and skill as they did, that was true. I really admired them ... Especially when we raked hay first into a stack, then onto a cart, and at last into the barn. They could stab a whole houseful of hay onto their pitchforks and hoist it from the ground onto a haycart or

*Come back here! (pronounced with a strong Slovene accent)

from a cart into the loft – while standing on a ladder!... Such a big bale that I couldn't wrap my arms around it. And if I hugged it too tight, I'd start to feel its thorns... I heard talking outside, Vati's weak voice... Was it already so late? Had I slept?... Mother had covered me in damp rags, causing me to shiver even more from the stinging cold... Uncle Karel came into the room. He was wearing his hat and his jacket was unbuttoned. He was entirely white in the face. This was the first time I'd seen him like this... expressionless... He was carrying a plate with a sausage, a big pear, and a thick slice of bread on it. He had come to pay me a visit. Like in the hospital. "Here," he said, setting the plate down on a bench. He patted me on the shoulder and kept patting until I smiled at him and he smiled, too. With his whole mouth this time, causing the tips of his mustache to quiver. He stood next to the bed for a while. We looked at each other... His eyes dried up and there was less and less of a smile in them... Oh, I knew we would never be friends!... Then Vati came and sat beside me. "Du mußt jetzt arbeiten, weil es die Zeit der Ernte ist," he said. "Ein halber Tag bei Stritz Josef, die andere Hälfte beim Karl. Dann, wo du bald in die Schule gehst, wirst du nur dem Karl helfen."* ... Something shifted in the small of my back. An indentation on one side and a protrusion on the other... "Schau nur, was deine Grobiane von Brüdern mit dem Kind angestellt haben," mother shrieked like a siren. "Wir müssen ins Krankenhaus."**

*You have to work now, because this is harvest time. A half day for Uncle Josef and the other half for Karel. Then, when you start going to school soon, you'll just help Karl.
**Just look at what your loutish brothers have done to our child! We have to get him to the hospital.

She hugged me with her arms, her breasts, her belly. "Beruhige dich, Lisbeth. Es heilt sich von selbst, so hat es der Doktor gesagt,"* Vati said to her... So had some doctor been here during this time? While I'd been sleeping?... Mother refused to calm down... She stood in the middle of the room. She was trying to illuminate the whole room like an arrow, a storm with her anger, her voice and her gestures... "Laß das, Mama, die Leute lachen uns aus,"** I said angrily.

After that Karel took me along to a livestock auction. To assuage a bad conscience, out of remorse? Unfortunately he planned to sell Liska there... She swatted her tail back and forth behind us on the path over the train tracks as we led her uphill and alongside a road. First him, then me, by turns. With her in the middle and one of us on each side, not together... At the market, in simple pens there were hundreds and hundreds of cows. Some horses, mostly dray horses. Pigs. Goats. A lot of fowl, too. Noise, dust... plenty of good manure went to waste under hoof and underfoot at the market that day. I studied the peasants, the laborers, the shepherds big and small. I stood next to Liska... actually, I sat on a box of feed belonging to the next peasant over... Liska was not in a good mood. She wanted to lie down and have a good nap... Uncle Karel came back with some company. He brought me a bottle of *šabesa*. This was a sweet drink with lilac and lemon that instead of a cork had two little balls in the neck of the bottle... Everyone was covered in sweat, as though they were dying. I saw some big

---

*Calm down, Lisbeth. The doctor said it will heal itself.
**Quit, mother, or people will just laugh at us.

money ... oh, let me tell you about all the banknotes, enough to paper whole walls ... going from hand to hand ... Overall, though, the peasants were low-key. Karel didn't sell anything ... Though he tried ... He called on God as his witness ... I saw him as if on a stage: his earnest face ... his cheerful face ... his clever face ... We went home. We tied Liska up to a tree outside the railway station and went into a restaurant where insects were flying around the rotten potatoes and it smelled of hard liquor ... He ordered two servings of goulash ... and rolls, a whole mountain of rolls ... The goulash was too spicy for me, even though it was delicious ... But the rolls! This was the first time I'd tasted white bread in three months! ... The taste of their soft centers reached my nose, my eyes, almost my brain. Karel started to drink with a group that had gathered. I went out to join Liska ... ripped up some grass for her ... and came back. My uncle was drinking with his buddies at a round table. He introduced me, and the bowlegged peasants took as much interest in me as I did in them ... He forced me to drink a little glassful no bigger than a thimble ... with a swallow of brandy at the bottom. I didn't like it. He laughed, but again his eyes were not laughing. Oh God, was I scared. This was really a bad sign ...

Then I was outside during a storm for the first time. We were pulling up turnips in the rain in Karel's field on the far side of the tracks, not far from the shack of the crazy woman down from the bright house that stood up there as if it was on stilts. We threw a whole expanse of their tousled leaves, their long mottled feathers up onto a cart ... a first one, a second, a third ... It was pleasant, I was wearing my shorts, and the rain and dirt had done a thorough job of soaking and spattering me ... Everyone was grinning ... we had a common enemy, the downpour ... "Bubi, quick ... what fun!" they shouted. My happiness was showing through all the layers of mud ... but I also took care not to say anything ... That's just what they're waiting for! ... The sky was literally bearing down on the black woods like an enormous log of coal ... then some terrible flash ... white! blinding! – as though God wanted to show us an X-ray of some enormous lungs full of black clouds, or the fury in his eyes through lightning ... Click! Click! Click! ... Ka-BOOM! ... as if some huge porcelain marble had just shattered to pieces. And the rain ... whole rivers of rain. We were all soaked to the skin, it poured onto us as though off an eave. Stanka was wearing some sort of light gown ... with all of her contours showing through, her breasts, her hips, her rear end – so the beauty had a body, after all! ... The rain was as hard as a body ... it stuck to everything, and we almost couldn't work our way through the furrows back to the cart ... But the most important thing was the thunder, the downpour, the lightning, and that no one was afraid, nobody hid, we were all just grinning like fools ... I hopped around in a puddle on one leg, I didn't care ... I opened my mouth wide and guzzled the water that came streaming down off a broken branch ... Others came and joined me, I wasn't alone. That's what was important! ...

One day Vati finally moved. He had found a job at the headquarters of the Elite Company in Ljubljana. He had also found a room. He left on a Sunday evening. He promised to come back every Saturday and bring his week's wages. Or send it by mail. It wouldn't be much, since he would have to deduct his room and board ... He also took his wicker suitcase with him on the train. That's where he kept his hides and the last of his furs from Basel. He would use these to sleep on, since the room he was renting was unfurnished, because that way it was much cheaper. But in his free time, he said, he was going to sew muffs out of animal skins, fur hats, collars ... whatever the world wanted of fashion at the moment, and he would sell them from door to door ...

Now mother, Gisela, and I were alone ... without him. Mother told me, "Du mußt slowenisch lernen, daß wir uns mit den Stritzen besser verstehen."* Of course I wanted to, but ... On Monday morning there was a lock on the well, so that we wouldn't be tempted to draw water out of it in spite of the ban ... Consequently, every morning I went first thing down to the spring, so that I wouldn't run into anybody. At first with a bucket, then with a bowl, and finally with bottles ... I had to put up a healthy supply ... who could say what Karel would think up that day ... he might, for instance, lock us into the house, or he might lock us out of it ... The water flowed between two marly stones ... and was as pure as crystal ... with a little fish swimming in it every now and then ... you had to be careful not to dirty the water ... Now and then the woodsman came walking across the footbridge. He was a muscular, red-cheeked, gray-haired man. He wore a kind of gray uniform with a green stripe on his knickers. He tended the forests alongside the railway line all the way to the end or the start of the Krka. This well, which everyone was welcome to draw from, was also his ...

---

*You have to learn Slovene now, so that we can communicate better with the *stritzes* (uncles – Slovene)

He stepped across the narrow footbridge in his leather leggings. I pretended not to have seen him. In our room mother cooked on a small round stove. She was short of lard ... and she didn't want to subject herself to the humiliation of asking Karel for more. Neither did I. I just knew when I needed to head out to pasture ... with Liska, and Gray ... and when I needed to clean out the barn. That was all. I snuck into the kitchen. With a spoon I swiped a bit of lard out of the cupboard in the entryway and evened out its surface at the top of the black pot. And if they did notice ... then it could also have been rats, which had already consumed a quarter of what was up in the attic, anyway ... Mother stayed in our room and constantly complained. She would pace back and forth, nervously balling her hands into fists. "Warum sind wir hierhergekommen ... Warum sind wir nicht nach Saarbrücken gegangen, zu meinen Brüdern nach Saarlouis. Was für ein Dasein! Was für ein Misgeschick!"* I couldn't stand to listen to it anymore. Everywhere we had been, she had just complained ... in Basel ... in our upper floor room in the Gerbergässli ... in the old house next to the park with the police station in it ... in the nice building next to the Christian brothers' school ... on the Elizabethplatz ... in the rue Helder ... even the rue de Bourg, where we had a whole floor to ourselves ...

SHE WROTE to Neunkirchen, Saarbrücken and Saarlouis asking for help. To her sisters, her brothers ... That's where she was born, that

---

*Why did we come here ... Why didn't we go to Saarbrücken, to my brothers in Saarlouis. What sort of existence is this! What a disaster!

was her home, she knew all the people there, had gone to school and grown up with them ... She would tell me about that place ... and it hovered in a sort of cloud in my head. A small town with red roofs ... a big central square ... the nine towers of Neunkirchen on the horizon ... Her mother was French with the surname of Fraigunau, her father was German, a tailor named Faist. They'd had twenty children. This was because her mother would always send her after her father, so she knew where he was. And why did she have to go after her father? To get him to come home? Yes, exactly! ... She had nineteen brothers and sisters. And in addition they had five tailor's assistants and a maid in the house. On Sundays when they went to church, all the men – her father, brothers, and assistants – were identically dressed and likewise all the women – her mother, sisters and the maid ... "Da kommt die Faistkompagnie heranmarschiert ...,"* people would say ... They had a big house and out front it had a sign that said "Adolf Faist, Tailor ..." And in the back there was a terrace ... embroidered curtains and everywhere little cushions and pillows ... That's where she and her brothers and sisters would gather, that's where they played and laughed their way through so many things. Oh, the games they had played and the pranks they had pulled! ... As a little girl she had a special box where she kept a globe, a pencil, and a pretty little cask. The cask was her secret and she showed it to nobody. Once she lost it and couldn't find it again. She cried and was disconsolate for a full year ... The fact that she had once been a little girl intrigued me most

*Here comes the Faist crew in full formation.

of all … She also had a photograph of herself from then, taken at her confirmation … a browned image on cardboard, with the name of the photographer written in silver. She was kneeling at a prie-dieu, with her prayer book bound in white leather lying open atop it. She herself was dressed all in white with a veil gathered in a bunch on her head and a cross made of cypress wood hanging around her neck … Her face, which was younger than mine, already showed features of the woman she would grow up to be … This girl, who was roughly my age, had given me birth – not this woman standing next to me now … I studied the girl's face, her eyes, her little nose, her mouth, her hands gloved up to the elbow … At the age when this was taken, even though she was already a first communicant, she would have played with me and understood me. Just think what time had done since then, when she was perched on her knees on a prie-dieu with the arch of an old-fashioned door in the white background … Time had galloped off with her like a horse through all kinds of misty landscapes and set her down here … In her accounts of that time you could hear the silken rustle of their satiny clothing, the kerchiefs and Brussels lace, which was so delicate that the slightest gust would carry it off the terrace and into the neighbor's garden … Her father had been a good and fair man. In his photo he had a mustache but also seemed gentle in his high stand-up collar. Her mother was a stout woman and wore a ribbon around her neck with a small watch hanging from it. Both pictures were gray, rough and murky, probably because both of them had died long ago … Then there were photos of a brother, a soldier wearing a Pickelhaube who had fallen in the war, a sister at her wedding, and her oldest brother, Hagedorn, who ever since 1900 had been a wild game hunter in India and wore a helmet made out of cork... Soon came the time when mother got engaged. He had been a non-commissioned officer with red hair, the cashier of some unit in Saarlouis... "Ein Kassiermeister. Er sorgte für die Geldkasse seines Regiments,"* mother said. I got the impression she still thought about him. "Er war immer ein so betrübter Mensch,"** she said. I imagined him in his green uniform carrying a metal cash register under one arm... such a giant that his head nearly touched the ceiling... She had told me about him so many times that I already understood she was secretly still bound to him... It's best to be nineteen or twenty years old, she would say... If she had married the army cashier, he would probably be my father now... and I would have been born into a completely different family... and would be looking through some other window than this one, with its view of a growing dung heap and the Krka... I would be sitting in some other room, which would be warm, with other furniture, in another city... in a city with red roofs and nine churches... where a little bell would jingle and I would go downstairs into a dimly lit dining room for supper, where other sisters and other brothers would be sitting around a table covered with a white tablecloth... all of them unborn... "Und dann kam dein Vater,"*** mother said. Yes, Vati had turned up in the course of his second trip to Saarlouis... he had come from these parts here... and

---

*A paymaster. He was responsible for his regiment's payroll.
**He was always such a sad person.
***Then came your father.

as a certified tailor got a job working for Lisbeth's father ... Things grew dark in this part of the story – as though some black shadow came out of a narrow side street and crossed the main square toward the big house on its far side. Vati! He who would henceforth be at fault for everything. The lout who understood nothing. The egotist! ... He was a short, thin, pale young man with very bushy hair and dressed like a dandy ... Tight-lipped. And he worked from morning to night in the workshop. Anyone could easily imagine what he'd been like ... "Was wahr ist ist wahr ... er war ein braver Arbeiter. Aber als Mensch ..."* He fell in love with her and wanted to get married ... but she didn't want to have anything to do with him ... She was in love with her non-commissioned officer ... Vati went chasing after her all through the house and town ... "Er jagte mich durch das ganze Haus, er griff immer nach meiner Hand, ich lief die Treppe hinauf zu meinen Brüdern und Schwestern. Wir lachten über ihn ..."** That part was really unnecessary. That part really hurt! Thank God her father was smarter than her. Because Vati was a conscientious and exceptionally talented worker, he ordered her to be a lot nicer to him from then on ... She had to go out with him for walks around town, down the avenue, to dances, and she remembered one Sunday as they were walking down some side-street two women at windows up above saying to each other, "Schau was dort für ein häßlicher Mann

---

*There's no denying, he was a good worker. But as a person ...
**He chased me all through the house, he would reach for my hand, but I ran upstairs to my brothers and sisters and we laughed at him.

mit der Lisbeth geht."*... My God, how ashamed she was. Only tall, stout, powerful men counted as handsome and trustworthy in those days, and he was such an unappealing little scarecrow... I couldn't swallow this. Not just because I felt sorry for him, but because it wasn't true! Sure, he was quiet, and thin. But he was also handsome! All you had to do was look at him... A great head of hair, a really fine face... and a lissome build... "Ja, heute ist er schöner, als er damals war, jetzt bin ich abscheulich...,"** she said. Robert, her paymaster beau, was still counting on her... How was that? Well, they still got together once a week under the arch of some side street. He would stand there and wait for her every day, whether she came or not. Each day she had just a ten-minute window. "Und nachdem kam es zu einer Tragödie..."*** What tragedy? How?... Robert came under suspicion of having misappropriated his regiment's money, which in fact he hadn't done. He killed himself. How? "Ich weiß nichts mehr..."**** She got married to Vati and then moved into a small apartment in a suburb of Neunkirchen. At the beginning they supported themselves by sewing buttons onto military uniforms. Every week a cart with buttonless uniforms stopped at their door and every week it left and returned to the barracks with a cart full of uniforms with the buttons sewed on... Then they moved to Belgium in search of more remunerative work, and that's where Clairi was born, in Brussels in 1910. Two years after

*Look what an ugly man that is walking with Lisbeth.
**Yes, now he's handsomer than he used to be, and now I'm the fright.
***But later that ended in tragedy.
****I know nothing beyond that.

that they took little Clairi and moved to Basel. Things weren't much better there ... Vati took on a lot of short-term jobs while she let out rooms to boarders ... she only rented to opera performers, including the famous singer Maria Petri, who later committed suicide. Then they rented a house with a store on Rue della Couronne. In 1914 ... "Es war damals gerade ein paar Tage vor dem Kriege ..."* Swiss Germans marched through Basel, breaking display windows and shouting against the Serbs. They came to Rue della Couronne and demolished the whole house, the store, and beat up Vati ... In 1916 Margrit was born ... I saw a photo taken during mardi gras when both girls attended a masquerade party disguised as a Gypsy couple, one taller, the other shorter, with tambourines and wearing big earrings ... Both of them had mother's nose, but only Margrit had inherited Vati's eyes. There was also a photo of mother and Vati with little Clairi when she was four years old and they'd just moved to Basel. Vati was seated in a chair looking pleasant and young, while mother sat in another chair already looking older, with her hair done up in something that looked like a two-headed pillow ... The time when they really started to make money came after the war ... when Hagedorn arrived in Europe from India ... and they worked out a deal where he would send them the finest furs for half price. Vati passed an exam qualifying him as a master furrier. Their assets began to grow ... a house and two stores ... half-page advertisements in the newspapers ... their own stand at the international "Kürschnermesse"** in Leipzig in 1925, a phonograph with a

*That was just a few days before the war.
**Furriers' fair.

horn, a violin and piano for the girls ... Clairi and Margrit began going to their first dances ... If only father had been a better manager ... but he just perched in his workroom and sewed ... he didn't like mixing in company, he didn't want to join the "Gewerbekammer"* ... it was something important if you were a member of it ... he declined Swiss citizenship because he wanted to move back to his homeland ... And the money! Somebody came from the Yugoslav embassy to ask him to donate to help build a Yugoslav club and then disappeared with the money. It amounted to a lot of franks ... And then all the money he paid up front to suppliers! In 1928 I entered the picture. This was the part that most interested me! ... Though he was up to his ears in debt, Vati was practically delirious with joy ... that day he flew through the workshop, overturning tables and shouting, "Ein Bub! Ein Bub! Einen Sohn habe ich bekommen!"** ... It warmed my heart to hear it. Because I was German on mother's side and Slovene on his, he wanted to give me a special name beside his own. Samson is what they entered in the baptismal certificate ... "Und dann kam es zur Überraschung!"*** Namely, the great crisis of 1929 ... when everything went wrong ... and that was it for the house, the store, Gritli's and Clairi's parties ... and they were back to trying to earn enough just to live ... "Und du warst ein großer Lümmel und dann zwei Jahre krank,"**** she said ... First Hagedorn died and then all of the other siblings but four ... "Ich

*Chamber of commerce.
**A boy! A boy! I have a son!
***And then came the big surprise.
****And you were a terrible brat and then sick for two years.

weiß nicht, ob jemand überhaupt noch lebt..."* She asked them to help, composed a long letter – as thick as a pillow... she was one of the oldest children and in Saarlouis had always had to look after the younger ones... At last she actually sent the letter but never got a response. Nor did the letter itself get returned to sender... Now she always had to wait for Vati to come back or for him to send money before she could buy stamps. But even then she would hesitate before dropping them in the mailbox, because at bottom she didn't expect any answer... "Gewiß sind sie alle unter diesem blöden Hitler gestorben oder verreist..."**

Two old women, tiny, white-haired sisters who were remarkably alike, lived on the riverside down from Karel's house. Home for them was a little, half-wooden, half masonry cottage. They had one cow and somewhere far away from the village, in Prečna, a decent-sized potato field... One of them had lived in the country forever, while the other had worked much of her life in town as a servant, and she knew German... One day the two sisters ran into mother at the spring. They invited her over and encouraged her to bring Gisela and me along. The house stood right next to the Krka, which meant that their yard got flooded every now and then. It had a terrace made out of wooden battens. That's where we sat with the little old ladies. They were so much

---

*I don't know if anyone is even still alive.
**With that stupid Hitler in power they've probably all either died or emigrated.

alike that I could only distinguish them by the fact that one of them spoke better German. Occasionally they brought supper up from their house for Gisela and me. A big slice of bread slathered with lard and cracklings... "Das ist ein slawischer Baum, das aber ein deutscher..."* said the one who used to work in town as she pointed to a linden and an oak that grew in their tiny yard... I felt more strongly about the linden, although for mother's sake I chose the oak. It was pleasant there with the breeze blowing off the water. Gisela and I would sit down by the water's edge, next to a hole-ridden boat. How could we fix it?... It was filled with water up to the top, though you could still see its seats. A stubby, white, undamaged oar had been leaned up against the linden... That's what intrigued me, the thought of rowing off down the Krka, far away, as far away as possible... I remembered the rowboats, sailboats and steamboats on the Rhine... The tugboat "Fleur des carrieres," which came puffing its way out from under the bridge every day. In its belly and on its decks it transported a whole ironworks, with all manner of hellish cranes and rods sticking out... And the small boats that the water kept scooping up on all sides... The tour boat that took us on a trip through the vineyards. Even if all I had was the tiniest little boat with its prow constantly leaping up in the air!... My imagination carried me off and my head hurt from daydreaming...

Across a wide, muddy path that led from the yard of the two sisters to the inlet where we watered the horses, just behind a stand of

---

*That is a Slavic tree, and that one is German.

trees stood the woodsman's big house ... which was also masonry on the ground floor and wooden above, but imposing ... There were already a lot of children living in it, mostly girls. The woodsman's oldest son, dark-haired and pale, was always inventing something ... mills, model airplanes ... Following plans he assembled a radio with headphones, stretching its wires from the peak of the house to a shed by the water ... on the way down the slope it was supported by trees, beanpoles, more trees ... Everybody went there to listen ... They put a scratchy gray headset on me. Everything outside got quiet and then from far off I heard, as though l were listening to that big seashell that we kept on the credenza at home in Basel ... music, the music of violins and mandolins ... It wasn't like anything else in my world ... A whole orchestra ... My head was swimming in sounds ... The lanky technician was in love with a blonde beauty, the girl from the new house with the red roof next to Karel's meadow. But his parents and hers were like cats and dogs ... The house belonged to the postman, who wasn't a typical mailman, but an official who worked in a telegraph office ... You got to the house over a gravel path where the veranda with the big, beautiful vase was ... Their windows had dainty curtains on them ... and the smells coming from their kitchen were of dishes that I'd once had at home but that the peasants here didn't cook ... Roasted potatoes, chicken, veal roulades, cutlets ... the sweet smell of boiled marmalade, potica and puddings ... of all possible sauces and soups with noodles ... "Heute gibt es bei ihnen Kalbfleisch mit Blattspinat,"* said mother, who had a nose for cooking ... We ate

*Today they're having veal and spinach.

soured corn mush or browned flour soup ... sometimes macaroni and bread, if we had it ... The smell came straight out from under their pinned-up curtains ... Lord, what a ravenous appetite I had when we lived there ... I devoured every crust of bread I could find, turnips, carrots, every drink gone bad, fennel root, I chewed on wheat grains and corn ... The smell of the puddings and meat literally became food for my head ... since my goatskin of a stomach couldn't have made sense of them, anyway ... But if only I could have had a bellyful of all that abundance just once ... The postman had a wife and daughter. Both were fine-looking and blonde ... except the mother was older ... small and as round as a wine cask. But the daughter! ... Her hair, her red lips, her face like a doll's, her eyes like blue candies ... The beautiful hands that drew the curtains aside on Sundays, so you could see the brightly polished cupboard and the gold clock standing on it ... Her whole head radiant amidst curls ... Whenever I caught sight of her, I either froze or ran quickly away ... She was studying to become a hairdresser ... and sometimes she wore her blue flowing smock ... She and the woodsman's son, the technician, were in love ... But the most they could do was nod at each other whenever they met. Once my two cousins and I were down by the washing stones. The woodsman's son was beside himself, flushed, angry, tearful ... He threw himself down on the grassy path, on top of one of the molehills. He began to convulse and simulate making love to a girl. Ivan and Ciril didn't move ... They stood there and watched without saying a word ... until the woodsman's son got up and put his thing, which gleamed like one of the nipples on an udder, back into his pants ...

T̶HE HOUSE WITH BIG WINDOWS and a garden cottage that stood amid fields on the far side of the railway tracks belonged to the engineer ... I had seen him: he wore a wide-brimmed hat and a black cloak. He knew Greek and Latin, they said ... Knowing several languages meant you could change the world, your surroundings even more, and in other ways ... let's say the woods by the train tracks ... In short order they could become an ancient forest with pagan gods and bulls that knew how to speak ... Pavlica, his wife, wore her kerchief differently from peasant women. Just a touch higher, like the housekeepers in Basel when they came out to beat their carpets ... And their rakes, hoes, shovels, and watering cans were all vividly decorated, resembling playthings ... Besides blooms of all colors, shapes and kinds, the flower beds in their garden also had glass balls ... that were big and all the colors of the rainbow, as though for Christmas ... They changed your body and face, made you look skinny ... Mother hurried over to visit the engineer's wife with a whole armful of fashion magazines that we'd brought with us from Basel ... She hoped to get an order to sew a dress for her. This time for money, not barter ... And following the latest fashion, at that ... Despite her nervousness she was fearful and tight-lipped. Oh, but she did know how to behave with clients. In Basel she had hosted various customers ... whether wacky, wealthy, serious, or revolting ... She pulled together everything she had in those old stacks ... various flounces, patterns, blouses, lengths, widths, skirts, laces ... even an ocean of silk. What people were wearing, what was in and what wasn't ... no more pleat on the right side, but down the middle ... this sort of cuffs on the blouses, the décolleté square now, big buttons made out of glass, a new sort of sleeve ... Meanwhile Gisela and I played with the lady's children ... and others from the neighborhood ... In their garden shed, which was filled with chairs, side tables, useless tools, also a big dynamo, an engine cylinder, some technical handbooks ... I taught them to drum ... I made faces imitating the masks that our Waggis wore and other disguises from the pre-Lenten parade ... I had them bent over with laughter ... Wrestlers from the amusement park, a magician, a weight-lifter, a fire swallower, contestants in the bicycle races ... a canary pecking from a feedbox labeled "Zukunft ..." All of it done with just sounds and gestures. They laughed so hard they sprained their mouths ... Then I showed them how a bull had jumped up on one of Karel's cows ... from on top of a table, where I depicted the whole business, I leapt up onto Gisela and mimicked the bull while Gisela imitated the cow ... They were rolling on the floor with laughter ... guffawing like trumpets and horns. Then suddenly they were all quiet! ... In the doorway the engineer's wife had appeared ... With her eyes practically bulging out of her head. "Hinaus! Out!" she shrieked, brandishing a red feather duster ... All the others were on their feet staring at us. I was already familiar with scenes like this from school. I picked Gisela up and practically flew with her in my arms out of there, to the train tracks ... right past the the duster's red handle ... Before long everybody had heard everything about the theater in the garden shed ... mother, Karel, Mica ... Ciril, Ivan, Uncle Jožef ... Stanka, Anica, Minka, the woodsman ... Suddenly there was nobody left who didn't burn holes in me with their eyes whenever I met them ... That was the reward for fun, for acting silly ... If I had at least been dressed for mardi gras, like a Harlequin at the fair ... they would have applauded me and I would have gotten a hatful of coins ...

Poldka was the name of the crazy woman who lived in the little house with the black roof ... She would stir a long, rusty fork in a big kettle, like a witch ... She cooked using water that she collected in bowls and buckets under her eaves and in kettles set out on her roof ... She amost never came outside ... I actually liked her. Despite the fact that her face was always sooty and her hair was just a black fringe. She would sit leaning out the window of her little house. I would chat with her ... half using words, half with gestures ... Especially about masqueraders, which would make her laugh. She was a kind woman, I could sense it. Not until during one of our conversations when I picked at the cinders did I realize that her house was built out of logs, not sheets of tin ... But what was it that kept accumulating in her room behind her? Some bags or other, like in the photos of trenches at the front during the war, and rusty hoops. What was behind all of that? ...

There was a little white house that stood above Karel's turnip patch. With a fine view of the whole village. It was as though it stood there on stilts ... a childless man and his wife lived in it ... She was a big, fat, ruddy woman. She had a head like a red pumpkin. He was short, inconspicuous, slight ... and practically bobbed around in his jacket and big, baggy pants, as though he were wrapped in a cloud. Sometimes he shouted, or sang ... He drank elderberry wine. He would stand stock still out in the turnip patch. He couldn't find the right words for his fun ... he just pointed at something and kept grinning. He was his own best parody ... Once I saw him standing next to an ox on some stones on the slope beneath the postman's house ... The ox was hauling logs. The little fellow was hauling off at it with the fat handle of a whip. Smack! Smack! ... On its muzzle, its nostrils, on its withers and neck. The ox stayed standing amid the stones like a colossus. Smack! Smack! Something like blood streamed down its muzzle ... it spurted ... and the forester's children appeared at the fence. Alongside the furious little stick puppet of a man, the ox was as beautiful as a water sprite compared to an old witch ... And it had to endure that revolting elf as it kept hitting it on the muzzle ... No! I picked up a stone and ... ping! ... it flew straight into the gargoyle's armpit ... "Oowww!" he shouted ... But then the ox moved forward ... and the forester's kids attacked from the rear ... They rescued me ... Then one afternoon there was a sudden commotion with lots of shouting ... everybody ran uphill to the house ... The fat woman had taken an axe to her sadistic wimp of a husband! ... Everyone came running uphill over the turnip beds ... they were shouting as though they'd been skinned, as though they were late to the amusement park ... Men, women wearing a hundred skirts, children. Hurry! Hurry! A gendarme was already standing there, brown and red as a cockatoo. He was shouting at them and into the entryway behind him ... The woman was sitting at the table in her kitchen ... half naked in her linen underthings ... arms propped on the table, supporting her head, which was splotchy and red halfway down her back from the sun and from drink ... with a liter bottle of brandy ... and an open tin of marmalade ... With one hand she spooned marmalade into her mouth ... or scratched her belly ... then glug, glug! from the bottle ... There was a puddle under the table that kept creeping forward ... Blood! The axe with its long handle, the kind Karel used to teach me to split logs and branches, stood by the door ... The gendarme and forester lifted her up ... She clutched onto the table as she tried to get upright ... and the bottle and marmalade went crashing into the hearth ... They brought her a blue coat from the main room with a little wooden heart attached to the collar ... And they led her downhill. To a strange, closed wooden cart with two horses whose manes had been cut short ... The woman kept scratching her big belly and holding her head back ... Everyone stared ... The whole hill was awash in horror ... They pushed her into the cart from the rear, like some broken thing ... everyone crowding around the door ... Nothing was visible, except for its gray wall ... The gendarme tromped back uphill ... This was the first time I saw a murderer, a murderess ... The whole time I was waiting for everyone to jump on her, or attack the gendarme to rescue her ... I was waiting to see how far they would go in their rage ... from what depths they would draw it ... But nothing! For a full week that was all they talked about ... They were simple ... Sheer gossip-mongers ... All they had inside them were bruises, cheap wine, and howls ... Nothing but meaningless junk ... But the women were different ... They at least kept all of their music ... the moments of great emotion, the moaning, the tears ... Everything in my surrounding that was far off and that I didn't know well enough stayed the same after this murder ... But the pear tree in front of the house, the garden, the barn, Karel's meadow, the turnip beds all refused to change back to the way they were before. They didn't want to be tamped back into their shells. The shade under the pear tree was black ... it ate right into the grass and deep into the dirt ... It took a week for me to somehow regain my composure. But I still didn't feel safe. Not until Sunday, when I went with Karel to mass. I had to. To Prečna on foot ... Clusters of peasants were walking down the road. Wearing black shoes, neckties, hats, pocket chains. To hear the word of God ... Uncle Jožef drove his carriage past us with his children and wife. He and Karel didn't exchange greetings. They had been at each other for some time now ... I only said hi to Ciril and Ivan, who saluted me back ... The church was packed with people singing the holy songs. It stank of cheap wine, tobacco, lavender, and soap. And on account of the soap, that much more strongly of dung, which their shoes had tracked in ... Nothing bothered them. What sort of God was it that they imagined, anyway? The priest, wearing a gold-edged scarf over his white shirt, spoke above a stove that had two books lying on it ... Calmly, like a teacher who always says the same thing. His voice echoed in a way that was supremely grotesque ... But he should have been scolding them, he should have shaken his fist at every last one of them down here, thrown books at their heads, or a cross, or the angels that hung from the stove ... Nothing. It was only the high walls that made his voice echo and a few times his eyeglasses flashed in a way that made me think: here it comes now! No ... His steady voice put me to sleep ... I started to doze ... After mass Karel weeded a bit around his parents' grave ... otherwise he stood with his head thrust up like a construction crane. That mound was where his mother and father were ... not that far down at all ... He ought to do something! Establish some contact with them! ... The whole cemetery had a fine, intensely sour scent to it, despite all the flowers ... If you took a deep breath of it here, it would follow you out onto the street ... Then Karel tried to get me to go with him to a tavern ... I didn't want to go inside with him, I resisted, because I knew he was going to force me to drink brandy again ... I stayed on a bench outside, waiting ... There was a crowd in the tavern ... A whole bunch of women were inside ... wearing headscarves, the town ones wore straw hats with lots of flowers and hard-edged barrettes ... the peasant men wearing hats ... They talked like animals, like the fabled town musicians of Bremen ... with loud barks and belches ... They were like dogs, hens, tigers, wolves, donkeys, lice ... The best you could hope for from their likes was scabies ...

One Sunday the postman came by on his bicycle and hollered "Telegram!" into the kitchen. I ran outside ... It was a wire from sister. "Komme Mittwoch abends ab 7 Uhr. Eure Clairi."*

CLAIRI GOT OUT AT THE STATION. Quickly. With a suitcase and wearing her white coat, like the last time in Basel. My heart leapt at the sight of her ... "Jesus, wie schaut ihr denn aus!"** she gasped in

---

*Arriving Wednesday after 7pm. Your Clairi.
**My God, look at you!

shock... Mother wearing a smock for work in the fields... me barefoot and in a ripped undershirt... She picked up Gisela, who was wearing nothing but a long undershirt... hugged her, kissed her, rubbed her face against hers... "Gisela! Gisela!... Ihr seid alle so braun!" she said over Gisela's head, "abgemagert und älter, ganz verrunzelt..."* She had brought a lot of luggage along. Uncle Jožef, who drove all three of us back in his carriage, studied her with great curiosity and surprise. Clairi was definitely beautiful. Dark curls of hair showed under her white hat with its wide, light brown ribbon, she was wearing white shoes with high heels and she had countless bracelets and rings on her hands... She smelled like the best and most expensive part of Basel... How old was she? She never told anyone. All I knew was that she was eighteen years older than me, so she must have been twenty-seven then... She shook Jožef's hand energetically, though she didn't like short men. "Ich habe auch deine Federdecke mitgebracht,"** she said after she gave me a big kiss. The comforter I slept under in Basel? That big, soft, fluffy bag with my name on it?... When she entered our room she closed and then opened her eyes. "Was, ein so armseliges Zimmer?... Ihr meint doch nicht im Ernst, daß wir alle vier in diesem Bett schlafen werden?"*** Mother just nodded. "Der Bubi wird auf dem Heuboden übernachten, jetzt wo es

---

*You're all so tanned. But emaciated and older, and completely disheveled.
**I brought your down comforter from Basel
***What? Such a miserable room? You can't possibly seriously think that all four of us are going to sleep in that bed?

noch warm ist."* Uncle Karel looked on from the side, but his eyes were practically bulging in admiration. When Clairi caught sight of him, she batted her eyelids a bit ... "Ein ganz anständiger Onkel!"** Aunt Mica nodded her inflamed head ... Clairi hesitated before shaking her hand. She seemed disinclined to touch anything ... the bed, the door ... as though every touch was a kind of boundary. Ciril and Ivan were exceptionally surprised by their new cousin. They danced attention on her ... Anica was bashful and hid ... Stanka and Minka looked at her with a mixture of admiration and contempt as she stood by the well outside Karel's house in her dazzling dress sewn with dot-sized buttons ... It was as though she had dropped down into our midst from out of the sky, but she was also trapped, because now she would be under their watchful eyes forever. Clairi didn't realize this yet, but I sensed it as they milled around her and talked ... As we walked through the village, they were out front, leading her like a bride. By turns Clairi's face showed surprise, dismay, pleasure and tension ... At Uncle Jožef's house the slices of corn bread were once again out on the table. "Das ist nicht Bisquit, weißt du ..." I warned her, "sondern Brot aus Kukuruz."*** I explained the photos on the wall to her: grandma, grandpa, three uncles from America ... "Wohin führst du mich?"**** she asked skeptically when I took her outside. "Ich werde

---

*Bubi will sleep in the hayloft while it's still warm.
**Such a handsome uncle!
***Be careful, that's not sponge cake, it's cornbread.
****Where are you taking me?

dir alles zeigen,"* I said. We took Gisela with us. I showed her the shed, the hayrack, the dovecote, the horses... In the village I took her along the train tracks to the pit where Karel had buried foodstuffs in case of a war, and then to the washing stones. A thistle in the grass stuck her. She ought to have put on different shoes. So we went around to the path... The dung heap was too close to the house... she would have preferred it to be farther off, in the woods... And the toilet was just a plain shack without any water or chain to pull... just a board with a hole in it through which you could see a huge pile of excrement going back a full year... She entered the barn as though it were a prehistoric cave dwelling. "Ist das möglich?"** she asked. She was seeing cows for the first time and they frightened her. It would have been more natural for her if she'd been able to approach them out in the pasture... I showed her she didn't have anything to be afraid of... and how we milked them. I took her hand and used it to stroke Liska on her withers... Was that bad? "Not at all," she said in delight. I told her stories about Liska and Gray... what they were like out at pasture and how they behaved at the fair... She told me how many towns and villages, houses and forests she'd seen through the window of the express train... handsome towns where she would have liked to stay, where she could have just gotten off the train. "Wenn ich aber die Augen aufschlug, sah ich immer einen kupfernen Ring im Abteil, immer den gleichen. Ich denke: in vierundzwanzig Stunden werde

---

*I'm going to show you everything.
**Is this possible?

ich die Augen auftun und ein anderer Mensch sein."* Then she said quietly, "Wie der Vati arm lebt in einem Kellerzimmer ohne Bett. Das darfst du keinem erzählen..."** I drew her along by the arms toward the woods by the train tracks. "Ich fürchte mich vor den Tieren und Räubern, Bubi."*** "Räuber gibt es nicht!"**** Even so, I showed her a place where snakes usually gathered... One just happened to be there in among the roots. "I don't look back!" she said. I pointed out the mark that I'd carved into a tree for myself, mother, and Gisela, so that none of us would ever stumble into one of their nests by mistake... You had to feel sorry for snakes, since they were deaf and all they could do was crawl. When we reached the point where the forest almost crossed the train tracks onto Karel's meadow... we ran into the red-haired forester in his uniform, with a rifle slung over his shoulder. "Guten Tag," he took off his hat. "Er hütet den Wald,"***** I explained. She was happy to have met someone in the forest who was wearing a uniform. The forester looked at her in a way that made me instantly aware of how he was looking at her... He showed us some places in the ferns and bushes where he had set out fox traps, but also traps for rabbits and bears. He had hidden some fox traps in the ferns and

*But when I opened my eyes, I saw a copper ring in the train compartment, always the same one. I thought: in twenty-four hours I'm going to open my eyes and be a different person.
**You can't imagine how poorly father is living, in a basement room with no bed. You mustn't tell anyone.
***I'm afraid of animals and robbers.
****There are no robbers.
*****He guards the forest.

bushes. "Ich fürchte mich, Bubi,"* she whispered to me ... When we came out of the forest, some Gypsies were just then driving a small wagon with a canvas roof over the crossing. Their little horse was hauling bundles and clay pots, and the Gypsy who fixed pots and umbrellas sat on the box ... A few little Gypsy kids running behind the wagon raised their arms, "A dinar! Cigarettes, pretty lady!" ... Claire was frightened. "Was sagen diese Leute? Ich bitte dich, gehen wir zurück in den Wald!"** ... Sweat was beading up on my forehead and I angrily waved the Gypsies away ... I showed her the postman's handsome house and the even handsomer house of the engineer way out in the fields. And then the house in the turnip patch where the woman had killed her husband. "Ist das möglich? Eine regelrechte Wildnis, nicht wahr?"*** she said somewhat apprehensively, but showing excitement. I took her to meet Poldka, who was leaning out the window of her little black house. I introduced her, "Zis is my zister." Clairi liked Poldka quite a bit. "So habe ich mir immer die Hexen vorgestellt,"**** she said ... Then I took her to see the spring and to visit both of the elderly sisters who lived on the Krka down from Karel's place. What pleased her most was that she could chat freely with both of them, and they were so weak that they couldn't have aroused fear in anyone ... Toward evening, when I rode Jožef's bay past the fence where she and Gisela were picking flowers, it left her speechless. She couldn't believe

*I'm scared, Bubi.
**What are those people saying? Please, let's go back into the forest.
***Is this possible? This is a regular wilderness, isn't it?
****That's how I always imagined witches to be.

her eyes. "Spring hinunter, sonst beissen dich die Pferde, Bubi,"* she shouted. Everything showed on her broad face as if in a mirror: astonishment ... joy ... fear ... anger. That evening she went outdoors: the barn, the house, the dung heap between. "Mir ist zumute, wie einem Gefangenen, Bubi. Mein Gott, was für ein Einfall ... Werde ich am Ende ewig hier leben müssen?"** ... We poured out some oil and lit both of the lanterns ... She took the things she had brought with her out of the suitcases. For Gisela a doll that said "mama" and closed its eyes. For me a wind-up frog that croaked and hopped. A steel strongbox for Vati, without any money of course. A round embroidered tablecloth with fringe for mother ... decked out in flowers of all colors, embroidered in the very best silk. And my feather bed! Big, white and puffy with the first letters of my name in red. Everything else was gone, but this feather bed remained. Nobody had made it the way they would a tablecloth, a frog, or a doll, at least not that I'd seen ... Time itself had delivered it when I had to move from my basket into a bed. It never grew old or went out of fashion. It lasted longer than everything else ... and it took me into itself and went with me, and I could count on it warming, enfolding, and protecting me for a long time to come ... But when mother put it on the rustic bed, it suddenly occurred to me that I was going to live longer than it ... Clairi wanted to keep one of the oil lamps burning till morning ... As a result, in its light the sky outside the window remained dark blue all night, almost

*Jump down from there or the horses will bite you.
**I feel like a prisoner, Bubi. My God, what a thought: am I going to have to live here forever?

transparent... The next morning we were already in Karel's vineyard in Prečna. We carried the grapes in buckets and tall baskets to a barrel standing on a cart in the road. Clairi carried her grapes in a wash basin... and she wobbled wearing somebody else's work shoes. She didn't complain, because the work was just as hard as any other. But something pained her that came from inside. Tears welled up in her eyes without her being aware she was so close to crying. "Warum weinst du?"* I asked. "Ich?"** she said, startled, her mood becoming normal again. The church bells rang noon and Clairi got carried away listening to Vati's bell. "Ich kann das gar nicht glauben. Daß das wirklich Vatis Glocke ist, wo er doch immer so ein Heide war."*** On Sunday Karel distilled brandy outside his house. Vati, who had come for a one-day visit, drank a good deal of the hot, pure liquid... We watched him use a long beanpole with a net tied to its end to pick the last pears from the tree... He staggered all around the perimeter of its wide crown like a bad tightrope walker. Everyone laughed, even mother. Clairi couldn't believe it. "So was... daß ich den Vati einmal betrunken sehe..."**** The decision had already been made that she would work with him for Elite in Ljubljana. They would both live together in father's tiny basement room. They would not come back on Sundays to visit, because that would use up too much money. Instead, they would send us a part of their salaries by mail.

*Why are you crying?
**Me?
***I just can't believe it. That that's really Vati's bell, when he was always such a heathen
****I would never have thought I would ever see father drunk.

Finally the time came for me to start school. I was given a small canvas backpack instead of the briefcase with shoulder straps that all of the other students had. I was as frightened as an animal. One morning I went with Ciril and Ivan through the cornfields out of the village ... across a footbridge over the stream ... along a footpath that led uphill and then down ... through the quarry where the Gypsies camped with their wagons and horses ... they were still asleep in the morning, with just their dirty yellow feet jutting out of the tents toward their campfires, which had gone out ... From there we followed the path uphill ... past the cliff with its chest thrust out ... then through willows and birches along the Krka ... that part was really nice! Then we climbed up the steep path we had come down on that first night and that led through a tunnel to a wall on the road up above ... It took us barely thirty minutes to walk the route that had taken more than two hours to cover on our first night ... The school was a gray, square, monotonous building. Like a dirty circus bigtop stretched taut in front of the sky. I could barely see its roof. It was nothing like the mission school in Basel ... that red cathedral with towers and a huge clock ... Its single classroom was on the top floor just under the roof ... a short but wide room with benches of various heights and colors ... I sat in the highest bench, which was as high as a pew back, between Ciril and Ivan ... The blackboard was white from overuse. The teacher was a Mr. Alojz, a man with wavy blond hair. There was something tomato-like about his round face ... Red, sluggish blood. The blond hair curling over his ears and cheeks lent him the aspect of a carrot, too ... The pupils were of various ages and sizes ... They half-blocked my view of the blackboard and Mr. Alojz ... The place smelled like a barn. Some of the kids lived even farther away than my cousins and me ... They had to walk two or three hours each way ... After leaving me alone for two months, Teacher Alojz began to work with me seriously ... He would call on all of the pupils, big and small, to contribute, to say something ... He wrote all the words on the blackboard in big printed letters ... which were easy to read ... And beneath them a translation. Big and small, young boys and adolescents all had to repeat them together over and over again ... in unison, keeping the beat ... The first time I spoke up, they laughed, then also the second and third ... I opened my mouth wide ... acted as though it was about to come out ... But nothing did ... Not a sound, not a syllable ... So I closed my mouth ... The experiment had been completed ... I was left in peace during the following lessons. "In good time, Lojzek, Lord willing!" Mr. Alojz greeted me during the break. Perhaps he was at his wit's end, a little bit desperate, but still well intentioned ... I felt sorry for him ... it got a bit on my nerves when he called on me ... Couldn't he just leave me alone? At last he sensed my fear or resistance and he stopped pushing. I knitted my forehead. I growled when he called on me ... I didn't take my coat off, not even during lessons, because they barely fired up the stove at all. Sometimes I dropped off to sleep if it got too warm in the coat. Ciril and Ivan moved to sit with the older kids, the ones their age. Now I was sitting alone. The others around me would play various games during lessons, but not me. I was no fun. During the break the others would group together in the hallway. They brought their lunch with them, little bundles containing unpeeled potatoes, corn mush, sometimes beans ... They ate at the window alcoves that had views out over town ... peasant houses, a peasant church, a wooden bridge. Better a proper village than this sort of town. I was as hungry as a wolf... Mr. Alojz patted me on the shoulder now and then as he walked by, clutching his grade book and papers under his arm ... He would whack others with his stick, but not me. I was a kind of guest ... It was autumn, so it was rainy and muddy. At home there was a single umbrella, Karel's ... Most often I walked alone to school and back, holding a scrap of an old horse blanket over my head ... At noon when I came home by way of the Krka and through the quarry, now and then I would be accosted by the Gypsy kids who otherwise darted back and forth among the older Gypsies out cooking in pots on the fires ... In the morning they'd all still been sleeping the sleep of the dead, but now they were full of vigor and ready for battle. They chased me all the way to the footbridge ... but they didn't dare go over the stream ... That's why I would skirt the top of the quarry on the way home. I knew that it would still be a while before mother would cook anything in that round stove, so I looked through the grass for all possible edible saps and grains I could chew on.

After two weeks Clairi came back from Ljubljana ... She had lost the job she'd been given as an assistant seamstress. Now all four of us slept in the same bed – Gisela and me at one end, mother and Clairi at the other. At least that way we kept warm, even if there were too many legs under the blanket. The down comforter loomed up over us like a white mountain ... light and warm. It reminded me of all my Basel haunts ... the park, the streets, the drumming school, the Rhine ... our places on rue Helder and rue de Bourg, next to the movie theater before the St. Elisabeth Church. The comforter was so out of place that I really ought to have hidden it. It refused to blend in with Karel's house. It covered our narrow bed like a cloud, but this cloud had been plucked from some other climate, over some other town ... I began to dream about a witch who lived near my friend Friederle. She would wait in front of our building for me to come out. She would attack me ... and chase me until up on the square I found a balloon I could escape in.

Vati sent us a postcard from the hospital, where he had been admitted for his lungs. The message was nearly indecipherable, written with a ballpoint pen running out of ink ... The cold, his unheated room, bad food, all this had taken its toll on him. Now he was laid up in a ward with twenty tubercular men and young boys ... Mother was beside herself again. "So ist es, wenn man dumm ist ... Und jetzt wieder diese leeren Magen!"* Where were we going to get anything to put in our mouths? There was nothing left to cook. Vati's steel strongbox in the corner of the room, which we had begun using to store foodstuffs in, was empty. I had succeeded in removing a loaf of bread from Mica's cabinet in the entryway ... Bread! We wrapped it up in

*That's what happens when you're stupid ... And now I've got these empty stomachs to feed again!

some laundry and hid it, so that Karel or our aunt wouldn't discover it during one of the searches of our room that they periodically conducted when we were out of the house... One Sunday Clairi and I went to see the priest in Prečna, where Vati's bell hung in the church belltower. We wanted to ask him to lend us some money. If we didn't get that, then we were going to ask for some groceries. The wooden steps to the rectory door creaked as if in a barn. The priest sat wearing glasses in his wretched office like a peasant in his attic smokehouse. This was the first time I'd seen a priest in civilian dress. He looked like Jožef and his desk was only slightly bigger than a feed bin. From his pantry he gave us a paper bag of beans and a big chunk of homemade bread. But Clairi insisted on money. She was so brave in her persistence that I had to admire her... At first he didn't want to give us a cent. Then he relented and took ten coins out of his desk drawer. That was enough for us to buy two pounds of lard and bread to last us another ten days... We were even able to send Vati two dinars in a letter envelope... Oh, if money grew in fields, we could have dug it up like we did potatoes. But two weeks later we were beggars again... This time we went to visit Uncle Jožef. I didn't feel like going in with her to plead. I also didn't feel like listening to any arguing, even the nice words that Clairi would exchange with our uncle. I couldn't stand noise anymore. While I waited for Clairi in that hidden nook off the trail where Vati once sat to pluck all the raisins out of the priest's potica, I went through the possibilities: Had she said it by now or not? Had they given her something, or not?... Minka, the nicest of them all, came out the door nearest the barns and Uncle Jožef went to the granary ... Then Clairi started calling me ... she had potatoes in a borrowed basket, a whole pot of lard, flour, two bunches of carrots, milk, half a dozen eggs and a big cut of dried meat ... This was luxury, provisions that would last us nearly a month, and I skipped the whole way home ...

Shortly before Christmas mother and Clairi got sick. They had come down with angina and a high fever, just as they had every year before that. They constantly spat their mucus out onto dry leaves that I set beside their beds and changed several times a day ... I had to use the last of our money to buy aspirin at the pharmacy in town. When they had angina in Basel, they would both spend a whole week in bed ... The doctor, old Dr. Fritz Goldschmidt, would come to examine them. Gisela and I made our bed on two benches alongside the window ... I gathered some twigs and branches ... and made quite a comfy nest for us. It reached from under the window practically up to the ceiling. All nicely snapped and bundled. But Vati's strongbox was empty again, with not the tiniest bean left in it. This was going to be our first Christmas without a tree. The kind sisters from the house down by the water brought us four pieces of cake and a bowl of mush, plus spoons to eat it with. I boiled up some tea in a saucepan. They had lost all their strength and couldn't eat hard food. They wanted me to fix them a thin flour soup with a beaten egg mixed in. I thought I was going to burst from worrying about them. I wasn't inclined to ask Jožef for help, much less Karel. Anyway, nobody in the house showed any concern for us anymore. Early, before anyone in the house got up, I crept out to the henhouse built out of an old wardrobe. I climbed up its doors and felt through the straw. There was nothing. Then I went down under the threshing floor. On an anvil, hidden beneath a bundle of straw, there were three newly laid eggs. That was a surprise! I was just on the verge of picking up two of them … when behind me, snap! … there was Karel with his whip … I burst out crying, and not from the pain … As distinctly as I could I said that my mother and sister were seriously ill and that I had to fix them some burnt flour soup with egg to help them get their strength up. "Zurick!* Put the eggs back! Damn thief!" Karel shouted. I set them back down. "March!" I ran. "Thieves! Damn thieves!" Karel kept shouting. "They'll steal everything they can get their hands on." Both of my sisters stepped out of the house and the young hairdresser looked out her window. The whole world was being informed about my shame. "Zurick in die Schweiz! Zurick in die Schweiz!"** Mother and Clairi were shaking and colorless, having propped themselves up on their elbows in bed. "Was ist denn? Was hast du wieder angestellt?"*** "Eier geholt."**** "Warum bittest du nicht die Schwester da unten oder den Joseph?"***** I bit my lip. I wasn't about to try to explain anymore if the women didn't get it … What if I asked Ciril and Ivan, instead of uncle? We weren't such good friends anymore … we didn't even talk to each other at school during breaks … There wasn't a

*Back! (German, pronounced with a strong Slovene accent)
**Back to Switzerland! Back to Switzerland! (in German with a Slovene accent)
***What is it? What have you done now?
****I was fetching eggs.
*****Why don't you ask the two sisters down by the river or Joseph?

scrap of food left in the house ... There were two locks on the entryway cupboard with flour and lard, one in front and one on the side. I couldn't go to the old sisters ... They had already given us too much on their own ... The forester's children looked at me from their terrace when I came to get water. Probably the whole village had already been informed in detail about my perfidious deed ... That afternoon Poldka handed me a small basket of potatoes and carrots through her window. It was enough for a soup. Mica was baking bread when I got back ... "Shoo! Get away from here!" she chased me away with big oven tongs, afraid I was going to swipe one of her just-baked loaves of bread, firm and grainy, cooling under a sheet on the table. Saliva practically flooded my mouth ... That's when I decided to do something that might have cost me my life if I'd been caught. I was going to steal some meat from the attic! While Karel and Mica were out tending the pigs, I climbed up in my stockings ... one, two, each step separately. I pushed the hatch open and entered a world of hanging hams and sausages ... I pulled off a long, moldy salami and even a ham with the hook still embedded in it. And if I ran into Karel? ... I'd kill him! Flat out, like an ant underfoot. Plant my foot on his chest so that he'd – wham! – go flying back down the stairs! ... I had such wide eyes that I had to wonder where this place was ... This was the life I experienced ... its raw, exposed nerve ... There was no one in sight ...

After that smoke suddenly began coming out of the stove ... Every day. The smoke would billow into our room ... it stung and we coughed and choked. We opened the window ... but the icy wet cold of the snow and the Krka surged in from outside. "Der Karel hat etwas in den Ofen gesteckt."* We went to have a look at the smokehouse that the vestibule had become, but we couldn't discover anything. Gray smoke enveloped the room and crept over its ceiling like steam over a forest ... "Das ist eine Verschwörung,"** mother said ... One day she came to pick me up at school because my fights at the quarry with the Gypsies showed no sign of abating, and as we reached the train crossing heading out of town, one of Ciril and Ivan's friends began pelting us with stones and shouting, "Hitler! Hitler!" Mother ran on ahead, but I didn't want to leave this debt unpaid ... I picked up some of the granite ballast from the track bed and began throwing it at him. I wouldn't relent. They said that Hitler wanted to take over the world. The *Patriot*, a newspaper that Karel got every Sunday, had pictures. One of them showed a soldier in a resplendent uniform ... in his helmet, boots and ribbons, with a pair of binoculars, standing in front of a crossing barrier, on top of which stood another soldier not at all like the first, in a leather helmet with a metal spike on the top and an old-fashioned rifle. "That's how it started with Austria," was the caption under the picture. They said that Germany was going to march into Poland or Czechoslovakia ... A lot of people went to the forester's house to listen to his son's radio. Bit by bit people began to avoid us. "Warum," I asked mother, "hat niemand auf der Welt die Deutschen gern?"*** "Weil sie hochnasig sind und immer Krieg

*Karel has put something in the stove.
**This is a conspiracy.
***Why does nobody in the world like the Germans?

wollen,"* she answered ... Barely would we try to light the stove again than that suffocating wool would permeate the room. That was our punishment from Karel for the ham. I had hid it behind some masonry stones out in the barn wall. I would go there to slice some off, and throw the pieces into a pot with barley and beans. The mixture produced a really hearty soup ... "Wo hast du das Fleisch her?"** mother asked. Some I got some from Ciril, some from Jožef, and some from the two sisters, I tried to extricate myself. Oh, if she had known that I'd snatched it from Karel, she would have taken me by the ear straight to him ... One evening, when he and Mica weren't home, I took some ladders from the shed to the back of the house ... I set them up by the steps that were overgrown with nettles and climbed up ... The rotten wood of the gutter had burst. The black straw roof was covered in ice crystals like the fur of some dog. I grabbed onto the ends of black straw and yanked out a big handful the size of a roofing tile and then on my knees, elbows, and belly somehow made my way up to the chimney. I reached inside ... it was cold, but also warm, sticky, dry, hot ... I couldn't see or feel anything ... So where was the stuff that had been causing our stove to smoke so unbearably? ... Mother got up out of bed and, still dizzy, walked through the vestibule into Karel's part of the house to talk with him. It was warm and airy there ... For a few days there was no smoke, then all of a sudden – whoosh, whoosh! –

*Because they're arrogant and they always want war.
**Where did you get the meat from?

back it came through the stove door, the seams and three other places in the stovepipe...

At last on some Saturday when he was released from hospital Vati appeared... Pale and haggard in his thick winter jacket, his eyes watery and his hair grayer and thinner. He was barely able to walk the whole way home from our train stop... especially not with that ridiculous skipping walk of his. Once in our room, he had to lie down immediately and then again every so often, or at the very least sit down... He had brought along a paper bag of bread rolls, already half stale, that he'd saved up during his last days in the hospital. They dissolved in coffee, and if you put them in water and mixed in some groats, it made a particular kind of food that did a wonderful job of filling our stomachs... Mother immediately told him everything about the stove and the smoke... Vati got up and went over to visit his brother in his place... In his and mother's presence, Karel pulled a round piece of painted metal out of the stovepipe. This open admission of his perfidy was an unusually brave act on his part... The stove stopped smoking... but it can't go on like this, mother told Vati. We can't take it here any longer. It's not working. We have to go to Ljubljana. And once we live together, our living expenses are bound to be less, too... Vati had arranged with the train engineer to take him to Ljubljana and back in the luggage compartment for very little money. That was an adventure I envied him for... riding in with the packages, letters and bundles. On Sunday evening he had to go back to Ljubljana so he could be at

Elite first thing Monday morning. A railway man helped him up into the green mail car and then slid the door shut ... He was going to sell some of the furs from his wicker chest at a loss, he promised before he left, and send us the money for train tickets ...

My first semester grades were excellent. How they got that way was a mystery to me. My Slovene was full of mistakes, my notebooks a mess of ink, partly because I wrote my assignments in my bench, sitting on the floor. I was fine at arithmetic because it was simple. Drawing and gymnastics, too. History was all incredible fairy tales ... Only the big wall map made me afraid ... so many different kinds of details, lines, spots, dots, and stripes for such a little country, as though it were the entire globe. Was anybody still allowed to walk on the earth without having all these maps, rivers, mountains, and parallels in his head? ... After school I would go with Clairi and Gisela out to the woods to gather kindling. But also to avoid running into Karel. Still, we stayed close enough to have the yellow house in the meadow with its black-traced windows constantly in view, especially when we left mother home alone ... In winter the pine forest wasn't as dry as a deciduous forest, which turned into a big skeleton on its snowy blanket ... One afternoon Clairi was out in the woods with Gisela when I got home from school. I ran into them out in the biggest clearing, where the tracks started to turn. They were talking with the forester, who stood in front of her in his fur hat ... All the color had drained from Clairi's face. "Was mir der Herr Lokar gerade erzählt, ist unglaublich ..."*

*What Mr. Vorester here is telling me is just unbelievable.

"Ist Wahrheit … Vater von Vater, prapraded, Urgroßvater von Herr Alojz und Karl war Zigeuner …"* "Hörst du das, Bubi?"** Clairi asked, looking faint … I looked at him as though he weren't in his right mind. "So ein Zigeuner, wie die da … die im Steinbruch leben mit Zelten und Pferden?"*** Clairi asked, her lips trembling. "Ja, ja," the earnest forester laughed. "So ist's. Aber schon lange Zeit her … ein Jahrhundert!"**** … I looked out at the road in confusion … The Gypsies I fought with every day … that ate horses, lounging around with their wagons and their women, whose bare nipples showed through their colorful rags … those were supposed to be our ancestors and relatives?! … Clairi left the forest looking like she'd been felled … "Bubi, das darfst du auf keinen Fall der Mama erzählen. Höchstes Geheimnis!"***** she said severely. Then she laughed, "Und doch … bin ich ein wenig stolz darauf … Veilleicht, weil ich so ängstig bin …"****** She brandished her bundle of branches around her. "Auf wilden Pferden reiten … immer in anderen Orten … wandern … Feuer machen. Uh!"******* She started to dance a little … excited and enraptured … This thing about the Gypsies was news to me …

*Is truth … Father of father, great-great-grandfather of Mr. Alojz and Karel was Gypsy.
**Do you hear that, Bubi?
***The same kind of Gypsy as the ones that … live down there in the quarry with their horses and tents?
****Yes, yes! But already long time ago. Century!
*****Bubi, you mustn't tell this to mother under any circumstances. Top secret!
******Still, I'm a little proud of it … Perhaps because I'm so anxious otherwise …
*******Riding wild horses … constantly in new places … roaming … making campfires. Mmm!

But I still kept fighting with them... Full force, so that we toppled over like bowling pins... They'd swing at my eyes, I'd swing back at them, they'd leg wrestle me, I'd kick them back... they'd grab my thumb in their teeth, I'd rip a whole hank of lice-ridden hair from their scalps. Nobody could have pulled us apart...

In March Clairi and I gathered kindling... it was already dry... It was strange, but somewhere far from here, but not far from where Vati was in Ljubljana... the dark Führer... the thin man with his stubby mustache and his hair parted to one side, with the belt strap going over his shoulder... had marched into Austria once again at the head of his glorious army... Into the city that mother sang about, "Wien, Wien, nur du allein... city of my dreams..." There were photos in the *Patriot*... A whole forest of upraised arms, flowers, black swastikas like crossed-out gallows or broken extremities in the white circle of their flags... And the tanks, the cavalry, the Heinkel bombers. A whole army of young boys carrying their little Hitler flags, in capes and with drums. The Attila Youth! These kids even had medals pinned to their chests... All of this was in the air... like an invisible, gray soot falling on the Krka. He called to the people, so that they came running down to the Krka to listen to the radio through headphones... Nothing was clear to me... Not far from the clearing we ran into the forester... He whistled softly from behind the trees and took a big portion of cracklings wrapped in newspaper out of his leather shoulder bag. For us!... Clairi and I didn't know how to thank him... "A kiss," said the forester... "OK, but only a peck on the cheek," Clairi said. But barely had she puckered her mouth when he took her in both arms, with his whole uniform, and squeezed her against him... Smack! Smack! went the kisses... He grabbed ahold of her rear end, her breasts... I was there when Clairi finally fought her way loose, jumped, and shoved him away... flushed red with anger and the abrasion of his whiskers... She stood amid the big clearing, rubbing herself... "Adieu, Herr Lokar... Das dürften Sie nicht machen..."* And he had always seemed to be such a decent man. Respectable. Well dressed!... I picked the bag of cracklings up off a tree stump... there was no way I was going to leave them there for the snakes or foxes... Suddenly a stubborn silence dominated the area by the spring near the forester's house... I would break the ice with a stone in the mornings to fill a pot with water... The forester's children came toward me over the grass and surrounded me. They were standing so close that I knew right away what that meant... But I didn't understand why, because they were good, decent boys and girls otherwise...

The day before our departure we still didn't know how we were going to get our things, our suitcases and the rest to the train stop... There was nobody we could ask in the village. Not even Jožef. Anyone who might have helped us would be getting on Karel's bad side, is what mother said. What about the Gypsies? Mother and I went to the quarry to get a hitch with a driver... Meeting with them didn't worry me, because the Gypsy groups often changed in the ravine.

---

*Farewell, Mr. Vorester. You shouldn't have done that.

Sometimes there were more of them, other times fewer, and sometimes there was just one of them perched there, picking his lice off. On the marly stone where the ground was level and smooth there were tents and campfires ... while their carts and horses stood on the gravel and sand. Now I saw the Gypsies differently from before ... They were like circus performers, magicians and dancers from an amusement park ... Chicken thieves, horse thieves, thieves of clothing, perhaps. But robbers and murderers by no means. With their ridiculous necklaces, bracelets and rings in their ears, with their sticky coin purses around their necks, sideburns straight out of fashion magazines, their funny and colorful clothes, their shawls, headscarves and hats they gave the impression of mardi gras characters. Moreover, they were only slightly worse off than we were and the granite walls of the quarry differed only slightly from the cold walls of our room ... And ours did leak when it rained, we would have had to admit ... There were old Gypsies here too ... gray-haired, barely mobile, with white fur on their chests, the faces of old doctors ... old women with the collapsed cheeks of grandmothers ... and fat women who resembled the rich fruit vendors at the market... I was amazed in their case and couldn't fathom how they could live out in the open, instead of in houses, in rocking chairs and hospital rooms ... Everything would have been fine, if they just didn't stink the place up quite so much ... cooking awful brown sludge in their pans ... pretending to work ... banging away at stones with their hammers for the municipality, sitting on the short handles of crutches wrapped up in rags ... Mother and I finally agreed with a fat Gypsy woman that everything we left behind would be hers ... some skirts, blouses, a straw tick, a pair of shoes ... if she drove us with our luggage to the train stop ... The evening before we left was corn shucking time in the vestibule ... everyone from Uncle Jožef's house, some villagers and Karel. They had all become good friends again ... Some of them were sitting right next to our door while the whole lot of them brawled at the top of their voices. Karel, Jožef, Stanka, Mica, some village women, Ciril and Ivan ... We didn't dare leave the room ... As soon as we said anything or moved, they would become alert ... They would stop talking and start listening ... We had to pack our things quietly, as if we were in some sort of hospital ... They talked, sang, cracked jokes, and laughed. Then I sensed that their voices, at first quietly and one by one, then in chorus, began to mount. As though you were putting logs on a fire ... first one, then another ... until you end up with a pyramid and light it ... Blam! a corncob came flying straight into the door at the height of their chatter. Laughter! Blam! came another ... "Zurick in die Schweiz! Heilhitler! Heilhitler" they hollered ... "Still bleiben!"* mother warned us. Gisela was afraid. Clairi was rigid with fear ... How was she going to get to the outhouse ... I sat on the strongbox, sorting through my school supplies ... textbooks, pencils, notebooks ... But inside I was boiling ... Two to one, only counting the grown-ups, but otherwise we were outnumbered three to one. This wasn't fair, this broke all the rules ... Suddenly ... flutter! flutter! plunk! ... the door opened and something black fell into the room ...

*Keep still!

and the door slammed shut behind it ... The black thing was not a stone. It collided with the wall and slid down ... then got back up ... as light as a feather ... A sparrow! It was back on the floor ... I tried to catch it ... but then ... pitter-pat! ... it fled away from my fingers ... It took off again ... I climbed up on the bench to catch it ... but it had already flown away and fallen on the down comforter. Carefully I reached across from the side and got it. Look! As light as a petal. It stuck its head out between my thumb and index finger. I lifted it up. But strange, under its eyelids there were just little pits ... Somebody had gouged its eyes out on both sides ... and they were hanging alongside its beak like smashed raisins ... I tossed it out the window toward the tree. Rage, horror, and disgust mounted within me to the top of my head ... and began squeezing my eyes out of their sockets. I kicked the door open and literally flung myself out, as though into water ... Onto a heap of tassels and cobs. I saw everything now in a particular way ... Their faces ... I started swinging ... Karel, Mica, Ciril ... I howled ... Thwunk! I got hit by a corncob in the head, in the back ... All of a sudden so many hands! ... I grabbed Karel by the neck ... He was grinning ... Then I squeezed ... He shrieked ... I flung myself this way and that ... I wouldn't let go ... He fell back off his log ... He bit me in the arm, the pig! ... Ciril came to help him ... One more head ... I leapt at Karel and gripped his chest between my legs. "Bubi! Bubi!" mother and Clairi shouted at me ... The others surrounded me from behind, shouting and cursing ... Somebody kicked me in the back ... then hit me in the neck ... followed by a gob of spit out of Stanka's mouth ... They threw me back inside the room ... Clairi, mother, Gisela ... their long faces in front of me like dripping candles. My hands, my face, my legs and everything inside me was shaking ... Only now did I feel all through my gut their blows, kicks, and bites ... I was broken ... my ribs wobbling, my teeth chattering ... My heart started pounding so hard that I couldn't hear the noise anymore ... I threw up ... My knees gave out ... and I dropped to the floor ... What if I'd killed Karel? ... I would have liked to be able to cry ... but some sort of cramp seized hold of me ... I had attacked everything there was and couldn't stop ... Oh, how I wished I could have killed all of them! ... With a scythe, a hoe, an axe! ... I would have smashed the whole straw cutter over their heads! ...

The next day all four of us sat waiting for the head of the Gypsy horse to appear at the window, with the Gypsy woman sitting on the box ... Everything had been closed, locked and secured with padlocks ... There was nobody else in the house ... We climbed through the window to get to the outhouse. I could barely turn my head ... everything was still boiling inside me, and everything was broken. The Gypsy woman drove to the back of the house, practically overturning the wagon on the steep slope ... Karel had forbidden any Gypsies to approach the house from the front ... We handed all our luggage out through the window ... the comforter, the suitcases (canvas, cardboard and round), a bag of laundry, the steel strongbox, the pipes we had removed from the stove, because they were ours ... and set it on the wagon. Mother made a stack of a sweater, some skirts, a pair of shoes and the straw tick for the Gypsy woman, who examined them closely ... held them up in the sunlight, unfolded them, tried on the shoes ... She wasn't satisfied with what she'd been given, it wasn't adequate payment for her effort ... All the way to the train stop she muttered angrily and complained in her language ... we went around the house through the fence by the postman's house ... past Poldka's little house ... the engineer's villa ... down over the long road past the blacksmith's ... There was nobody anywhere, except for some kids in some yards ... Because the little wagon was so fragile and the diminutive horse so skinny we didn't ride in the cart ... It went slowly. It took an effort to reach each of the trees along the way, one after the other. Over and over ... It was raining buckets when we reached Ljubljana that night and Vati met us on the platform. The streetcars had stopped running, and he couldn't take us and the luggage home with him on foot ... So he ran out to hail a taxi ... He argued with the driver over the fare. Finally the driver agreed. By then we were soaked through to the skin ... A black, square car with red arrows for turn signals on both sides drove up to where we were ... It had a huge spare tire on the running board blocking the rear door ... so we all had to pile in through the door on the other side ... The train station vanished along with its lights ... Despite the rain I could feel the wheels revolving along the asphalt. Thank God, we were back in the city! ... The driver turned on the overhead light. Now we couldn't see anything outside anymore. That little light set in felt captivated me ... maybe because I was sitting between the seats on the floor ... The taxi swayed as it drove into the black hole of night, full of the downpour and gritty puddles that spattered the windshield and windows ... on the sides, at the back, in the front ...

"Mein Zimmer liegt weit draußen in der Umgebung der Stadt,"* Vati said.

All he had was a black pot, a plate and utensils for one person. The bed, a table, a chair and the stove in his basement room had been borrowed and belonged to the landlord. "Ein pensionierter Zahlmeister – bei der Marine,"** he explained. The only furnishings that were ours were the wicker chest and the sewing machine that Clairi had brought with her from Switzerland.

The first morning we got up very early ... The first thing I actually saw through the window was a miracle. A miracle of red roses entwining some green sticks that had crystal balls on them amid the thorns, reflecting the sky's blue and the blue house ... Right across from the window, which was barely an inch up off the sandy ground! ... I had to get outdoors as soon as possible ... "Paß auf!" mother put a hand on my shoulder in warning ... My God, the house was so big, three stories tall ... Blue, with its windows and doors outlined in white and white bands at the corners. It stood on a big lot of white sand that was neatly and carefully raked ... Behind the flowers there was a round pond full of water and a wooden gazebo painted green ... The trees behind it were arrayed in thick grass that had been well soaked by the previous night's rain. The road was visible on the far side of an

---
*My room is way out on the outskirts.
**A retired Navy paymaster.

iron gate set in a high, sculpted hedge ... God, where had we come to? A castle, a villa, the estate of some wealthy count? I didn't dare move from the spot ... As though I had downed some concoction, starch? ... I just stood there. But there was something else ... something that flickered and buzzed in the air ... What was it? I couldn't guess. Behind the house in the middle of the sandy yard there was a big green well, with a gigantic handle jutting out like a train signal ... To one side of it, tucked away, was a shed made of boards and white cardboard. I didn't dare go there yet ... That's where the forest began, which probably wasn't big ... and at the edge of the forest was a wooden hut, an outhouse, and a lime pit. Behind the gazebo, from the lime pit on, a narrow path led alongside the woods to a brown chapel. The Chapel of St. Roch with his dog ... The saint was depicted in the garb of a Roman soldier with a sword made of mosaic tiles. He was standing in a desert and pointing to a wound on his thigh. He had blue eyes with rings around the pupils ... No matter if I stepped to the right or the left, the saint's eyes followed me ... I went on ... behind the hedge was another road, full of dust that intersected with the first one behind the iron gate.

I watched Vati while he shaved, washed from a bucket and put on a celluloid collar. He and Clairi took off for town. To the Elite factory. Just for one day, so she could help him catch up on his backlog ... Once they left, we could move quite comfortably around the room ... But I ran after them. So I could see more! I walked with them to the intersection of two roads, where there was a smithy in some courtyard and a light affixed to a telegraph pole ... They were going down the main road that led straight past fields of grain and clover into town... From there I saw the castle on the hill again, as I had a year before. The grayish brown walls with the square tower and green cupola and the bell tower of who knows what church down below.... Here on the righthand side there was a wall running through the wheat and potato fields into the distance. A path past a gravel pit that had a wheelless wooden wagon in it led that direction. Crosses and tombstones jutted up over the wall. So this was a cemetery...

But the most unusual thing of all was the air, which shimmered... It smelled of water, which must have been flowing full force and in huge quantities through some riverbed somewhere close by... It smelled of the rocks and vegetation that must grow there. Was this why the trees quavered in the air like reflections in water? Some sort of noise surrounded my head on account of it: everything shimmered, moved, trembled, scratched, swarmed, repeatedly making contact in a repeating vision... As though instead of the treetops there was a creature perched on the trees... nature itself, with the folds of its vegetation exposed on all sides... There, in that wet field, in the dense shadow of the trees on the far side of the pond, I was suddenly on some separate planet: quiet, light, mute, unhearing, with no resonance and no echo... How was this possible? As though this was no longer me... This quiet space was somehow contained between the corner of a small stand of forest and a gap in the hedge where, beginning on the far side of a small bench, some quarried rocks lay scattered alongside the road: but from there on, beginning at a house with no stucco and the same gravel pit where I'd seen the gray wagon, that noise and the shimmering of the clear air came back and enveloped me...

Mother rearranged our room. It was five paces from the door to the window and two and a half paces across. The window was big and the walls were blue, with little flowers on them... From now on all four of us were going to sleep in the bed, she said, and Vati would have the table. The stove that was there had outlived its usefulness. A small cooktop with at least two burners and an exhaust pipe for the oven would need to be bought at a rummage store. A chiffon curtain would need to be sewn for over the window... So we wouldn't have to constantly be going out and in, we would keep a bucket full of fresh water in the room. Its place would be here by the door. Bubi, you are going to look in the woods for a short stump or something similar that we can set the bucket on. Whether or not there was a woodshed we didn't yet know, so we were going to keep a stack of wood here in the corner and under the stove. Our clothes and underwear would stay in the suitcase for now. We would nail several catches to the door... We would have to be careful in the toilet. It was just a latrine! Each tenant had to clean it once a month with a poker on a pole. So... "Ihr zwei müßt brav sein," she impressed on us. "Mit niemandem reden, außer das notwendigste. Keinem etwas erzählen über unser Leben. Mit niemandem eine zu große Freundschaft schließen! Still und anständig sich benehmen. Die Leute in Ruhe lassen."* Gisela, who

*The two of you must be good. Say nothing to anyone, except when it's absolutely essential. Tell no one anything about how we live. Make no close friendships with anybody. Behave modestly and with dignity. Leave people alone.

sat on the bed, washed and brushed and happy, was impossible to stop. Even if she did get into mischief, anybody would have forgiven her. It warmed everyone's heart just to see her. She was like a daisy gleaming in the grass... "Now to the water hole," mother decided. So out the door... and to the well for water... into that glorious world I had no idea how to navigate. On tiptoe? On my head? On my hands? When you still don't have any idea to what or to whom you're going to belong... Clatter! I set the bucket down on the drain and took hold of a pole hanging down from the handle. Screeeaaaa... it squeaked... it squealed all through the courtyard, the garden, the forest, the sky... I stood there petrified... Already I'd committed my first transgression against peace on earth...

There was never a light on in the vestibule. Steps led from it into the courtyard. I flew over these one-two-three when the baker came calling in the morning, "Kaiser rolls! Sesame rolls! Bread loaves! Baguettes! Croissants!..." The baker was a little man riding a bicycle. With a huge basket on his back and a slightly smaller one over the handlebars... He pulled a cloth off the basket to reveal thin loaves jutting up like lances among the croissants and rolls. I bought a small loaf of cornbread for two dinars... Every morning he pulled up like this outside our courtyard door and announced himself. As though he were paying a call at some landed estate... Who all lived in this building?

At the far end of the vestibule, in a slightly larger room next door to ours, lived a young dark-haired woman with her son named Enrico.

Her husband, a mason, built houses all over the country and was seldom at home. All three of them had fled the Littoral after Mussolini came to power, settling in Ljubljana. Enrico, who was a sickly boy, knew Slovene only slightly better than I did, but he spoke it as if he were singing a song, which made it harder to understand him. At first he didn't like me, because he thought we were Germans, and Mussolini was great friends with Hitler. Then that got straightened out. He began coming out to the woods where I would spend time. Most often at lunchtime, carrying his plate, which was laden down with delicacies he wanted to share with me. The best food of all was little fried bits of polenta. Like me, Enrico was a little mixed up from their move ... He hadn't found his bearings and he was afraid. He didn't know where to go to find friends, and so, for the most part, he stayed at home with his mother, shut away in their room. There he drew and read out loud to her from comic books in Italian, while she, always beautifully dressed, knitted or ironed ... Across from us in a room with a kitchen that had a proper brick stove, lived a many-headed family named Baloh. Father and mother with six daughters and sons. All of them heavy-set, pimply, with low foreheads and dense jungles of hair, and very pious. Every evening when the Ave rang at the cemetery, they would pray their rosaries aloud, kneeling around the stove in their kitchen. You could hear the murmur through the door, as though in a church ... Outside, in the courtyard, an old woman, formerly a waitress, lived with her young, pretty daughter in a tarpaper shack ... That was everyone ... Except for the owner, a former naval officer, and his housekeeper. Looking in through his window from the road you could clearly see a gold compass, a ship's wheel, and ship's rigging hanging in his nicer room ... Wearing a white cap, his servant cooked, cleaned and took care of him ... In the mornings he came out into his garden down a staircase with a railing that had a stone ball on it ... dressed in a robe that was only a shade less blue than the house ... An utterly white, thin, old gentleman with sparse hair, wearing a white cap with a celluloid visor. Even his eyes were blue, as were the lenses of his sunglasses ... He carried motorized model boats in one arm ... little cruisers and destroyers ... At the pond he would set them down in the water ... That was interesting, but I could only watch from a distance, from behind some flowers ... Other times he would come out without anything ... taking a seat in a chaise longue in the gazebo, where his maid in the cap would serve him at a small table. The first time I saw him, I had the feeling that it might be Mr. Perme, his embroidered robe or something else about him that caused that noise and shimmering in the air ... Vati introduced us one Sunday morning. When he heard the footsteps coming down the stairs, he called us, "So! Jetzt!" And all of us went over to where that ball was at the bottom of the staircase railing. Vati was a little nervous. Mr. Perme stopped in his tracks. He spoke like an officer. In short, abrupt sentences, to the point. We were not to play on the sandy paths, he said, looking at Gisela and me with his slightly faded blue eyes ... And if we did, we were to rake the sand every evening before we went in ... If we wanted to pull some weeds, he said, we would get apricots as a reward ... The forest, over there on the far side of the lime pit, was for playing in. Then he came to the bottom of the steps and shook hands with each of us ... And though he smelled of perfume and was all silky smooth in his embroidered robe and smooth shaven underneath his white cap, somehow or other he seemed less clean to me than the peasants in Cegelnica ...

So we played in the forest. The Baloh boys and girls went there, too. All of them strong, healthy, and wild. The nicest among them was stocky Štef, whom I made friends with because he was so bold. Of course, Enrico also came here, although somewhat reluctantly because of the large number of kids. Then there were the three Pestotnik urchins from a tall, half-completed building that was going up practically in the forest. They were members of the Falcons. Sometimes they would come racing out of their construction site wearing their red costumes or colorful soccer uniforms. The Balohs were Eagles and soon they would spend whole days debating with the other three ... At the sound of a whistle all of them would leap at a ball, pounding the muddy ground for all they were worth, jostling with each other and slapping mud into their mouths and eyes ... Some people who lived in their own handsome houses down on the road that led toward Ljubljana also belonged to the Falcons ... I had already seen the pretty lace curtains that hung in their windows, and had once even heard a real piano being played there. Imagine that! ... Two pale, freckled, red-haired boys who were nearly identical would also show up. They lived in the unplastered house next to the gravel pit and their last name was Jaklič. Quick, nervous, and as variable as the weather. Then there was easy-going, lazy Mirko, who lived with his mother in that wooden wagon at the bottom of the gravel pit. Then two blond boys named Slabe, with noses like boxers, who came from a long, one-story house a little farther on from the Jakličes. Their father, a scrawny man who had worked a long time in France, was called the Frenchman ... Farther on from his unplastered house, which stood right in the middle of some lettuce and bean patches, a new, white, four-story building loomed up on the top of a hill that the road skirted. There was just one tenant living in it, a Mrs. Gmeiner with a sickly son about my age. He never came out to the forest ... But from a house by the road, where they lived with their parents in the cellar, two tall, lanky, long-haired brothers named Žikič would often come out.

G<small>AMES OF EVERY POSSIBLE KIND</small> took place in the woods below the construction site ... soccer, shoot the goat, slingshot tournaments ... It never got boring. One day I went with the Balohs, who had brought along some rope, down to the Sava for firewood. One Slabe and one Jaklič brother also came along. I had no idea which, the younger or the older ones, because I didn't know any of the four very well and they all looked a lot alike. Enrico didn't come with. He avoided groups that went anywhere with some definite goal in mind. And he had enough firewood at home. Whenever his father came home from one of his construction jobs, he would bring along on a tricycle or a pickup truck a few gunny sacks full of wood. Bits and sawed-off ends of struts and masonry scaffolds from construction sites. Such nice yellow chunks that it made your mouth water to think what all you could do with them if you just had a hammer and nails at hand ... Past the four-story house on the hill we came to the first feed barns, hayracks, and farmsteads... These weren't really proper farmsteads... they were half town, half peasant houses. The people who lived in them had half and half faces to match... If those were peasants, then I was a native Parisian. There weren't even any dung heaps in front of the houses... Some fields, a horse here and there, but mostly just a few pigs and hens. And what about their fields?... Small plots of potatoes and beds of lettuce and onions and cabbage and beans. Now and then one Baloh or another would pounce on a patch and come out with an onion in his teeth... Oh, they wouldn't have gotten away with that in Cegelnica... Everywhere there was lots of laundry out drying, in front of every house and in all the courtyards and meadows... Under the eaves stood the same tall, yellowish brown, two-wheeled carts that I'd seen on the day we arrived, on the main street outside the train station. This is where the laundry women live, Štef explained, who do the laundry for the rich folk in town... When we went down to a meadow that was full of trees and bushes, that smell, noise and breath that always encircled me grew stronger and stronger... And when we got to the edge of the meadow, I saw paradise... the Sava, bluer than the sky and flowing through three big, distinct channels with banks made of smooth, snow-white pebbles that otherwise only existed in dreams!... I almost keeled over in amazement. This was too much! I sat, unable to move ahead. The river was racing at tremendous speed! So this was the source of all that had seemed so mysterious in the atmosphere... Such air! Such unbounded shimmering! And the scent! Of gravel, of wet sand, of the wood, the branches, the willows, the stones that the water flowed through...

Two hills ... that stood in a field of blue on the far side ... two furry tents, a dromedary ... also belonged to this paradise ... On the left a short forest, on the right mature willows ... Too much for one pair of eyes ... Such beauty was almost impossible, such a thing must surely intoxicate people, change them completely ... turn them upside down and set them on their heads! ... But I had to get up. My group was creeping ahead over the gravel without looking at anything around them, as though only the cord and their gunny sacks were important. We waded across the first channel, which was stagnant, then we stepped into the second ... Its rapids ... I could clearly make out the bottom, which was paved in brilliant light and dark stones of various sizes that would just lift up and float away if you kicked them. Such detailed inlay! ... I could barely keep my balance on them ... I thought that the water was going to fling me up toward the sky ... suck me down ... slice off a foot and carry it off ... it raced with such force, as though I'd been caught in a powerful eel basket ... I triggered a whole avalanche of stones that quickly floated away like a school of fish ... The surface smelled like nothing else in the world. Like an incredibly huge bowl of ice-cold stewed fruit ... Willows, rusted pots, sand in dried-out tree trunks ... with their short roots and branches they were like bathyscaphes or naval mines washed up from the bottom ... and dandelions, dandelions and more dandelions, as yellow as lemons ... And on top of a heap of stones lay a long, yellow, narrow skull with hollow eye sockets that the wind blew through ... "A horse!" said Štef ... Like in the wild west! "Es ist zo nice here!" I forced out, but immediately realized I'd blown it. Red-haired Jaklič next to me broke into a broad grin that involved all of his freckles and all of his teeth. Rats! I softened. For a second I turned my head toward the dense forest to calm down ... Just let him poke at me one more time, and I'll let him have it, I'll give him a knock-out punch straight into the Sava ... Štef and his crew, his younger brother and Marija, were already heading across the third, deepest channel to the other side ... That was where the best firewood was supposed to be, that got washed up by the Sava and that nobody ever gathered ... The wind was blowing over the water for all it was worth. At first the water was up to my knees, then suddenly up to my navel, my chest ... It hurled into my shoulders, my hips, my knees, shoving me to the right, where the currents of both channels, this and the weaker one, joined up together and formed an enormous whirlpool beneath a high, eroded bank, a downright demolished earthen wall ... As though a merry-go-round had been flung out into the rapids ... Štef reached an arm out of the raging water ... mother would have died if she'd seen me ... and grabbed me by the belt around my trousers ... Now I was in water up to my chin. My heart was beating not just in my throat, but in my chin. I was going to drown! I didn't know how to swim. But I was ashamed ... One of the Jakličes was skipping down the left side with his hands clasped over his head, like some girl dancing ... Then there was Marija with a scarf on her head. And she was a year younger than me. Then she shouted ... The water had carried her scarf away ... She was screaming ... The white rag was already floating away past the eroded bank ... It vanished and reappeared ... It could no longer be saved ... The bank rose up like a wall ... I climbed up on all fours, clutching onto the wet sand ... There was as much wood here as anyone could want ... just waiting to be collected. Washed up into a heap, scattered to all sides, tired of waiting, even dust had begun collecting. Branches like you couldn't find in the forest anymore ... Boards from old fruit crates ... Boards from old fences, still painted ... Real traces from a wagon rig! ... Nice looking yellow floorboards, as though they'd just been planed down ... We hauled everything up into a heap, made bundles out of it, and Štef even made a kind of raft out of the traces. He was going to sell them to some peasants in Tomačevo, he decided. Marija was shivering in the cold. She had lost all her color and her nose and her ears were dripping. She knew what awaited her at home on account of the scarf. Her father's belt, her mother's anger. Štef paid her no heed. That was his sister's problem ... Each of us hoisted a bundle up onto his head. I was going to drown, I knew it, just as soon as I stepped back into the current ... if I carried this thing on my head, I would lose my footing ... I went as far as the water and froze. I couldn't make myself move. They were already out in the middle of the water, with only their heads and bundles sticking out, closer to the far shore than to this one ... "Do we need to carry you piggy back?" Štef shouted over his raft ... I knew where that would lead. I shook my head. I wanted to show I was worthy, despite not knowing the language ... I stepped into the water ... step by step I veered to the right, as far to the right as possible, so that I would come out on the other side as far as possible from the place where the two currents met ... The water was raging ... A shower of stones amid flakes of froth threatened to crush all my bones. My head shook, swayed, rocked ... Every second could be my last ... Without my hands to row and with the bundle on my head I was like an invalid. Should I throw it away? No! It perched on my head with an easy weight, even though the wind kept slamming into it, if I threw it aside and forded through with my hands and feet, I would remain intact. No, I had to carry that wood across to dry land ... yes, I had to see it under the stove, at home, whatever the cost, it was my plunder ... The water was reaching up to my chin. The wind carried off a few crate planks, so long! ... But then my head rocked, shook, and suddenly slammed into the gravel on the bottom. Then I was upright again, minus the wood. And then a terrible avalanche of sand accosted me ... sifted me ... I'm going to drown ... Disgusting! The flood is going to carry me off. I saw Marija, Jaklič and Stabe all running soaked over the gravel ... and shouting. All their effort was in vain. The raging water flung me to the bottom once more, then carried me back up to the top ... in a flash I could see them all on the bank talking about how I had drowned ... With me floating past in pieces ... For an instant I wasn't aware of anything, and then something hit me hard in the chest and began squeezing me around the neck. It was one of the horse shafts, which Štef was holding on the other side ... They dragged me up onto the hot sand, among the dandelions, willows, and nettles ... Every part of me hurt, but most of all my belly and toes stung from the stones. "The Sava isn't for you yet," Štef said ... Fine! At least I had gotten a thorough bath ... Štef waded out into the middle of the second current. He scooped water up in his hands and drank it. "To trink?" I asked Marija, startled ... "It flows over seven stones," she replied ... What? Over seven stones? What kind of stones? Big ones? Where? Up at its source ... I had never before drunk water that I swam in.

I SHOULD HAVE KNOWN: as soon as mother and Vati were together, the complaints, accusations, shouting and arguments would begin again ... "Warum hast du damals die Schweizer Staatsbürgerschaft nicht angenommen? Warum hast du damals diesen Lieferanten alles Geld anvertraut? Warum bist du damals nicht in die Gewerbekammer eingetreten?"* And Vati's grumbling, which got louder and louder ... he would start by talking quietly to himself in some corner, getting ready for the alarm, drilling for the fight ... and then ... I knew it from the rue de Bourg ... from the Gerbergässli ... from rue Helder ... I knew all the arguments and counter-arguments by heart, alway pronounced in precisely the same way, they were like mummies and couldn't hurt me. I held my hands over my ears. What I heard was always the same: the voices pitched high and low, thundering and whimpering, and the crash of various objects that seemed to get hung onto them ... the iron, a hammer, scissors, wood blocks for fur hats ... then fell and started rolling around ... Once when I was still little I saw both of them, holding hands, fall to the floor ... and then get up again. I thought they were playing. No, they were

*Why didn't you assume Swiss citizenship back then? Why did you trust those suppliers with all of our money that time? Why didn't you join the chamber of commerce when you could have?

wrestling each other. Vati stood upright, his eyes bulging, shaking his clenched fist at mother like the handle of a ladle. And mother, red in the face and smaller, whimpering, shouting, and shuffling through the room. It happened more and more often that I would come floating in somebody's arms ... mother's, Clairi's, Gritli's ... into the blizzard surrounding Vati ... and, because everybody was afraid of him and shouting at him, I shoved my fist at his shoulder and his shaggy face, causing his spectacles to fall like saucers ... When the fight died down, mother came to me all in tears. She would sing some song to entertain me, or Vati would unwrap a little piece of cheese from some silver paper. Essentially they both had a heart, as did I, only that's not what counts in life. Mother and Vati ... were the kind of couple about which anyone could have instantly said that they didn't belong together. Uncle Jožef was a little, scornful man and his wife was a tiny, malicious woman. Mrs. Baloh was small and pious and Mr. Baloh too was short and a believer. Enrico's mother was dark-haired and pretty, just as her husband the bricklayer was handsome and swarthy ... But mother and Vati didn't fit together in any respect. Not in their hands or their feet or in their faces or postures, they didn't even go together in the way they worked. Only in their anger and bickering ... Even now. Especially when they learned from whoever it was about my adventure on the Sava. I could have drowned! Both of them were beside themselves ... Who was responsible? Him, for spending his days sewing at Elite, which had unceremoniously fired him, or her, for being at home all day anyway? Her, because she wasn't minding us, or him, because he didn't earn enough to buy her even a meter of firewood?... And again they started throwing things at each other... boxes, covers, promotional scissors that Vati got for free at the autumn fair. Clairi quickly closed the door and stayed standing in front of it. She covered the door, I covered the window, in order to insulate our walls, to separate them from the world, to prevent them from pushing their way out of our little room into the hallway... Each of them on their own, that was still manageable, but not together. The greater the distance between them, the better it was for both of them and the rest of us, too... When Vati showed up in the cornfield on his way home from Elite, that meant the beginning of a difficult hour, a regular hurricane. Or: when I was having a good time being with him and she came limping up wearing her floral smock, all red in the face, that meant the good time was over.

Out in front of the house, where there was some grass to walk on, the women usually sat sewing or knitting, with the owner's housemaid working on some embroidery. The first few days we were there mother joined them with her sewing. She had curled her hair for the occasion and ironed her smock. She felt a little awkward on account of her legs, which were covered with the black balloons of her varicose veins, so she hid them under the bench. But she was most ashamed of her toothless mouth, because of the stumps and the worn-down fillings. Whenever one of them asked her something with a German word, a gesture, or laughter... she would cover her mouth with her hand... It was good for the poor thing to be able to spend some time in company and chat with people at least a little bit... But on the days after that she didn't want to go back onto the lawn. She stayed in our room. That was a bad sign ... Gisela picked flowers around where the women were sitting. With her long hair and in her little brown dress with its yellow polka dots she was so cute that the women sitting there couldn't help calling her over, passing her around from lap to lap and fondling her ... Mother sat on pins and needles at her sewing machine without touching it. "Was haben sie dich gefragt?"* she asked as soon as Gisela came back in. Where is her daddy? And whether we really left our furniture from Switzerland at the railway station?... Mother turned pale. "Habe ich dir nicht gesagt..."** She sat down on the bed. She was going to explode any second, I could tell, or else faint ... Oh, she was prepared to sew anybody a dress, a blouse or whatever for free, just as long as they didn't start nosing around. And now that had happened ... Her face shook with rage, but also with fear. That was infectious. I could even feel it start to fill me ... Was I supposed to cut myself off from the world just like that? From the courtyard, from the Sava, the woods?... Mother no longer left the room if she heard the women outdoors. And if it happened that she ventured outside when they happened to be there, she dashed into the woods or the garden as fast as though lightning were striking all around her ... She stopped going for water, too. Particularly ever since the morning when she caught one of the Pestotnik boys at the trough. He was lurking there with a ten-inch knife, waiting to ambush one of Štef's younger brothers as soon as he showed and take

*What did they ask you?
**Didn't I tell you ...

his revenge for having thrashed him with a wooden board the night before... "Das sind alle nur mordsüchtige Luder,"* she whimpered as she lay on the bed. For the first time in my life I tried to comfort her. It was more powerful than me. I put my hand on her shoulder... "Warum sind wir hierhergekommen? Wo wir doch die Wahl gehabt haben, nach Deutschland oder Jugoslawien zu übersiedeln,"** she said without feeling me touching her... She would stand motionless at the door or the window. She was trying to listen. "Was sagen sie wieder? Über was lachten sie eben?"*** She wouldn't wait for me to translate. She understood the language like music... bangs, splashing, some bells tolling... Mocking... overjoyed... most of all threatening. "Sie werden mir einmal etwas anstellen, weil ich Deutsche bin."**** The women began to complain about Gisela and me. About me because I had spilled water from the bucket onto the steps. And about Gisela because she had dug up all the sand with her little pail and shovel. Because we played with boats that I folded from paper at the pond when the owner was away... The women pointed out the steps to the maid, whom they didn't like because she was the owner's lover, as well as the sand excavated down to the dirt in the yard... Old Mrs. Baloh went to complain to the landlord because I had dragged a whole tree crown from the forest into our room, dropping leaves and branches in the vestibule on the way... Mother was

*They're all a bunch of murderous low-lifes.
**Why did we come here, when we had the option of going to Germany?
***What are they saying this time? What were they just laughing at?
****They're going to do something against me because I'm German.

called upstairs. When she came back, she turned and shouted, "Das möchte ich sagen: ihr seid alle unverschämte Leute!..." Gisela and I dragged her inside ... she was as strong as a motorcycle. Then she punished us. She struck Gisela on the hand and then she slapped me in the face, her full wooden mask, and then she thrashed me with the bamboo cane that Vati used to beat animal skins. Everybody in the house could hear the stick whistling through the air and me wailing. "Nichts anstellen! Und wenn dich einer etwas fragt, nach mir rufen..."* I told her that was easier said than done. If somebody asked me something in the woods, what was I supposed to do? "Das wird die Mama antworten..."** From then on Gisela was supposed to play with her pail by the window, so that mother could have her in view the whole time. If anybody stopped and spoke to her, mother would stick her head out the window. "Was möchten Sie von dem Kind?"*** she would call out irritably.

Whenever she ran into somebody she didn't like when we were out gathering firewood, she would disappear quickly into the denser brush. Others she would nod to from a distance, and some she would greet with a Guten Tag. There were just a few she would stop for a moment and chat with, but for no longer than she herself saw fit. I tried to ascertain from the people ... by how attractive they were, or their age or their clothes ... why she afforded some of them more friendliness and others none at all ... Even afterwards I could never

---

*No shenanigans! And if anybody asks you anything, call for me.
**My mother will answer that.
***What do you want from the child?

figure out her behavior ... and I couldn't depend on her opinions, which weren't even interesting in the tiniest bit ... Women who weren't yet mothers were the same with everyone ... a kind of perpetual source of universal kindness ... But mothers, no. They were tight-lipped and stern ... stupid or the kind that constantly sang ... still others that carried themselves like athletes or nuns ... and some whom their children obeyed at the twitch of an eyebrow or who shouted their throats out at them ... Only Enrico's mother was friendly and quiet, like the image of a real mother in paintings ... All of mother's attempts to socialize with people or hide from them went over my head ... but I had to keep pace with her like a locomotive ... Out in a clearing she ripped through old clothes set out on newspapers and made new ones out of them. For Clairi, for herself, for Gisela, for me. With amazing speed! She would glance curiously up at the new four-story building where Mrs. Gmeiner lived ... She was a German. She would have liked to make contact with her. As soon as possible ... She waited for the right opportunity, she didn't want to be pushy, the opportunity had to come of its own. I understood this ... When she had washing to do, she did it far away from the others, on the far side of the lime pit, practically in the woods. She hung the laundry up on rope stretched between tree limbs, half in the sun, half in the shade. "Bleib bei der Wäsche, daß sie sie nicht schmutzig machen oder stehlen."* I sat under the laundry ... thank God other boys also sat under their mothers' laundry, so this wasn't anything strange or

---

*Stay with the laundry so they don't get it dirty or steal it.

unusual. For instance Enrico, with whom I talked a lot. He told me about the harbor in Trieste, where he'd been. About the sea and how enormous it was. About waves as high as a six-story building, about seagoing diseases. He knew his ships well. Navigating them, too. He had seen a three-master that had collided with lighthouses and sailed into port without its mainmast ... Some steamship covered in frost that freighted nothing but huge ice blocks from Russia. And submarines! And fast, white torpedo boats with projectiles that sped through the water to sink submarines ...

On Saturdays I scrubbed the room. Mother went to sit and sew on a bench that was near some quarried cliffs where all of us residents were allowed to go, but few ever did. Occasionally she wrote to Margrit or to her relatives in Neunkirchen. She would leave the paper on the bench and pace around with her hands in the pockets of her smock. That's when she would be thinking about what lines she might add to her letter. First she thought about them, then she wrote them. Sometimes she even recited the lines out loud, changing the sequence of the words ... Once the room was dry, Gisela and I would spread mother's embroidered floral tablecloth on the table and set a bottle with a flower on it. To cover the opening on the stove I cut a lace napkin out of paper. Even though all of it was going to have to disappear from the table and stovetop in half an hour. But for a little while the room looked like it had been assembled from a kit.

Vati only went out to the woods now and then to get some fresh air. Usually for no more than an hour, because he had so little time. He liked for me to go with him. He wouldn't say anything as I walked alongside him. He kept quiet. He didn't ask any questions, either. I should have asked him some, but didn't. Sometimes he'd exchange a few words with a worker out spreading gravel on the road or some woman working in her garden. If we did exchange any words, it wasn't in Basel dialect, but this new, Slovene language that I was gradually learning. This changed him into some other person. What sort? More accessible, or less?... I couldn't figure it out... The new language we spoke to each other was something peculiar. Like some unfamiliar, half-cooked, still raw food in my mouth. If we had wanted to tell each other what we thought of the unpeeled potatoes we were just then chewing on, whether they were edible or not, we could have found no better way of expressing it. I already knew a few words and what they meant. Except that they still lacked a heart and a mind... Not far from the new four-story house there was a clearing full of tree stumps. That's where we sat. Vati had on his only good suit, a blue one, with a necktie under his celluloid collar, the only one he could afford. He had his own way of keeping it clean, white and like new... He would work two or three layers of a special wax for dying hides into its cracks... That held for at least three months... and protected it from impurities in the air, fingerprints and sweat. He used that same lotion, which had a cellulose base, to treat the linen collars of his two other shirts... In the clearing he took out a pocket knife with a thick red wooden handle that he had bought at the train station... this was the most Slovenian thing about him. He used it to trim his nails, which grew fast, yellow and curved like the windows of old taxi cabs... The rage that possessed him when he was talking with mother or Clairi subsided ... Outwardly he was quiet and said very little ... He walked slowly, with his hands clasped behind his back, far away from the houses, way out in front of me ... a bit off to the side, uncertainly, as though he were stepping over shards or avoiding bugs or puddles on the road. His feet would recoil and his ankles would twist, causing his soles to twitch right and left before he set a foot back down on the ground ... I had to call to him and only then would he stop and wait for me to catch up with him. He said nothing. I would barely catch up with him before he turned around and went on. Was he a kind man or what was actually the story with him? I wanted something to happen. "Laufen wir!"* I shouted. I took him by the hand and raced off down the road with him. But after a few meters he would lag and say, "Laß mich los! Laß mich los,"** and sit down, all out of breath ... His lungs worked like a rotten bellows and a dry froth appeared on his lips ... He was completely gray, as old as a grandpa. He was fifty-five years old, as I reckoned, when I arrived ... and mother almost fifty ... That was a Methuselamian age ... somewhere way up ahead in life, or way at the back ... He didn't like me to be too energetic ... If I started jumping over a stick that I kept setting higher and higher, he turned and looked away. In the past he would at least pay attention when I showed him how agile I was, but not anymore. I wanted to learn something from him ... whatever it was ... that would be essential to me in life. I didn't know what to ask him about that he

*Let's run!
**Let me go! Let me go!

would know how to answer. Yes, he knew a few things about Hitler, Stalin, Mussolini, Chamberlain, and Roosevelt ... But of course he knew nothing about military affairs ... armored vehicles, bombers, and fighter planes ... submarines ... various kinds of rifles and automatic pistols ... what their trajectory was and how to handle them ... All of that was important for war! So that's why I described the specifications of various kinds of weaponry and waited for some spark of curiosity from him. It didn't much interest him ... It wasn't possible to convert him. He was different from others. In every way. Nobody else had such a tiny, fragile frame. He was handsome ... Handsomer than in his photograph with mother where they were sitting in wicker chairs, holding onto little, fat-headed three-year-old Clairi between them ... or than he was in the yellowed group portrait at the end of his tailoring course in Trieste, where he stood lined up with other young tailors in an auditorium, surrounded by old, stout master tradesmen sitting at little tables with tape measures and protractors. Thin, with sideburns and a thick mustache ... A handsome, elderly face with a beard ... it was amazing how much he resembled the patriarchs in church paintings ... His light green eyes behind glasses that he repaired using yarn would dart this way and that, big and expectant if anything darted past, or they would suddenly become cleverly focused when he fixed them on something that interested him, for instance a fur. I would look at him, because, quite simply, he was always silent ... Sometimes he would exercise a bit ... He would hop extending his arms up and down ... which looked funny, like some sort of running in place. I would quietly check around to see if there were people nearby who might laugh at him if they caught him doing that.

Much later, several weeks after our arrival, he and I set out for an air show at the airport... Old Baloh, Štef and Marija also went with us... We took side paths and shortcuts and snuck through a beech grove so we wouldn't have to pay admission at the airport... The meadow was full of banners and people. The planes did all kinds of acrobatics and flew flags on their tails... sky-divers jumped out of them... and gliders released pigeons from cages... Vati discovered that the handiest thing to do was to lie down in the grass and look up at everything flying and doing loops, at the cupolas of chutes opening up in the air. That's when I got in the practice of lying down to look at the sky, at stars and clouds...

Back at home everything was out of joint again. Bang! Vati sat down at the table with his back turned to mother and began sewing a fur with a thread three feet long... jerking his arm way up over his head. Whirrrr! mother started nervously working the pedals of her sewing machine... That the two of them had ever hugged? Impossible... Vati kept carping the whole time at Clairi about Gisela. But she wasn't afraid of him. She would walk right past his chair to mother or me, as though Vati wasn't even there... Clairi would come home from Elite completely worn out... on foot, more than an hour's walk, in order to save the money she would otherwise have spent for a streetcar ticket. Her heart was acting up. It was throbbing all the way up near the armpit. She had to lie down... She always held her hands turned forward when she walked, or turned up when she was lying down.

While she was resting, I was tempted to turn them over at the wrist, to correct her posture ... but I left her alone, because she would have hit me if I did ... She had a tremendous desire to eat her fill of a variety of fine dishes, especially cakes. For lunch she and Vati would always sit in the park and have some slices of bread and a bit of salami, and now and then they would treat themselves to an apple ... "Heute," she told me when we were alone, "bin ich einem älteren Herrn so sehr aufgefallen, daß er mich eine Stunde angestarrt hat ... aber Vati saß leider die ganze Zeit bei mir. Vielleicht, Bubi, werde ich einmal einen feinen älteren Mann treffen, der mich trotz Gisela heiraten wird. Dann wirst du etwas zu staunen bekommen: uns allen wird es wie durch einen Zauber gehen..."* She believed that eventually somewhere in the world she was going to meet an understanding man who was smart and not too old, who would give her everything ... clothes, a decent house, travel, perfumes ... and with whom she would have a nice life, not like mother and Vati's ... "Nur warum wurden wir auf die Welt gestellt von diesen zwei, die sich nie verstanden haben?"** That was too complicated. That part I didn't understand. Welt, monde, svet! That part was nice! A garden with shiny globes, paths, flowers, roses, gazebos, striped lounge chairs, swimming pool ... a forest, fields,

*Today I made such an impression on an older gentleman in Tivoli that he stared at me for an hour ... but unfortunately Vati was sitting with me the whole time. Maybe, Bubi, one day I'll meet an elegant older man who will marry me in spite of Gisela. Then you'll be amazed: we'll all live an enchanted life ...
**Why did we have to be brought into the world by these two, who have never gotten along?

and the Sava flowing through white gravel ... The world was magnificent! It looked boldly up at the sky like a baby ... Clairi pressed me to herself, as though I were her husband, and rubbed her cheek against my shoulder ... Was I supposed to believe that she was just my sister, a child of Vati and mother like myself? ... I couldn't ... She belonged more to people who were constantly arguing ... that jungle where eyes got lost even close up ... where chaos came to life in the most colorful way, and which excluded any sense of rules or regular patterns of repetition ... I fled to join the boys and girls from Jarše in the woods, where at least something was happening.

On the far side of our landlord's back hedge there was a one-story house of unplastered brick. So carelessly thrown together, with the bricks jutting out of the walls, that I could have built it better ... One afternoon, several days after we arrived, I noticed an unkempt dark-haired girl in a red dress who looked exactly like Anica. She was standing on the other side of the gap in the hedge, looking at me. I pointed my hand toward the area between her legs and dropped my shorts. She lifted her skirt up and pulled down her panties. Due to the leaves I couldn't quite make out her bun or she my pee-pee ... She waved for me to come around the hedge and join her ... Her mother, I'd heard, had once been a cook at the royal court. But which one? The court of the Austro-Hungarian Emperor Franz Josef or the castle of the young King Peter, who parted his hair on the side like Hitler? ... Next to the road before her house there was a brown wooden shack with curtained windows and a sign that said POP - ŠABESA. A young woman lived in this wooden structure who wore a wide, flouncy, rustling skirt of coarse silk. They called her the "basket" and said that every night a different man stayed over in her shack, which had once been a sweet shop ... In front of the cook's house there was a field with kale and beans. The girl resembling Anka, Adrijana, was already waiting for me there ... The house was as sooty and scabby as a barn ... the dirt floor littered with cinders ... Straps and hoes hung from the unfinished walls in the vestibule. Adrijana had a little and a big brother, who was a baker and had a new racing bicycle ... She wiggled her blackened fingers at me to come in ... In the middle of a big room with brick walls whose floor was also scattered with cinders, there was a big stove made of stone, resembling a well, with its stovepipe leading up through a hole in the roof. With little scoops, rakes, rusty shovels, chisels and black pots hanging everywhere ... In a corner beneath the paneless window there was a bunk under a big heap of rags ... I stopped and had a good look around. That's what I always did to get used to a new place. It wasn't the poverty that frightened me, but how hollow the house was. So this was the home of a woman who had once worked at the royal court, where everything gleamed golden and alabaster. I wasn't surprised, because as early as Steinenvorstadt I had seen lots of people – rich merchants, including Vati – who lost everything overnight and then lived like beggars in some miserable room ... Adrijana took me by the hand and led me over to the stove ... It contained a whole wheelbarrow full of fatty soot and ashes heaped up to the edge ... When I leaned over to look in,

Adrijana squeezed my balls in her hand, causing my pee-pee to hurt, and I squeezed her bulge through her skirt. I was looking around to find some corner of the room we could go to hug, when Adrijana led me to the bunk... Then something stirred and rose up... and the face of the dwarfish cook looked out of the rags... broad, flat, tiny and so covered with spots that it resembled a pan full of dried cracklings... I said *Koot tay* and ran out of there as fast as I could.

No, I had imagined girls differently. Clean... wearing cute dresses and colorful knee socks. And button-up shoes. Light blue cardigan sweaters. A chain necklace and light down in the hollow at the back of her neck. Glossy, brushed hair without any ribbons or braids... In plaid skirts in winter and a little coat with a fur collar, boots, and earrings under a woolen cap... If I ran into a girl who was wearing at least one of the items on my list, I turned to wood, as though bewitched... Štef's sister Marija had a gray face, slate-like eyes, scraggly braids, hair so thin you could see through to her scalp, and a smock made out of the material used for umbrellas... When her kitty died and we buried it in a shoebox in the meadow next to the gravel pit, she was so sad as she made up its bier of daisies and cherry pits and she cried so unstoppably that she became cute and lovable... The blacksmith's daughter was also pretty, reminiscent of the postman's daughter in Lower Carniola, who was already sixteen. She had a lot of blond hair and a round face with apricot skin and a nose like a baby's. She was prettiest of all riding her new bicycle... when she came racing by, sitting upright, her front wheel in the air and the rear wheel on the road, her arms crossed, not touching the handlebars... When she got pregnant by some boy, her father punished her. He waited for her at the crossroads near the street lamp on the telegraph pole. Belt strap in hand, he forced her to get off the bike, kneel on the ground and crawl on her hands and knees from the pole around both roads to the smithy courtyard ... her face smudged and her dress filthy with dust. Once they finally reached the courtyard, he began to lay into her with the belt ... People came out of the neighboring houses to watch and nobody said a word. That was the father's right, they said, a daughter who's brought shame to her family has to crawl home on her knees ... Those were the young ones. But the other, older women in the neighborhood! ... Mirko's mother, for instance, from the wagon in the gravel pit ... She would sit Turkish style in the grass, cleaning lettuce, and because she wore a short skirt and her stockings were fastened below the knee, I could see her full, white legs ... almost up to the point where that unusual black bridge between the hips began, and I gasped like a bellows ... I just took care not to look her straight in her gray face ... and to avert my eyes from her crotch, but my head kept turning back there all on its own ... Those were women who were suitable for bed or the outhouse ... I felt like pulling her skirt up over her head ... becoming coarse, grabbing her hair and shaking her like a pear tree ... sniffing all her various smells, baring her big, supple butt that moved closer and closer to the ground ... As I had that old hag when I was stealing potatoes from a field near the airport ... We thought those potatoes were for the taking, when suddenly a peasant appeared out of the forest, and on horseback, at that ... Everybody was out of there like a streak ... I lagged behind, I stayed, I only had about five potatoes in my sack ...

and I ran around blindly on those side paths near the airport and got lost... Finally I reached some rough-hewn shack standing off by itself in the brush... and noticed a fat woman in just a slip on the far side of its hedge. She was sitting amid trash and worm-eaten peas, trying to thread a needle. She had a face like an udder, eyeless, noseless, mouthless, even hairless... She couldn't get the thread to go into her sewing implement. She scratched her thighs, under her belly where the furry depression showed black, and her nipples, which stretched taut as planets... She resembled the miller's wife from the fairy tale, Lucifer's mother, whom the hungry young man went to visit... To get him to stay with her and love her forever, she conjured up a richly laden table for him every day with all kinds of exquisite dishes and drinks... I was immediately ready to live with this hag, the way you live at night in your dreams... I would caress her and love her, night and day I would lie next to her fat body in bed... And I would eat, eat, and eat!... Sweet twitches passed through my little pole... and I imagined shoving it into the gray forest, that strange mouth under the belly, as if into dough... I couldn't tear myself away from the hedge, I shoved in and out, as if I were with her under a comforter, until I finally felt some end and it all passed.

I could imagine all women like this, except for Enrico's mother. She was too pure, beautiful and bright for me to imagine without her clothes on... With naked breasts, bottom, and belly... The skin of her face was so white. And her hair, with waves on both sides that seemed like a single curl, a big treble cleff. The ring in her ear cast a violet reflection on her cheek and neck... I couldn't imagine her long, pretty arms in anything but motherly caresses ... nor her pale lips, which weren't painted into a rectangle, like they were on other women ... she didn't use makeup at all ... kissing anything but a cheek or a forehead ... nor did the big, almost lonely brown eyes of her long face ever become harsh, cold or hateful ... You never heard the sound of squeaking bedsprings coming from her room, like you did from the Permes' upstairs or the shack selling pop ... When she wore her low-cut blouse, it would never have occurred to me to pull the front down to see more, and when she sat, I never once glanced at her knees ... With her, everyplace else was as pure as her face and her hands. She was almost an angel, perhaps even a nun at one time, ready for nothing more than friendly squeezes, pleasant smiles and heartfelt talks ... The bricklayer could be happy to have a wife who was such an aristocrat ...

MAY CAME ... I was on my way with the Balohs and others to the new church in Moste for devotions to Mary ... At a crossroads before we reached St. Martin's Road we suddenly ran into the Pestotniks and other Falcons and girls ... They were on their way back from exercising at the National Home ... We spotted each other from a distance and as we drew close, both sides got ready ... It started with taunts: "Hey, owls! ..." "Falcons! ..." "Clerical curs! ..." "Red rubbish!" Shouts, arguments, then blows ... The path was narrow. We went first then they had at us. We shoved each other into the grass, the clover, the wheat ... The girls started squealing like cats. And went running to the houses with pianos for help from adults ... We pushed toward the property markers and the telegraph poles. Once you get slugged in the face, the hatred comes from somewhere deep down. And it floods everything. And it's so deep that a bit of it stays in you ... They threw themselves on each other ... twisting, rolling ahead, rolling back ... Two girls grabbed at each other's hair, too, by the ribbons ... The Falcons knew some good punches and in their gym clothes they were lighter, too. Our guys shouted too much, and Štef wasn't there ... I didn't feel like getting involved ... I'd gone with the Pestotniks to the Falcons' exercise grounds in Moste a few days before ... I'd seen the brothers and sisters dressed in red and white carrying a big flag like a carpet between them, and the decorated portrait of King Petar. A brass band played the anthem. They shouted "Hail! Hail!" and sang ... I didn't like it ... all that defiance and rigidity came out of nowhere ... perhaps from the high schools ... Some tall, skinny guy from a small house by the road was approaching ... I acted as though I didn't see him and let him get close. When he leapt at me with his arms stretched out and his right leg extended ... I didn't wait anymore ... and I slugged him in the chest for all I was worth and kicked him in the shins, so that he howled and began hopping around like a frog ... He was out! ... Then one of his girls came running up and started whining and sniffing around me ... I stretched out an arm ... Brats are the same everywhere in the world ... if you don't strike immediately, nothing works later ... Spoiled mamas' boys and cosseted baby girls ... We wiped off our faces, slapped the dust off our shirts and picked the straw out of each other's hair ... The church in Moste was full and we had to stand on steps along the side wall. The church was new and very white ... only a few statues and paintings, all very bright, stood here and there in niches or hung on the walls. It wasn't like a church at all, more like a whitewashed hangar, or synagogues in Africa that were white so the black people could see each other more easily. Somehow God couldn't be here. He had to be in dark churches, so dark that there had to be lamps or at least candles burning in order for you to look around. So that darkness descended on you when you entered and you couldn't see a single person in the pews ... So you could pray or think as you saw fit ... Here that wasn't possible ... You saw all the people, and in the light of day as it fell through the clear windows all the faces were as alike as under the open sky ... I didn't care to go back there for services ...

In the woods we made paper airplanes and each of us was supposed to mark his with his country's flag. I wanted to draw a white cross on a red field on mine ... all the others were either Yugoslavia, England, America, France ... or such far-off countries as Holland and Sweden ... "You're competing for Germany ..." Pestotnik said. "No, I'm koink to pee Zvitzerlant ..." "Others have already got Switzerland." They stood there glaring at me, the pains. So I took my plane and on its wings and tail drew a swastika, which I didn't like because it was so prickly, like four linked gallows ... Coats of arms with swords, lilies, or lions were completely different. We assembled along a line in front of the building site. Three heats. The plane that flew the farthest and longest would win ... In one of the heats the winning plane bore the sign of the swastika ... So I had won.

Out of the blue old Slabe, the Frenchman, started coming out to the woods, a toothless old grandfather in a white shirt, white cap and white tennis shoes ... He taught us fencing ... At first we each smoothed off a stick and attached the cover of a box of shoe polish at one end as a foil guard to protect our fingers ... In the clearing he showed us the various basic thrusts ... eight in all ... and especially a trick for assuring victory in a match. In the usual course of crossing foils, instead of going after and parrying your opponent's tip ... you plant your foil diagonally into the floor in front of him, while your opponent, whom you've tricked while he's holding his foil in a horizontal position, naturally strikes downward to protect his legs, but just as he does that, you lift your foil up, striking him in the chest on the heart side with its tip. A kill! ... All of us learned it and it would have been monotonous if we didn't know other basic attacks and didn't use the trick at various intervals ... Somewhere in the middle or at the end of a round, after several warm-up lunges on the ground as we leapt from stump to stump while fencing. But your eyes had to be quicker than your opponent's ... The Frenchman's wife, a tiny woman in an apron fastened across her breasts, who raised flowers and vegetables to sell at market, would get angry at her husband and make fun of him ... Every so often she would call to him from on top of the flat roof of their half-built house to come home and get to work, her shouts echoing all through the woods, but he would pretend he was deaf ... Others made fun of him, too, but everyone liked him more than they liked his wife ... After every competitive round he would solemnly praise us after lining us up. He also taught us boxing. Not knockout punches, which each of us already knew, but hooks and uppercuts and how to block punches. Word was that he had once been a wrestler or trainer, and ultimately a referee too ... he showed us a photograph on a scrap of a French newspaper: him dressed in white with a black bow tie. What was he like? You couldn't make fun of him. He went jumping around so earnestly when we practiced. And his gray eyes bulged so severely whenever we broke a rule that we had to take him seriously. Mornings he would already be waiting for us, as we'd agreed, past the bushes in the clearing, all dressed in white and with the wet gray fur that grew out of his ears ... He would ask if we'd slept well and then we were off, repeating the previous day's lesson after him. There was no difference between him and the kids, we could address him informally ... When occasionally he had to go watering flowers with his watering can and we had to wait for him over in the clearing he would be red in the face with embarrassment ... Once mother, Gisela, Clairi, Vati, and I were invited to his house for a visit ... Vati didn't want to go ... He never liked paying visits, or formalities ... The Frenchman's wife showed us around their house. Everywhere you looked there were colorful things ... variegated curtains, multicolored furniture, rainbow bedcovers and curtains, yellow, red, and green throw pillows ... it was as if you'd walked into the wagon of some circus performers. I liked it ... From their flat roof, where his wife always called to her husband and the Frenchman was supposed to finish the house by building another story, if only he hadn't been so lazy and run out of money, there was a beautiful view: over the grain fields all the way to the forest and then across more fields to the cemetery and airport. They were constantly at odds with the Jakličes, who wouldn't let them take the road across their property ...

so the Frenchman's wife had to take all her flowers, which grew near the neighbor's beds, and take them on a cart back to the house and only then set out on the road into Ljubljana ... She brought glasses of lilac juice which she herself made out to the garden for each of us ... She smiled a lot, she didn't seem at all as hard-hearted as she did on the roof, and the Frenchman told a few jokes from Paris ... During our visit mother constantly kept looking over at the new four-story building where tall, stout Mrs. Gmeiner lived. Now the one boy, who was my age, was joined by a brother who was a student of engineering. According to the Frenchman's wife some bank officer, a Slovene, was also paying occasional visits. Mrs. Gmeiner was reportedly from Vienna and an Austrian, but she kept very much to herself and hadn't even exchanged a word with the Frenchman yet ... One day I ran into her. It was pouring buckets and I was coming home from school without an umbrella and soaked to the skin, when I noticed her in a shiny black leather coat holding an umbrella in one hand and a cape in the other, running through puddles past the houses across from the school, which was on St. Martin's Road. Her little boy was just then coming back by a shortcut nearby and she shouted out, "Mein armes Büblein!"* An instant later she had him wrapped up in the cape. I was jealous. My mother would never have done anything like that ...

One fine day we finally got to meet her. How? Had mother tried to pump her for money or had she sold her some fur item of Vati's? ...

*My poor little boy!

The lady came down to the road with her friend, the bank officer, and her younger son, where we were waiting for them, as she and mother had agreed beforehand. Together we went down a road past grain fields and clover to some neat little houses, then back to where the farmsteads began and finally down the road into town. I wanted to talk to Leon who knew Slovene really well, since he had been here since first grade. But he was too fragile and delicate for me to get any halfway lively conversation going. I could barely get him to go with me onto the grassy escarpment over the road, where it was nicer to walk. We looked at the castle, all lit up and crystalline in the early twilight, and the bank officer, who was wearing a white raincoat and had a black mustache and sideburns... he appeared to be quite the cosmopolitan gentleman... explained what a nice local practice it was, "alte Schlößer und Monumente am Abend zu beleuchten."* At last they invited us over for some stewed fruit. Everything still smelled of mortar and our footsteps echoed through the big, empty building as we climbed up its modern staircase. It was a handsome apartment with big windows, and her son the student was drawing some schematics in the kitchen on a big drafting board. In the living room, which was full of rugs and armchairs, Mrs. Gmeiner wound up the gramophone... "An der schönen, blauen Donau,"... "Wien, Wien, nur du allein...."** Mother sat fearfully in a chair, her arms nervously folded, while Clairi, who was all excited, began swaying on the

---

*... to light up old castles and monuments in the evenings.
***The beautiful blue Danube*, and *Vienna, just you alone*

sofa in waltz time and humming along and clicking her tongue, "tsk tsk tsk..." At his mother's insistence, Leon showed me a box containing arrows and a target... we played for a while... After the stewed fruit we left. The lady from Vienna and her bank officer lay down on the sofa in the living room and Leon, whose health was fragile, soon went to bed. I stayed for a while in the kitchen with the older one, the student, and because I liked drawing, watched as he used charcoal and a fountain pen to shade in big and small turbine screws. Through the open door I saw feet resting on the edge of the sofa... coarse male feet in polkadots and hers with their tiny heels in silk stockings, which excited me. I also heard her voice as the springs squeaked, "Laß mich in Ruhe, du! Laß mich in Ruhe..."* Women really did have it rough... Suddenly something began to rumble as if out of hell. Military planes, one, then another, flew right over the house... almost touching the roof with their wings... They were fighter planes, that much I guessed right away from the machine guns alongside their cockpits. The panes in the windows growled and a whole avalanche was released through the upper stories, causing my mouth to go dry... The airplanes vanished together with the lights on their wings in the direction of the airport... All of us jumped up, except for the student. "There's going to be a war," he said as he continued to draw. "The Germans are going to come any day and send this whole Yugoslav circus to hell..." It was the first time I'd heard somebody saying in Slovene that Germany was going to destroy Yugoslavia. And with

*Leave me alone, you. Leave me alone.

such zest! That had a strong effect on me... But the young man's face was so focused and serious when he looked at me that I believed him...

M̲rs. Gmeiner was like my teacher Roza. She was just as big and powerful a lady, except that she always wore clothes of black or purple satin because she was in mourning for her husband... At the beginning of summer Vati got me re-registered for the public school in Ledina, because the one in Jarše was too full... The school in Ledina was much grander than the one-room school I'd attended in Lower Carniola... There was strict discipline and tidiness in the hallways. Between the windows and doors to the classrooms there were framed pictures of famous men in beards, all of identical size in identical frames. While I was waiting for Vati, who was in the principal's office, I read the names under the pictures: Prešeren, Stritar, Cigler... Kersnik, Jurčič, Mencinger... Levstik, Slomšek, Dalmatin... The hallway was like a temple and as I walked back and forth, the eyes of those great men followed me through the gray ash of their hair, their mustaches, their beards... They were probably doctors or judges... Then a teacher came, tall, broad, stout Miss Roza all dressed in black but with red lips. She spoke to Vati, who looked like those learned men with long hair and beards in the pictures, and as he held his hat behind his back, standing in front of this woman who was nearly twice his size, he seemed to visibly shrink with stage fright... She kindly pressed me to herself, to her blouse covered with frills and patches. "If he studies as hard as he did in Lower Carniola, he won't have a thing to worry about ..." she said. My fellow students were all perfectly combed and dressed. Miss Roza introduced me from the platform, with her hand on my shoulder. Here is your new classmate. He came here from Switzerland over a year ago. He attended the first form there. He was seriously ill and spent two years in hospitals ... Her voice sounded clear, sweet and maternal ... His Slovene is bad, she went on, so be nice to him and help him ... The brats were staring at my long hair that my parents cut at home ... Despite my embarrassment and the teacher's sing-songy voice I immediately spotted two ass-kissers and a few who had already declared pre-emptive war on me ... A whole train car full of mama's boys and and conceited know-it-alls! Then the teacher had me take a seat in a bench by the window. She sat down and her bosom with all the various decorations affixed to her dress made her look like a portrait bust set on her desk. Above her was the famous young king in a fuzzy photo, looking gently down from under his black profusion of hair ... Oh, he had whatever his heart desired ... During the main break the other students snacked on chocolate and rolls with marmalade or thin slices of cheese. My head was practically spinning from hunger ... They would leave their leftovers under the benches ... halves of breakfast rolls jutted out among the briefcases stowed on the shelves and I felt like nabbing them. But I knew that theft was punished harshly at school ... A few busybodies came up to my bench. How's it going? Why were you in Switzerland? Some of them behaved decently, but one of them, a fatso, started interrogating me with his hands in his pockets like some bank director, and his head was all bulging out, too, "So why did you come here from Swtizerland if you don't know any Slovene?..." This was another one of those damned lumps who feel just super duper dressed in their nice sweaters and corduroy knickers... because they know all about something or because they have a train set under their bed at home or because they already know they're going to get a gold watch for their next birthday... "Bah! He can't even answer my question!" he scowled. You just wait, I'll land you such a punch, you'll be looking for parts of yourself around the schoolyard for days!... My immediate neighbor, named List, was different. Calm. Independent. With a thin, dark red face, like mountain climbers, a bit cross-eyed, always wearing checkered shirts with white suspenders... While I answered during the first period, everyone had a good laugh. But that was nothing, I expected as much. Miss Roza found a way to silence them immediately... not with a look and not with her hand or with anything that I could notice... it was very elegant. I didn't know anything... well, maybe my drawing and handwriting weren't so bad... When Miss Roza asked me a question, I stood up and didn't answer. All right, then, next time, she said and gently motioned with her hand for me to sit down... All my homework was written in chicken scratch. I didn't have anyplace to write... when we'd finish eating, Vati turned the kitchen table into a work table and then later into his bed... In between times I had to steal a corner of it for my notebook or some sheet of drawing paper. But that was an excuse. I knew nothing because I understood nothing, and sometimes because I didn't feel like thinking...

Across from the school there was a fur store ... with a fox made of red tin walking across its signboard. In its display window there were muffs, collars, coats and a pretty mannequin dressed in a moleskin jacket. This store was like a memento of wealth and of Basel ... I would go over to look at it. I felt like I was back on Gerbergässli. Every day I had the long walk to Jarše and then from Jarše to school ... I had to get up especially early. Off of St. Martin's Road there were soldiers who lived in a wooden shack in the middle of a field guarding the army's crops ... Every morning I gave the guard a hand salute ... But then: past the long wall of the lime factory to the railway overpass and from the Dragon up toward Tabor to Ledina ... more than an hour! The washerwomen were already out before seven pushing their two-wheeled carts with bundles of laundry down the shoulder of the road into town ... At the steam oven bakery, I'd occasionally see two bicyclists engaged in a tussle, usually an Eagle and a Falcon who had run into each other on their bikes ... One was riding into town, the other out of it. As they rode toward each other, one would wave an arm or an umbrella, causing the other to fall off his bike ... He left his bicycle in the middle of the street and ran after the other, grabbing at his rear fender ... if the other didn't manage to escape, he kicked at his pedals or the bike ... and then it began ... they grabbed at each other, writhing through puddles, rolling over the grass and then back out into the street. It was comical to watch these grown-up, wobbly grandpas locked in some childish wrestling hold. People stared and either left them alone or walked on ... At St. Jožef's hospice I always waited for List, who lived somewhere close by. Those few minutes before school were the nicest of the whole day. Sometimes his older sister would bring him in on her bicycle. I liked her, because she was cheerful and like her brother and she always wore checkered skirts with suspenders ... A few times on the way home from school we stopped at St. Jožef's morgue where the dead lay, the old men and women from the hospice ... There were wreaths and flowers all around where they lay. What were they like when their souls left their bodies? They had white faces and cardboard shoes that lay just as flat as them. We sprinkled holy water on them but there were some lowlifes who, if a corpse had its mouth open, would take all the little sacred objects set out on its clothes and stuff them into its mouth ... I wasn't afraid of them, I was just afraid that some soul floating around in the cold crypt that resembled a dirty garage might touch me ... slide into my mouth like a cold snake and whisk everything out of me. Teacher Roza asked me a little bit every day and finally rewarded me with a smile ... as though I were suddenly some model student ... She had a son, they said, who apparently was such a prize student that he skipped some grades and was already in high school ... After school she would often take me or some other student along to the market so we could help carry her baskets ... She put on a black straw hat with glass cherries ... She always wore a skirt that almost reached to the ground ... Velvet, taffeta, satin, twill ... I knew my fabrics well ... Everyone said hello to her ... on the bridge, at the market ... I went with her from stall to stall where meat was sold as she made her selections. I listened to her talk to the master butchers. I was curious how such a learned lady would act in the midst of everyday life, at the market, with all its shouting and bargaining over price. She just smiled, enjoyed herself and was cheerful, like a true lady ... she could have easily been the queen of China or Spain or Monte Carlo ... She had her special vendors and peasant women ... for potatoes, for lettuce, for apples, eggs, cream and flowers ... Everyone was happy to see her. I was proud and felt it an honor to be able to walk with her through town ... When she got on the streetcar outside city hall, she always waved goodbye to me through the window ...

Once after school I got to go visit Elite ... It was a big sewing workshop, full of machines and men in vests cutting, measuring and sewing around a big extensible tailoring table ... Vati worked around the corner, with the work in his lap, because he didn't have a place at the table. Clairi sewed in the back behind some thick, brown tarp. She had to hide, I don't remember from whom ... the boss, the owner or the police ... because she was working illegally ... I didn't understand ... All I knew was that the men in vests at the big table were paying her directly out of their own pockets, because she was helping them. I went with both of them to Tivoli and then once with Clairi to visit her friend Marica, who worked in an ice cream parlor on St. Peter's Road ... This was a big establishment that had to be electrically lit even in daytime. Marica was pretty, blonde, and dressed all in white like a hairdresser ... Not only did she have blue eyes and black eyelashes, but even her eyelids were blond, like a forest maiden's ... She brought each of us a piece of cake at her expense and then chatted with us as though we had paid her ... The way home was much longer ... and if I didn't stop by the shed with the soldiers, all the more so. Mother cooked beans and potatoes or macaroni, if she had any, and mixed in an egg every once in a while. But our biggest holiday was on Saturdays, when they both got their pay from the tailors ... I went out as far as the light at the intersection to meet them and when I saw the loaf of bread and the package of butter in Clairi's shopping net, I immediately broke off a whole heel, even though my sister tried to prevent it.

By the end of the school year I hadn't passed. Teacher Roza assembled all of us for our final lesson. It was quite ceremonial. In a vase there were red and white roses with a tricolor ribbon wrapped around them. The boys were on pins and needles, red in the face and all of them sweating. Each of them had brought some present for the teacher ... downright elegant little packages with a ribbon, or at least a bouquet of flowers. Miss Roza called out each name separately ... You're going to have to repeat third grade, she said to me when she handed me the big, rigid report card ... all ones and twos, barely any threes ... I was a little disappointed. This big document ... with the stamp of the government and the white royal seal was going to trigger a tragedy, if I thought about my parents ... After distributing the report cards Miss Roza gave us a short speech. All year long I've been looking at one of the boys in this class, she said, and thinking for the longest time that he had a terrible blemish under his forehead. Then one fine day I realized that he has such big, dark eyes ... "Who? Who?" everyone shouted right and left. Our Lojze, the teacher said ... So that meant I was handsome?! I realized to my delight ... It was hot as I walked home and I was hungry enough to eat even wild chestnuts, if there had been any, even though they're as bitter as soap ... I went straight to visit the soldiers out in the field, guarding their crops from their shack ... They were true giants with upturned mustaches, big shoes and caps that made them look like they were wearing pots on their shaven heads ... But they were so friendly, you would have thought we were the same age. They knew as little Slovene as I did and that's why we got along. I sat in their dark shack, with them reclining on their metal cots, which were for the cavalry. Now and then they would offer me a piece of toast left over from breakfast, because they were hungry every day, too ... they showed me their rifles ... such clumsy ones that they would go off when they took them down off the wall, or wouldn't when they tried to shoot them. They looked at my catechism with its color pictures of the creation of the world, the garden of Eden, Adam and Eve ... everything that happened up to the birth of Jesus ... and then the pious widows who accepted the infant John the Baptist in the New Testament ... I said that I would sell them the catechism, which belonged to the school, for a fourth of a loaf of bread or, in other words, a day's ration of army sourdough ... I sensed I was doing wrong, but I had to gather some strength ... At the far end of the field was a barrel of water that they called their rain gauge. I hesitated a bit. "One must pay the utmost attention to documents, all one's life," mother had always stressed. She was thinking of passports, birth and christening certificates, various receipts, papers, and confirmations. I folded up the stiff report card and submerged it in the water barrel, then I tore off a white wad of it and shoved it into a molehill ... At home nobody asked me about my report card. Mother didn't remember about it until halfway through summer. "Hast du die Klasse bestanden?"* "Ja," I said, "das Zeugnis bekomme ich im Herbst."** Well, at least I would have some peace until then ...

Mr. Perme had his model cruisers and destroyers out in the pond on maneuvers ... That afternoon Hitler gave a speech. I heard his angry, piercing, percussive voice ... the cheers ... the fanfares ... applause, as though all the hands were articulating bits of slogans in some big, probably beautiful assembly hall far away in Germany, all of it sensitively broadcast by that little box. The radio sat on the ledge of the landlord's window and he and a few other refined gentlemen sat in the garden listening to it. When there was another round of applause and cheers, and you could hear them all getting up off their chairs (there had been 30,000 people assembled, according to reports the next day), one of the gentlemen in the garden said, "Here comes the ultimatum, the declaration of war. Now it's France's turn, or Poland's ..." War ... tanks the color of leaves and dirt, airplanes, demolished houses, people tied up, like in the photos from Spain ... meant the end of a beautiful life. It affected me even more when I considered that I had flunked the third grade ... Of all the furious shouting I only understood a word here and there, even though the radio volume was turned all the way up, resounding as far as the

*Did you pass third grade?
**Yes, and I'll get my report card in the fall.

· 200

woods on the far side of the lime pit ... The voice contained that unusual boldness, when you needed to take just one more courageous step ... the step that left you speechless in Tarzan movies or Popeye cartoons ... fantastic, impossible, unpredictable ... that lured you to that place where others could only shout terrified, "Stop!" "Dieser Feigling wird alle Leute in die Grausamkeit stürzen,"* mother said.

Clairi was spending days at home again, because it was summer and the tailors at the tables didn't have enough work even for themselves. The Elite also furloughed Vati until the fall ... He took everything he had out of his wicker basket ... sleeves, collars, fur caps, short women's vests, everything except for a big opossum hide, which he was keeping for really hard times ... He put these items in a small suitcase and began walking around town trying to sell them ... but he sold nothing. Someone gave him the address of the conference of St. Vincent de Paul, a philanthropic organization of the Church of the Sacred Heart, where we went to ask for groceries ... The mother superior, who answered the door of the white building, sent us around the corner to the monastery's public entrance where the sisters had their garden and kitchen. The entrance was next to a gasworks. The nun minding the entrance was tiny, old and nice. We were allowed to collect the uneaten bread that the St. Vincent's nuns had left over from supper, emptying them out of the baskets on the long cellar tables into a paper bag. Mother would mix groats in with those crusts, producing an excellent dish. But we used up the five-kilo bag

*That coward is going to plunge the whole world into horror.

within two or three days ... Hunger returned to our house ... dropping its sticky, invisible net on us again. I was so hungry I couldn't stand upright anymore ... I went to lie down in the cool grass under the trees at the back of the garden. My head was spinning ... I saw ghosts ... and it seemed like the world came and looked at me: the trees assumed barky masks ... the sharp grass ... little white tears on the blades that kept dropping off ... and the awning attached to the angled timbers over the door ... I started shaking, so I went to lie in the sun, but then I got hot, so I retreated back into the shade ... I was like a freezer or a blast furnace or a barometer ... there was no way I could get rid of the painful oozing of saliva in my mouth, or the putrid stench belching up out of my guts and cramped stomach ... The others, mother and Vati, lay in our tiny room so they wouldn't move around too much and thus make themselves even hungrier ... I went to check in on them twice ... first out of amazement that they were lying together, and the second time in fear that they might have died. Their heads were leaned up against the headboard and their feet hung out over the end of the bed, and they were dozing or sleeping with their hands folded over their stomach ... as though they were dead ... I went out to the grass growing at the edge of the road to find ears of grain to chew on ... tree bark and acorns in the woods were too bitter ... The worst was that we didn't have a single friend to help us ... maybe if we had told somebody ... Mrs. Gmeiner owed mother something, even though she had pawned the hides ... She didn't dare go to her house to ask for an extension, let alone another advance ...

In the middle of July Vati's lungs got worse ... They wheezed so much that it was truly disgusting. He spat out blood everywhere, onto the dusty road or into small bits of paper. When he went to see a doctor, they made him stay in the hospital. He lay in a big room with lots of other patients. They were always pleasant and said hello whenever I went to visit him. Real skeletons. They lifted their heads and waved at me over their pull-up bars or at least bared their teeth. They were so meek ... gray, not dangerous in the least or aggressive like healthy people were, I felt so good among them. If I ever became a doctor, then in addition to the respect I would enjoy in endless supply, I would also have a peaceful life ... Vati would give me the bread left over from his supper, breakfast and lunch, which he hid from the sisters of mercy in the drawer of his night table. In return I collected butts for him, the ends of stogies and cigarettes ... I always found the greatest density of them scattered near the Moste movie theater on St. Martin's Road, next to the sidewalk, and outside buildings that housed taverns and restaurants. I folded little pouches out of newspaper to put in my pockets, to make my collecting more efficient and keep my trousers from stinking of butts. "Not a word to your mother about ... (he didn't want to actually say about what), Bubi!" Vati exhorted me. He looked at me uncertainly ... doubting my word. But because we spoke Slovene to each other, our conspiracy remained under a double seal of silence, more confidential and hush-hush than the White Prince's secret writing. Out in the hospital garden we unwrapped the tobacco remains from their papers and leaves and dried them out on the cement of a fire hydrant ... it produced quite an exemplary heap of assorted tobaccos ... yellow, black, dark brown ... as fine as grit or as coarse as crepe noodles ... if by some miracle that heap could have changed into food, into rice or spaghetti ... that would have been something! ... Vati wore an old, oversized, patched pair of pajamas and a striped robe that belonged to the hospital. He looked a little eccentric, like a crazy person or a masquerader. Behind his baggy hospital clothes he was even skinnier, shaggier and more naked than Christ on the cross ... The most he ever saved from a meal was three slices of bread, sometimes a breakfast roll hard as a rock ... It was a long way home and I didn't always succeed in practicing chivalrous restraint ... now and then I arrived home with just two pieces of bread, or just one.

B<small>ALOH AND</small> I would go to the Sava for firewood ... to old Jarše to steal heads of cabbage ... out of a little field around the power line, where the peasants had to run too far uphill to be able to catch us ... and to more remote destinations, like Štepanja Village or near the airport for potatoes ... One time we nabbed a whole wooden bucket of lard out of an unlocked granary ... and another we brought a half pound of plums home along with the basket ... It was a time of legumes and vegetables, which could be prepared in a hundred different ways ... But the lot of it lasted for barely more than a supper ...

Clairi and I took all of the finished items and the better hides ... except for the opossum skin ... In order to be able to sell them, we wrapped each item up in its own attractive package made out of newspaper and we put all of them into a bundle, because the suitcase would have been too small for such a selection. We left early in the morning, because Clairi was ashamed for anyone to see what we were living off of. She sent me into the courtyard first, so I could sneak out while everyone was still asleep, and I ran through the grain field to the road, where I waited for her. Each time she sent me a little farther out ... until at last we agreed I would wait for her by the wall of the railway overpass next to the Dragon factory. I hoisted the bundle up and we set off on our rounds, basing our calls on the appearance of a given house, whether it looked well-to-do or at least had something distinguished about it ... the front door, a doormat, a curtain. We also paid calls on furriers ... But the furriers ... the four or six of them on both sides of the Ljubljanica ... didn't have any work or income, themselves, aside from storing their clients' furs for the summer. Clairi would ask, and I would translate, whether they had any work we could take home to do, no matter how basic or trivial, but because the summer season was at its height ... I sweated streams under the weight of that stifling bundle ... they had laid off all their workers and they didn't anticipate "any increase in demand for furs on the part of clients during the autumn" ... so naturally they didn't buy anything from us. Mrs. Rot, a fat blonde lady, owner of the largest fur store in town next door to city hall, was impressed with our expertly finished items. With Clairi's permission she cut open a collar lining, which she then gave to one of the girls working for her to sew back up in the workshop that was over the store, which had a mannequin in a fur coat in each of its five display windows. She examined Vati's stitching on the skin and then the fur on the other side ... he always used a collection of various pieces, patches and remains of pelts to sew an entire fur hat, a muff, or a vest ... in such a way that the fur of the various pieces of pelts was aligned with respect to color, composition, and density, making it look as though he had made each item out of the whole pelt of a single animal or just from the backs of a few larger animals ... "Das ist wirklich ein großer Meister,"* Mrs. Rot said. That made Clairi and me feel good, even if we didn't sell her anything ... if we could have left just one item with her to put in a display window for a week, alongside one of her black and silver crystal name plates, that would have meant even more to us. Then we could hope that somebody would buy it sooner or later, and of course Vati's prestige would be recognized, too ... The whole time Mrs. Rot examined our items, I examined her, too ... especially the neckline of her silkily billowing smock ... and what big, white, dreamlike high breasts she had, from her neck practically down to her waist ... my little pole stood right up, as if ready to fly over the counter ... The other furriers, all men, were like Vati ... a little pale and wearing smocks that were full of needles and fur ... Smudged with various leather dyes, they came out of their workshops past hanging foxes and bunches of little dormouse furs to get to their counters ... But they had proper establishments ... display tables, small tables and chairs for their customers, new magazines, a cash register, a little rubber dish for the change ... everything that a real merchant needs ... It would have been a great honor to us if they had taken anything to display in their windows or if they had

*This is really superb, masterful work.

promised Clairi some work for the autumn ... We left each stuffy little storefront more frustrated than the one before. Nothing. There was nothing. Where else could we go? We had written down on slips the addresses of all the furriers in town ... We decided to go from door to door in the neighborhood of the courthouse, the one that had towers ... Clairi walked a bit in front of or behind me, because she was ashamed ... she asked me to carry the bundle when we walked down beautiful Miklošič Street, which led to the train station ... several paces ahead or behind, just not even with her ... We rang the doorbells on every floor and when a door opened ... and they were all alike, inlaid with wood of a different color ... Clairi would start saying in her Swiss German mixed with some French that we were selling various furs ... chokers, muffs, hats, stoles, boleros ... the whole kit and kaboodle ... for winter, for dances, for everyday wear ... for very little money, practically for free ... For the ones who couldn't understand the language I translated her offer in my moronic Slovene, which sounded like I was echoing out of a kettle or a pipe. We were met with all kinds of looks ... startled, as though we'd just fallen out of the sky and they or we were just dreaming all of this ... piercing, as though we'd escaped off some train ... derisive, as though we were circus performers ... Some of the more fortunate ones would just start to laugh and call the other homebodies out from the kitchen and bedrooms to come have a look at us. There were also the harsh, rejecting faces, as though we were burglars, and the looks that practically smoldered with hatred and sliced everything off ... our hands, our ears, our noses ... The hostility from the eyes of a bare-headed young man with a small mouth was like a wave that billowed into us, forcing us a step back toward the banister ... Clairi said indignantly that this wasn't called for, we hadn't done anything wrong ... But we had to pick up our stuff and get out of there fast, because the loon or falcon or eagle was getting nervous and the piano that someone was plunking on in the apartment suddenly went silent ... Some younger woman invited us into her apartment with a vaulted ceiling ... it was a big, round room in a tower next to the Fig Tree restaurant, where through the windows you had a great view of the articulated streetcars as they writhed and slinked passed each other in the round intersection like snakes in their nest. The building's facade was quite elegant, all green bricks and blue carnations ... but inside it wasn't so perfect. Old divans with grease-stained covers dangling down to the floor, yellowed books with no covers, stinking of glue ... I set the bundle down on a carpet that had practically eaten into the floor and the woman inspected our things ... We unwrapped each item from its newspaper, but the lady wasn't satisfied. She knelt down and her lemon yellow house robe opened, but she had nothing on beneath it. Embarrassed, Clairi smiled. "Schau nicht hin, du Dreckfink!"* she said. But I wanted to see her furry hole and it was awful to see but not see it ... Somehow it parted and something jutted out ... The crazy lady didn't want to buy anything, so we wrapped everything back up ... she offered each of us a yellow candy out of a tin box ... Clairi didn't dare put it in her mouth. She went down the stairs so fast that I had to shout after her, "Clairi! Clairi!" I only caught

*Don't look there, you little guttersnipe!

up with her in the lobby. "Wirf den Zucker weg!"* she ordered me. She flung her piece of candy into an ashcan. "Nun machs!"** I felt bad about it, but I threw it out ... and I felt even worse when I saw ashes stuck all over it, it probably had some liqueur filling. "O mein kleiner!"*** Clairi pressed me to her chest ... All the buildings in the street behind the courthouse were handsome. "Lauter Advokaten! Die haben Berge von Geld."**** We went into a building that had a white marble statue of a mother and child over the entrance ... Next to the doors there were whole rows of plaques ... black, white, blue ... announcing a lawyer's office.... In a bright room there was a gray-haired doctor, a lawyer, sitting at a big desk ... A gentle face, gray hair, the wide shoulders of a trained boxer. He spoke exquisite German, "hochdeutsch" ... Clairi just stared at him ... her nostrils quivering ... This was the husband of her dreams! Gray-haired, not too old, attractive, intelligent, rich, courteous, educated ... But when he got up from his huge desk and stepped away from his gold-studded leather chair back ... I couldn't believe my eyes ... He was short, not just shorter than me ... but a dwarf ... even though he kept the broad shoulders ... Now Clairi was more beside herself than ever ... He crossed the gleaming parquet floor to where we stood, smiled at me as one man does at another ... such teeth, like blue porcelain! ... and clasped both of Clairi's hands in his. "Kommen Sie einmal nächsten Donnerstag, am

*Throw the candy away.
**Do it!
***My poor little guy!
****All lawyers! They have mountains of money.

Abend, neee?"* he said in his perfect German ... "Ja, gut," Clairi said, quickly turning to leave. She could barely find the handle in the thickly upholstered door. Once we were back outside she regained her composure. "Hast du das gesehen, Bubi? ... Solche Armmuskeln im Stuhl und dann ... Was für ein Knirps! Aber doch: wie intelligent, reich, apart ... Aber was meinte der Mistfink doch, als er mich eingeladen hat, ich soll am Donnerstag abends kommen? ... O, das soll er sich gar aus dem Kopf schlagen. Fällt mir im Schlaf nicht ein ... Aber es ist so etwas Feines an ihm, nicht wahr?"** She was unsure ... We headed towards Tivoli ... the whole way there she kept talking to herself, shaking her head or nodding ... On the third floor of a red building next to Tivoli a long, skinny, heavily freckled, nice woman answered the door ... as thin as a reed. She said right off the bat that she wasn't going to buy anything ... but then she asked me where we were from and when I told her, she invited us into her bright kitchen for a bowl of cold stewed fruit ... "Ich bin Lehrerin,"*** she said. It took my breath away. She had a light green book edged in black on the table titled "Slovene Grammar" ... notebooks full of tables ... and different colored pencils ... It was too much for me ... She asked Clairi and me

---

*Won't you come back next Thursday evening, hmmm?
**Did you see that, Bubi? Such arm muscles when he was sitting, and then ... What a runt! And yet, how intelligent and wealthy, how striking he was! ... But what did the little creep mean when he invited me to come back next Thursday evening? ... Oh, he'd better get that notion out of his head. Not in my wildest dreams ... But there is something very refined about him, don't you think?
***I'm a schoolteacher.

questions. Her German was quite good ... "Vielleicht kommt Ihr Bruder einmal in meine Klasse."* That would be nice, but ... "War das eine nette Frau,"** Clairi enthused about the kindness of Mrs. Komar. "Bubi, est gibt wirklich viele ordentliche Menschen auf der Welt und es ist nur Schade, daß man sie nicht schneller aufspürt."*** A little old man in a sweater and hat who was just then out in the flowers doing something with water let us into a house with a garden ... He called Clairi into a separate room behind a glass door ... Through the milky pane I could see she was modeling some of the items for him ... I heard her quietly squeal then screech at the top of her voice and shout ... she came flying out all flushed in the face. "So ein Schwein."**** She was holding a choker in one hand and a bolero in the other ... I quickly stuffed it all back into the bag and made a beeline behind her through the garden. I only managed to catch up with her at a railway crossing, because she'd sat down on a bench there ... We wandered through several intersections, an underground pedestrian crossing, a glass corridor that had an excellent draft, some narrow streets, side streets, thoroughfares ... and a peaceful neighborhood of villas on the far side of the Roman wall where the sidewalks were cooler under long rows of trees ... My feet started to blister in the old pair of

---

*Perhaps your brother will come take my class sometime?
**Now that was a nice lady!
***Bubi, there are really so many decent people in the world, it's just a shame we can't find out who they are sooner.
****What a pig!

street shoes that I'd had to put on at Clairi's insistence so I would look more respectable ... I cooled them off in some ditch ... and all sweaty under the well spigot of a deserted garden restaurant ... The fur scratched at my back ... all those damned remains of times past were just too pathetic, disgusting, annoying ... We didn't rest, there wasn't even enough time for me to pick up a chestnut or a stick ... as though our customers were everywhere waiting impatiently for us at their windows ... The trees started spinning around me ... Was it worth it? Even if we did sell them ... it was strange how grown-ups suddenly struck me as disgusting for getting so excited about buying all that furry crap and then actually wearing it ... At last all that was left to us was the pawn shop on Poljane Road ... from one side of a barred window you found out how much you would get and how long you had to buy your things back ... All the men who worked there were as pale as death and wore black sleeves, I had been once before with Vati to this room with counters and windows, resembling a bank. He got a small sum of money, which we immediately exchanged in the bakery next door for some bread ... but they gave you so little time: you had two weeks before you lost your collateral, and then you had nothing ... Vati had brought several collars, fur hats and a whole child's outfit made of white rabbit furs, for a girl ... In one building, in its courtyard where there was a dry cleaner, we got lucky. Above the ironing shop was where a skinny little old lady lived, who was German. Clairi began her pitch from the top ... mindlessly and a little unhinged by now ... you had to wear the customer down under a hail of words ... An incredible opportunity ... satisfaction guaranteed ...

The customer was supposed to succumb to your talking points, lose their common sense. "Lassen Sie doch das, liebes Fräulein,"* the old lady suddenly boomed in a deep voice... She invited us inside to get cool "hinter den dicken Mauern meines Hauses..."** Good lord, it was the old empire everywhere you looked... carved side tables, cabinets, tasseled curtains, a vivid fresco on the ceiling... angels with trumpets... around a gold fixture that a chandelier hung from. And something even more incredible: rifles with dates carved on their stocks inside a glass cabinet, swords on the walls, khanjars, shields like the one the White Prince carried... She gave us some cookies and ice cream... her daughter, who was the owner of the dry cleaning and ironing shop and a big linen store, had an actual machine for making ice cream... She smoked a cigarette in a long mouthpiece and bought a muff and a chain necklace from us... but probably more out of pity than need... She took the money for them out of a velvet purse that was attached to her waist... "Kommt mal wieder vorbei,"*** she said... She tucked a colorful volume of *Die schönen illustrierten Abentever***** into my pocket... That was the kind of grandmother that the White Prince himself would have had as his sidekick in a castle under siege... If Clairi and I could sell at least one little fur hat each week, our six-day quest around town would pay off...

*You can skip all that, dear.
**...within the thick walls of my house.
***Come see me again sometime.
*****Beautiful Illustrated Adventures*

213

On Fridays Mirko's mother from the wagon in the gravel pit would put on her worst rags and set out from home carrying a handbasket to go begging. The boy had to go with her, no matter how much he resisted ... Friday was beggars' day and when they came home at noon, they brought all kinds of things with them ... once in a while, even toys, whistles, mirrors, broken harmonicas ... Once they gave me an arrow with a rubber tip ... Mirko tried to get me to go with them and even his mother tried to persuade me, claiming that Mirko got bored without company ... One Friday we set out together. And then several times after that ... His mother didn't paint her lips like she did at home. She put on a worn-out skirt that you could see all of Jarše through, and a blouse she had darned, she tied a blue apron around her waist and covered her head with a black kerchief down to the eyes so that she looked like a penitent ... We went barefoot in single file. His mother's hips swayed just over the cornflowers and poppies as we crossed a field ... with each gust of wind her big rear end bulged in her skirt like an enormous onion ... What might await us in town I had no way of imagining ... Now, with nothing in hand, to get something, anything at all? But you could squeeze something out of a number of stores ... even some that sold toys ... if nothing else, a paper cap with advertising on it, sometimes a balloon or at least a catalog with color pictures ... The selection was wide and the city well-supplied with surprises. We weren't allowed to ring our bells outside the buildings that had blue metal signs over the door that said the owner contributed to the foundation for the poor of the municipality of Ljubljana. But we could outside stores and workshops ... On the sidewalk approaching the Dragon Bridge, where we were ringing our bells, a woman looked at us through a half-opened door... her eyes, when she noticed us, suggested that we were worse than the trash cans on the sidewalk. "Don't you even know how to read?" she asked acidly. And indeed, under the house number there was a blue metal sign. How had Mirko's mother missed that? The woman slammed her door shut and for a moment I lost faith in Mirko's mother's expertise. "I just thought we'd give it a shot," she shrugged, laughing... The Šarabon department store across from the hospital was the most tolerant of beggars... you just had to hurry so that the other cadgers didn't beat you to it... the tavern drunks, the morons and idiots from the municipal poor houses, who knew the city's more charitable hearts well. You had to be there the minute the shutters over their doors got rolled up... The big store was the shape of the letter L. We went in and said what Mirko's mother had taught us to say, "In God's name, please give a beggar some alms..." I was supposed to go to the checkout window, she went to the grocery counter and Mirko went around the corner where some interesting housewares were sold... Those were the orders his mother had given us. That way one of us might get something, she said, or maybe two, possibly even all three, but there was no way, if there were three of us, that none of us would get anything... I stood in front of the tall pane of the cashier's window and it took me a while to twist my lips into a kind of snail. "In kots nehm bleez..." "Huh? What did you say?" the cashier asked, who had a dreary face framed in a permanent, like schoolteachers. Either I'd said nothing or she hadn't understood me. How on earth was I supposed to get anything off of these well-stocked shelves, display windows and drawers up to the ceiling... with nothing at all, just for some words... after all, this wasn't Childermas, where kids got to cane presents out of adults... Easier than talking would be just to snatch a candy or a packet of vanilla powder... I stepped back a pace from the glassed cabin when the cashier called me. "Are you with them?" she asked. "Yeees," I nodded. "Here, you can have this..." I couldn't believe it. The kind woman pushed a 25-para coin out through the gap onto the rubber mat on my side of the window... Outside Mirko's mother got angry with me. I didn't say a word. "You have to say nicely: in God's name please give a beggar some alms. Then you bow your head and wait..." She put the money in her apron... and everything else... a small tube of toothpaste, some shoe polish, a lollipop, and a little metal frog in the hand-basket... At a bakery Mirko and I had to stand next to her, as though we were both her sons. The baker looked at all three of us and grabbed some pieces of yesterday's bread lying in the corner of an empty shelf, and mother tucked them into her bag. "May God reward you," she said... At the dry goods store it was all about money, because they wouldn't give you enough material for a handkerchief, or at most a couple of buttons... at the delicatessen, amid the mountains of ham and cheese you might get a salami... and a broken pretzel, a box of matches or a thimbleful of brandy for her at a restaurant... Out on St. Peter's Road we ran into others who were coming to beg... revolting little women all carrying empty, bag-like baskets... a tall, skinny man with a violin case... he at least played the fiddle for alms... Mother pushed us to get moving ... she had a few kind souls on this street ... a barber, a watchmaker, a dairy attendant. She couldn't afford to have the others beating her there ... We sprinted and went under the noses of some old women through the open door of the barbershop, in among the glinting mirrors and barbers dressed all in white. Now it got easier, because she told us to just say hello nicely when we went in and then stay close to her without saying a word ... At Mayer and Sons, where they had gigantic carpets lying on the floor, the sly-faced salesmen, all of them dressed in nice, gray suits, chased us out the door, waving their hands ... At Krišper's they had nothing but toys in the basement ... train sets, dolls, musical tops, racing cars, tanks, boxes of tin soldiers. Mirko and I looked over them while she was upstairs in Housewares ... Each of us got a small notebook with a red cover from the lady who sold picture postcards ... "It'll be ten soon," mother said. At ten all begging had to stop. Not until late afternoon, from five o'clock until the Ave Maria could beggars come out and beg again. We still had the market ahead of us, you could always get something there, if not from the vendors, then out of the baskets and crates of refuse ... Mother took off her black headscarf when we reached the Kolin factory on the way home ... The play was over, no more mardi gras ... The walk home to the gravel pit was hurried and impatient ... Mother unfastened the padlock on the wagon and shook everything we had got out of the basket onto her bunk, which was at the far end of the wagon. Between it and the other end, where there were pickaxes, shovels, and clothes, there was a shelf of pots, a kettle with a lid, a quite decent stove and Mirko's bunk ... I didn't get much, most of it stayed with them, and almost no money ... but that wasn't so important. More important than the tiny stacks of change and the colorful junk on the bedcover was the fact that the woman then sat down cross-legged on the bed, so that I could see up her white thighs ... Or when some item escaped from the little piles and rolled into a crack or a wrinkle in a sheet and then, as she went looking for it crouched with her knees on the bed, her breasts hung down like a beaver's, their tips touching a pillow ... I felt feverish at the thought of being able to see and do even more ... all I had to do was take hold of her skirt and I'd have her over my head, just touch her blouse and kerplump! her breasts would fall out ... just tug on her a bit and she would shake like a pear tree ... I left the wagon all dizzy, envying Mirko for the fact that he could be alone with her. I couldn't believe that she was his mother and he was really her son ...

W<small>E MUDDLED THROUGH</small> the first half of August, that most beautiful month of the year, as best we could ... I read to Gisela from the big little volume of *Die schönen illustrierten Abenteuer* (Wien 1933) that the old lady who lived over the cleaner's had given me ... It was really an exceptional artifact ... the little one was intrigued by the princes and especially the princesses riding around in their coaches, attending dances at the royal court ... Each story was richly illustrated ... with everything, down to the last detail, before our eyes. I especially admired the drawings, then the colors ... scarlet, green, pomegranate red, a knight's armor with rubies ... It was masterful work! The best picture of all was one in the middle of the volume ... a mighty battle stretching its whole height and width. Two-humped camels, elephants, Knights Templar, heathens in desperate flight ... Gisela picked some daisies and grass and strewed them all over the book.

Then beginning in the middle of August it started to rain for all it was worth and we couldn't go anywhere ... A number of things happened during those rainy days.

First, one afternoon a soaking wet gentleman from the St. Vincent's conference knocked on our door ... When we opened it, there he stood, tall, with a dark mustache, wearing a hat and a camel hair coat ... so elegant we didn't know what to do with him. He filled the whole room ... taking all its light and air for himself ... We grew afraid ... was he the police, had he come for us? He held an overstuffed briefcase and had a board wrapped up in brown paper under his arm ... He set something down on the table and something else on the bed ... "My name is Vladimir Kompare and I'm from the St. Vincent's conference," he said. "Your family has returned from living abroad?" I nodded, whatever he said. "In the name of the Society of St. Vincent de Paul I've brought you some beans and a devotional icon," he said. His mouth made such strange shapes, like a boxer's after a knockout – mostly twisted, causing his brushed mustache to shake.... But he had the same sort of bent nose as the Arab merchants or the barbarians at the bazaar in my book ... He wiped the sweat and raindrops off his face ... he must have had to walk very fast from the streetcar stop near Holy Cross ... No, he hadn't had to walk that far, on the road outside, next to the fence, was an old, rectangular car with a canvas roof... Targa-Florio 100 HP... So he was this wet from that short walk to the house... His briefcase was full of pieces of paper and newspaper clippings... he set a cloth bag down on the table... and an old, gray paper bag. He unwrapped the picture and threw the paper under the stove. "Where shall we hang it?" he asked. We didn't have a single nail in the wall. "It will look nicest here over the bed," he said. I looked for a tack for stretching skins and Vati's pliers. He picked up the paper that he'd thrown under the stove and spread it over the bed. Then he climbed up... He had wide shoes, which were in style and looked like submarines... and he began to hammer the tack in. It didn't take the first time, second time, not until the third... Then I handed him the picture, which had been printed on cardboard and put in a wide, shallow, brown frame with rounded corners. It was the first time I'd held a holy icon... on the back it was all scribbled with receipts, stamps and signatures... The man got back down and looked to see if it was hanging nicely... God knows I didn't see him as a real person. His fancy hat and camel hair coat were completely mismatched with his distorted, fleshy afterthought of a face... If this wasn't a disguise, then he was just strange. He took a document out of his stuffed briefcase. "Sign here. One kilogram of beans and one reproduction of the Mother of God." Mother signed in Gothic script. Then he went to the Balohs to deliver the bag of flour. At that very moment they were kneeling around their stove, praying their rosaries... I went outside... through the small celluloid back window of his car I could see a whole stack of old cardboard pictures in wooden frames... "Ein komischer Kauz!"* Clairi said ... "Die machen so eine blöde Reklame für das Kirchenamt,"** mother said. The beans were the main thing. But they were so old, gnarly, and tough that even after cooking them several times and gnawing and grinding at them like peach pits, they wouldn't soften and we had to throw them away ...

Second: suddenly, because we hadn't paid him the rent for three months, Mr. Perme threw us out on the street. Clairi went up to talk to him, but halfway there she turned back. "Er ruft mich ... ich müßte zu ihm hinauf kommen ... ich weiß, was das bedeutet, ich gehe nicht,"*** she told me, her face flushed red. I understood what the old man wanted from her ... On the day when we were supposed to clear out of the room by evening, Clairi and I put some things in bundles and headed over to the sugar mill to ask if we could spend a few days under their roof. "So, jetzt sind wir ans Ende gelangen ... nur die Armenanstalt bleibt uns übrig,"**** Clairi whined the whole way there, making me cringe ... First we had to go to city hall to get a document called a "poverty certificate." I didn't want to go upstairs with her and have to listen to her laments all over again ... I stayed downstairs in the main courtyard entrance, among the cannon and mortars from World War I ... The big, old Sugar Mill building was near the boat locks ... it had at least a thousand dark windows ... Its wide wooden stairs ... where we met all different kinds of people carrying

*What a strange bird!
**It's just stupid advertising for the church.
***He's shouting that I need to go up to his place. I know what that means and I won't go.
****So now we've hit bottom ... the poor house is our only option.

washbasins, cooking pots, baskets full of tomatoes and lettuce on their heads ... were so worn down that they frayed under each additional footstep as if it were a pistol shot. First, at a window in the entryway, they registered us, then we proceeded to a big office where rows of little female officials worked – gray-haired ladies who handed us a ticket for three beds ... The dormitory upstairs was a long, vaulted room with twenty iron cots, all of them nicely made up with bedding. I rather liked it ... It reminded me of a hospital or the sanatorium in Urach ... We set our bundles and hand baskets down on the first three reserved beds by the door, and then we went back to Jarše ... That evening at six, when the deadline arrived that Mr. Perme had given us for clearing out of the room, we handed the key to Enrico's mother to take upstairs, and we left ... We went as though we weren't going. Even though we were. It was like a tasteless joke ... Suddenly it occurred to me that we had become unrecognizable, barely a memory, and that from now on we had nothing to be afraid of ... and that nobody would find us ever again, not even Vati ... I pulled my hood made out of a bag way down over my eyes to my chin ... this is how death walked around in its monk's habit at the time of the plague and in my vivid green picture ... Mother and Clairi took turns carrying Gisela and one other bundle. At the St. Peter's Bridge a raincloud suddenly burst which almost broke their umbrella and whisked it away ... we were all soaked through in an instant, with fountains and rivulets gushing all around us ... We weathered it out in a little park right under the the nose of the sugar mill ... the boat lock was on the verge of exploding in the onrush of water ... We went up the wide vaulted staircase. I knew which door ... opened it: the dormitory was full of people ... a regular circus ring ... Some fat woman in a slip was brushing out her braids ... three or four men, either idiots or beggars, were sitting on chests at the back in their long underwear ... there were a lot of fruit vendors or Gypsy women along the wall ... with green and red eyes ... who were bathing a child in a wash basin as the water sloshed out. A strange world ... never before seen ... some sort of crazy picture ... "Nein, da gehe ich nicht hinein!" mother said. "Und wenn ich auf der Stelle sterben müsse."* She was as white as a sheet and shaking. "Nimm die Sachen! Wir gehen zurück!"** I was sleepy and my soaked clothing stuck to my skin ... but worst of all were my shoes, which were full of water and threatening to float off of my feet ... "Warum nicht?"*** Clairi stared at mother as though she were seeing her for the first time. "Nimm das Zeug, Bubi! ..."**** I picked up the two bundles and baskets that Clairi and I had set there and closed the door ... I had no idea what to do next. We stood on the staircase landing for a few moments like statues ... As alien to ourselves as strangers ... The rain was pouring and streaming out of all of the big building's gutters. We waited behind the half-opened doors of the wide entryway for the storm to dump all its rain and supersaturate everything ... Gisela slept on the bundles, which we set in a cart fastened to the wall with a chain so fat it could have been used for a

---

*No, I'm not going in there. Even if I have to die on the spot.
**Get our things. We're going back.
***Why not?
****Get our things, Bubi!

223 ·

drawbridge. Mother sat the whole time without saying anything ... "Gehen wir"* she said. Clairi wailed, "Wie..."** "Ich habe die Fenster im Zimmer offen gelassen,"*** mother said. It was a long way and we had to endure more on the way back than when we came down ... We waited the weather out under a railway overpass with sooty bundles billowing through it ... It wasn't so much raining anymore as misting, but we were still soaked from before, we were shivering, and we were muddied up to the waist when we got to the vicinity of Jarše ... It was as though we had suddenly returned to our former bodies, that we'd come back to life; but we were afraid. On St. Martin's Road we stood in front of a deep, water-filled depression before we headed down the old path through the wheat fields ... It was eleven thirty ... We carefully pushed the iron gate open so it wouldn't squeak in its hinges ... we walked down the sand path on tip-toe ... the windows really were open a crack ... We pushed them open and one by one we stepped from the window ledge onto the sewing machine and from it down onto the floor ... "Wir werden da hinter dem Bett schlafen,"**** mother whispered. We stretched a rope from the stovepipe to a nail over the bed and hung a sheet over it so that the owner wouldn't catch us first thing in the morning, we pulled the mattress off of the bed and made it up behind the sheet, from corner to corner ... Quietly, very quietly, so that the Balohs, who liked to snoop

*Let's go.
**But how?...
***I left the windows open.
****We'll sleep over there behind the bed.

around, wouldn't hear us ... against the wall by the stove, on the other side of which Enrico and his mother had their room, we could breathe and talk a bit more normally, because the two of them would never give us away ... "Ich muß hinauf," Clairi whined with resolve. "Wir können uns doch nicht so einschleichen und wohnen, wo wir doch nicht gezahlt haben."* Mother said nothing. "Schlaft jetzt,"** she ordered. All four of us retreated behind the sheet, which let through the feeble light from the window like the screen in some cheap movie theater ... I woke up late that next morning, the sun was already out ... actually, Clairi woke me with a cup of warm milk in one hand and a fresh breakfast roll in the other. The sheet was gone from the rope. Was everything that had happened last night just a dream? I couldn't believe that ... "Wie denn das? ..."*** I asked. Clairi blushed deeply, then went pale, her lips quivering and her eyes misting over ... She threw herself straight at me, past Gisela, who was still asleep ... She hugged me so hard that I felt jabbed in the ribs ... Her hug almost smothered me, and she smooshed me with kisses ... I was suffocating ... pushed her away ... objected ... shrank back. I didn't want to shout, or old Mr. Perme would hear ... I wriggled loose, but she latched onto me again ... and everything started all over again ... A regular avalanche of affection ... I nearly broke my back under all her crazy kisses and hugs ... My face turned into mush ... I couldn't find my nostrils ... "Bubi! Bubi!" As though she were begging me ...

*I have to go upstairs. We can't just sneak in and live someplace where we haven't paid.
**Go to sleep now.
***How did you get this?

She began crying somewhere inside, from very deep down... She was completely beside herself... The old man upstairs was going to leap out of bed... Finally she calmed down a bit. "Iß nur!" she said. She must have done something. But what? Had she sold Vati's opossum skin on the sly? Had she gone upstairs to Mr. Perme's, to that room with the compasses? What had happened? Where was mother?... I wolfed down the milk and roll... and got more of each, in the same portions, while Clairi kept looking at me very nervously. Then I got yet a third breakfast, which left me lying knocked out...

We took down the rope, replaced the mattress on the bed, and once again we were living in our room. But that wasn't everything. There was milk, bread, lard, meat and cheese on the table, all wrapped in paper, freshly bought at the store... Mother came in carrying a bucket of water. She cleared off the table. Then she aired out the bedding. Then she began scrubbing. Furiously, stubbornly... That evening everything was neatly organized and put away. She became a different person. She was ashamed.

Then Vati sent some fellow patient who had been released to tell us that he was coming home soon... We went to wait for him outside the smith's house. He approached alongside a cart loaded high with shucked corn, which he would hold onto and lean on as he went... he was more green than pale and his head spun like a little drunk's. He didn't get his job back with Elite... They had fired him once and for all... "Der Vati will neu anfangen," Clairi said... Yes, he wanted to sell everything of any value that he had in the wicker chest, except for the opossum... move closer to town... open a workshop, a kind of repair shop ... A few days later we had to go back with our bags to the St. Vincent's breadline. The doorkeeper nun already knew me. Vati waited around the corner ... the way Charlie Chaplin as a jobless glazier waits for his son Jackie Coogan, who is throwing rocks at windows ... he watched as I banged the knocker on the door. I had seen that movie with Margrit several times in the Clarmont Theater in Basel ... it was the only one that they let children see ... and that scene was inscribed in my memory ... The doorkeeper let me in ... "Oh, it's you?" she said, pleased. As she had the time before, she led me through their handsome garden of geraniums and touch-me-nots, across their tidy courtyard into the sisters' dining hall in the basement, where I was allowed to gather pieces of bread out of their breadbaskets and put them in a paper bag. On the way home Vati and I took a short-cut off of St. Martin's Road that led past fields and cinder heaps to our road in Jarše and suddenly we were in the middle of some army maneuvers. Soldiers in helmets, all wearing shoulder straps, gas masks, with shovels and cartridge belts, were lying all agitated and flushed amid the molehills or in trenches and shooting, bang ... bang! with blanks, raising a lot of noise and dust all around us. An officer with a red stripe on his trousers and a bare saber in hand was shouting like a pottery mender ... not at us, but the soldiers. We jumped aside and fell straight into another trench, behind some soldiers in ambush who were firing across the road ... the whole field was full of gray buckets ... we barely managed to save our bags of bread ...

That fall Vati went to look at apartments around town and found one. A room where we would have both a workshop and a kitchen.

We moved to Bohorič Street. We rented a hand cart and made the trip three times ... first with the suitcases and chest, then the sewing machine and table, and finally the bed ...

A butcher named Ham, the building's owner, was a rich man. He had stables with horses and cows in the courtyard, a delivery wagon with rubber tires and an enclosed carriage, a butcher shop on the main floor and another one in its own wooden building at the market ... Three of his assistants lived in rooms over the stables. His apartment was covered in Bukhara carpets and paintings ... it was on the main floor, and whatever he rented out was in the upper floors of the building ... aside from us there was only an old woman and her daughter who lived there ... On that first day when we moved, Mr. Ham invited us down for tea ... In the middle of the living room amid sofas strewn with throw cushions and embroidered armrest covers stood a black piano with the lid open. It also smelled really nice ... His eldest daughter played "Trink, trink, Brüderlein trink, laß nur die Sorgen zu Haus'"* ... because they thought we were Germans. They wanted to get in Germany's good graces through us. We were supposed to feel proud for mistakenly belonging to a nation that was constantly throwing the world out of joint ... Other people were always trying to hurt Germany or take revenge on it through us ... There was lots of other music on the piano ... Lucia di Lammermoor,

*Drink, drink, little brother, drink, leave behind your worries.

Rusalka's Song to the Moon, Werther... those were songs his daughter was still practicing... Our hosts wallked around with my parents drinking tea and chatting... it was fantastic! Mother and the butcher's wife, who was wearing a rabbit fur lined with red velvet, were chatting in the most refined tones. All the worn-out words changed into magical formulas... The music and all the rest gave me the feeling that we'd arrived in some other country, some sort of theatrical play where entirely different, quite decent people performed... The Hams' two youngest children, their seven-year-old twins Peter and Andrej, were tumbling all over each other on one of the sofas. They would insult each other by calling each other owls. Like their parents, they were both for the Falcons. The butcher's wife was a ruddy-faced, chubby woman who had no clear connection to the piano, the carpets or the paintings... Mr. Ham, who resembled his daughter, had a pale face and a long, narrow head without a single hair that made him look like a doctor in his white lab work coat...

Our apartment was in the attic. It had two windows and a kitchen out in the hall. The hallway led under a slanted ceiling to the far wall, where the faucet and toilet were. Across from the stool was the attic apartment where the older woman lived with the pale girl who was her stepdaughter or foster child... Whenever I went to the toilet or ran the water, the old woman would push the curtain aside on their hallway window and watch in case I spilled anything under the stool... Her head was just as big as the little pane of glass she looked out through... It was all right the first, second, tenth time. But then I started to get nervous, because I could always feel those eyes on my back and the play of expressions on her face, so that I couldn't help spilling some water when I impatiently pulled the pot away. Then the woman would come racing out. "If you spill anything, boy, you have to mop it up," she said sweetly. I didn't want to go to the faucet anymore and I began pleading with Clairi to go instead of me.

Our kitchen was so dark that the light had to be on even in the daytime whenever mother cooked something in the oven or on the stove ... The room itself was bright and good-sized ... With the money from the furs that he sold, Vati bought from an antique dealer two chairs, a table and two hammocks for the bed, which we set up at night using the beech blocks for making fur caps, so that we could sleep two and two together. He still preferred to sleep on the table rather than in bed. It was better for his spine. In the morning we took the hammocks down, set them by the wall and covered them with a blanket. In a courtyard where a public auction was held when a small shirt company went under the hammer, we got for a ridiculous price a dozen nice, big, hard, canvas-reinforced boxes with metal handles and little compartments for cards describing the merchandise. Vati put furs and other items in them and I wrote in each little frame what the box contained ... during the day our attic apartment looked like a real workshop, where things were sold, too ...

Bohorič was a desolate street, and would have been even if there had been anyone to do things with ... In the ground-floor entrance of one little building there was a news stand and across the street a dry goods store, Bojadamič, where I went for five dekagrams of salt or sugar, which the lanky owner would chop off of a cone on the counter ... Farther on, toward the far end of the street, there was a place in a courtyard that sold heating fuel, coal and wood by weight or pre-packaged in hundred-pound bags ... and at the very end there was a bakery and across from it some tar-paper shacks inhabited by a motley rabble of jobless people and Gypsies and right behind the shacks was an apartment building with vaulted hallways all around that was called "Mexico" ... At our end of Bohorič, across from the butcher shop, was a hospice. It had old people sitting around in its yard behind a fence ... strange, goitered, half-crazy women, and men who would grin and froth at the mouth or spray spittle through the fence gate ... Next to the hospice there was a stretch of grass with a few houses where I gathered dandelions ... At the very end, which was already in Moste, there was a military hospital. That's where I'd go with Vati, who went out of nostalgia for his army days, partly to save money, but partly because he was hungry for army bread, which he could buy from the sick soldiers out milling around, half a loaf of thick sourdough, enough to fill you up as much as two regular bakery loaves ... You just had to bide your time next to the hospital, first until one of them who had bread on him came to the fence, and then until the sentry withdrew to his guardhouse on the main road ...

When we bought the boxes, Vati also contacted a young woman who had put an ad in the paper saying that she wanted to apprentice to a furrier and was prepared to pay a modest amount for it. And so one day we got a visit from a young girl, quite small, dressed in a long sweater and with healthy, ruddy cheeks, as though she was just off the farm. That was a holiday for me ... at last somebody was crossing our threshold from the outside, a stranger who was about to come to life in the midst of our eccentric home... We completely changed the way we behaved, especially Gisela, Vati and I, though not so much mother or Clairi. They complained and kept looking at her. I couldn't understand that, considering what a ray of sunshine she was, this quiet, reserved young woman. Neither then nor later could I ever understand the animosity between women in situations like that.... There had once been some young ladies living with us at home in Basel, that both of them liked, and although they were pretty, I couldn't stand them... Still waters, who knows what she's got up her sleeve, they kept saying about this one... She didn't have anything up her sleeve, you were scarcely even aware she was in the house. In the morning when she arrived she always seemed a little surprised, as though she were lost or had taken a wrong turn. Then she sat down on a metal dye cask that we covered with a blanket, because we didn't have enough chairs... if you asked her anything, she'd be at a loss. She sewed the tiniest fur patches, veritable cobwebs, ruining her eyes... You could have confided anything to her and she would have kept it to herself. So suddenly we had a new girl sitting in the middle of our room and I had the unbearably wonderful feeling that we had a forest sprite in our house... I liked her tremendously and I also felt sorry for her. I knew that once Vati had taught her to sew, he wouldn't be able to employ her, because he didn't have a cent to his name to pay her with. It also concerned me that she could have learned a lot more from some other furrier in town who had a workshop and lots of equipment. After a week spent dealing with needles and furs the girl left us. She brought Gisela and me one cream cake each. She hugged Gisela good-bye and then me too. For a while I just lay – because she was still sitting on the tall cask – with my head in her lap, feeling her soft, gentle belly, in which there were two hearts beating ... the one up above resounding through both palaces of her breasts, and that other, secret one that lay below her belly ... like a clearing in the woods with the murmur of a stream emanating from it ... Then came her hands, which covered my eyes. Even though they did smell of furs, her hands were pink from the sun that shone through her ... Beginning that next Monday she no longer showed up and once again my burden pressed down on me, but with added weight ...

I WAS LEFT WITH just Peter and Andrej, who were too young for me to spend time with. I played with them both in the entryway, between the courtyard and the wooden barrier of the entry gate ... We played marbles next to a tree that grew out of a concrete ring ... the only leafy green thing in the vicinity ... played hopscotch ... dueled with sabers that I made on the Frenchman's model. We talked, by now I already knew quite a few words ... Peter and Andrej had been named for the king and his younger brother ... They were for the Falcons, like their father, mother, and sister ... the way all the more affluent people in Jarše were for the Falcons ... The merchant across the street, Bojadamič, was also for the Falcons ... You couldn't separate falcons from gymnastics and nice houses ... They were all gymnasts and all athletes were usually raw material ... like perpetually running engines and race cars they dashed around mindlessly ... one huge eruption of meaningless motion ... of blissful, unthinking running. The Eagles came from poor houses ... they smelled bad and they spread a sour stench like the Balohs, the smell of poverty ... At home they got their hair shaved instead of cut, on account of the lice, and they smeared them with sulphur on account of scabies ... They went to mass instead of gymnastics. They were stupid, submissive, and pious. Even though they kept betraying God and sinning against his commandments, they would then go repent on account of it ... they never went too far ... they betrayed their teachings and then they immediately went to confession ... those big, dark, shiny cabinets that I was forbidden to enter because I hadn't yet been confirmed ... As for the Falcons, I didn't know how far they went from gymnastics, parades and their nice houses ... if they sinned, did they go straight back to their gyms or what?

Peter and Andrej were two tenacious cartridges filled up to their snotty little noses with Falconry ... Their mother had Falcon outfits sewn for them that were appropriate for their age. Proper uniforms: red shirts with high collars ... a jacket that had braided cords hanging from the left shoulder ... a tall cap with a falcon feather ... Two regular little Lilliputians that looked like they'd jumped out of their big brother's pocket. Every day a funeral procession went down Bohorič Street toward Holy Cross at least once and occasionally several times ... The black processions would turn off the little street that ran perpendicular to the Hams's entry gate ... They would drag on, bristling with heads ... as many as there were dead people in the cemetery ... First a policeman would appear in the intersection to stop the horse rigs, bicyclists, the occasional car... Judging from the policeman Peter and Andrej could quickly guess whether a Falcon or an Eagle had died. If the deceased was a red, they would stand on the sidewalk outside the gate, take off their caps and wait at attention for the tall black carriage drawn by two horses with plumes and the first small group of mourners to go past... if they determined from the constable that an Eagle had died, they went up to the fence and spat through the laths and the leaves onto the sidewalk, shouting "Boo! Hiss!" Because I felt sorry for dead people, I deliberately went out to stand on the sidewalk and quietly wait for the whole funeral procession to pass... not just the tall carriage with the little black angels in the patched pillars, but also the last couples, usually dressed in everyday street clothes, as they strolled here and there in the direction of Holy Cross... This was the cause of countless fights between the twins and me. "You're an Owl! An Owl!" they railed at me... I wasn't an Eagle... actually, I didn't feel like I belonged to any group, which was the worst and most desolate feeling in the world... except that now and then I may have felt I belonged to God... or rather, to the conversations I had with him in the air around me, not that he ever answered or filled the emptiness with his presence...

The twins weren't appropriate company for me... that didn't exist anywhere on Bohorič Street... except for a few little girls and boys who were even smaller runts than they were. There wasn't a single house whose front door you'd see a boy or at least a girl my age, ten, if not already eleven, coming out of... Bojadamič's son, a stuck-up giant, was already in high school... I had nothing in common with him ... he led a different kind of life ... out in his magnificent yard with its flowers and trellises he had everything, a set of parallel bars, colored rings, model airplanes ... I also didn't have any connection with the people up there ... in the tar paper shacks behind the fences, where temporary workers lived among heaps of old metal mixed in with jobless people, beggars and Gypsies, so I didn't take a step in that inhospitable direction ... Around "Mexico" ... I would go there to read the newspapers posted on the bulletin board, so I could tell Vati the news from the Spanish or Abyssinian fronts ... riding around the building on bicycles or kicking a ball in the yard were the children of better parents, who were a little too self-satisfied and conceited for my taste ... Living in the houses and villas with gardens nearby there were just mamma's boys carrying pails and shovels ... So I had to go down Bohorič in the opposite direction ... toward the military hospital to flush out anybody who was to my liking at all ... I was hanging around some dreary houses when one afternoon I heard the voice of a boy humming an aria from the opera Carmen coming out of the vestibule of a house standing where the street narrows ... This was Zdravko, three years older than me ... a real athlete and, judging from his speech and his build, already a young man ... We sort of became friends. What bothered me about him was his thick neck, which suggested a kind of coarseness and brute force ... He confided in me that he planned to become an opera singer when he grew up ... nothing less than a singer, a soloist – the lead soloist in a major opera company ... He told me about various opera stars, about Caruso ... his great successes ... his voyages across the Atlantic to America ...

the beautiful women who chased after him ... He would practice in vestibules and hallways where there was a good echo ... and I even tried it myself, I let him teach me, if only I could have had a little bit more time with him ... Unfortunately we weren't able to forge a more durable friendship, because he was older and didn't have time, because every day when he wasn't in school or helping his father, the driver of a brewery hitch, he was taking voice lessons with a teacher in town ... That hitch of his father's frequently bolted, spooked by wood-burning trucks, and went racing down Bohorič, the reins flying in the air, as the stacks of barrels fell off the wagon and exploded with a bang on the pavement ... while his father, a powerful, ruddy-cheeked man in a leather apron down to his ankles, whip in hand, raced after them ... Sometimes when he was coming home from school or his voice lesson, he would sit down beside me by the fence for five or ten minutes ... "So brav müsstest du sein, wie er, etwas lernen, was dir Freude macht,"* mother would set him up as an example for me ... Once when we were sitting like that, a boy wearing the lace- and embroidery-adorned clothes of a knight suddenly appeared on the sidewalk, looking so brilliant it nearly blinded me. He was wearing a high ruffled collar around his neck and shoulders, and the cross of the Knights Templar showed black on his chest. I got up and followed him, both Zdravko and I went, because that was on the way home for him ... He was a regular White Prince from the *Beautiful Adventures*. He wore a wide-brimmed hat on his head with a plume that bobbled and

---

*You just need to be as diligent as he is, learn to do something that gives you pleasure.

he had low-cut shoes on his feet and gloves on his hands that went up to the elbow, like the ones for hunting with eagles ... Besides all that, he was carrying a spear with a split flag that also had the Templars' cross embroidered on it in silver ... And his trousers! All threads, hems, patches, and braids ... "That's a crusader," Zdravko explained to me unphased ... "Ant vehr do zey ket zose krate univorms?" I asked him, beside myself. "From the Franciscans ..." "You chust ko zehr ant zey kiff you a speer ant ze cloze?" ... "No, you have to apply, attend mass a lot, distribute literature door to door ..." Zdravko ran off home, but I followed the crusader to the end of the street, followed him to the train tracks ... the military hospital ... across the bridge ... all the way to some ugly building that he entered like a ghost from another world. I couldn't believe my eyes. Something like that really existed? I wanted to become a crusader like that ... They also had shields, Zdravko explained to me, and they carry swords in processions ... That was something! To change your clothes and yourself! That's what I wanted! It was like becoming Tarzan, Robin Hood, a gangster ... If only I could bring myself to go there, to the Triple Bridge and the Franciscan brothers.

At the start of the school year Vati had to show up at school. It was there that he found out that I'd flunked the previous year and was doing third grade over again ... He was standing in that hallway beneath the portraits of learned men and talking with teacher Roza ... I stood way off to the side, because adult conversations interested me less than the dirt beneath my fingernail. To this day. Miss Roza was as pleasant as she'd been the year before, when we lived in Jarše, and all flushed in the face ... I saw Vati flinch at the news ... and his hand drop while holding his sooty hat ... how much grayer he was ... Yet another jolt. After so many had assaulted him that he'd broken into splinters ... I couldn't bear to watch it ... I could have spared him this blow ... Oh, yes! I couldn't stand causing anyone pain. I absolutely forbade myself any malicious act ... I would sooner have let any mischief, treachery, greed, or cowardice pass than have to be the cause of someone else's pain ... I would rather have committed harakiri or cut off a finger than see anyone have to cry on account of me, as I had to cry on account of others a number of times ... I hated the devil, Satan, that vicious freeloader ... I wanted to go up, and I strove and sought and longed for God and heaven ... I didn't want to go to hell for things that depended entirely on me ... "And the report card?... He destroyed it?!" I heard Roza's voice ... Getting a certified copy would require rubber stamps, running from courthouse to courthouse, it meant yet another expense ... This was bad!... Miss Roza was beside herself ... she called for the new teacher who was going to teach me, Mr. Marok, to come see her ... What would this one be like?... The door to the teachers' lounge opened behind my back ... He was here ... Oh God ... he looked like he'd stepped out of an antique store! Broad-shouldered, stocky, big belly ... a fat head with no neck and regular feather dusters for a mustache, with sideburns that flowed down into his wide shirt with a dirty necktie and the dirty necktie into a sweater the color of kohlrabi ... But his voice, I have to admit, was beautiful, like a basso profundo's ... Vati kept blinking as he listened to both of them ... and I could practically feel the fury shaking inside him ... electrifying his hands. I knew I was going to be punished ... justly so ... I would endure it ... But I would show them my teeth if they were going to try to drag the beating out into infinity ... Then finally back home! Everyone sat stunned ... mother, Clairi, even Gisela, who was worried how much blood the rod would send spurting this time ... Their mouths were all open, as though the news was so big it wouldn't fit in. The staring and disbelief lasted the whole day, until evening ... and then a whole week ... They couldn't get their mouths shut, as though their jaws had come out of joint ... I couldn't sit or lie down for all the bruises ... "Hör zu," Clairi said to me ... "Wie kannst du so schlecht in der Schule sein, wo du so ein Köpfchen hast? Und lügen dabei? Und ein wichtiges amtliches Papier vernichten?"* She was shocked, furious, pitying ... she looked at me in disbelief ... me, a gargoyle, a phantom who stood somewhere beyond Hades ... "Du wirst dir das Leben versauen ... Sie werden dich ja in die Erziehungsanstalt oder sogar ins Gefängnis stecken ..."** She was at her wit's end. Vati left me alone ... but oh, how he shook the table, the boxes, and threw the pliers on the floor ... Mother didn't want to have anything to do with me, she couldn't bear to look at me ... There was just Gisela ... she was my angel of

*Listen, how can you be so bad at school when you've got such a bright little head on your shoulders? And lie, to boot? And destroy an important official document?
**You're going to mess up your life ... They're going to put you in a reform school or even in prison.

God... And of course Clairi. She would thoughtfully wake me up in the morning... twist the lamp so I could find my socks... spread the lard thick on my bread, if there was any... She would try to arouse some interest in me for the day's classes... Kiss me in the doorway... She became a regular nuisance!... I knew that I'd lost a year of my life. Oh, if I just could have rolled up in a ball like a hedgehog.

Mr. Marok also taught handicrafts... basket weaving using different colored papers, sawing little shelves, crocheting. Drawing was hardest for me. Marok drew a ship on the blackboard, a big pot with holes for the cabins. I drew a similar one, only I added everything I'd seen on steamboats on the Rhine: in addition to the smokestacks and railings I drew signal masts, little flags, the captain's bridge, and all around the boat swarms of tugboats and freighters like little bacilli... My bench neighbor, Bajželj, had drawn a steamship in perspective... with its prow raised and its stern low as it sailed on the horizon... Pot-bellied Marok came padding over in his slippery suit and kohlrabi sweater... he was excited about Bajželj's drawing on account of its perspective... this was something... he pinned it up to the board as an example for everyone... Bajželj got an A and I got a C. It didn't help to do what they said, or be disobedient... I had no head for other things... I calculated everything wrong on the abacus... my language assignments teemed with mistakes.... my handwriting was all smudged and I could barely read... Rote answers to questions while standing in front of the class... would have to be heard to be believed... It was torture to pronounce each word... they were like little stone cubes that it took all my effort to push out of my mouth with my tongue...

out of my throat, the corners and hollow of my mouth ... There wasn't much I could do with them, least of all express myself ... I couldn't like anyone, get mad or laugh at a joke with them. All the words were wrapped in thorns or compressed into balls of tangled threads ... there was no way to take hold of them or turn them around, much less disentangle them ... It just wouldn't work! It was a mystery ... One of my schoolmates named Robert also lived on Bohorič. He was a pale, blond boy. It was strange that I hadn't become aware of him before. His father was a train engineer ... Once he invited me over to their house. They had a big, bright kitchen with four windows on two sides, with every possible dish simmering and sizzling on a big range ... His mother was a pretty, freckled lady whose red hair and little green apron suited her perfectly ... I sat on a painted cabbage box and watched as, kneeling beside him, she tried to feed my colleague beef soup with light groat dumplings one spoon at a time. The boy refused and his pretty mother had to beg him with each spoonful. A spoonful for daddy, a spoonful for grandma, and on and on ... I couldn't believe it! I couldn't remember the last time I'd been like that ... maybe in Basel or when I was in the hospital, but even then I must have been hopeless with asthma ... His mother served me with hearty pastries, which were golden inside like her fine skin, and had a brownish crust like the little roof over the secret little house that she hid under her heart-shaped apron. Between Robert's mother and the atmosphere filling that prosperous white kitchen, I had enough scents and colors to keep me satisfied for a full month.

At home they were now allowing me my own tiny place at the table to do my homework. I felt a resistance to numbers ... to the arithmetical symbols + − × : themselves ... I would furrow my brow when they looked at me from the page, because that's how one thought ... you couldn't just lure your brain out with limesticks ... My resistance to school got stuck on them like some little toad. I didn't have the slightest inclination to illuminate the darkness inside my head like some castle hall. It would have made my head hurt ... There was nobody I could ask for help with anything – not mother, not Vati, not Clairi ... They didn't understand the rules of arithmetic, much less of grammar ... I jotted down an equation and answer based foremost on how elegant they looked. For the answers I would choose numbers that didn't appear in the equation above or, if they did, I would change their sequence. It developed into a kind of drawing. I scribbled out the writing and grammar assignments hastily, from the topmost to the bottommost letter in my notebook I could see my hand moving deftly and with childish ignorance as I wrote them ... as though it were playing in sand. One day I'll master these things the way I breathe ... without any agony. I would have preferred not to have anything more to do with these notebooks, erasers, and pen holders, even though big, fat, juicy ones with tails on them, the kind only Marok knew how to draw, kept glaring at me from out of my notebooks ... In the morning before classes some of my schoolmates would hastily copy the star students' homework. I could see fat Marok going from bench to bench, reading them and assigning good grades, without those knuckleheaded cheats having to lift an eyebrow. That was cheap, tricking Marok, because he was ugly enough as it was and all he had in the world was his beautiful voice... My backpack began to stink of classrooms and benches, as though I were lugging the whole school home... I threw it into the farthest corner. That was enough for one day! I wanted to have some peace in the afternoons... I went out and looked at what few interesting things there were on our street. At least that was something, even though I still didn't have any friends...

Zdravko all but disappeared for a time and sickly Robert was always out on errands with his mother. He needed a lot of air... I was left with Gisela, the twins, or the old monkeys over behind the hospice's fence. I couldn't understand how a person could become so old and decrepit and still feel like living. Particularly in as messy a yard as that. If only the old folks were at least a little bit nice. But sometimes their eyes would start glinting as though a whole madhouse had just opened up in their heads. They also sang now and then, sometimes in the middle of the night, like monks... I could hear them through the wall. They didn't have bad voices.

Finally I gave myself a kick and headed over to the barracks. I climbed up the fence and looked in. What utter poverty! The wooden shacks were as shabby as those plague-eaten horses in the pictures of my illustrations... Heaps of rusted metal, pipes, strips, and sheets... And what wasn't strewn around the gate... motorcycle tires, holy icons, horse collar padding... But they had piglets in pens, with chickens pecking around, and rabbits in warrens... There was a brilliant sign on the fence: "Cunt and prick make little Dick," next to which there was a picture of something like poop dropping into a potty ... A few boys with bowl haircuts came out accompanied by girls. I wasn't afraid of them ... they seemed to be shyer than I was. I particularly liked one of the girls. She was wearing a skirt that probably belonged to her mother, because it reached to the ground. Her ass almost bounced like a ball. Dark hair. With a little ring on her tanned hand ... They invited me to come on over the wall ... Lots of interesting wrenches lying around heaps of old metal, some of which would have made fine brass knuckles. And cleaning rods like arrows. Unusual package-like parts of machines. And fat rubber bands for slingshots and tanks that you could make out of spindles. Sheets of aluminum. Glass liquor bottles ... I kept close to my Gypsy girl. She let me know that she liked me. She was like Adrijana and Anka rolled into one ... We scaled a few little fences and in an empty, abandoned pigpen with high walls we kissed each other on the dry cinders; she put her tongue in my mouth ... she stroked my balls so hard, with both hands, the way the little Gypsy girls in Cegelnica begged for a dinar, and I stroked her cherry with its little groove. Her little sisters and brothers exploded with laughter. They made fun of our caresses by rubbing themselves between the legs and kissing the air with big, puffed-up cheeks, as if in some big movie ... When I came back the next day, firmly resolved to see our nastiness to its end, my girlfriend was gone ... she had moved ... It was always like that: either I moved or others did.

At the end of Bohorič Street on the other side of the railroad crossing was the Salesian Home, which housed the Kodeljevo movie theater. This building and the playgrounds below it is where you would see some strange boys, all of them religious and a little crippled. They would kick the ball in a restrained, oddly tame sort of way under the watchful eye of their trainer and referee, a young priest in a cassock, with a whistle clenched in his mouth, who kept jumping around among the spectators ... Their founder was the blessed don Bosco, the educator priest whose life I was familiar with ... The players ran around their shallow clay-covered depression in pathetically baggy uniforms like harlequins ... The goalie was leaning up against the goal, probably because his position gave him some peace and quiet that he could use to think about things. He didn't like it when they disturbed him and he always let the ball go by ... Toward the end of the game they looked like staggering statues of clay ... The reason for the bad match was probably that they didn't have any real opponent. They were playing against themselves. They were so light and thin, just skin and bones like me. They almost didn't weigh anything ... when they attacked, if the wind picked up speed, they would go flying over the edge of the field with the ball ... If I compared them to the Falcons' team across the train tracks in Moste! The way those guys marched up the embankment, well-fed, each of them carrying a soccer ball under his arm, with their captain out in front, the whole team in their pale pink uniforms contrasting vividly against the blue sky ... The Salesian Home was as much home to gawky boys and girls as the new church next-door and the movie theater it contained. They always showed movies from all different times there ... black and white ones, old-fashioned sepia ones, modern ones in color. And always two at a time: an adventure movie and a comedy, a detective story and a tragedy, an operetta and a serious drama... If I had a spare dinar, I would go sit in their big, red auditorium... The Salesian boys and girls acted like they owned the whole building. They ran around the place with bunches of keys to various main doors and side doors, to cabinets and closets, entrances and exits and various stairways... They didn't behave like some closed little society that doesn't let in any outsiders, but they did act as though they were themselves a bunch of Errol Flynns, Mickey Rooneys and Shirley Temples, day after day entertaining the public from the screen in the big auditorium... They had their own little rooms or classrooms with benches upstairs, where they studied, played and ate snacks that were brought up to them in laundry baskets... I couldn't have joined them. One day I listened to them talking out on the soccer field. They were talking about sports and goals, about Biblical parables and piety in church... in fact it was neither the one nor the other, but some cross of the two. It was stupid and hypocritical.

Ham's assistant lived in the butcher's courtyard, in a little room over the stable. He was an Eagle, a member of the Slovene Lads. His red-stitched brown uniform, belt and hat with an impressive eagle's feather hung from the wall. He played a small drum in the Slovene Lads' brass band, and in the afternoons or evenings he would practice with his drumsticks on a piece of felt that he set over the drumhead, in order not to make too much noise. I told him that in the drumming school in Basel the beginners first practice on wooden footstools. That seemed to really interest him. He let me bang out all of Vogel Gryff... the introductory march of mardi gras in Basel. Only the piper was missing, so

I whistled along ... He was really impressed with the rhythm, because it conveyed the melody even without the winds. He tried it himself and mastered it in no time ... I went to visit Jože a number of times. You got to his room by a stairway ... He was a nice, honest guy from a farming family. He trusted me and I him. There was a picture of his girl, Tončka, on his night table. He had Vati make a choker for her out of lamb's hide. He had a stack of other photographs showing him with his band. He kept an army style revolver on the shelf in his wardrobe. A formidable caliber. He had brought it back from his service in the army. It was wrapped in a thousand sheets of newspaper. He let me hold it. I spun the barrel, causing the hammer to go "click! click!" With the bullets that he kept in the box next to it, I could have ripped the whole room to shreds and put holes in all the chimneys ... Mr. Ham made a little fun of Jože, especially on Sundays when he would dress up in his Eagles uniform and, with his drum in a sling on his side and his drumsticks in a holster on his belt, head off to practice or a meeting of the Slovene Lads in town. But because he was such a good worker, it wouldn't have occurred to Ham to fire him ... He and Ham worked so well together, you would have thought they were both owls or falcons. Even the twins held their tongues around him ... Jože and I once hitched a team to the delivery wagon with its tall sides and drove to the slaughterhouse ... All the cows and even horses they had standing outside in pens under the acacias! ... Inside there were big, cool rooms with white tile and red floors, perhaps so the blood wouldn't be so visible ... I watched them slaughtering cows, bulls, calves. The butchers were dressed in white from head to toe, with masks over their mouths and noses like surgeons. Jože preferred not to look. He even turned his head away, toward the pegs in the coatroom. The butchers, all giants with faces as plump as women's, grinned at him, not meanly, but in a way that showed they respected him ... They killed the cattle with a rod that had electricity in it, or with a tube that shot out a little dart as thin as a needle. They looked for the place on their foreheads: bzzzz ... and in an instant the animal, tied by the legs and horns, toppled onto its side ... Sometimes it also staggered, each of its four legs separately, like a mardi gras horse with two men hidden inside who can't agree whether to go straight or in a circle ... The animal collapsed and stretched its head far forward ... like a skull drying on the Sava's gravel ... At first I thought that it had passed out, but then I saw that it kept pressing farther down onto the floor, as though it wanted to sink through it. It really was dead ... They dragged it off like a swollen carpet over the floor, to skin it ... Then they sprayed water on the floor and brought in another. Sometimes an animal would resist ... while it mooed they would shove it from behind with a kind of ram and pull it from in front by the rings in its nostrils. Sometimes the calves would bolt ... and they would have to go chasing after them all through the hall ... Meat and skins alike hung from hooks ... like clothes in a closet ... the horns, the hooves, bits of tail would be stacked up in the corners by individual butchers ... Jože gave me a pail to collect hot blood in ... they made a strong soup out of it ... now and then I also got a piece of meat, some tripe, a soup bone ... On Saturdays there would be crowds of poor people and women holding assorted pots standing out under the trees around the slaughterhouse ... You always got something, if not for free, then for not much money ... At times I did fine as I watched the gigantic animals fall to the floor, as if hit by lightning ... yes, this was proof that death was the same for all ... at others the recollection of Liska, Dimka or the warm, sticky smell of blood drove me out under the acacias to vomit ...

T̲h̲a̲t̲ f̲a̲l̲l̲ we were penniless again. Summer and early fall, "die billige Gemüsenzeit,"* were over ... That table, both hammocks, the chairs ... in one of them, which was upholstered, Gisela and I had our hiding place in a gap under a spring ... everything we'd bought when we moved had made such a hole in the family's wallet that we were still feeling it ... In response to an ad that Vati had placed in the newspaper *Jutro* there had not been a single customer ... Again we had to take groceries from Bojadamič on credit. Again we had to borrow to pay for heating fuel ... we had long since given up on gas, which came through a coin-operated machine. The main room got its heat from the kitchen. That's where we went to warm our hands and backs. When our mouths began watering unbearably, that's when they sent me down at a gallop, list in hand, to the woman who sat in the newsstand ... All I ever saw of this woman in her little witch's hut were the downy wrinkles around her mouth or her hand when it pushed a pack of cigarettes toward me under the window ... I compiled the list

*The cheap vegetable season

myself, in cursive and Slovene translation as mother dictated it. According to it, we were pawning a rabbit fur ... a fur hat ... a choker ... for so and so many dinars in credit. The lady unrolled the list that I had rolled into a scroll. Sometimes she gave me money for nothing, and sometimes she needed some enticing collateral. "Yes, the choker!" she said. I raced back upstairs and brought her the choker, made of angora rabbit fur and nicely wrapped in newsprint. She inspected it in the gloom of her little house and counted the money out onto the rubber mat ... one, two, three ... we counted together, out loud ... Soon it transpired that she had more of Vati's furs in her newsstand than tobacco and cigars ... I immediately ran with the money and gunnysack to "Fuel" just several doors down the street. The rumor was that the owner of the company was a communist. The communists were on the side of the poor and wore red neckties, because they lusted for blood ... When the salesman, who had his shoes wrapped in gunny sack on account of the cold, weighed the full bag out in the courtyard, the owner was always looking out the window of a sort of granary that loomed up high over the mountains of logs and the streets of stacked boards ... He would run down and check to see if the scale wasn't showing less than the actual weight of the bag ... Vati came to meet me, so that we both carried it back. The bag was at least twice my size and so heavy that it made me stagger. Finally I almost had to carry both of them ... the bag and him ... up the steps, when he suddenly went pale and almost collapsed near the fence ...

That fall mother finally found a friend ... Mrs. Guček from Moste ... a tiny, toothless woman in a broad-brimmed hat with thickly made-up lips ... She lived in an apartment building near the railroad crossing barrier. She told us about her son, who, when he was returning home from his military service, couldn't wait to see her and instead of waiting to get off of the train at the station, jumped off the car at a ramp, breaking an arm and a leg. Her son was a little, powerful fellow with short hair, a baker by trade ... Mother had met Mrs. Guček while out at the store buying buttons, and she brought her home ... Mrs. Guček played a small clarinet, which she carried with her in her bag. In better times she had also played the piano ... Vati couldn't stand her. Nor could I ... She wore thick knitted mittens on account of her sensitive hands. She never took her hat off ... She spoke in fine phrases and with exquisite care. She'd had a very good education, we noticed that right away. Her father had been a corset and glove merchant ... Before the great war he had had six employees. The door to his atelier was constantly opening or closing. He was wiped out in the financial scandal of some bank in Vienna. Her husband, a government official, Peter's father, was dead ... Everything that Mrs. Guček had to say turned into a wistful dream ... She drank tea and often had supper with us, although she must have noticed that we didn't have anything ... Most of all she liked to take a spoon and scrape the scorched cornmeal mush or macaroni stuck together off the bottom of the pot, which was also what I liked to do and why mother always set it aside for me. So this made me resent her even more. But she did play the flute nicely. Like the early morning twitter of birds in the woods ... the splash of water ... a pan pipe ... the sorrow of an abandoned girl ... that's how it sounded ... She had a wide repertoire. She would sit on the barrel with her legs crossed. Or right on a skin on the floor ... She got more and more reckless. "What would you like?" she would ask. "Ein Walzer," Clairi said. Sometimes she would mimic an entire ensemble, an orchestra or, with her hands cupped around her mouth, a trumpet ... she kept time with her foot ... "Cuckoo!" she would say to Gisela, who would be hiding under a blanket. Outdoors she would wear a veil. On account of her skin. She would come uninvited, out of the blue. She and mother spent a lot of time chatting, getting angry about things, crying together ... she was ready to cry at the drop of a hat ... She would talk about this and that, she knew a lot of people. And when she didn't she would say, "The rumor is that ..." She even knew the old lady who kept watch at her window to make sure I didn't spill any water, as well as her stepdaughter, who would call her stepmother to the window the instant she saw me ... About the bishop, who was fond of drink, which is why he was bloated and flushed all the time, and who also had ... and from here on she whispered in mother's ear, but so loudly that it thundered and I could hear everything: had women, nuns, the sisters, ladies from some of the better families ... Despite the fact that she was annoying and made us angry and that we also laughed a lot at her expense, mother couldn't get by without her ... She told her about the theater, the opera, dances ... she was very well-versed. Mother had a weakness for actors: once, in Basel in 1913, on the Elizabethplatz, she had had the actress Maria Petri as a boarder ... and she still had photos of her ... later she killed herself over an unhappy love affair ... One evening Mrs. Guček napped in a hammock next to mother until eleven at night, when they both left for the movies, a special showing just for adults that young people weren't allowed to see ... Mother came home at two in the morning, for the first time in her life and in a carriage, at that, which Mrs. Guček got for her through a friend who was a driver ... All of us shot up in bed when the hitch stopped outside our house.

One day Clairi – as a result of a humorous incident in which, on the street outside the hospital she was startled by a streetcar and dropped a box of furs that she was taking to offer some customer in Tabor – made the acquaintance of an older gentleman who picked up her items for her and helped her repack them in a park on the other side of the street. A white-haired gentleman, all furrows and wrinkles. He invited her out on a date at the Tabor Café and she took me along, because she didn't quite trust this casual acquaintance ... He really was a white-haired, wizened man, but to me he seemed more like an old show-off, awkward and not very bright, at that, which I inferred from the fake way he behaved, but most of all from the unsavory jokes he was constantly cracking ... On top of that, he talked in a falsetto, and if only his hair, though in Clairi's opinion quite attractive, had not been cut in a ring of fringe at the top like the fathers ... So this was the suitor I'd had to bathe, brush my hair, cut my fingernails and sit as still as a statue at a wobbly table for, and on top of that translate his inanities for Clairi and hers back to him. He didn't care much for me, either, I noticed that instantly, I got in his way ... oh, I knew what he wanted and I could tell from looking at Clairi that from one minute to the next he was becoming less and less to her liking. He ordered cake and raspberry juice. I got nothing out of the whipped cream or the syrup, because everything was so polite and forced. When he paid, he pulled a sheet of paper out of his pocket, which contained a banknote folded in three... Only then did my eyes open, only then did I begin to feel sorry for him and I felt ashamed. But it was too late for me to become any nicer toward him, at least not outwardly.

Then Clairi got to know a military family. Actually the Croatian wife of a non-commissioned officer at first, a stout woman with a broad face and lots of hair, Spanish-looking with lots of earrings and a beauty mark under one eye. She had brought Vati her red fox fur to mend. She knew how to tell fortunes from coffee dregs and cards... read palms... and she knew a whole bunch of superstitions... she knew lots of unusual Balkan dishes and bloody love stories. Her bracelets would clatter like castanets when she told them and her voice, her hair, her hands, her breasts, all of her would quiver. Clairi was drawn to exotic and romantic things... freedom, wind, fire. This was something for her! A free life in which every sign in the heavens and on earth has its own hidden meaning, every gesture its hermetic secret... Clairi would stare like a child. "So was?... Was Sie nicht sagen... Ist das möglich?..."* She believed that our great-great-grandfather might have been a Gypsy after all... That was probably why we were constantly on the move, living from hand to mouth... why we liked fire, wind, trees, rain... and why we would never lose our will to live. At the same time in her mind she was cautiously assembling a judgment about this exceptional person... What an army dimwit...

*Well what do you know... You don't say... Is that possible?

what a schemer, trying to get her tasteless fur, those "twelve worn-out foxes on one sow" mended for little or nothing... this vain, pampered shystress of fortunes and oracles. But then again... some age-old wellspring of faith in the instincts, in the senses, in the inextricability of phenomena... a door grown over with vines, beyond which there was another door, and beyond that yet another... until you finally ran into the grace that bestowed its revelation on you... Mira's husband was a sergeant. One Sunday the sergeant came with her. He was a short, handsome, swarthy man reminiscent of Valentino. He wasn't an officer, but still... He had white gloves and a saber, and from the saber's hand guard a number of tricolor ribbons hung down. He hadn't come empty-handed. He brought a bottle of brandy and some bacon. He sat down at the table and talked with Vati half in Serbo-Croatian, half in German, with a bit of Slovene thrown in. He was for Hitler... Vati was, too... Hitler had two roles to fulfill, so claimed Sergeant Mitič. He was bringing abundance to all the poor of the world and in order to do that he was also strengthening the offensive capabilities of his army... The world has never seen an army like this... powerful, mechanized, disciplined. He's going to defeat all his opponents and establish a new order... And something else: Hitler is going to beat it into all the weaklings' fat heads that only the person who is least afraid wins. Nobody is going to be able to hold out against that kind of force, which arouses such terror in weaklings. They will all be ground into nothing!... And as proof that all this is going to happen, take the German people. Whether by trick or courage, it doesn't matter – they have to see the thing through to the end... the time has come for all nations to pass a test of their viability. A human arm can be transformed into a club ... cowards have to change into heroes, unbounded creatures ... Hitler says, "Wir wünschen alles zu machen, daß die Form Mensch nur ein Zufall bleibt und eine Übergangsphase! ..."* This ought to become the plan and goal of every nation ...

The sergeant lived with his wife Mira in a modestly appointed room of a villa near the railroad tracks ... next to the Falcons' gymnasium ... Aside from a wardrobe chest and their bed, the only furniture consisted of several big, gray-green wooden suitcases with heavy locks ... The fact was the officers and NCOs were constantly on the road, first in one Yugoslav province, then in another ... They had big, embroidered sheer curtains on their windows ... I was amazed to see that military commanders had such poorly furnished homes ... It bothered me that they lived in accommodations as makeshift as ours ... It would be fine if these were fortifications, shacks, guard posts at the front, or in disputed territory ... But to live like this with all their dress uniforms, sabers, braids, and medals ... The sergeant had a friend who was also a sergeant and who enjoyed seeing Clairi ... I didn't see that either one had a pistol, a machine gun, or an automatic rifle ... They hung their sabers over the knobs on their night tables. What kinds of commanders were these? ... They had big diplomas, solemn oaths in frames hanging on their walls ... with the royal coat of arms in gold and crossed swords ... "I will defend and protect the Kingdom of Serbs,

---

*We want to do everything necessary to make sure that the species called human being remains nothing more than an accident, a transitional phase.

Croats and Slovenes, the Yugoslav homeland ..." I stood looking at these, full of admiration and doubt. How was it possible that they had these solemn vows on their walls for all to see, when all of them were against the king and the state ... when they had no intention of protecting and defending the border when Hitler attacked ... When all of them supported *him* ... I looked at both sergeants and others who came to visit them ... These couldn't be real soldiers, commanders ... True, they wore the uniform, but more the way any woman wears a fur coat. I didn't want to believe this ... I found out that they did in fact have pistols, which they would take out of boxes to clean the hammers, polish the barrels with oiled cleaning rods, and shoot with, too ... I saw one of those decorated commander's uniforms come off once, revealing skin like other people had ... vaguely disgusting, white human flesh with black bristles, devoid of taut muscles, tendons, any firmness at all ... a kind of lazy, disintegrated human machine like the bodies of ice cream parlor attendants or cooks ... And finely articulated hands with polished nails, as though they never did any work and just picked their noses or something. These were supposed to be warriors? ... I couldn't believe it ... but then they got back into their coarse uniforms, put on their belt straps and sabers ... the soldiers outside the house saluted them, all turned to stone, as though they had gods in front of them! I was full of doubts ... they gnawed at me ... everything was so fuzzy, double and triple ... If these weren't actual, loyal soldiers, they weren't actual sworn enemies, either. If they were traitors, they couldn't have been true friends of the enemy, either. They were nothing ... neither civilians nor soldiers, not people, not men, not priests, not Gypsies ... I still enjoyed going to visit them, because I kept hoping that everything I'd seen on my previous visits had just been an illusion or a deception, and that any day now ... I was going to stumble onto their true image as warriors ... firm, decisive, hardened men, full of plans and concerns ... old Indian souls who had a vision of life and could show you the right way: Sky ... Earth ... Clouds ... But instead ...

One Sunday all five of us had our picture taken under the arch of the railway viaduct, so that it looked like we were standing in front of some fortress made of hewn rock ... At least they would have that to point to ... Then we went down to the restaurant next to the quarantine hospital ... along the way the other sergeant kept putting his arm around Clairi, but she gave him no sign of encouragement. Soldiers were like Gypsies for her ... completely undependable people ... plus they could get killed at the front. "Heute da, morgen Gott weiß wo ..."* The tavern was noisy and smoky. Someone was playing the accordion. And they were singing. And dancing. All of them had faces as red as tomatoes. Even Jože was here in his best suit, with Tončka. Clairi's friend Marica from the ice cream parlor with her big, fleshy fiancé, an insurance salesman. We ate pretzels and they gave me a glass of wine to drink ... All three women kept talking about dying their hair. For the first time I felt a cloud in my head and something as hard as a rock pressing against my forehead ... I mumbled the songs that the others were singing ... Jože and Marica's fiancé asked me to

---

*One place today, God knows where tomorrow ...

sing something ... Over a full ashtray that still had smoke coming out of it, I sang the aria from Carmen that Zdravko had taught me ... "Toréador, en garde, toréador, toréador ..." and when I finished half the tavern applauded ...

ONE DAY a small package containing a wristwatch arrived from Basel. Margrit had sent it. The watch had a gray wristband and was packed in cotton. I put it on when I went to school in the morning ... Now I was almost like the other students. If I'd had boots, corduroy knickers, a light blue sweater with a white shirt, a leather briefcase and a Pelikan fountain pen, I would have attained the ideal ... But I had a pair of Vati's old trousers, a shirt that mother had made for me from one of her blouses but that still looked like a girl's shirt, and the same old canvas backpack for books ... Worst of all were my shoes, which a nun at the St. Vincent's conference had given to me. They had high, narrow heels and you fastened them with little hooks way up over the instep, practically over the shin. And if you added my strange accent and the way I mixed up genders and cases when I talked ... which made my classmates laugh ... I wasn't just funny, I was hilarious, a regular laughingstock ... The heels on the boots from the nun were so high that I rubbed clay on them to make them seem shorter, so that people at least wouldn't tease me around town, because I was as wobbly walking in them as I would have been wearing stilts ... Now I had a watch ... All my schoolmates came flying like bees to honey to look at it on my wrist. This watch was the height of fashion, even though it told time the same as any other watch ... One morning mother asked me to leave it at home, because they didn't have any other timepiece. I reluctantly took it off my wrist. She hung it on the nail in the wall, which was where she kept the electric bill ... When she hung it up, I wanted it back, but she soon got me to change my mind ... Every day when I came home from school, the first thing I did was look at the nail over Vati's head, to see if it was still hanging there by its band ... One day the nail was bare. I broke out in a cold sweat ... "Sie wollte nicht mehr weiter. Wir mussten sie zum Uhrmacher tragen ..."* mother said ... That exquisite watch had broken down? ... I didn't know what to do. "Wann wird sie repariert? ..."** "In einer, zwei Wochen ..."*** It took a long time ... A week passed. Which watchmaker had they taken it to? I asked ... if they had taken it to the arcade under the Skyscraper, the repair would cost a fortune. "Die Frau Guček hat sie zu einem befreundeten Uhrmacher in die Altstadt getragen ...,"**** mother said. Mrs. Guček, that crazy old loon whom you couldn't trust with a pin ...

The second week passed, then a third ... There was still no sign of the watch. One day I noticed it on the wrist of the merchant Bojadamič's long-legged son. He was out playing in the yard. He was walking along the ledge of the wrought-iron fence, holding onto the uprights, when I noticed the gray watchband with the big chrome

---

*It stopped running. We had to take it to the watchmaker's.
**When will it be fixed?
***In a week or two.
****Mrs. Guček took it to a watchmaker in the old town who's a friend of hers.

onion on his wrist... "Vehr to you haff zat votch fromm?" I asked him respectfully, because he was an awful dolt... "What do you care!" he answered with the same dismissive sneer on his pale face that I'd grown used to from this sort of boy... He squatted down and fixed his button-like eyes on me through the fence until I gave up and went back to the other side of the street... Pigs! So they'd given it to the merchant because they owed him for groceries... I stormed upstairs, kicked the door open and yelled, "Ihr habt..." I summoned heaven and hell down to earth... I raged like Vati... rammed my head into the wall... bit my tongue as I roared, so that it swelled up like a donut... ran out into the hallway to catch my breath... and there was the old lady already with her stepdaughter, come out of their broom closet to enjoy the fun... I stormed back inside... blood was trickling from my lips, it was getting dark before my eyes... I was suffocating and felt I was losing consciousness... "Nein, nein, wir haben die Uhr nicht mit dem Spezeristen umgetauscht, wir haben sie nicht verpfandet... sie war so kaputt, daß der Uhrmacher mit ihr nichts anfangen konnte... lauter Räder und Federchen..."* mother said... She was lying, that was obvious, it was written on her forehead in big letters... They were all lying! It was only my indignation and rage that gave them cover not to feel anything... They had sold the watch or bartered it for food that I, too, had eaten... "Gritli wird dir eine

---

*No, no, we didn't trade the watch with the grocer and we didn't put it in hock... it was so broken that the watchmaker couldn't do anything with it... nothing but cogs and springs...

andere schicken..."* Oh, sure, that's exactly what she'll do!... I ran downstairs suddenly ... The old lady and her ward were still standing by the faucet, though enjoying themselves less ... I almost flew across the street, I was so pumped full of rage ... I walked up to the counter. Big-nosed Bojadamič came out of the back room. Do we owe you anything? I asked... "Not anymore, everything's been settled..." I began to feel afflicted ... "Die seelischen Qualen sind stets erhabener als die körperlichen,"** Mrs. Guček had told mother... I had stopped going to buy things at the store up there, the biggest one on the block and in the whole neighborhood, because they had once caught me trying to steal carob beans ... There was another, smaller store on the other side of the street, close to the train overpass ... In a small, dark window amid little painted cardboard cases hanging on threads, for such was the marketer's art ... there were stacks of carobs, walnuts, almonds, hazelnuts, prunes, and little chocolate truffles ... I went to the tobacconist lady and, without looking through the slot at her puckered mouth, I said that if she could lend me seven dinars on my parents' account, I would use it to buy a bag of firewood ... She gave it to me without any hesitation and without a receipt ... I bought a whole bagful of carobs, a bag of almonds, a kilo of prunes, cinnamon, chocolate-coated bananas ... Across from the store there was something like a little plot with a well that had dried up ... I brushed the powdery snow off its ledge, it was the end of October, and I spread my

---

*Gritli will send you another one.
**Pangs of the soul are far nobler than pains of the body.

sweet banquet out ... the saliva and juices were collecting all through my head ... my body craved tons of sugar ... I devoured it all in an instant ... I did manage to put one of each item in a bag for Gisela, which I was going to put in our hiding place for her, the hollow space under the cushioned chair, from which later, when no one was left in the room, we would take things that we meant to hide from the grown-ups ... A week later I went back to the tobacconist lady ... this time with a sheet of paper rolled up into a little pipe, and I asked her for twice as much money as the first time ... I ate quickly ... a half kilo of marmalade this time ... which I ate with my fingers straight out of the wrapping paper. This time I sensed I had overstepped the bounds of what was permissible ... my punishment was already waiting for me with no right of appeal ... it was already descending ... I headed out onto St. Martin's Road to invite one of the soldiers from the hospital who were always selling me sourdough bread to go to the movies with me ... None of the orderlies, all of whom I at least knew by sight, were anywhere to be found. So I stopped across from a soldier who was standing outside the front wall of the Šlajmer Clinic, looming over the foliage of a laurel hedge that reached up over the sidewalk, cleaning his comb with some leaves. "Živio!"* I greeted him. He was wearing a cape, and under its hood a cap with a badge and thick combat boots instead of the usual foot wraps. He was from an upland division, the mountain artillery ... I would have preferred an infantryman, because I didn't know the gunnery side of the army

*Hi! *(Serbo-Croatian)*

that well. He was glad to have company. "Do you want to go with me to the movies?" I asked. He was immediately in ... they had released him from the hospital and now he had the whole live-long day until his train departed. At last I had company, too ... We went to the Kodeljevo Theater, I bought two tickets in the first row and we ate two portions of Turkish delight in the lobby ... I was very pleased to be able to treat him and he was embarrassed, but grateful, then went back to normal, then was surprised once again as he sat next to me in the chilly auditorium, wrapped in his cape, showing me his bayonet and eating more Turkish delight out of wrappers ... I was proud and full of joy when during the movie I observed in the glow of a heater that showed through some hole in the wall the effect my manna was having as I continued to shower it on him from the sky. We watched a double feature ... After the show I walked with my mountaineer in his studded army boots to a building that had a fresco of the four seasons on its facade ... there I quickly bought him three Ibar cigarettes, we shook hands and he said goodbye ... he went marching off to his train ... it was the end of a beautiful day and I returned home completely worn out ...

The tobacconist lady called to me through the gap in her window when I sat down outside her newsstand. She was demanding her money "immediately." I instantly deflated ... The next day when I came home from school at noon, Vati and mother were already waiting for me in our room, bamboo rod in hand. The tobacconist lady was standing there in the corner ... she had closed her newsstand over lunch ... she was short and undistinguished without her newsstand, but she had such a wide, muscular rear end that I got excited and began fantasizing about something dirty ... I had just enough time to throw down my backpack and race back down the stairs head over heels. I had no idea where to ... I ran toward the train station, racing without any let-up, as though all the tobacconists in Ljubljana were on my heels ... I stopped outside the fence of the freight station. I kept my hands in my pockets ... Stood first on one foot, then on the other. Amid all this my pole stood up like a thumb in a glove ... I watched the trains going past ... freight wagons, tenders, tank cars ... There was a distinctive building on the other side. The Hotel Miklič, as its vertical sign proclaimed ... That was where we had stayed overnight two years before, when we still had Swiss francs in our pockets ... People were sitting in the waiting rooms with the intention of traveling. Travelers. Different from those on the street, who just walked around for no reason. Peasants with wicker handbags, with backpacks, with cardboard suitcases, with baskets ... The squalor consoled me, felt good. I sat down on a bench next to a railing and fell asleep. When I woke up, there were two bearded beggars, two well-liquored old men leaning against me. Where was I? I got up, shoved the shaggy dwarves, those bearded children who would never grow up, away from me ... The steam that the locomotives emitted ... "tssshhhhhh" ... turned into cold, stinging fog. It reminded me of the souls in a drawing that I'd once seen in some old German book: in a rocky, barren landscape, vibrant little clouds came out of the mouths of dying knights, then narrowed into naked, white angels or black, finned devils who blocked out the sky, the sun, the stars, the moon ... I went to the market.

There I saw the open butcher stalls where I used to help Miss Roza do her shopping. Under the counters next to the chopping blocks there were empty spaces where I could spend the night. But there was such a stinking, rotten chill dominating the place, gnawing at my wet feet and especially the slit between my trousers and long underwear, which had been sewn by its elastic band to my pants where I was exposed, that I had to get back up … It's bad when you can't find any possible place to breathe, one corner was worse than the next … I walked around in a daze … in the park near St. Peter's Church I had cold sweats … I cruised from bench to bench, sitting on each of them for a short while … I made two circuits. In Jarše, in Lower Carniola, in Basel, in the mountains around Urach there were places, sanctuaries, hollows where you could hide and live, albeit with cows or young wolves of my age … Finally I shoved off and boldly headed toward Bohorič … Once past the fence and in the yard, I wanted to go up the ladder to Jože's, but as if I was cursed, the ladder was gone and his room was dark. The horses neighed, it was warm there … But the stable door was locked. The house was asleep. Stars shone over the courtyard. They glimmered way up there, white and cold … sending each other ironic little arrows … I crept up the staircase … Here outside our room there was at least a kind of house rag that served as a doormat, and I could wrap myself up in it. I put my hands under the back of my neck, tucked my head in between my knees … Barely had I managed to doze off … to slip into a world of pleasant, warm darkness with no people … when light sliced into it: mother and Vati in their coats, Clairi in her brown sweater, and a cop with a big belly.

A commotion of voices ... They'd been looking for me all over town, trumpeting my shame to all four corners of the world ... It was three in the morning. I felt worst of all for Vati's sake. He always got up first ... He immediately went to the kitchen to shave. I stood motionless at his back while the commotion continued around the corpulent constable. My throat was all knotted up. He looked askance at me, then continued to busy himself with his knife ... Clairi went all the way to the far corner ... she wanted to have nothing to do with it all. The policeman left. Mother got undressed and then, "ganz still, bitte,"* she whacked me on my cold butt with the bamboo cane, which proceeded to get hotter and hotter. Gisela woke up and started to cry. She tried to protect me by throwing herself in between, and then the cane stayed in midair ... I lay down beside her in bed. Gisela pressed close to me, hugging me tight to warm me ... It didn't hit Vati until morning ... He shook the table and the boxes ... muttering monologues to himself. Bankrupt! ... Hooliganism! ... War! ... Jews! ... Blackguards! ...

"V<small>ON WEM HAT DER</small> L<small>ÜMMEL</small> nur das schlechte Beispiel?"** mother asked, as if I weren't in the room ... It was a harsh blow ... the whole house found out about the scandal, the whole block ... From the hospice to "Mexico" ... The twins disappeared whenever they saw me ... I didn't dare show myself to butcher Ham, who was always

*Hold still, please.
**Who on earth ever set such a bad example for the lout?

· 268

so nice to me ... not to mention Jože, whom I hid from like a needle in a haystack. I shook passing the newsstand as if it were my tombstone ... I would have preferred to spend days and days in bed, hidden under a blanket ... Slept or died. But you can't afford a luxury like that living together in one room. I had to get up and go to school, that ludicrous chaff cutter ... The tobacconist lady told mother, "Dieses Kind wird Ihr Unglück sein, liebe Frau ... Schon jetzt ist er durch und durch verdorben ... Ein elender Bub ... Ich habe mein Vertrauen in ihn gelegt ..."* Those were her last words ... Mother was afraid she was going to take us to court, even though she'd gotten furs as compensation ... that she would have me locked up ... She didn't dare respond. She and Mrs. Guček discussed whether or not to put me in some institution ... yes or no? At length they weighed the arguments for and against ... "Ach, wenn der Lausbub nur wüßte, wie Weh er Ihnen tut ..."** Mrs. Guček said. Yes, the very same fright with the shriveled eyes of a mad crow ... "Die einzige Rettung ist die Erziehungsanstalt,"*** mother concluded, fixing me with her eyes ... The old woman and that girl of hers by the faucet now had a free hand ... to go at me with even greater zest ... I spilled water on the floor when I set a bucket down ... Of course I would first take the bucket back to our room and then come back with a rag ... No! Up went the blinds ... the foster child or stepdaughter pressed her elliptical, pimply face to

---

*That child will be your undoing, ma'am. Even now he's rotten through and through. A wretched boy. I trusted him.
**Oh, if the lout only knew how much pain he's caused you.
***Reform school is the only solution.

the glass pane. She said something back into the room, informing her aunt, and the next instant the old lady had leapt into the hallway and begun shouting at me... Mother came out... she brought a rag along with her... and more or less came to my defense... I was boiling... with rage at the old hag, but even more at that pale, anemic puppet of hers... A few days later I finally ran into her, just as she was coming up the stairs. She pressed flat up against the wall, so as not to brush against me... that low life and wild man. She was taller than me and four or five years older. I stood right where I was on the steps up above her and suddenly landed her such a wallop, a full wooden mask, that it deafened me, too, for a while. At first she almost fainted... then the tears started to pour... as pale as her face... amid sobbing that was so miserable that it touched my heart. She ran upstairs, sprinkling the hallway, the walls, the support beams as she went... At that very moment mother reached for the bamboo cane again...

CLAIRI WENT BACK several times to visit the old lady who lived on Town Square over the dry cleaner's... She also got to know her daughter, Mrs. Hamman. She was the owner of the dry cleaning shop, which included ironing and alterations, as well as a linen shop selling bed covers, quilted blankets and window curtains... Then mother began going with Clairi... She curled her hair for the occasion and put some rouge on her cheeks. Since she didn't have any proper blouses, she sat in her coat through the whole visit, with it buttoned to the top and a scarf that she wrapped around her neck to make it look like a blouse collar... When they came back, they talked about Mrs. Hamman and some gentlemen who were there... and always fell silent when I came in... They would let me hear about the impressive furnishings of her rooms and salons. "Das Nipptischchen in der Mitte, ein herrliches Louis XV. Stück,"* they enthused. And the ladies... the Duchess Thor von Thorfels, Miss Ana-Maria, who was slightly cross-eyed, Miss De Lambistes, a relative of the Italian ambassador... Mr. Hoffmann, Dr. Haras... The most distinguished, most influential set in town. Just hearing about all these exquisite objects was enough to cause a delicate crystal to form in my ears... On the ladies they recognized all the best pieces from the workshops of Ljubljana's furriers. Choice "jackets," little chokers and stoles. They even knew what they cost... And how a lady wasn't really a lady until she wore fur! How nice the things looked on them. They had been charmed... And once again they headed out for a visit. They had their urgent courtesy calls to make, and now and then even Vati had to go with them, whether he liked it or not. He ironed his trousers, bleached his collar... Wherever it was they were headed, it was mysterious and a long way off... As mysterious as if they were heading into the fog... especially because all three of them kept coming back more and more worried, as though out there, beyond the confines of Bohorič Street, they had experienced a shock, a disaster...

Around this time I had to start attending preparations for the sacraments of the holy communion and soon after that preparations for

---

*The little bric-a-brac table in the middle, a beautiful Louis XV item.

confirmation in the St. Peter's rectory. I was the biggest disgrace in my class, because I hadn't yet had communion. And because I hadn't been christened until I was eight years old, as the certificate of baptism said, in St. Paul's Basilica in Basel. All of these things got delayed because Vati didn't like priests. During our last year in Basel mother had me christened on her own initiative ... On that occasion in the park across from the church, the priest of St. Paul's handed me a yellow envelope containing a gold twenty-franc coin. My coin was immediately confiscated at home ... ever since the bailiffs had repossessed nearly all of their assets they needed every last sou ... They always took everything away from me ... there was nothing to prevent this, it was their right ... I recall how the ministrants performing the liturgy in that wide, dark church, all wearing white shirts, giggled behind their music as not an infant, but a regular giant was lifted up over the christening font, and how I howled when they poured ice cold water over my hot noggin ... And even though I got the name Alojz Samson at the time, my family kept calling me Bubi ...

This time, of all the kids getting ready for the sacrament of holy communion, I was the oldest once again ... The old vicar and his young assistant priest taught us stories, commandments and songs ... The assistant priest was a tall, skinny, waxen priest in a cassock. We sat on chairs with high backs in the rectory's vestibule, among portraits of bishops and past priests of St. Peter's, and we sang: "Sing, ye mountains and valleys ... sing with us, all ye plains ..." "So, what did you like most about the hymn?" the young priest asked us as we sat in the open doorway between the vestibule and the room with the piano. I decided that I was going to open my mouth and say something for a change, something I didn't do even in school. Because the words of the song had truly captivated me. "I like ze mountains pest off all ..." I said. "Why?" the priest asked, his lips showing the grimace of disgust at my accent that I was already used to seeing from everybody. "Pecows ze kow, ze flow ..." I stammered. "They don't flow, they sing," the priest brusquely replied ... this time with more obvious repugnance in his voice, because I hadn't understood the words. Just like my Slovene language teacher!... Once again I'd let myself be lured out onto thin ice ... I'd opened my mouth and babbled ... Don't ... say ... anything! That was the best counsel of all ... Whenever I didn't speak and kept mum, I could let my eyes wander wherever my heart desired. No sooner did I say anything than I awoke the sleeping dragon ... got entangled in disputes and rejection ... I looked at the priest, because based on everything that the catechism said, he ought to have been a living rebuke to all the highfalutin and hurtful miscreants in the world ... But he had such an ordinary, puckered-up face that I couldn't believe this was supposed to be a servant of God, one of the Savior's elect, that he could have eyes seeing the inner truth. And even all around me ... not in this wide heavy table, nor in the piano, nor behind the cheap silk curtains concealing St. Mary with the emaciated Jesus just off the cross in her lap ... there was no sense of any presence of the all-highest ... except, perhaps, in the cleanliness of the old cabinets and the smell of the holy water that was already stagnant, in fact. Where was He? Nowhere! Not even here, where the priests slept, ate, and bathed ... when in fact this is where he ought to be before anywhere else, certainly before that palace with bell towers next door, the big, white church ... That's where the altars, organ, candles and icons were ... a sort of dance hall ... And what about the mountains and valleys that were supposed to be singing? What sort of far-fetched nonsense was that, what sort of dangerous games of the imagination!... If they really believed that the mountains sang and didn't go, then that ... aside from the fact that they liked to eat and drink far too much and far too well, something Jesus would never have permitted ... was the greatest depravity of all. In that case something had to be wrong with their spirituality ...

On the day before that Sunday Vati spent all night long sewing my first confirmation suit out of his own black suit ... By morning it still wasn't finished and he sewed on its right sleeve with just a few stitches. With a white ribbon and a bunch of lilies of the valley tucked into my sleeve cuff I came running into the church at the last minute ... I was already late and I had to push my way through the crowd of excited and flushed parents who had come to watch the first communicants and therefore had filled up the entire back of the church ... I shoved my way through them, under their bags and bouquets, and suddenly my sleeve came off at the shoulder, slipping over my elbow like a stovepipe, and I only caught it at the last minute ... the cotton or horsehair or whatever it was that served as a lining poked out at my shoulder ... "Gottverfluchteterteufel,"* I swore like Vati ... I had to shove the sleeve back up toward the shoulder and press my arm to

*God bloody dammit!

my side, as though I'd just been inoculated... The vicar looked at me furiously with those charcoal-rimmed eyes of his... only my communion candle was left on a little covered table... I grimaced in pain in an *I just got kicked by a horse outside* posture... Idiot! Life was always veering off into some comedy or other... you would have burst with laughter if something like this happened in a movie... Another problem was when we went in a long, fingery line, our hands clasped around candles, up to the communion table. One row got up, then the next one left and caught up with it... The light, the reflections, the organ, the singing and the spectators all blinded me... For the first time my tongue was going to feel the light touch of Jesus, who was contained in a white, thin little disk, and my mouth instantly swelled... He was going to break into me like the highest saint of all saints, without there really being anything for him to find in me, in this dark little cell crammed full of perversion and greed, in this heart of a murderer... and I had to reassure him that nothing awful was going to happen to him, that I would try to protect him from the evil forces of my soul and body... tuck him away in some quiet corner of myself, where he would be shielded from me... But what was going to happen to me when he really entered me, taking over my body, my soul, my whole being?... Was I going to change, become illuminated, behave more nobly?... was his light, bony hand going to guide mine, would the future be brighter and nicer... From now on was I going to feel the lightness of strength and faith... Would I get to perform some glorious feat in the process... would I become a model student, build a house for Vati, a garden for Gisela, would I tame mother, find Clairi a husband? Would I become a soldier? Awaken the love of a beautiful princess and become betrothed to her, and be in her heart as she was in mine ...? A massive table in the rectory was laden down with delicacies ... there was a cake in the middle that was as big and white as Mont Blanc with a layer of sand ... there were cookies already out on plates ... and dishes of cherries in sugar glaze ... I could barely wait to sit down and dig in. Then they took a picture of all of us ... white candles in hand ... the girls wearing their little wreaths and veils ... mine was the only black suit in the picture amid all the white ones ...

Had I told the priest everything at Saturday confession? No, I hadn't! What was I going to tell that fat bag of flesh, that red crocodile hide in his black cassock who could barely breathe on his dark side of the grill! I wasn't going to tell any of them anything about the delectable things I did with my pee-pee and repeated over and over again until the little thing was just a poor, skinny fuse ... Nothing about Anka or the little gypsy girl, nothing about my shoplifting, or the tobacconist lady, nothing about my angry thoughts. That stayed in my head. I couldn't and wouldn't put it out in the open ... and then he wouldn't have understood my accent, anyway ... God already knew what sort of a labyrinth I had in my head. I wasn't about to confide anything to the blacksmith bellows rasping behind the bars of that little cell, even if it smelled of flowers and ambrosia itself ... No, I didn't believe that even one of them was Jesus's apostle. They were ordinary people in uniforms who made faces ... like the police, or sergeants, or train conductors, whether they were talking about ordinary things or singing hymns ... I'd sworn, I'd lied, that's what I'd told him the last time ...

One bright morning in the middle of the night, two dead boys got up to fight... Those were the kinds of things I'd confessed. Once the hurt priest said to me, "Oh, how Jesus is crying now!" There was something relaxed in his voice, like a storyteller's... I could practically see twelve-year-old Jesus in his little shirt, shedding tears over the storm gutter at the corner. I almost opened my mouth to tell him everything, that's how much the humanity of his voice moved me... but thank God, I didn't... Once outside I assigned my own penance, more than the priest had given me... Instead of one Our Father I prayed ten, instead of two Hail Marys I recited twenty... That was for all the infractions that God alone knew about and for that reason were his concern only... "You must have had a lot of sins, if you had to do that much penance," my schoolmates said when I came back out after half an hour... they judged the sinfulness of your sins based on how much time you spent confessing in church. They were determined to mark you one way or another... Oh, then I began to finish my prayers in a flash... I didn't pray my real penance until I was back outside... sometimes crouching behind the fat entryway pillar that supported a golden painting over the doorway... And from there I would move to a bench in the park. Did it count if I prayed just in my head? No... surely not, I had to at least move my lips as I prayed, otherwise it would be too convenient... Nothing, not a single thing counted for anything if you didn't use your muscles in the process...

Then every Saturday afternoon I began having to attend the pieties that were designed to prepare you for holy confirmation. At confirmation you became a soldier of Christ... that was something real that you could get enthusiastic about. The preparatory pieties were held in a different place each time ... first in the cathedral, then in a church in Trnovo ... We prayed, sang and studied, listened to the sermon of a priest who told us that there was a fog in our souls that we had to cut through with a knife. That provoked some laughter, because it was true. Now I began to look differently at the paintings over the altar, especially the ones on the ceiling ... Jesus conveying the big golden key of St. Peter on the rock ... A big, handsome ship sailing through shadows ... full of sails to the very top of its masts ... setting about for Mount Ararat ... All of the townspeople were on its deck, all of them calm. Among them I recognized some dead people from Basel ... I even recognized the man holding onto a camel and the one who was at the wheel ... Captain Noah ... He had his mouth open. He was shouting commands ... The ship went on ... With my whole heart I followed it across the whole ceiling ... On the far side was Jesus, resurrecting Lazarus in some cramped room ... A banquet. Troubadours playing for coins. And women around a king, giving him all kinds of advice ... a whole mountain of advice ... Bloody women, they were always spoiling eternity ... I'd had it up to my ears with their gossipy tongues ... The Last Supper, Judgment Day ... I believed in the paintings that depicted events. But I didn't believe the modern ones that just had one saint standing with his hand raised in an oath, as if he were in a telephone booth where just one person could call ... My sponsor was a student, an owl, the St. Vincent's conference had assigned him to me, Vati explained. I was promised a new suit, underwear, and shoes. I went to get measured. In the nuns' garden, amid the geraniums and touch-me-nots, a skinny, pious tailor measured me for a belted jacket and three-quarter pants made of mottled cloth ... I also got shoes with soles that stuck out on the sides and looked like submarines, and a white shirt with a collar that reached halfway down my chest ... The confirmation took place in the cathedral ... This was the first time I got to see the bishop up close, the one that Mrs. Guček and the whole town knew liked looking at women, and had a red nose because he was fond of drink ... There was no other bishop in town, so this had to be the same one that everybody picked to the bone ... This was the first time I saw the bishop, whom they called pastor ... he really was dressed all in gold ... with a tall gold cap, a gold cloak and a gold, curved St. Nicholas rod. He didn't strike it as hard as they'd threatened he would. The blow wasn't manly or athletic or feminine or anything at all ... My student sponsor in his outgrown sport coat and wide necktie stood behind me ... There were street vendors outside and he had bought me a bag of candy and oranges ... Then we went to some little house in Moste next to a factory, where we played roulette for prizes ... The whole sidewalk outside was packed with us and it took us nearly an hour to get inside. There were ten of us who'd had sponsors appointed ... We gathered in some room at a round table. The grand prize was a pocket watch on a chain that was hanging over a chest of drawers. At first we won tea and potica. When my turn came, I tossed a little ball onto the red spinning wheel with silver numbers on it ... The ball kept bouncing crazily back and forth before magically stopping on the number that had also been assigned to the pocket watch on a big label ... The grand prize! Incredible!... God was shining his grace on me! Then a nervous conversation, a brief argument erupted between my sponsor and a little man in a black necktie and hat who was the organizer... I was holding the watch, which was silver with a green dial... "The watch," said the little man, "cannot be his, because he's from a different precinct." What did that mean? I could see my prize, my treasure disintegrating. I have to admit, my sponsor offered a spirited defense, even though he was quite undistinguished and gesticulated a lot... but he was just a lowly youth, a student, and he had to give way to the little man's arguments. I had to return the watch through a whole forest of hands so they could put it back over the chest of drawers... I really was on the verge of crying... Instead I got a different prize, a kilogram box of "Dr. Francek's Chicory"... At home Vati fulminated. "Diese Schweinhunde von katolischen Pfaffen..."* Mother and sister searched through the bag... aside from a few jellybeans, lollipops, hazelnuts, and one orange there was nothing... not one single dinar, not even a cent. I gave the whole bag to Gisela. All I had were the shoes and the suit, which, because the fabric was cheap, mother predicted would fray, wear out and fall to pieces within very little time... First communion and confirmation were behind me... without too much pain I'd passed one subject at school: religion.

VATI WENT EVERY DAY to read the *Morning* and the *Slovene* on the bulletin board across from the baker's where they got posted... After

---

*Those Catholic clerical pigs!

school he would send me to read the afternoon edition and the *Slovene Nation*. I was supposed to read just what he specifically told me to read: the war ... foreign affairs ... the want ads, the for sale ads ... the prices. I couldn't always find everything or understand it ... There were too many maps and headlines, especially on the first few pages, which were full of exclamation and question marks ... I liked reading the captions under the photos best. An armored division in Spain, where fat General Franco in that silly army cap had won ... little Japanese tanks somewhere far away, on the other side of the world in Manchuria, where rice grew with snakes all around ... a complex roller device that Hitler's bomber pilots were using to learn to hit their targets more accurately ... One day toward the end of August there were a lot of people crowding around the bulletin board ... a dark thicket, in trench coats, shirtsleeves, caps, holding ice cream cones ... I stood at the back, unable to see anything through a layer of people reading that was ten feet thick ... They were standing so close together, leg to leg, pocket to pocket, that I couldn't squeeze through them ... This had to be big news, because everyone came away with faces that looked like what they'd just read was some sort of food they were still trying to swallow ... From the end of the fence I began to move toward the start of the bulletin board ... from the last page of the newspaper toward the first ... They wouldn't let me get near it ... they were leaning into the board with their arms ... their heads dangling over the front page like pears, as glue continued to drip thickly off the board from under the newsprint like honey ... Finally I shoved my way past the front edge to the row of pages ...

and was greeted by a lot of grumbling, they wanted to chase me off to the children's corner ... A picture showed Hitler and that other scary man. The one with the low forehead and the fringe-like hair from the caricatures, who led the Jews and the communists, Stalin. NON-AGGRESSION PACT BETWEEN THIRD REICH AND SOVIET UNION ... A photo showed German foreign minister von Ribbentrop in a uniform and Mongol-faced Russian minister Molotov in a black suit ... "Has Europe been divided into spheres of influence?" it said ... At the bottom of the page was a picture that showed Hitler in his short mustache and Stalin in his bushy one, each grabbing from either side parts of a jigsaw puzzle labeled "Poland" ... Vati was so surprised when I told him about the pact that he dropped everything and ran outside in his house robe to look at the bulletin board ... He came back looking confused. "Juden und Deutsche zusammen! Im Traum hätte ich das nicht geglaubt ..."* The tavern on Bohorič buzzed like a beehive ... Everyone was buying newspapers ... crowding around radios ... talking in clusters on the sidewalks ... trench coats fluttering at the street corners ... Two superpowers had united ... Now it was Poland's turn! ... What response would England and France have? Chamberlain and Marshal Pétain? ... And America? Roosevelt? ... I knew we were going to move soon. That worried me a lot more. To Town Square, the house of Mrs. Hamman ... into a big apartment ... there in the center of town Vati's fur business was going to prosper a lot more. They coached me for it ... from now on I was going to have to

*Jews and Germans together! I would never have dreamed it could happen.

work harder and be a lot better behaved... Or else they would put me in a reformatory, and that sort of education – oh boy! – that was like being in the army... for every infraction the schoolmasters beat you with a belt... they had already got me transferred to my new school, Graben... There at the very least I was going to have to earn Bs, not like now when my report card showed nothing but Cs... I had already asked around about the man who was going to be my new teacher, named Mlekuž. A strict, unbending man! He would have what it took to tame children...

Then, after the big news that had struck everyone like an axe to the head, the newspaper wrote: Blitzkrieg... Germany attacks Poland... A photo showed Polish cavalry consisting of white-clad horsemen with lances attacking German tanks... Bombardments. Stukas. Two pursuit aircraft flying over Warsaw... The Germans dismantling a border crossing... Germany gained 190,000 square kilometers, the Soviet Union 180,000... of Poland... Great Britain and France declared war on Germany, but they didn't help Poland... Vati and I went to Šiška to sell furs to a merchant who had a house near a train crossing... His pink round house with columns and a grocery store on the ground floor stood on a corner... upstairs the merchant had his nice home: a big living room with oil paintings in frames. While Vati and he were talking, his son Oto and I played tag all through the house... up and down the steps that wound like a snail shell... outside in their yard, with bags and crates lying around... among the columns that we designated as home... Nobody scolded us, nobody shouted... Oto walked into the store... bottles of champagne, fish, foie gras in mayonnaise lined up on the shelves and in the display cases... He took a tall jar of chocolate candies off of a shelf and gave me a whole handful... the saleswomen stood by with their hands behind their backs and didn't even say "boo"... It was immediately apparent that, when his father wasn't around, Oto represented the owner here... That's how I would have liked to live... have a well-stocked grocery store several paces away where I could go whenever I felt like it and take whatever I wanted... The merchant was still a young man and serious. "What had to happen has happened," he said to Vati. He pointed down to his courtyard where the bags and crates were. "Now at least for a while my people need to keep their mouths shut..."

We moved after ten p.m. when the streetcars ran less frequently and there were no gawkers out in the street to make fun of our meager worldly possessions... So long, faucet and old witch! So long, Mrs. Guček! Tobacconist lady!... Goodbye, Jože! Mr. Ham! Zdravko!... We moved using a cart that Mrs. Hamman had loaned us... the tables, the hammocks, the chairs, the wicker chest, the boxes, the sewing machine, the bunches of patterns, the box with pots and eating utensils... We had accumulated quite a bit... We had to make three trips there and back... Carrying our clothes, bedsheets and Gisela, Clairi and mother walked on the sidewalk behind Vati and me as we pushed the cart... When we arrived in the vaulted entryway of the wide house, which had a glass-enclosed porch framed in white-painted wood as part of its facade, and began to carry our things up the dark staircase and then down the long, squeaky courtyard veranda protected by a glass roof and metal poles (there in the corner was where old Mrs. Hamman lived), through a vestibule into a big, empty room with two windows that faced out onto Town Square, from which a streetlight cast a dim glow onto the dark parquet floor, where we set each item carefully down, to avoid hurting our hands, but also so they wouldn't drop and wake up the people who lived in the house ... I remembered similar moves that we'd made in Basel ... from the green house in Gerbergässli to the ruin that we lived in in Steinenvorstadt, from there to the Rue de Bourg alongside an arcade you could take to get to the Rhine ... from there to beautiful rue Helder with its fountain in the middle of the road, and then from there to the square near the Mission school and finally back to the green house in Gerbergässli ...

In the darkness we used matches to quickly inspect the apartment ... From the veranda a glass door led up steps to a long, cold, high-ceilinged room where the red plaster was peeling ... A bit farther on, under a vault, was the true, legal entrance to the apartment, a door with a window that was covered with waxed paper printed with roses ... First was a dark hallway ... the kitchen with a gas stove to the left, and on the right that big red room and next to it a spacious cave for the bathroom with no tub ... Then there were two doors ... between the first and the second was an antechamber with built-in cupboards ... which led into the big room where we set our things down ... Outside the windows there were cables, the trolley ran here ... Each of the houses on the right and left sides of the square had at least one shop in it ... This reminded me of the house I was born in on Elisabethplatz.

I spent the first few days leaning against the window ... As a trolley went by, the wires tautened all down the street ... On the other side there were shops: Zos's for ready to wear and shoes with a little arcade in the middle ... A delicatessen, a barber, a hairdresser, the Fischer grocery store with its cardboard parrot on the door ... A tobacco shop and the Šmalc variety store with its corner of black marble ... A goldsmith and watchmaker ... A fur store, housed in a palazzo of mirror-like marble. The Shmied department store ... Everything, from the doormats to the door handles, was elegant. The stores were all lined up one next to the other so that you didn't so much walk as fly down the sidewalk ... But nowhere was there a single patch of greenery or dirt for me to spit into. Day after day around here I was constantly going to have to wear nice clothes and well-polished shoes. All I had to do was remember the Sava, its gravel riverbed, the fields, the airport and my throat would constrict. When I leaned so far out over the ledge that I nearly fell, on the top edge of the "Hamman" shop sign I could see the pigeons padding back and forth over the letters and cocking their heads to the side to look up at me ... This also reminded me of the Elisabethplatz in Basel, and the window where they used to carry me as a baby to look out at the street, the people, the children, and the pigeons on the window ledge. With all my horizontal weight I could sense that the raucous little creatures weren't any danger ... Now I was suddenly there again, looking out on a city square with its crush of stores, and the pigeons were once more keeping track of my behavior, as they had on Elisabeth Square. They looked at me appraisingly, as if assessing what and how many things were going to happen to me here in this new environment. I felt as though I were locked up in a classroom or a hospital ward ... I made myself quieter and less obtrusive than the window panes, in order to make out from their cooing as many of the good and bad things that awaited me here as possible, and not miss any of their predictions, particularly not the bad ones ... They would scatter at a loud noise, fly up over the wires and then perch on the windows opposite, so that I couldn't make them out any more, or new ones would land, with other prophecies, warnings and news ...

    I didn't dare go out in the street. There wasn't any decent company for me out there that I could discern, anyway ... I played with Gisela. We played telephone: I unwound a spool of twine, running it from the main room to the other, long, high-ceilinged one near the courtyard that had plaster crumbling off its walls. Shoe polish tins served as our speakers and receivers ... I stretched a sheet out in the corner by the stove and made a tent for us that was so high and spacious that I could lead her around on her wagon under our big top, and still we were hidden from the adults. We played button store and staged a mass on the wicker chest. We also performed a play and various farces for the adults in the doorway to the antechamber. We dressed in mother's clothes, put on Clairi's shoes, adorned ourselves with chokers, fur hats and muffs, and painted our cheeks with rouge. Gisela participated in all of it with lively enthusiasm. We told funny stories, played pantomime, and tumbled all over each other ... Gisela's pale, little down-etched face and silky brown hair were made to order for the role of a princess ... But gradually I got tired of these contrived entertainments ...

At last I summoned some courage and went out to stand in front of our glass apartment door. It had been pasted over with waxed paper that had a checked pattern with red roses. Just like the distinguished doors of affluent residents! There was a small space outside the door. The vaulted exit led on one side to the courtyard veranda, and on the other it led up a polished stairway to the apartment of the mysterious Mrs. Hamman... Sometimes we ran into her... A big, powerful woman with charcoal eyes and black, wavy hair. With something rigid inside her... She would stop in the middle of the stairway under the vault and shout orders back upstairs... to her cook or her maid in German and Slovene... At times she was accompanied by a businessman in a black necktie and green hat, occasionally even by two of them, who wore the same kind of ties and green hats and almost had to run to keep up with her... One time it would look like the lady was following their lead, and the next as though they were obeying her... There was no way of making that out... I always managed to do a sort of double double-take whenever I saw her. The first on account of her beauty and elegant clothing and capes flapping behind her, and the second at the resolve and nonchalance that she showed to the world... I didn't know whether to greet her with "Good morning, ma'am" or "Grüß Gott, gnädige Frau." So I greeted her with a bow. Once she bowed buoyantly back at me, but mostly she just hurried on out of the house, her jaw clenched tight.

Here, at the short end of the courtyard veranda, was also where the nice old lady lived, her mother, who had given me a copy of *Die schönen illustrierten Abenteuer* a year before. What wouldn't I have given to be able to have another look at those guns engraved with the years of manufacture, or the collections of sabers and shields on her wall... and run my hands over those objects from noble times that I could only fantasize about... One day I ran into her just as she was airing some rugs out on the veranda, each of them bearing its own noble coat of arms... She was standing beside them, leaning on her cane and smoking out of a long mouthpiece. Her white-haired head, refined face, hooplike bracelet reminiscent of cells in a castle dungeon... and the cane with its beak-like silver handle on which she was leaning... all of it literally etched itself into me... It brought to life for me images of palaces atop cliffs in olden days... even those times of the rich past in which Vati, mother, Clairi and Margrit had lived and which for me were only a fairy tale, like everything that had been in the world before I was born... I said hello to her with all the awe that informed me... humbly, placing my hand on my heart, the way real esquires showed respect to their ladies... Oh, how I hoped she would one day invite me into her chambers...! She greeted me back with a strong, good-hearted nod, which sufficed for the moment, as her good will enfolded me like a veil beneath which I would either perish or take flight...

The veranda ran all around the rectangular courtyard, above which the trees of castle hill inclined, their bushy crowns and powerful trunks descending from the castle onto Hamman's Dry Cleaning, Pressing and Alterations like a primeval forest... Through the long glass pane of the workroom, only the bottom half of which was frosted, I could see the laundresses, seamstresses and female assistants, all wearing caps and white work smocks. Sometimes they sang in chorus, as if up in a choir loft... Beneath its glass roof the veranda would squeak and rattle noisily whenever anyone walked on it, and the girls would lift their heads and look out over the frosted glass to see who was there. If it was me, I turned red as a beet and took off like a madman... A glass-enclosed porch hung like a basket on the wall at a right angle to the veranda. Various gentlemen and ladies would walk around and take their seats in armchairs inside it. They had eyes that they used to observe the courtyard, although they were different from the knobby eyes of the workwomen... Thus there was no refuge for me on the veranda, because you could never be alone and completely free there...

The best thing to do was get away from there... Through a wide exit doorway you came into a square hallway with doors surrounding oleanders in the corners and a rug in the middle. Thank god, it was quiet and dark there... Here at last was the vaulted door to the staircase, illuminated by real streetlights protected in wire mesh. The wide, eroded steps made a sharp turn as they followed the thick wall... That's why I always descended them carefully or shot down like a bomb... A sunny day with street noise shone into the vaulted entryway through the wide door, only one side of which was opened inward. I stood there for a while and looked at the people... all conceivable types were walking across the square as though in a live toy box of figurines... I felt drawn outside... Next to the door was the goldsmith's and a lamp store, then the clothes designer's studio and a shoe store, then an optician who also sold binoculars, and then the Rot fur store. That one I knew. I stood outside its display window, hoping to see the tall blonde lady who aroused my desire, but I couldn't find her. After that came city hall with its gigantic striped poles for flags on each side of its entrance. There was a statue on its steps: a short-maned, stocky horse ridden by the old King Peter I as he fled into the mountains of Albania... Both of them had been fashioned in rough curves out of gray rock... The handsome old king in the same sort of army cap as any Serbian soldier would wear was so alien in this environment... city hall, the square, the whole town, it might as well have been the statue of an Apache chief here on the steps... This startled and made me feel uncomfortable, because the old king's face was so noble that I liked him immediately... Behind the barred windows of city hall were those cannon and mortars from the first World War that I had already looked at before. If the gate was open, I would slip into the cool, dark entryway to feel their barrels and carriages like hay carts on wooden wheels and the soft, still-oily bundles of rags on their ramrods... Beyond that of course was the cathedral... then a florist's shop, and the Falcon and Spinning Wheel Inn... an old man, a junkman who sold odds and ends in display cases in the entryway... buttons, children's watches, toothpaste, shoelaces, scarves, the board game *Mensch, ärgere dich nicht*, yoyos, belts... I'd already been to Šenklavž's, also to Krisper's, that time when I went begging with Mirko and his mother. I was careful not to let any of the sales staff recognize me. Then there was yet another furrier in a narrow building, a regular palace built out of black marble... The elegance of the street... the artificial flowers, the toys, the pretty odds and ends in the display windows, the neckties on shirts, the veils, mountains of hams with parsley, wigs of all different colors ... practically lifted me off the ground, so that I could scarcely feel myself anymore and it seemed I could swim through this ocean of silk, necklaces, fine shoes, gold cufflinks ... Town Square ended where the buildings got narrower and Old Square began ... which was dark, crowded and grim. I didn't go there ... Here, on the border between the two squares, a barber was standing outside his diminutive barbershop with an outsized copper plate for a shop sign hanging over his head ... Here was also the sign with the red Turk smoking a hookah ... Here porters with braids over their shoulders and numbered tin badges on their caps waited for work ... here a swarthy shoe shine man crouched behind a mirrored box, a brush and open tin of shoe polish in hand ... The bridge that went over the Ljubljanica was called the Cobblers' Bridge, it was white and had handsome lamps on it. The path that followed the river was called the Gallus Embankment ... This is where the antique stores were all lined up, with rummage in their windows, their doorways, out on the street ... Furniture, nails, mattresses, pots, cast-iron stoves, radios, flower stands. All of it old, disgusting junk that repelled me. Gargoyles of cast lead in the window and in boxes arrayed along benches, in front of them dragons, phantoms and devils ... Everything great or small was inside in the windows or outside and under the chestnut trees ... The antique dealers, women and men and their children, sat on stools, armchairs, beds and divans that they were also trying to sell. I wanted to figure out if these city kids were anything like the ones in Basel ... if they were better or smarter than the peasant kids in Lower Carniola, or in Nove Jarše for that matter ... I went from face to face, searching. Here was one like

Anka, but too chubby and done up. Farther down from the chestnuts in a vacant sandy lot some boys were kicking a ball ... They were too self-contained a group for me to be able to join them. I was drawn to some sabers and old mortars displayed in the windows, along with knives, swords in ornate sheaths ... armor, lances, helmets with steel face guards ... If only one of those things could have been mine ... But the antique dealers kept an eye on everything and gave me dirty looks, as though they'd guessed my intentions ... Around here, I concluded, there was no chance of finding company or making friends ... The neighborhood was too gussied up, but also quite desolate ... I went back along the wall toward the bridge ... There were several trees in the sand ... Carts leaned up against the wall ... the wide iron gate of a warehouse ... The Ljubljanica flowed lazily between its high walls. The whole of it wouldn't have made up for one single branch of the Sava, its gravelly riverbed, the woods, the potato fields near the airport ... I didn't come across a single scamp my age anywhere ... I walked down short, narrow Locksmith Lane, between an inn and a warehouse which exuded a stench of dampness, rotten fruit, paper and old dirt, with flies swarming around ...

After that I arrived back at Town Square ...

Alongside the jewelry laid out on velvet in the goldsmith's display window next door to the Hammans' front gate I suddenly caught a glimpse of myself, so changed that I didn't even resemble anyone I knew ... I felt such despair, fear, hopelessness, and confusion within myself ... but the windowpane showed a thin, wiry boy with disheveled hair and the muscular legs of a soccer player or boxer ... An athlete trained almost to the point of deformity ... I had to step close to detect in the shadows of my eyes and nose some of that hopelessness and confusion that were inside me ... All the rest was some unknown brat, whoever he was, who could very easily also have been my enemy, but under no circumstances my close friend ... more likely an obstacle, the way other boys I tried to avoid were obstacles to me ... Good God, how disappointed I was with the appearance I'd been stuck with, and I felt even more crushed than just shortly before ... I wished I could literally extract me out of myself into the light ... grab onto the air and pull myself out of that unfortunate shell into the open ... I didn't want to look anymore, otherwise I was afraid I could lose all partiality toward myself ... I was one of those kids I had to run from because they were constantly blocking my path ... I thought it would be best for me to quit studying, make myself invisible and unheard, and avoid people, or else sooner or later they would gang up on me. ... I breathed a sigh of relief when I was back on the other side of the door again, no longer visible to myself or anyone else. I was free ... and curious once again ...

Most often I went to the area just before the cathedral. Because that's where the smallest store was that I had ever seen: the rummage man's little display cases in the courtyard passage next to the inn. He also had several cases out on display on the steps and on the sidewalk outside the passage ... This was my world ... on a micro-scale. Toys, straps, buttons on cardboard, little toy pistols, combs of various sizes ... and then rosaries in every possible color, toothpaste and powders in tubes and little jars ... two taffeta corsets that got me excited, little balls of yarn and seven tiny cups on a silver platter, six of which were gilt, but not the seventh ... These glass boxes crammed full of wares from all over aroused more interest in me than the display windows of the biggest stores in town ... They were like colored cartoons, variegated kitsch, comic strips from the *Most Beautiful Adventures in the World* ... Barely had you noticed one thing, than another showed up unexpectedly beside it ... next to a bowl of pearls there were race cars, behind them there were trumpets and English horns with a Mickey Mouse and a child's two-barreled shotgun for the jungle, affixed to a piece of cardboard showing, against a field of blue, a lion's head with a silver mane and a gaping, fire-red gullet ... beneath it was a gray wind-up elephant ... The owner, the rummage man, stood or sat in his passage, always wearing a jacket and hat ... He was an old man and slightly decrepit. All of this merchandise belonged to him. I didn't pay any more attention to him than I did to any other uninteresting person on the street ... He, on the other hand, noticed and remembered me when I stopped by every morning to stare into his cases on the sidewalk ... Once he came up to me. "Since you seem to be so interested," he said in a thin, wheezy voice, "come help me sometime when you're free ..." The thought electrified me ... I was hired on immediately and was standing outside the passage the first thing the very next morning when its doors were still locked ... The merchant arrived on an old bicycle and handed me the key ... I opened it and set out a sign under the house number that read, "DRY GOODS AND

MORE. Jurij Velikonja" ... Then I helped him take the little display cases from their stacks, unlock the padlock on each of them, and set them out one on top of the other up to the ceiling. I hung polka-dotted belts, whips, dog leashes, necklaces and different colored rosaries out on pegs, pinned scarves to lines strung across the ceiling, always in the same order ... striped ones for everyday wear, then white, then silk ones for Sundays and checkered for special occasions, and after them scarves of red damask, scarlet taffeta and still others of green taffeta ... set out on a big tarp two big pillows for gentlemen and ladies, two smaller ones, and then two even smaller ones ... then Velikonja put a cardboad vest over my head that had buttons of all kinds ... metal, glass, ivory, monochrome and multicolored, for clothing and linens ... I walked around in that costume as advertising outside the cathedral and back and forth on the square ... I had to admit that the display cases and the wares in them were redolent of age. But I enjoyed selling. Selling and business became my goal. At home I even made a sign "We sell everysing here" and had to replace the "s" with "th" ... Old Velikonja was nice ... we talked about this and that ... but not at all about me, nor was he inclined to talk about himself ... so not about anything personal. We mainly talked about the most urgent things connected to selling. He acquainted me with simple bookkeeping. On one sheet he had a precise list of what he had of this and that, let's say scarves, and on the sheet opposite how many of them he'd sold. For everyday record-keeping purposes he had cardboard tabs that hung from the display cases where you just marked off whatever item you'd sold. As a reward for good work in my first month he promised me his best cork pistol and a box of corks ... We tended to have few customers. Out on the square I might occasionally sell a set of buttons for underwear ... And in the passage, every now and then a housemaid might come for hair clasps or a ring ... and would spend a long time choosing among all the rings displayed in various little boxes: little hearts made of red stones, a greenish anchor made out of aquamarine, gold stamped rings ... The women bought hairpins and every now and then a scarf, the younger men bought belts, ties, a cigarette lighter or case ... old ladies might buy a white prayer book for a girl's first communion or confirmation ... Nobody paid any attention to the Japanese ocarinas made out of bakelite ... Velikonja toted up the number of items sold from the charts and put the money into a ceramic milk dish ... At noon, when the church bells rang, he turned toward the stairs at the end of the passage that led up to private apartments and prayed. Then he went to the inn next door, the Spinning Wheel, for lunch. During that time I handled sales on my own ... Once in his absence I sold a whole set of buttons for a man's suit and roughly a meter of satin to some woman ... though by then I had a good command of the inventory, there were still a few things that challenged me ... I was most drawn to the little watches, toylike little things for kids on elastic bands. One afternoon I couldn't resist anymore ... although I knew that the watches were made out of tin and celluloid and weren't real ... still ... and this should testify to my stupidity ... I took out two of them that were attached to cardboard at the back of one of the cases ... one to wear myself, and the other to give to Gisela ... That was the end! That evening or the next morning, after checking the sales or the lists on the cases, Mr. Velikonja, who was very precise, noticed that he was missing two silly little toy watches ... When I arrived the next morning, he just gave me a rude glance and said nothing ... I sat down on the shoe grater next to the steps, but Velikonja went in and out past me as if I were thin air ... I could feel his resentment like a sort of sad, lazy spell reminiscent of sleep. That's how two stupid little toy watches cost me a friendship ...

So that was how I managed to cut off my own path to the cathedral ... I headed back down Locksmith Lane to the embankment. I could sense, I could smell that boys met there ... Outside the locked door of the warehouse there was a big, sandy area with thin trees growing on it, lindens ... I sat down under one of the trees, determined to wait for the first boy who walked past so I could establish a friendship with him, no matter if he limped, was an idiot or had lice ... if need be I would even have been happy with a girl my own age ... I looked at the sapling for any similarity between it and the tall, mighty trees that grew along the Sava or around Cegelnica ... It was too tiny, it was deficient in chlorophyll ... it made more the impression of a little box of soup greens than a proper tree ... The houses were deficient, too ... both on this side of the river and the other. Otherwise, on the other bank there was a good-sized building, the gray blue Matica movie theater, and beyond it was Congress Square and the Star Park ... Some chestnut trees were being cut down there and the base was being erected for a monument to King Aleksandar I, who was the son of Peter

I and was also going to be riding a horse, but one twice as big. Nearby was a casino with a garden restaurant and a music pavilion where an orchestra played in the evenings ... But all of that was meant for the elegant world, the grown-ups, not for kids ...

My waiting finally paid off ... I noticed two boys carrying a big box across Cobblers' Bridge, then they turned past the Kolman porcelain warehouse onto the embankment ... They were walking so carelessly, one of them taller, the other shorter, that I immediately figured this had to be their home turf ... Just to be safe I had put a stone in my pocket ... Something in their faces immediately changed when they noticed me ... They sped up and I tautened some muscles so I could get out of there fast if they attacked me ... They set the box down close by, both of them taller than me, long-legged and long-necked like storks ... "Where do you come from," one of them asked ... He seemed to have some difficulty speaking. Now the burden was on me and I had a test to pass ... "Ve moofed here from Pohorič Street," I said ... The taller one was looking at me out of deep-set eyes. The pucker around his mouth was swollen and golden brown, but his forehead by contrast was white and bulging, making his head look naked ... a moron? an idiot? The shorter one was made of other stuff, even though they looked and were dressed alike. In blue work aprons, like two little businessmen ... fruit farmers, produce vendors ... I got up. This required delicacy, because I was the one infringing on their space. Of course I was shorter than either of them ... The other one, Karel, had a skinny, triangular face with jutting cheekbones. There was something unpleasant in his unblinking, narrow, gray eyes and around his thin lips, something that radiated through his skin ... He was more dangerous than the tall one ... "Where are you from?" he asked harshly. "From Moste, Pohorič Street," I answered. He sat down by the box, clasping his long arms around his legs ... He lowered his pointed head between his knees so that the vertebrae stood out on his back ... Then he lowered his eyelids so that only the pupils were visible. This was now a matter of instinct ... distinguishing between a thousand changes of tone in what could be a friendship. Both of them needed to find out as quickly as possible that I came from a long way away and that I was absolutely no threat to them ... "Ve came from Zvitzerlant sree years ako," I said ... The younger one opened an eyelid and started looking at me a little differently now ... "Are ze two off you broders?" I asked quickly. I was in a hurry so they wouldn't think better of this, decide that I wasn't worth a cent and leave ... "Yes, we are," the taller one said enthusiastically ... "Ant zis? Vie to you haff zis?" I pointed to the big box that seemed to be full of strips of different-colored paper. I wanted the younger one to answer. The older one waved toward the bridge. "That guy who puts covers on books gave it to us." ... "The bookbinder!" said the younger. "Let's go! ..." My mouth suddenly got dry ... "Vill you come out zometime?" I blabbed, full of hope and doubt ... "Maybe," the younger said ... They went into a yellow house that had a shop sign on it that said "Prinčič Fashion Salon" ... Oh, was I ever happy, even though they never showed up near the warehouse again. I skipped with joy as I went home ...

That's how I got to know Ivan and Karel ... They lived in the same house where their mother and both sisters had a small hat shop. They only put one hat out on display in their store window at a time and changed it every week ... one week it would be a hat with a veil, the next week without ... then a hat for mourning, followed by a hat with cherries and next one with bouquets or swallows ... If you went into their little store, all around you there were mirrors and among them a big print of The Angelus by Jean-François Millet, as the caption said down below ... Past a wooden wall you came into their workroom and past the workroom there was a vestibule and from the vestibule you came into their room, where all five of them lived ... Their mother was tiny, thin, and dark-haired ... She reminded me of Mrs. Guček. Both sisters resembled the two brothers. Silva had a cylindrical head like Ivan ... and the younger one, Ivka, had the same sharp, gray, bright eyes as Karel. They had yet another brother, the oldest, who was a barber and no longer lived at home ... There was one hugely important difference between Ivan and Karel. Ivan was enrolled in special education and was very religious, while Karel went to a regular school and didn't care about anything ... Ivan was the first to get up every morning, so he could go to the Franciscan church, where he helped the priests and other ministrants first in the sacristy, then at mass ... He would clear off the pews, put out the flowers, trim the candles. Now and then, under the supervision of an older attendant, he would serve as a ministrant in one of the side chapels ... The others were all still asleep by the time he got back ... He would put the big prayer book which one of the Franciscan brothers had given him back into the night table, climb out of his good clothes and lie down next to Karel to finish sleeping ... Karel, on the other hand ... not just his name, but his pointy face reminded me of our uncle. Unblinking, cold, tight-lipped, inscrutable ... as though he was never going to let you see his true colors ... I had to accept that as part of the bargain ... I suspected there were quite a few other things I was going to have to swallow. I resolved not to bat an eye at any intolerance or disappointment ... I was prepared to sacrifice anything I had for this friendship ... even more than the White Prince in the *Beautiful Illustrated Adventures* ever intended to sacrifice ...

The next day I went to sit by the warehouse door. When they didn't come, I climbed up on the wall across from their business. The wall there formed a kind of box or balcony looking out over the Ljubljanica. Inside the box was a cart chained to a young willow tree that grew there ... My friends slept late, until eight or nine ... After that I couldn't hold out anymore. I went down Locksmith Lane and called to them through a street-level window that had an iron grate over it ... The room would have been bare if it hadn't had wardrobes against the walls ... They slept together on a narrow, brown bed in the corner ... two steps away from the big double bed that their mother and both sisters slept in ... I sent a big rooster parading around in their room ... Finally they heard me. They dug themselves out from under their blankets, where they'd been sleeping in their swimsuits, which inspired me, because mother had always forced me to put on one of her old slips overnight ... They washed next to a bucket in the vestibule, then came outside to the wall ... I felt badly only on account of the women ... I assumed they must be completely different from mother, Clairi, and Margrit ... I took care not to embarrass them.

Silva... a broad-hipped, diligent, boring woman... I had nothing to do with her... But Ivka! Whenever she poked her disheveled head out of the covers at my muffled whistle... she also slept in her swimsuit... I would freeze... She was like Karel in almost every respect. Exactly the same triangular face, the jutting cheekbones... the same thin, taut, pinkish skin... but especially the same sharp, gray, glaring eyes the color of slate... Now and then she would toss me a look or mumble something through her thin, pursed lips... something nasty, insulting, mean... at my expense, naturally... The feeling I developed toward her was similar to what I felt about Karel... except that it was so complicated and high up somewhere, as though it unfolded on top of some mountains where my eyes couldn't reach... I sensed a chilly revulsion... I would have given just about anything to be able to change that disdain in her eyes at least into indifference... Once when I walked into the vestibule by mistake when she was there washing her armpits by the bucket, I froze in fear of having perhaps embarrassed her... But she just kept washing as if I weren't there, and even though I calmed down, the feeling that I had simply been blotted out was surprisingly unbearable... I would have preferred it if she'd yelled at me... But then, she didn't pay much heed to other people, either... not to her sister, not to her mother... she and Karel communicated with little more than a short word or a gesture... probably because they were almost twins... The only time I saw her laugh was when her oldest brother, who was a barber, came to visit... She laughed aloud at his jokes... The oldest brother was a skinny, pale, dark-haired man with a haircut like Tarzan's, always artistically dressed... in a light blue sport coat with a scarf around his neck that was tucked into his checkered shirt ... While he told jokes and everyone laughed, with one hand he would give Karel and Ivan, who were begging him, coins from his pocket which was so full of change that it weighed his elegant jacket down, while with the other hand he kept constantly running a comb through his hair ...

When Ivan and Karel came out, we would go one place or another. "Vehr to?" I would ask. I would look at Karel, because Ivan responded to everything with equal enthusiasm, no matter what somebody proposed ... Karel wouldn't answer at all ... My attachment to him grew as fast as my revulsion ... only occasionally would the antipathy lag. I perceived his proximity ... from his head to his toes, from his eyes to his long pants belt that always flapped over his knee ... as serious, precious, and unbearably annoying ... Had he done anything to me? Not a thing! Had he done anything bad? No! But one day he would, and I had to get ready for that ... Gisela, whom I brought with me once to the embankment, talked and played with him as though he were air. I envied her that she could relate to him that way.

We went from the antique stores toward Žabjak and Breg streets ... that was a dangerous neighborhood, that's where boys hung out who were stronger or at least more numerous than the three of us ... You had to stay alert. One of those guys could come dog your heels, and if you didn't pay attention or turn around fast enough, he could give you a kick ... Karel and Ivan said that they were always invading the embankment, but if you just stepped on their territory, you'd get a rock thrown at you or delivered by slingshot. Ivan showed me where his legs had been hammered by projectiles... As soon as they hit you, they shout, "We declare war on you!" ... and you have to beat it as fast as your feet will go ... You have to do something so those wise guys stop harassing you or invading the embankment at the drop of a hat... An army ought to be formed that includes all the boys who live on that side of the water and nearby. If we have our own units, then nobody will ever dare touch any of us again, no matter if we go down to Trnovo or Žabjak or up to the castle... Creating an army on the embankment, I sensed, would be the secret glue that would bind our friendship together most tightly of all... I would have to think about that some more...

At that time we would go visit the public market... now and then some vendor or shopper would give you an apple... or we would climb down the ladders at the Triple Bridge to get to the gravel riverbed. Karel would slowly climb down the rungs one foot at a time, clinging to the ladder like a girl... it gratified me to see that... We undressed and waded through the shallow water to those catacombs under the road that used to be a dock in olden times... We drove the fish ahead of us and would try to bludgeon them with paving stones... Sometimes we succeeded, but the fish stank too much of the Ljubljanica and sludge... So instead we went looking for valuable objects on the bottom... once we found a burnt-out compressor that was as heavy as a steel cash register... When I went back to the gravel, I avoided the heap with Karel's pants, belt and undershirt, as if he were still in them... I felt as though I would get stung or catch something... Every day I would strain to think of shortcuts or detours

I could propose to strengthen our friendship ... At home in the evenings I would make plans for the next day in feverish excitement ... all kinds of imaginative games ... I would consult with myself about what direction to head out in ... what entertaining things we could try ... what I would tell them about myself and about Basel, and what I wouldn't ... what games we would play ... to the extent possible ones that I'd invented when I was all alone and had no playmates ... The closer the time for us to meet, the higher my temperature would get, and when we met, I would become like someone possessed. In those few short hours that we were together I had to try out all those games I had invented and planned. My fear that it would soon be evening and I would have to go home intensified the wild pace of the games and ideas ... But my apprehension about the short-lived nature of our fun sometimes took all the fun out of it. Besides that, I had to keep the reins on myself so that I wouldn't go completely out of control and turn into a tyrant ... Karel remained unfazed ... Just when I thought that we understood each other best, I would be filled with the greatest revulsion and hatred for his hidden aggression, which I couldn't flush out of him. Most of all I would have liked to do some irreparably nasty thing to him ... punch him in the nose, which would have been least hard of all. Once, for fun, we tried wrestling. I could have whipped him like a pussycat, even though he was older, and pinned him to the ground, if I hadn't always had second thoughts at the last minute about the force of some hold or blow ... When he fell, I didn't leap on his chest and force his wrists to the ground ... The thought of touching his skin and his bones repulsed me ... What sense did victory have if it was like a defeat? The tension stayed in the air like a burnt smell. But I couldn't have parted ways with him and I was haunted by the fear that some day I might actually offend him. Ivan, however ... he was a caricature of Karel. With him Karel's sharp voice and disdainful laugh turned into a kind of hiccup and grin from ear to ear ...

One day as we were headed to the public market, some delinquent from Breg started pelting us with rotten apples. Outside the bookstore there was a heap of tomatoes gone bad that the green grocers had dumped into the sewer ... I flung my first bomb, a tomato, at our attacker ... and hit a priest ... the cathedral canon dressed in a violet clerical vest ... just as he was about to go across the square ... when I turned around, Ivan and Karel were nowhere in sight. I could see that the tomato had exploded on hitting the priest's head, and because of the red juice running down him, I couldn't tell if I'd drawn blood or not ... I bounded around the edge of the square toward the butchers' stands and the Dragon Bridge, when I suddenly noticed that a long-legged produce vendor in a blue apron and a leather cap whom I knew by sight from the fruit market was following me ... I had to avoid a crowd, but he was faster and latched onto me just under the first dragon ... "I'll show you to steal from me! Let's go!" he shouted for all to hear, spun me around and with his hand on my neck propelled me back past the wooden stands and benches to his fruit stand. "You stole my money!" he said once he had shoved me in among his empty crates. I was surprised. "I titn't zteal anysink," I said. But I knew it was futile to plead innocent. He searched me ...

my trousers, pockets, shirt, belt ... my buttons went flying ... He shouted for a policeman, but there were none close by ... He wrote down my name and address in the notepad that he used to add up customers' purchases ... When he let me go, I didn't budge ... "I titn't zteal!" I howled at him. "Scram!" he leapt at me again with his huge shoes. "I titn't zteal, you cherk!" I repeated. At that point he lost all control and was on top of me with all fours in an instant, in his shoes and his felt gloves ...

O<small>NE OF THE MOST IMPORTANT THINGS</small> now was to establish our own army on the embankment ... Ivan made the rounds of all the houses on the embankment, Town Square and Jail Road to summon all the boys who could conceivably join our army. The assembly point was next to the cart by the wall. The first to show up was Franci, who delivered the *Morning* door to door and had raced past us on the embankment several times with his newspaper bag. He was a pretty solid kid. Even in the middle of summer he had a runny nose from the dust and drafts in the buildings where he delivered the paper ... His trickle of snot would harden into putty. For fun he would dig it out and swallow it without batting an eye. Not only that, but he smelled of mush gone sour. He infected everything with his smell ... even the trees and the grass ... He had an older brother and a grandmother. He lived on the top floor of the last house on the embankment, which had a furniture and carpet store on the ground floor. His grandmother was sick and couldn't leave the house. And on top of that she was quite cranky. When no one was home, he and his brother would have to tie her up so she wouldn't do anything to herself. Once he showed her to me: she was sitting tied with rags to an armchair, so she wouldn't fall out the big attic window that she always looked out of toward the dead end of Frog Lane and the Harbor Inn restaurant. His brother could have been twenty or maybe fifty. He was a little daft. He did things to help out the sexton of the cathedral ... he swept the courtyard of the bishop's residence, watered the palms in big pots, and in the mornings he delivered the *Slovene*. The two of them took great care to make sure nobody in the bishop's residence found out that his younger brother delivered the *Morning*, and to that end Franci only delivered his newspapers on the left bank of the Ljubljanica. Metod, his brother, was a fright to look at. Flushed, blond, with a big mouth that gaped like a fresh, wet wound, full of crooked teeth and bared gums ... He spent his free time in the afternoons at the Harbor Inn, from where he could keep an eye on their grandmother ... The Harbor Inn was a huge tavern consisting of just a single room in the shape of a big letter L, with a gigantic rustic stove at each end. It was where produce vendors, storekeepers, Dalmatian Croats, newspaper salesmen and delivery boys, drunks, Greta Garbo from outside the main post office, idiots and petty thieves liked to drink ... once I just walked into the place ... it was a real hellhole ... the long room with its huge rustic stove on which drunkards were lying, and a gigantic bar that was thick with smoke and people ... in that rubbish heap they played the accordion, whooped it up, clobbered each other, sang ... some of them even slept there. The mute violinist whom I'd run into on

Fridays when I went begging with Mirko and his mother would also be in the ostaria, playing... Franci was strong on account of constantly carrying his heavy bag, which had made one of his shoulders lower than the other... But he was a coward. You couldn't count on him at all. No sooner would you turn to him with a serious request than he would vanish, evaporating like dew off the grass on account of some other obligation...

The next one who joined us was Marko, who lived over a shoe store near me on Town Square. He was a little kid with such gentle eyes framed by a pale face that they were really, as books used to say, reminiscent of violets... something unreal, like out of a fairy tale... He brought along his little sister Tončka, who was four years older than Gisela, chubby, with tiny eyes that would melt away behind her high, puffy cheeks. When she decided she wanted a toy watch like the one she saw on Gisela's wrist, I gave her the other one that I'd stolen from Velikonja... Marko's family tended a goat in the woodshed behind their house. The boy once brought it along on a rope and it proceeded to graze around the lindens and the wall. We hitched it to the Prinčičes' hand wagon, which we loaded with rocks. That's when the idea of a battle wagon came to me that we could use in our attacks.

Firant came from the prettiest house on Jail Lane. He was a nervous, volatile boy like me. Right from the start something like fear, mystery, attraction, repulsion and pleasure reigned between us, as between two opponents facing each other in the front line of battle. Friendship was not possible. I was aggressive and so was he. The very way he walked and held himself was like an attack. He would drag one leg behind him, glance up at you with his head bent down, clench his fists. His otherwise collapsed face had a big mouth and a bony, jutting jaw, like gangsters in comic strips. The first thing he did when he joined us at the wall was to call me a German and challenge me to a fight. He wanted to know which of us was stronger. I wanted to find out, too. After a few initial feints we had each other by the shoulders. He won because, it seemed to me, he had reserves of some hidden, vicious strength. And also because he was fierce. In the second round I pinned him to the ground. He looked around angrily, with lots of white showing in his sunken eyes. The third round was a draw. The thing that got on my nerves most about him were his lower front teeth, his incisors, which stood out from the others and caused him to lisp ... I felt like knocking them, along with his jaw, back into his gullet. In spite of it all, he invited me over to his house, where his father worked as a women's tailor. We walked up the artfully winding stairs, where there was a potted palm on every window ledge ... all the way to the top, to the attic over the fifth floor. For me this was one more proof that annoying people always lived in the nicest surroundings. His father, who was constantly beating Drago with his belt, was a powerful, tough, curly haired fellow who looked like a priest in civilian clothes, while his mother was tiny, just skin and bones. There were colorful rags and swatches lying all over the kitchen floor that muffled your footsteps. Firant had his bed in the kitchen in a sort of alcove right next to his parents' bedroom door ... At night he sometimes heard what his mother and father were doing in their bedroom, moaning and making the bed squeak as they fucked. He talked about it so calmly that it amazed me, but then again not. He opened the door and showed it to me. In the middle of the room was a big double bed that in my imagination ever since then has stood for continual lust and delight. Next to the bed was a bassinet with an infant bawling in it, his little brother. My God, how he must have enjoyed hearing all that right next to him. He described it to me in detail ... Then one time next to the cart he solemnly promised us that he would take us all there some Saturday evening or Sunday afternoon to listen and watch through the keyhole as the two of them, Davorin and Pepca, his parents, did it in their bedroom ... But despite all this directness he was quite sneaky. You could sense how pumped full of deviousness he was and you could practically feel it leaking out of his mouth like hot air. You had to be careful around him, because he was always resentful about something and balling his fists. You also had to be pretty dumb if you decided to go look at heaven with him ...

Then, lastly, we were joined by good-looking Andrej from the most dilapidated house on Jail Lane. Without exception all of us recognized how exceptionally handsome he was. A thin, refined, pale face, small, dark, velvety eyes, and such a small mouth that you couldn't imagine how he could shove an ordinary spoon in there. What's more, he always spoke out of the corner of his mouth ... almost inaudibly, as if sipping each word ... Upstairs in the attic of the courtyard building where he lived with his mother and half-sister in one room, he had an open hallway that got narrower and narrower on account of some big supports, where he hung out whenever he was home alone. In the hallway there was a pantry and a stove with a long pipe attached to the gutter. His half-sister Neva was a strong, homely young woman who did temporary work as a salesgirl in various stores ... his mother, dark-haired with lively eyes, like him, loved singing love arias from operas, popular songs, chansons and hits from musicals. She lived on the pension that she had from her first husband. She knew how to tell every story she'd ever heard, she smoked like a chimney and was forever reading suspense novels that she checked out from the St. Jacob's library ... Here on this rooftop, she once told us, was where the cops chased after Hace, the famous burglar who stole from the rich and gave to the poor. The police climbed up on fire ladders to put him in handcuffs, but he just slid down a gutter downspout and lightning rod and escaped ... with a whole bagful of watches and rings ... I was excited. I couldn't look enough at the ridge of that roof and the fat chimney from behind which he was said to have taunted the cops. Now that was a bandit! A real Robin Hood! ... Now and then Andrej's mother and Neva would give me something to eat ... their asparagus strudel was especially good ... In the mezzanine next to them there was a tiny room where a young whore lived. Andrej's family had some sort of rights to the room, because they kept their wardrobe and two crates there ... Andrej told us how he sometimes looked through the keyhole when she had callers inside. She would dance around in a little ballerina dress, sometimes exposing her breasts. The men would do push-ups on top of her and then throw some money into a basin on the table. Whenever she made too much noise, his mother went after her with a coal shovel. He had even gone after her with a broom once, punishment had to be meted out! ... He showed me her little room.

It was like a monastic cell. There was a picture of Mary on top of a cask. Once, he told me, he and I were going to hide in the wardrobe and watch what the little whore did from close up, because the girl didn't lock her door, she would just fasten a hook on it ... and sometimes not even that ... the room would gape open all day long so you could go in and out like a breeze ...

All six of us together now made for quite a powerful group, even though you couldn't count on most of them ... Marko was too delicate, Franci too much of a wimp, Firant too sneaky, Andrej too handsome to fight without holding anything back, and Ivan too excitable and dimwitted. I just wasn't sure about Karel. Nobody really had him figured out. Was he brave? ... Of all of them I was most attached to the two of them ... possibly because our parents did similar work, both families had workshops at home and all three of us constantly had to cut, fold, dampen, crawl on the floor looking for needles, and clean ... and we were always decked out with every conceivable thread, yarn, fur, and ribbon ... But what mattered was that there were enough of us now that we could attack the Breg dwellers, who were constantly violating our borders on the bridge ... Perhaps we were already strong enough to declare war on Žabjak and Trnovo, but for sure we could prevent other armies from making incursions on the embankment ... Up in the old castle, for instance, there was a motley rabble living in the semi-dilapidated rooms that were propped up with beams. It was led by Sandi, the scourge of delinquents, who had already been under arrest for robbing an alms box in the cathedral ... If we could just organize our defenses like they did! They had a habit of lurking in the tree branches that jutted over the path and then leaping down on miscreants' necks like Robin Hood's merry men. It was in one such attack from above that they jabbed a pocketknife into one kid's neck ... If they caught one of their attackers, their practice was to tie him up to a tree trunk upside down and then take everything that fell out of his pockets ... Knights! Then they kicked him from the battlement walk all the way down to Streliška Street at the bottom ... Some of their sisters were also part of their gang, and they were nasty, wild, combative girls ... They wouldn't even let grown-ups into the castle, they chased everyone away ... nannies with children, school classes that went up with their teachers to have a look at Ljubljana, they sent all of them running ...

My idea for the coming battle was this: to use scrap lumber to hammer together swords of various lengths that we could hide in our jackets and trouser legs ... fill up some inner tubes with lead ... pool everything we had to get some brass knuckles ... buy up some popguns for visual effect at a distance ... fashion some bows and attach wire to the tips of some toy arrows ... In short, to create all the armaments that the others already had. Hammer some nails into shields made from old crates, with the tips pointed out. Change the Prinčič boys' wagon into both an attack and a supply vehicle for munitions. Equip it with sharpened beanpoles or stakes and then shove the wagon ... weighted down with paving stones that the driver would sit on, steering with his legs and wielding a slingshot, while a gunner would be free to throw the stones – downhill toward Žabjak ... As the wagon raced down the roadway, the slingshot-armed driver and the gunner would send stones flying at boys and windows ... The wagon would immediately be followed by infantry with slingshots and sabers ... This would have the same effect as the English desert tanks at Tripoli, Sidi Barrani, and Benghazi ... the infantry would paralyze the enemy exactly the same way the pictures in the newspapers showed Finnish ski patrols turning the Russian assault cavalry, old nags and all, into ice ... We began fashioning sabers and learned to fence following the Frenchman's instructions, we threw stones on the run, and we practiced shooting our slingshots with pots set out as targets. Fencing and throwing did not come easily to Karel: he would hurl a stone across the water or hit a dog with a stick like a girl ... Our first battle was with the Breg gang on Cobblers' Bridge. There weren't many of them, so it wasn't a real battle, more of a trial run, our first faltering gropes, during which our swords broke ... The real war was still ahead of us and that was with the castle gang. But they must have found out about us and our plans. Maybe Franci had blabbed something to Slavko Škerjanc, a friend of his from the castle, whose mother minded the public toilet underneath the Triple Bridge. Škerjanc helped her out at work and so spent all his days on our territory. They must have found out, because no sooner did we get to the steps leading uphill at the Scarp than they attacked us from behind the old fortress wall as others began racing toward us through the neighboring gardens to the upset shouts of the owners. We sword fought with them up close, then we just clobbered each other with baskets snatched off pegs that we still had in hand, until we finally retreated in the face of their superior strength ... However, we did manage to pay the Castle gang back, if only a little ... they showed up on our turf ... They were coming along the Ljubljanica from under Cobblers' Bridge, taking potshots with stones at the fish in the shallow water. Sandi was with them. They were walking in a long, drawn-out single file ... from staircase to staircase ... He was walking in the middle, wearing his red revolutionary shirt, as always. We shouted and got them to look up ... We shrieked that they'd better withdraw from our waters ... They shook their heads as though there were flies buzzing around them and went on ... Then we started to pelt them with stones and slingshot fire ... not straight out, so as to hit them, even though the fatheads deserved it, but just to warn them that we meant business ... The paving stones and projectiles struck in front of their column and behind them, sending the water shooting in ten-foot-high fountains up to the steps.... Sandi, who was a true leader, since the bravery or lack of bravery of his crew made no difference to him, pressed forward to get to the steps by the drugstore and climb up, but another, Slavko Škerjanc, one of his sidekicks, turned back toward Cobblers' Bridge where there was another way up across from the antique stores ... We couldn't under any circumstances let them come up, or else we would pay for it ... we had to drive them back upstream, toward Žabjak, the St. Jacob's bridge, and farther on to where Little Graben empties into the Ljubljanica ... to Trnovo. We ran on both sides of the river, on Breg and the Gallus Embankment, past antique dealers yelling at us, over their divans and past their mirrored cabinets, throwing stones at all the staircases. I knew that if they got a chance to poke their heads over the top, that would be it for my army ... Now we waited for the

payback, their revenge. I believed that we had to beat them to it...
We had to attack the castle before they could launch their offensive...

One day Vati unexpectedly received from the Swiss authorities the money that was left after they confiscated his property in Basel and settled his debts... There it wouldn't have amounted to much money, but here it was a lot... Vati began making plans to start over again, from the ground up, so to speak... Despite the fact that we'd been living in the center of town for quite a few months, and despite all his advertising, the business refused to get off the ground... He could count the customers who had walked in our door on the fingers of one hand. Mrs. Hamman, one or two friends of hers, Sergeant Mitič and the wives of other NCOs... But those were just repairs – blowing the fur, as they called it, to see where the piece was worn down or deficient... No serious orders. A fur coat. Or a whole outfit: a fur hat, a stole, and a muff... A jacket or a vest... "Die Leute haben kein Verständnis mehr, kein Gefühl für wirklich schöne Dinge," mother lamented. "Sie schätzen die feinen, ganz handgearbeiteten Dinge nicht mehr nach Gebühr... Man interessiert sich nur für den verkommenen maschinengezeugten Kram..."* In the display windows of the six or eight furriers in town... Eberle, Rot, or on the square, you could see yards and yards of muffs, fur hats, little caps. Miles and

---

*People have no understanding, no sense of truly beautiful things anymore. They don't appreciate fine hand-made things anymore the way they ought to... They're only interested in cheap, machine-made junk.

miles of them! And fur coats on mannequins! Always different and new, a regular multitude. The junk that mother saw that was quickly stitched together by machine not only made her sad, it gave her stomach cramps... And we continued to eat badly. Rice made a hundred different ways... steamed, with peas and milk... There was no butter on the bread... maybe once a month some beef soup... twice a week a little, thin disk of salami... macaroni mixed with egg, just one of course...

Vati was making his plans: to become a supplier of hides. He was thinking of building a rabbit farm. Rabbits of all different colors and breeds. Silver, Russian, angora, and silk... He would build his farm in Polica on Uncle Janez's property. We didn't know him yet. It was near Ljubljana. The gray fur of Russians, resembling chinchilla, for overcoats and jackets, and wavy angoran like yarn for children's outfits... We would have the furs and the meat, to boot... Mother and Clairi were against it... Mother kept vigilant against flights of fancy. A farm like that would be exposed to all kinds of opportunities for theft. And somebody would have to look after it. And then there was the expense of the hutches!... you couldn't just leave the rabbits out in a field or the woods. Then there was food for the rabbits, a special kind of bark, these rodents had an insatiable appetite... We have to think very carefully. It would be better to invest the money... But Vati kept pushing. I wrote in his name to Uncle Rudi in Polica that we would be coming for a visit on Sunday. We took the train to Grosuplje and from there we walked through a quarry and a road that ran through some fields... which I hadn't seen or smelled in a long time. It was like an outing...

Uncle Rudi was a short, broad-shouldered man who bore some resemblance to Uncle Jožef, but wasn't as caustic. He would ride his bicycle to Ljubljana and in the winters did road maintenance work in nearby Grosuplje. His house stood on a small hill with a winding path leading up to it like the kind in picture books ... He had a number of children, including some girls, and one of the boys was my age ... They were poorer than Karel and Jože, but they were nicer. They had just one cow, two pigs and a few hens. Their fields were all on the hillside ... But their barn was magnificent. The straw was hard and smooth and we could slide down it like a lumber chute, then tumble down the slope outside the door ... Vati chatted with Rudi about his interest in building some hutches on his property and buying some rabbits ... Uncle Ivan was for the idea ... We got a basket of fruit, lard, and some flour to take home ...

The train was overflowing with drunk and happy men and women ... There were so many of them that they sat on the floor between benches, in the corridor, outside the lavatory ... All of them were carrying bags, suitcases, backpacks, bundles, and wicker baskets ... with corn, beans, barley, sausage, and chickens ... "Well, boy, I'm going to need to empty my bladder here in a second," an excited little man kindly put his hand on my head. I drew in my legs so he could shove his way through to the toilet ... People were singing in the compartments ... including the women, flushed red, their shiny faces with necklaces that got lost in the fat folds of their pendulous dewlaps ... I had never before liked people so much as I did on that train. Every compartment had its own song, or several compartments would share one ... The luggage racks practically shook from the basses and sopranos and things fell down in our laps ... In the compartment next door people were of course talking about that ... the willy and wee-wee. That was interesting ... "Me, no longer able to do it?" cackled a man's bass. "Even after three score years she isn't satisfied ... Now when I get home, she'll start whining ... like you wouldn't believe. I'll tell her, look, here's a news flash. When I leave in the morning, you get one kiss, so in thirty days that's thirty kisses and after dinner I'll slap your bottom, another thirty per month, so that's thirty kisses and thirty slaps on the ass all together ... whoever wants more won't get any, that's bolshevism, skinning a man alive..."... "Ha ha ha!" ... "Score, one-zero, my favor!" On the platform of the last car where you had a good view of the tracks as they narrowed on the gray granite ballast the farther away they got, the happiest people on the whole train were shouting and playing an accordion...

Several times when I came into our room I found Mrs. Hamann standing in front of the table where mother, Vati and Clairi were sewing. One time there was even one of those gentlemen in the black neckties and green hats with her. The next time there were two of them, a short one and a tall one, both dressed identically ... Barely had I come in when they fell silent ... Sometimes a servant would ring the bell and Vati or Clairi or mother, and sometimes all three of them, would have to go upstairs to talk to her ... "Ich will mich nicht in die

Politik einmischen,"* mother complained ... They were sitting around the table, downcast ... "Sie werden uns glatt in ein Lager stecken, wenn wir nicht eintreten," ... I heard Clairi say. "Andererseits, wenn wir beitreten, bekommen wir eine Unterstützung..."** I didn't like it when they sat like that, made worried faces, mumbled to themselves ... that usually meant we were facing yet another misfortune or some decision that would propel us into even more hopeless circumstances ... a move ... no money ... even worse poverty. "Wo sollen wir eintreten?"*** I asked ... The mere fact that I'd entered the room caused mother unspeakable irritation. "Geh spielen ..."**** she said abruptly ... she still saw me as a stupid, frivolous, heartless child who was not to be trusted. But at school they all took me for a full-blooded German. The classrooms at Graben were ugly. They were full of stupid mama's boys and spoiled brats from Trnovo. There was no point in having anything to do with any of them. Just one boy in my class, Miki, the son of a drunken painter, small for his age, even came close to being likable. At least he didn't laugh at me. Otherwise the whole class would grab at their bellies guffawing whenever I was asked to write a conjugation or declension on the blackboard. The teacher, whose name was Marija Sajevec, seemed bright and pretty to me. She had reddish-blond hair that looked like a huge blossom, pretty legs, a

---

*I don't want to get involved in politics.
**If we don't join, they'll put us in a camp, no questions asked. On the other hand, if we do join, we'll get some support.
***What are we joining?
****Go out and play.

nicely made-up face, and eyes between her blond lashes that looked like aquamarines among onions ... But her prodding, silly questions exposed me to even greater mockery. It was in her nature ... The class got stomach cramps from laughing and I stood on the platform, as dumb as a log ... Then with her finger or facial expression she sent me packing back to my bench and recorded a big, fat F for me ... I didn't understand how such an elegant lady, who put me in mind of perfumes, dance dresses, and great beauties, could be so indiscriminately hard-hearted and rude ... And yet our form master, Mlekuž, was even worse. His huge, naked, white head with its shiny crest reached all the way up to the black frame of the heir apparent's portrait ... while under the table the orthopedic shoe on one of his feet rested there, big and black, as though it were some sort of old-fashioned photograph camera ... He walked with a cane. He was a confirmed Falcon and patriot. On the first of December, with fifth grade teacher Sirnik, leader of the Youth Organization of the Adriatic Guards, standing at his side, he delivered a speech in the gymnasium, which had been decorated for the occasion. He spoke about the twenty-first anniversary of the Kingdom of Serbs, Croats, and Slovenes, about King Aleksandar the Unifier and about the Germans who were threatening Slovene territory. He spoke briefly, clearly, not one bit loftily, while the one next to him in his white trousers, blue jacket and captain's cap on his head looked like a crooner straight out of a musical ... From the first day I knew that my classes with Mlekuž were not going to be easy ... From the very beginning he gave me sinister looks. Without the tiniest trace of a smile. He had bulging eyes and plump African lips. Otherwise he was quite emaciated, with the sunken cheeks of a fanatic... Even when he spoke Slovene with Vati, his eyes would bulge pronouncedly and his fat lips would strain and contort, as if they were one of the most disgusting amphibians... And his big red ears, with which he could hear everything, even a pin hitting the floor... His voice was penetrating and harsh. He could have delivered a sermon in the cathedral and everyone out in the market would have heard him... He would swat you with the rubber on the tip of his cane, but you'd also catch a good length of cane... Once I had to read aloud what I'd written in my notebook... He simply exploded. He shoved back from his desk and came limping toward me in his faded smock, swinging his cane, with which he smacked me across the shoulders so hard that I literally sank down into the bench... To top it off, some of the boys would wait outside for me every day. I was still safe as far as the main door of the school's disgusting entryway, which was painted all over with brown crawlers. But as soon as my foot came off the last step, I had to be on my guard... They would leap at me from behind... get me in a double Nelson... they even knew the holds!... so that all I could do was kick with my heels... or they dropped on me from above, from the threshold, the steps, causing my school bag to fly across the sidewalk into the street, my notebooks, erasers, some arrows... Two or three would hang onto me... they didn't just use holds, they beat me furiously, which was even worse. I had to defend myself and retreat long enough for some adult to show up on the sidewalk, but they usually weren't any help, sometimes they just egged on my assailants... They also ripped my school bag so many times that I had to sew it back up with a big needle in the afternoon. They were born brats, Hitler was just an excuse... I would have liked to see him there. Or King Peter II. Or an efendi, or the Aga Khan! There was another ambush waiting for me behind the Zois pyramid... That's where that miserable Firant sometimes lurked, who was always opposing me, as if it went without saying... allying himself with whatever side was the strongest... Now and then the blowhard was even the ringleader of the ambush... but he was never alone. My voice almost changed from the fury I felt when I saw him. They were all around me, two, three, four of them. Still, I kept heading straight for the pyramid. But I also began to get ready... With a stone that I always took with me to school that served as brass knuckles... I whaled at Firant's bony gourd, at the bocce ball heads of the other falcons and the knobs of the eagles... I threw him an undercut, a regular knockout punch with my helper, which made his gums bleed and his two bunny teeth up in front start to wobble... Not one of them was my equal. I promised Firant I would deal with him that afternoon when he came to the riverfront... When I got there, he would sometimes be crouching by the cart. He'd steer clear if he didn't happen to have an inner tube full of stones with him. Sometimes he'd ask from a distance, from the edge of the bridge, if we could be friends again and he'd walk toward Kolman's on the embankment with his hands up... Sometimes I'd wave for him to come, because I felt sorry for him as he kept circling a pump on the bridge and looking our way... I knew all too well how rough it was to be on your own, without any friends... But at other times I'd be unbending and wouldn't relent until Karel put in a word or

Franci came running to report Firant's request that we make up ... I knew that none of it would last very long ... at most until the next day after school ... School was one world for us, but the embankment was a completely different one ... Sometimes he came up to me all excited to report what he'd just heard on the radio ... that eighty German paratroopers had taken Fort Eben-Emael in Belgium, which was defended by three thousand soldiers ... Or that the Germans had advanced into Luxembourg ... The rat, devoid of any force of character or will, the parasite! I felt like telling him that if you're going to talk up the Germans so much, speak German, otherwise you're just a traitor ... Now of course there was no way I could think of a war on the Castle ... No exploits were possible with that clever and treacherous Firant, who could attack me from the rear ... It wasn't just the Germans in Belgium, the Russians were beating Finland. They had broken the Mannerheim Line, against which they'd fired three hundred thousand rockets in a single day ... They had also taken a fortress and waved with their rifles on top of it, like the Germans did from the Belgian fort ... strange friends.

Finally I got my chance to see the frescoes and rifles in old Mrs. Hamman's apartment again ... Clairi took me along when she went to visit her ... The old lady invited us to sit at a tall brown wicker table and served us cream. Oh, if only I could have lived in such peace and abundance! I would just read books and draw and never leave the house to go anywhere again ... The old lady gave me a little metal box that showed a sepia film of an African scene ... a hunter sitting on a fallen log in a tropical jungle ... and another film from an operetta:

female dancers in short skirts, with plumes on their heads ... There were two reels in the box that I could turn to make the film go forwards and backwards ... You saw the scene play when you aimed the device at the light ... That hand-operated movie theater allowed me to instantly strengthen my friendship with Karel and Ivan ... Now in winter practically nothing happened. Sometimes we went to the movies if we had the money for it ... Movies about stubborn pilots who didn't obey their generals and wore straw hats instead of helmets and then became exemplary heroes ... Outside the warehouse we built a fort with firing slits out of snow and poured water on it so it would freeze overnight ... What if we made a theater, it occurred to me. The red room, which was cold and damp, was still empty and we could build a stage in it. We could filch the boards from construction sites ... sew a curtain out of some sheets ... The Prinčičes' mother invited me inside ... Now I would sit with Ivan and Karel in the workshop behind the back wall of their store ... Ivka was there, and Silva ... all three of them sewing hat crowns. Both brothers and I would crouch on the floor near the stove, winding hat ribbons up on our fingers ... Sometimes the two girls and their mother would sing. Not hit songs, but real ones. About a Gypsy, an orphan who was driven away from home ... about a stepdaughter out in a cold storm and snow covering hill and vale, who falls asleep on her mother's grave ... Tears came to my eyes ... Then we told stories. I talked about Basel ... about its attractions ... the shop that we had on the Gerbergässli ... about Vati's assistants ... about the rabbit farm he was going to build in Polica next spring when the females got pregnant ... I could feel my prestige growing, but still I avoided Ivka's willful eyes the whole time.

Sergeant Mitič and Vati were sitting in the first room, looking at a map that the former had brought ... German tank units were approaching the Maginot Line, with British, French, and Belgian divisions all around. Now it was France's turn ... It had already lost its best divisions. The ones that were left were mediocre. Even their air force was nothing much. The Germans could attack with a hundred and twenty divisions and have another thirty in reserve ... The attack was going to be like a blow from a blacksmith's hammer ...

It was our topic of conversation out on the embankment, too ... War was in the air ... and sometimes so were airplanes. Yugoslav ones. They would fly in a starlike formation. Blue gray Messerschmidts and blotched Hurricanes. Sometimes they would suddenly appear in attack formation from behind the castle tower. Gigantic crosses with spinning screw propellers ... the bombers more slowly, the pursuit aircraft more quickly – flew over the square and Star Park ... their din drowning out the street noise. People became a kind of dough under these metal factories in the air, no longer significant ... at the Ursuline Church the squadron of crosses lifted their noses and flew up into the sky, like skaters heading out onto the rink of an ice palace ... If France, that distant country, fell, what would be next? ... "If Great Britain helps, then everything will be fine," I said ... Andrej had his own opinion ... which he'd got from a friend of Neva's, who was a mechanic at the airport ... Air power would be decisive ... if England contributed its Halifaxes, which were best at nighttime bombardments, and its two-engine Mosquitos, which were quicker than German pursuit planes, France would be able to defend itself before the onslaught of Hitler's tank destroyers ...

At that time a blonde girl from Breg whom Franci had seen before would often walk along the riverfront. She and her mother delivered newspapers door to door, not the *Morning*, but the *Slovene Nation*... Her name was Tatjana. She made herself right at home walking down the embankment. Starting at the Triple Bridge she would cover the whole territory down to Cobblers' Bridge, as though she didn't care in the least what we thought of it. Occasionally we noticed her from a distance when she turned past the ostaria. She had such pale blonde hair that her head was like a bunch of straw and she always wore clothes that looked like they had been sewn out of bed slips and throw rugs ... She waved her arms a lot when she walked. She never stepped on the sidewalk or roadway, she just always walked on the curb ... Once when we saw her coming our way again, Firant said, "Guys, what if this girl is spying for the Castle or Trnovo?..." That was entirely possible. We watched as she walked past the Black Cat restaurant ... "Hey, you! Stop!" Drago shouted just as she reached the trees. She immediately stood still and turned toward us. We were sitting in a kind of pyramid: some on the ground, a few on the cart, one or two on the wall ... Her face was wide and pale. Almost white, as if powdered. She had wide-set eyes and a small nose. She looked me straight in the face, causing everything to start flickering ... Firant stopped in front of her and I could tell from the way his head was cocked that he was about to hit her ... I couldn't take that. "Leaf her alown!" I shouted out. I jumped down ... shoved him aside ... he looked at me furiously and I knew he was going to pay me back with interest the first chance he got. I turned to face Tatjana. What eyes this skinny girl had! Watery, bulging, as though they were floating in a glass. Yet at the same time they radiated something powerful ... "You can kow here if you're in a pig hurry," I said. I should have said something else ... like what I might say to Gisela ... But there was a lump in my throat. The air would have exploded if I'd blurted anything else out. Firant puffed up his cheeks and punched them with both fists. Pop! If I hadn't known that was him, I would have looked everywhere to find out where that smack of air had come from.

That night I didn't fall asleep, because I kept having to think about her, that Tatjana. Just as I thought I was about to stop thinking about her, she would appear in some gray rainbow ... growing progressively sharper, even more than in daytime, and then some entirely new, unexpected detail would come floating along ... suddenly she'd be wearing a necklace, then she'd get a kitten on her shoulder, or a lace-trimmed skirt and a red jacket to wear ... if I had told anyone about what I thought, his jaw would have dropped and he would have started crossing himself from all the laughter ... The next morning I crossed to the other side, to Breg, to see if I could catch her somewhere ... I was afraid of meeting her alone, so I took Karel and Ivan along. I told them we were going to reconnoiter ... On Breg there were old, fat houses from the previous century, if not the century before that, standing all in a row ... resembling an enormous rotting forest, and people went in and out of the houses as though they had tree holes ... We inspected this courtyard and that courtyard, then all the passageways between the walls of buildings, where we'd find doghouses and old bones lying around ... In one courtyard I discovered a really nice pond made out of sandstone. I had to stand there for a while admiring it. It was almost surely from the times when the war between the Black and White princes was still going on and the knights climbed up onto rooftops and balconies on rope ladders ... If Karel and Ivan hadn't started yawning in boredom, I would have stayed in that courtyard for a full hour ... even if it meant running into Škoblar, the grocer's son who led the Breg army ... We strolled past the benches where girls sat and around the big red library that the bricklayers were still working on ... through the park with the bronze heads of composers outside the Music Academy ... There wasn't a trace of her anywhere, although some special air, some potable breeze blew on this side of the Ljubljanica ... there was something about it, there had to be something about it, it was in the air and that was that! I could feel the power of Tatjana's presence like a fire that had to be mightily burning somewhere ... The next day around the time when she usually walked down the embankment, I was sitting on the wall ... I tried in vain to produce any sound ... I was in seventh heaven and yet also in purgatory ... The whole time it took for Tatjana to walk away in her white dress, which had black stripes so that it looked like it was scattered with burned-out matches, my heart was in my mouth. The thousand invisible threads that tied me to her broke ... one after the other ... When she turned onto Cobblers' Bridge at the Kolman warehouse and then disappeared, I just stared at the warehouse door like a calf, and when I bumped into Karel's eyes and Firant's mouth, I jumped so fast that the cart tipped onto the street ...

THE GERMANS had made a hole in the Maginot Line: Rommel's 2,800 tanks, so wrote the newspapers, had defeated the 4,000 armored vehicles of the Anglo-French forces ... Bombs began to fall on London ... on June 14th the German army invaded France. On June 21st in an old train car in a forest Marshal Pétain, who had the face of old King Peter, signed France's armistice ... The Russians marched into Lithuania, Latvia, and Estonia, three tiny Baltic states that had once been the property of the Russian tsar ...

A mandatory lights out was ordered in town. The streetcars ran with blue lights, as they had in Basel in 1936 when the Spanish Civil War began. The oldest cars, wonderful summer trailers with their flapping, striped little awnings, drove without any lights, and school kids, students and boys would jump up on their running boards and ride two, three, even eight stops for free ... there and back ... We rode in total darkness amid a whole crowd of freeloaders, past flickering display windows and people with coal-black faces who lit their way with flashlights pointed at the ground ... This was a new kind of fun. A coal truck nearly plowed into a crowd, spraying all of them with hot steam ... At noon they would test the sirens on the castle, which were intended for air raids ... The mighty signal horn with its bird's head wailed so piercingly that everything came to a stop and all the din and clamor of traffic around city hall was concealed beneath the sound curtain of its howl ... My old stockings were rotting in my shoes. Vati had bought his rabbits and there was no money at home. I was hungry ... Across from the fountain, on the same side as the bishopric, near Jurij Velikonja's sundries store, there was a little ice cream and candy shop ... I calculated everything down to the second ... the minute hand on the city hall tower clock showed twenty minutes to twelve ... I walked in and had a seat at a marble-top table next to the door. In their display windows, on their counter and all along the walls there were savory scones ... white flour, rye flour, big and small, and cakes ... butter cakes, honey cakes, chocolate, pear, and almond cakes ... sliced or whole ... A waitress went from table to table. I ordered two cream pastries and two slices of pear cake. Once I had finished slowly masticating them and begun drinking some water, the alarm directly above city hall started up, an ear-piercing sound that completely filled the little sweetshop ... as if on command everybody turned away, holding their ears ... I got up and calmy walked outside. Everything there stood gaping, trapped between the motionless street cars and paralyzed horses ... The siren had not yet even reached the peak of its continually mounting intensity when I reached the monument to King Peter II ...

At home a package was waiting for me that the young son of Fischer the grocer had brought by. It contained white knee socks, a white shirt, a black necktie, a pin with a silver swastika on it, and under the shirt a silk armband: red with a white circle that had a black swastika printed on it, like a hooked, spinning wheel that drilled right into my eyes... "Das mußt du anziehen und übermorgen zum deutschen Konsulat gehen..."* This costume was of course the uniform of the Hitler Youth, which everyone, young and old alike, loathed and despised. "Schau, daß du das alles unter den Pullover oder die Jacke versteckst..."** "Ich will das nicht anziehen und ich werde nirgends hingehen."*** ... "I vont ko zehr!" I said to Vati. Vati raised an eyebrow and kept on sewing... "Du mußt dorthin gehen, sonst werden uns die Hammans noch aus dem Haus feuern...,"**** Clairi said. She was flushed all red in the face and upset, and she must have been crying before I got there. I couldn't sleep. The package on the table... white, black, red... was like a snake's nest... Mrs. Hamman's employees had sewn it together... in the courtyard I saw boxes with the remains of red and white scraps... two days later I put on the shirt, which had an H in the collar, designating Hamman's tailor shop. They knotted my tie, stuck the pin in the knot, put on my armband... and my arm went stiff like after a vaccination. This was an even more disgusting costume than the one the Falcons wore. I used my jacket collar to hide the tie with its hooked cross when I bounded out of the house. Like a traitor hiding a bomb in his pocket... Outside the school at Vrtača where the consulate was, there were about a hundred boys waiting in

*You have to put this on and go to the German consulate the day after tomorrow.
**Make sure you hide all that under your sweater or jacket.
***I don't want to put it on and I'm not going anywhere.
****You have to go there, or else the Hammans are going to throw us out of the house.

line. All wearing overcoats, dwarves and giants mixed in together. Lots of dark-haired boys, a few blond ones like Hitler required. All with their hair parted on the side, all of them children of better families... A youth in corduroy trousers who was hiding his tie pin under his trenchcoat's raised collar appeared to be in charge... "Das wird ein Ausflug und Besprechung sein," he said... We went in rows of eight through the underpass to Večna Path, where I suddenly spied two red-haired noodles in our column... It was the Jaklič boys from Nove Jarše. What?! How did they get here? I lost my voice from the shock. When the two brothers spotted me, they instantly blushed and turned away... What was all this about? Slovenes, Germans, mischlings? The youth marching alongside the column ordered those of us who knew it to sing "Die Fahne hoch"... They sang it out loud, straight up into the windows and balconies of the buildings... How dare they do this, when this territory is Slovene? Thank God, after a bad rainstorm there weren't many people outdoors. At the top of a slope beneath Rožnik, which was privately owned, we were supposed to form a line. "Ihr seid die Hitlerjugend, die Zukunft unseres Reiches..." the young leader began. "Ihr wißt, daß die friedliebenden Völker Deutschlands und Rußlands gegen die plutokratischen, imperialistischen Angreifer kämpfen: gegen England und die Vereinigten Staaten Amerikas... Darum müßt auch ihr üben!..."* We took our coats and jackets off and performed a defense and an attack... We fought in segments. First

---

*You are the Hitler Youth, the future of our empire... You know that the peace-loving peoples of Germany and Russia are fighting against the plutocratic, imperialist aggressors – England and the United States... That's why you must practice!

the attack, digging in, initial resistance, followed by a break. Then we continued. It was funny to watch two Hitler youths with red bands on their white sleeves wallop each other ... The Jaklič boys were going after each other as if this was real ... My opponent was a boy who smelled like a drugstore, a delicate mama's boy who was practically crying, he so did not want to fight, the poor thing. I let him be ... We gradually shoved our way out to the road. Alongside a creek that flowed through a ravine our commander said, "Seht, was man machen kann im Winter, wenn man keine Waffen hat und der Gegner nachstösst! Schnee in die Flüsse und Bächer schaufeln, daß sie afschwellend die Feinde festhalten!..."* My God, this was stupid!... The instant the leader summoned the boys back to assembly with his whistle, I stayed among logs up by the forest's edge ... I shoved the tie and pin and the threatening armband that was visible for miles around into my pants pocket and hightailed it out of there, taking shortcuts and detours ... I hadn't enjoyed being there for one minute ... that was the strangest part. But I had to go one more time ... to some auditorium on Old Square above the Salaznik Café ... There were a lot of older boys, younger men, even girls there, each in a uniform with a belt strap over the right shoulder. They were happy, all of them laughing with bright, handsome faces ... There were lots of other people there, too, grown-ups I recognized from around town ... a skinny old man who was always dressed in a hunting coat, a richly dressed lady covered

---

*See what you can accomplish in winter when you have no weapoins and the enemy counterattacks. Shovel snow into the rivers and streams so that they swell and hold the enemy at bay.

with silver bracelets and black earrings ... and other ladies and gentlemen ... Mrs. Hamman holding a tiny glass ... both of her gentlemen, who always wore black neckties and green hats, were in some alcove playing ping-pong ... In one of the rooms I even noticed Gmeiner, the young student from Jarše ... or maybe I just thought I did ... I felt as though I had entered high society. They called the young ones among us into a good-sized room to practice. They closed the door and we learned to sing out of a green book. Then we played some sort of gymnastic game ... while crouching, with our hands clasped at the back of the neck, we were supposed to go hopping from room to room ... including the auditorium where the older people were. They made room for us and shouted high-spirited encouragement ... Then it was time for the drawing ... The grand prize was a ticket to the Union movie theater. I drew the right slip out of the hat, but Fischer's young son objected. "Er kann es doch nicht bekommen. Er ist doch Slowener, sein Vater ist Slowener ..."* he told the leader. This leader was not the same as the one at Rožnik ... he wore corduroy trousers with a belt and strap and was a very considerate, smart fellow. "Und wenn schon. Seine Mutter ist Deutschin und er ist Mitglied der Hitlerjugend ..."** The film at the Union theater was about a German mountain-climbing expedition to the Himalayas ... it was full of snow and orchestral music ... after fifteen minutes I ditched it and left ...

I told nothing to anyone about these adventures ... not to Karel or

---

*He can't win it. He's a Slovene and his father's a Slovene.
**Doesn't matter. His mother is German and he's a member of the Hitler Youth ...

337 ·

Ivan or anyone else, because I was afraid I would lose their friendship instantly...

Finally, one day we set out to visit the Franciscans. Ivan had arranged it for us. Downstairs in the basement of the rectory there was a big room with a stage where among other things they put on puppet shows. Comedies involving Punch and Judy... First we prayed for peace on earth. Then father Chrysostomos, a short, fat, kindly priest, who was the editor of the youth magazine *The Little Light*, read us some of his poems. Some of them were playful and others were quite pious. I sat as if glued to my chair. This was the first time I'd seen a poet. I couldn't believe that such a corpulent man, who was a real monk dressed in sandals and a brown Capuchin habit, could compose published poems. He certainly had to have something that wasn't visible on him anywhere and that also made him so outwardly kind that we didn't have to be afraid of him... Then we watched some silent religious and documentary films that the father put on the projector himself. These included a film about Lourdes, about the sick people who descended on the healing waters there in droves, about Bernadette's house and the Sanctuary of Our Lady of Lourdes... then there was a movie about an agricultural school in Norway and two young people, a boy and a girl enrolled there. The most interesting thing was that they didn't carry a briefcase to school, but just took their books tied with a strap. We could have carried our school things tied up in a bundle like that, too... Then the young people boarded a train and found a place to sit on the platform of the last car... They looked at each other the whole time and laughed as the snow-white fjords moved by between their noses ... At one point, however, when they glanced at each other and their faces suddenly drew close ... probably so they could kiss ... father Chrysostomos put his hand over the lens and the screen went dark. "Awww!" everyone moaned. When he took his hand away, the train was already far away ... just a dot on the horizon ... After the show father Chrysostomos promised us that we would soon become crusaders. He had his warehouse in a small room next to the stage. The costumes lay rolled up into balls, and though they'd been washed, they hadn't been pressed ... There were no proper trousers for me and even the ones that fit were ripped at the thighs ... There weren't enough spears and he was also short of plumed hats ... No one had everything, except for the older crusaders who had taken their costumes home with them the year before ... By Corpus Christi, the priest promised, we would have everything on hand and could participate in the procession. In the meantime we were supposed to ask our mothers at home if they would patch and press the trousers. By Corpus Christi there still wasn't anything ... so we had to march in the procession deficient, some bareheaded and others without a spear, following behind those who had the complete outfit ...

Now it was also high time for us to attack the Castle ... War was in the air. We collected suitable stones for our slingshots, sharp arrowheads that we put in an empty road worker's box that lay unused among the carts ... We had target practice using bottles ... The day before the attack I went to reconnoiter. Carefully, without a single stone in my pocket ... first contact with the enemy should be like a first loving caress ... On the hillside above the path that a street sign called the Path Past the Fences I noticed a kind of trench, a meter-deep hole dug in the ground, covered with branches and surrounded with stakes strung with thorn bush branches ... A guardpost, a sharpshooter's nest, the enemy's front line ... The next day around lunchtime we headed uphill, as if we were going on a field trip ... The bunker in the hillside looked like a bush from a distance. We crawled up to it on our bellies ... as though the girl we were in love with had fallen asleep in a ditch. There was nobody in it ... We yanked out the stakes and threw the branches aside ... Well look here, they had some sort of piggy banks made out of bean cans, but there was nothing inside them, they were empty ... Then it struck me: they had meant to string noisy tripwires of tin cans around their trench, like the English had done on Crete, so that any paratroopers approaching their fortress would set off a clatter ... We continued uphill on the paved road toward Osoje. From here on the castle gang had their eyes everywhere, behind every bush, every tree ... I said that we should all pretend like we were gathering bouquets of wildflowers ... for science class, for our botany teacher ... Then an inner tube that Franci, that klutz, was concealing slipped out from under his shirt and trousers ... clunk! ... right onto the middle of the wide road. That was the alarm signal! Even the gabbiest of gabby people could have noticed that with the unaided eye ... We hadn't yet reached the foot of the ramparts when I saw Sandi in his red shirt running down the tree-lined path out of the castle ... Two or three others, including Škerjanc and a girl, were racing behind him ... "Slingshots!" We had to hold them back. Plink! Plink! the poor little pebbles went flying. We only stopped them for a moment, during which they looked around ... then they headed downhill through a ditch, behind some trees and through the grass toward the path ... By then Franci had already turned around ... he was running down from Osoje and dropping everything along the way ... the inner tube, his saber, the stones out of his pockets ... Behind me I still had Ivan, Firant, Karel, Marko ... Andrej a little farther to the rear ... The castle gang were already lying in the grass, testing their slingshots ... we had to get down on the ground and shoot our rocks from there, aim at the boards we suspected they were hiding behind ... Then all of a sudden, as if out of nowhere, a watchman wearing a green cap came running out of the ramparts ... waving a stick. "It is forbidden to walk on the grass!" Was he the father or an uncle of one of the castle gang? This broke all the rules! He was threatening just us with his cane, but not even looking at them ... cop justice! ... We had to withdraw from the grass onto the path, onto the gravel, while the castle gang could stay in the grass, he still wasn't paying any attention to them, as though they weren't there. The jerk! Just then Škerjanc's brother leapt out of the grass at me ... at least he had the same kind of nose and shaved head as Škerjanc ... I grazed his shoulder with the inner tube ... "Attack! Attack srough ze grass!" I shouted. When I looked back, Ivan wasn't breathing down my neck anymore, he was running away ... and a bit farther on I could make out Firant, Marko, Andrej, Karel. So he was a coward after all! The thought filled me with pleasure ... and for a moment it was as though I was free again! So now I was all on my own. This was going to be a regular fight of a canary in its cage! I had to decide! I had to attack! I began to shout. Only hot air came out of my mouth ... I threw a whole thing of stones at Sandi and the others lying in the grass, of whom all I could make out was an ear or a forehead here and there ... I had to take the offensive ... My skin was taut with anger, taut to bursting, like a drum skin, so that any blows would only have made dull thuds and nothing else. I charged straight ahead through the grass, throwing stones ... I changed into the victor, because now I wasn't the one who had done wrong ... They were in shock ... that's what I counted on ... I darted past their shoulders, legs, and heads as quick as a breeze ... Hop! and in a single leap I was on top of the ditch, right in the middle of their unconquerable boulevard where they staged their parades! ... At least I'd done that! They got up, shouted ... "Get him! ..." I saw reinforcements running down the tree-lined path ... a second group, the one that always guarded both points of access to the castle from the market, the shorter path and the longer one ... they always thought of everything! ... I had to get down via the path that went past the ramparts, that led through the woods to Karlovški Bridge ... The stones began to crumble to dust. I saw the red shirt amongst the rabble. I dashed off toward a turn beneath the wooded slope. "Go around! Catch him at the chapel! ..." If they caught me, they were going to take my pants off, this I knew. That was a lot worse than getting beaten up, it was psychological pain ... not anger, but sadness would dull all physical torment ... I didn't have a single breath left in my lungs. I looked over my shoulder: sky and red shirt. Around the turn. Yet another turn. A double turn like a snake wound up in a coil. I flung myself over the edge of the road down the hillside. Thump! Smack! What sound does a head make when it slams into a tree?! Down, down!... I rolled past trees, through ferns, bushes and undergrowth, all speckled and spongy, my arms and legs smacking against the trunks of trees ... The wall along Streliška ... there was no end in sight to it, I could barely make out a gap in it over the orphanage ... Some gentleman dressed in a cloak and a velvet hat was standing in the middle of the road holding a flower... The soup kitchen was just about here ... I was furious. That damned, cowardly gang! I may have been a hero ... but I had also turned tail... All scratched up, I limped to the riverfront to confront them ... Of course not a single one of them was anywhere to be found ... they'd all hidden, each one for himself...

On Christmas Eve Gisela and I got toys and clothes from the German organization in town. Gisela got a sweater that smelled strongly of perfume and some other girl, along with a black doll made of celluloid with a grass skirt and a ring through her nose ... really quite nicely made. I got a racket and shuttlecock and a red checked jacket, the kind that bad guys usually wore in the westerns ... I put it on right over my shirt and when I went out that evening to look at the toys on display in the tobacco shop's window, a policeman stopped and scrutinized me from the side. He thought I was planning to rob the store ...

The victories of the German army around the world had begun to surround me with friends. My schoolmates became more polite. Those victories and defeats of some army in the distant world were like bingo, where you'd win or lose friends ... It annoyed me that they surrounded me for things that smelled of far-off, noisy places that I'd never seen with my own eyes and where something was always exploding ... I wanted to get rid of random friendships like that ... I already knew how that went: warm today, cold tomorrow. It actually tickled me as I headed to school in the morning to see them crawl out of their houses so they could join me on the way up to Graben ... As though I wore one of those uniforms with the ribbons ... as though I were one of Rommel's tank drivers or a Stuka pilot. "The English have got more tanks," some kid named Bajec said to me. Now he was going to go on about the respective merits of German Tigers and British Churchills ... Even Karel changed. All of a sudden he was at my heels more than ever, without my particularly asking him to go places with me ... His mother invited me to their place for crepes with crushed walnuts. I sat at a round table at the back of their shop, which they closed over the noon hour, and ate with the whole family. Ivka smiled at me once. For the first time ...

The Germans were already in Bulgaria, where the communists had once blown up a church ... When Cvetković suddenly signed the Triple Pact in Berlin ... That was news! ... People crowded Town Square, jostling this way and that, they were completely shaken ... Mlekuž paced the hallways at school ... his smock fluttering, his cane furiously banging ... he spoke with the teachers, resting his bare head on the doorframe, haggard and quiet, as though he were looking into a hospital ward, not a classroom. You could feel it: Germany was coming ... on a hundred thousand motorized wheels ... black and horrible ... Then one morning General Simović defied the government ... and seized power. They called it a putsch ... Special one-page editions of the newspapers started coming out ... The heir apparent Peter II had become King of Yugoslavia ... He spoke on the radio. Suddenly, spontaneously, there were flags on every house and building ... even way up on the peak of the Hammans' roof, nobody knew who lived there ... there were coats of arms in all the store windows, the heir apparent's colors, his portrait ... among all the eyeglass frames at the optician's there was a big cut-out: the crown and scepter of the Karađorđević dynasty ... the Oplenac church ... When you turned away from a display window, the air was full of what everybody was exhaling. It swarmed with it ... Defiance of that arrogant house painter with the little black mustache! ... Music, young people, old people marched densely entwined across Town Square and shouted, "Bolje rat, nego pakt!" ... "Bolje grob, nego rob!"* ... From the post office to the Triple Bridge students carried litters on their sholders that were covered with white flowers, in the midst of which stood, like the Mother of God in Brezje, a big color portrait of King Peter II in a glass-covered golden frame ... still others carried on another scarlet litter the symbols of the king's honor. Some shop windows had been transformed into creches depicting the life of the royal family ... Peter, Tomislav, Andrej playing in a sandbox at Bled ... The streetcars were festooned with ribbons, the policemen all wore the tricolor on their sleeves, and flags waved in front of Aleksandar I on his big horse in the Star Park ... there was an indescribable excitement and bustle in

*Better war than a treaty! Better death than a slave! (*Serbo-Croatian*)

all of the stores ... the music pavilion of the Casino was all decked out in Yugoslav pennants ... a vase of flowers was in every window, even the most ordinary and rundown ... Great Britain and America were going to help us! ... If people were this genuinely excited, they also had to be noble ... And if it didn't matter anymore whether you were young or old, but everyone was equally young and old, then that made them even better and happier ... I marched with my school past the post office ... of course, everyone was looking at me askance ... it was best if I just went away. The young, exultant faces, the flags leaned up against the display windows, the newly forged friendship of teachers and students, the general rejoicing put me into a stupor, a strange, unbearable sense of being divided ... How were things going to be with mother and Vati now? I raced home and from home back out into the streets ... Vati was standing at a window, pale and entirely beside himself. In 1914 he had hidden just like this in the attic of their green house while the Swiss Germans trashed his store downstairs, because they assumed he was a Serb ... He had never thought that anything like what happened that day would ever happen again. He had left the Austro-Hungarian Empire when he was still young, and when he came back, he returned to the same places, but a different country. He was excited, defeated, speechless. He began splaying his feet even more when he walked and incessantly blinking behind his glasses. Was he glad or worried? And which one was predominant in his mind? I looked at him instead of asking, since that was the only way I could tell. If I'd asked him what he thought about all of this, he would have answered these were not matters for children. Or that everything that was happening was just froth, like on beer... Mother, of course, was afraid, and Clairi was shaking. "Der Hitler wird doch nicht aus Beleidigung die Stadt bombardieren?"* Mrs. Hamman was nowhere to be found. The shutters were down on her storefront... I was for king and country, but everyone around me was practically trying to stab me with their eyes... I was for the war that was coming, I didn't like Hitler, but I wasn't against the Germans... I would have preferred to change into a road that parades marched down, or a horse, or a tree on a hill... whatever, as long as it wasn't a person. The air shimmered with people, as though it were burning... it was strange that the housetops didn't ignite, that the tiles didn't begin to slide off the roofs and the asphalt to boil...

On Palm Sunday I went with Gisela and her basket of Easter eggs and oranges to get them blessed at the St. James church. I thought everything would be as it had always been. Girls dressed in white with blue sashes, as I told Gisela. Bundles of willow branches and wicker baskets of fruit that people bring to get blessed. Then, a week later, the thing I always enjoyed attending most of all... the miracle at daybreak: "Christ is risen..." But it wasn't like that at all. Miki, the son of the drunken painter, was waiting for me outside the door to his apartment. We had arranged to meet before mass. But then the siren started to blast. All of a sudden, way up high, almost pasted to the sky, the little crosses of airplanes appeared... A first flock. A second. A third.... Miki and I recognized them from the pictures on chocolate

---

*Surely Hitler isn't going to bomb the city out of resentment?

bar wrappers and from photos we'd seen ... Heinkels, Junkers, Messerschmidts, famous airplanes ... they roared steadily against the hazy sky ... one squadron after the other ... Their roar echoed inside the church like the buzz of the organ bellows ... everybody looked up at the painted ceiling, from which the chandelier was swaying on its chain ... at the windows that rattled, as though a worldwide deluge were pounding them. The sirens kept howling. Everyone stayed in the church ... And at that precise moment the sky over Belgrade erupted ... roaring and snapping everything from its place ... people, trains, tanks, infants, Gypsies and grandmothers, then followed more airplanes, one squadron after the other. And all of these bundles of branches and baskets here, and us with them. It came as though clouds had just opened up, one after the other. Flames, bombs, new flocks and the extinguished volcanoes of buildings coming to life again, crammed full of phosphorus ... Boom! Boom! The suburbs left hanging from churches, train engines from bell towers ...

Civilians reappeared on the streets with flowers and wooden suitcases ... Soldiers in helmets ... Because the trolley wires and power lines were too low, they all held onto a long flag as though it were a fence ... "For king and country!" Howtizers! Mortar rounds lay cushioned in hay in horse rigs and hay carts ... Sergeant Mitič appeared for a moment. In a helmet, with a gas mask and cartridge belt. "Još par dana i alles kaputt ..."* What was he ... a traitor, or not? ... We could hear cannon spitting hollowly into the sky, as if the sun were exploding

---

*A few more days, then it's all over! (*Serbo-Croatian*, then *German*)

behind the clouds: boomff! eeeee! boomff! eeeee!... There were no real classes at school. The newspapers came out on a single sheet, like flyers... "Germany marches on Greece and Yugoslavia!"...

We had several gray, cloudy days... One afternoon the air suddenly ripped apart... people began racing out of all the houses with hand wagons, carts, tricycles, horse rigs... they went to the garrisons and warehouses that the army had abandoned out on the edge of town... to grab flour, lard, zwieback, uniforms, blankets, pistols... Karel, Ivan, Marko, Franci, Andrej, everyone... Vati borrowed a handwagon from Mrs. Hamman... It was getting dark as we went past the sugar mill... the sky was displaying the magnificent glow of fires. Straw was burning by the bale... The long road was crammed full of wagons... There were only civilians now in the garrisons... men, women, children, old people... what a sight! As though rats had broken into a church. Bonfires raged that had been set with gunpowder... People were carrying boxes out of the warehouses down chutes and down the staircases inside the garrison buildings... they threw bags out of windows, which exploded on the ground, leaving the people below to walk through flour and macaroni. Was even one of them thinking about the army, about king and country? No, certainly not about them... the king and government had fled by airplane to Egypt, where it's always warm and there are pyramids... I pushed my way through with the wagon and Vati... who was dreaming about us getting lots of army zwieback... past heaps of smashed crates with zwieback that had been trodden to dust... over puddles of oil, skating rinks of lard... The warehouse door had been ripped out and lay like a pontoon bridge over a muddy lake ... We hauled one, then another crate of zwieback over to the chute, sticking our heads out every window to make sure no one had stolen our wagon ... We came close to not getting anything, because I kept deferring to older people out of courtesy ... People were setting their children onto crates to reserve them ... or dogs, jackets, scarves, umbrellas ... We were lucky to come across an untouched metal container of lard that didn't belong to anyone. Just the container alone was worth something, empty it could serve as a table ... We trundled our booty home ... along the way we saw some people repairing their damaged wagons, broken axles and shafts ... All of our heads were smoldering hot ... flour! lard! bread! ... "Dino brought a whole bag of eggs home," one woman said. "And just imagine, only one of them broke." That was incredible ... At home we quickly unloaded the cart and raced back to the garrison ... Once again we loaded up zwieback that was so good, we found some more flour in an open bag and picked some muddy horse blankets up off the floor ... A truck belonging to the merchant Šarabon drove through the gate pushing people aside like a plow ... It was blazing a trail for itself ... and the people shouted at it. "Jerks! Parasites! Gluttons!" I made way for it, because their cashier, that time when I went to their store with Mirko's mother to beg, had given me a dinar ... The truck stopped beneath the warehouse windows and some loaders immediately set about heaving bags onto it ... What sort of a store was this! ... as though you'd walked into the bowels of a dirigible with its gas chambers full ... I noticed an army belt and a brand new bayonet in its metal sheath on the floor ... That was a find! ... I fastened it on under my shirt. But there wasn't a single rifle anywhere, much less a pistol, just a few bullets and gunpowder in disks that people would throw on the fire to make it burn brighter while they searched and collected... People, wagons, hitches, motorcycles and sidecars were like lunatic outlines against a glowing background... Some people in the crowd were exceptionally polite. Some took father by the shoulders and gave him a cordial shake. "If you need any rubber Palma heels, they're back there by the locomotive," one man said and pointed to where the train engine was going tssshhhh, tssshhh!... Vati thanked him. In fact all of this was like a big present from the govenrment to its people... I saw Andrej and his mother, who was all excited and humming something, or so it seemed, Firant with his father, both of them all fired up... We barely said hi to each other, there was no time... At home Vati and I set the crates of zwieback on the bottom of the built-in cabinet and we immediately put the lard into pots... I hid the bayonet under the wooden floor in the place that was meant for a bathtub...

The next morning a white flag fluttered from atop the castle tower... actually it hung, because there was no wind... Probably the people most offended by that flag were Sandi and his castle gang... It was the end of the Kingdom of Serbs, Croats, and Slovenes. I knew it too little to be either happy or sad, I was just curious what would come next... the Italians, Germans, Hungarians and Bulgarians were pressing with tanks and motorized infantry from all sides into the country that on a map back in Switzerland had seemed to me very much like a thick bearskin... There were no authorities anymore, no soldiers, no police, not even any traffic cops... which meant people were free and could do whatever they wanted to each other... Mrs. Hamman and her two gentlemen came with swastikas on their arms to see Vati and brought him a German flag wrapped in paper that he was supposed to hang out the window the next morning... At the time I was at Marko's house over the shoe store. I was looking out their kitchen window to see what was happening on Town Square... All the flagpoles jutted up empty or had white flags on them, and bedsheets had been hung out some of the windows... Marko's father was leaning on the window ledge next to me and said, as if to an equal, "That's it for the circus show... Now things will be different... Hitler's going to bring order..." I looked him in the eye, because he was sizing me up. The adults were talking in the room where he, his wife, Marko and Tončka slept... they greeted me as though I were already grown up. My God, I was barely twelve... I sat down in the kitchen and waited for Marko to come back... Tončka came up to me... she still had the watch from Velikonja that I'd given to her... I reached out my hand to look at it, and she walked straight in between my arms and knees... she pressed her wide-cheeked face with her corn tassel hair up against me and suddenly put her mouth on mine... The whole kitchen swayed before my eyes from this miracle, this new feeling... Suddenly I didn't know where I was... in a kitchen or in some golden palace...

That evening the streets came back to life... people were going out to see who would come... the Italians or the Germans... At eleven o'clock Clairi and I walked toward the post office... people were standing pressed against the wall, in courtyard entries, in the doorways of stores, in case things suddenly started to pop … "I saw them in Trieste," I heard somebody say in the doorway of Slamič … "They're so short … dwarves, really …" When it began to rumble, everybody stepped forward: motorbikes! It wasn't the Germans, it was the Italians on motorcycles with sidecars driving in a long column down Tyrševa Street, three to a vehicle. It wasn't until they drove under the blue light at Bata shoe store that I noticed their green helmets, round as gourds and sporting black feathers.

Town Square filled up with soldiers of a different sort … wearing dark green riding breeches and strange horn-shaped caps … a jeep with a German crew and a dusty motorcycle with a side-car were parked outside city hall … The monument to King Peter I had been covered from head to toe with an Italian flag … and up on the Castle a red, white and green flag with a crown and the crest of Savoy fluttered, like the flag from some fairy tale involving princes … People, mostly men and boys, were gathering around the German patrol … Of all of them the officer was the most attractive … covered with dust, young, restrained … People were straining to think of some word in German to say, which struck me as childish but also moved me … The patrol was happy to show them their weapons … machine guns, grenades, and bazookas, which they had whole stacks of right at their feet, next to the steering wheel … They explained how to shoot them, from the shoulder, but before that, how you fit one ring into the next to make the weapon lethal … "What decent people!… One of the soldiers slept at my house last night ... In the morning when he shaved, he didn't leave the razor blade on the window ledge, no! ... he wrapped it up in newspaper and took it out to the toilet in the courtyard ..." some slightly daft old man explained to the crowd ... In Maribor the tanks and motorized units were welcomed with flowers, flags and music ... Even Hitler paid a visit. Pale, the collar of his leather coat turned up, in an army car. Then from the balcony of the city hall he announced that they were going to make Slovenia German again ... Many people thought that the Germans were going to come to Ljubljana too. In Lower Carniola peasants carried a sign that read "Da ist das deutsche Reich"* from village to village ... almost into Croatia ... Everyone wanted to live under the Great Reich ... nobody wanted the spaghetti eaters. The Italians delivered flags by truck from street to street ... Mrs. Hamman, who had distributed German flags and ordered them to be hung from every window, was crushed. Her two gentlemen looked rather grim too. Her house was one of the few in a long row of houses that didn't bask in the sweetshop colors of the Italian flag, instead she put out the deadly serious red flag with its black twin gallows in a white circle ... the banner of attack, discipline, war, and death ... the four-footed cross that turned like a screw, crushing everything in its path ... I had a vague sense that a certain distinction existed in this friendship between Italians and Germans ... I understood differences in friendships well and I felt sorry for the Germans, because they'd probably been tricked ... Italian martial music filled

*This is the German Reich.

Town Square, reaching all the way to the monument to Napoleon and the Casino. They played "Giovinezza"... The drum major tossed his baton with its silver knob as high as the second stories of the buildings... People stood on both sides, laughing, clapping, pleasantly surprised... Elegant Italian officers and their wives went shopping in the stores... Civilians wearing foppish outfits, with handkerchiefs in their coat pockets, strolled in groups of two and three. These were detectives, questurini... The soldiers wearing black shirts and caps with tassels were from Mussolini's division of Arditi... The uniforms of the Honved officers were odd: instead of buttons they had wooden wedges and on their shirt fronts across from them loops, and they wore square caps with feathers. The carabinieri wore Napoleonic hats... The Germans in their close-fitting uniforms that looked like they'd been poured into them were the only ones that resembled real warriors... In a serious city that was full of books and learned people, the Italian soldiers seemed more like clowns... What they cared about was the women. They bowed right and left and outside the shops they would tip their hats... "Che bella biondina!..." "Che bella signorina!..." They blew kisses from their trucks so intently that sometimes they even fell out of them... They would stop groups of girls on the street and strut around them in their baggy riding breeches, one looking like Stan, the other like Ollie... The girls liked it... they laughed at the Italians... they hadn't seen soldiers like these ever in their lives... they would retreat from them walking backwards and laughing so hard that they soaked themselves with their tears... Around town... in courtyard gateways, on corners, in stores you could hear various foreign languages being spoken ... a regular Babel, like Basel ... The whole world descended on Ljubljana ... That buoyed my spirits and I felt relieved ... People, antique dealers, porters on Jail Street, women, the Prinčičes' mother, Andrej's, Asipi the bootblack ... stared, admired, and talked on sidewalks up close or shouted across streets to foreigners wearing a variety of uniforms. The city changed into a different kind of emporium, a different kind of capital ... Portraits of King Victor Emmanuel and the Duce wearing a helmet appeared in the shop windows. There was new money in circulation, too, lire. But the bread that we bought from the baker on Jail Street, that was worthless. Like boiled flour, burnt corn. A loaf of it would disintegrate along its furrow. And when you brought it home all you had left in the bag were sticky lumps of mush ...